Just One Weakness

By: D.L. Ptaszynski

I dedicate this book to my all of my wonderful friends and family who continue to support me in my writing ventures. Thank you all for your help and encouragement. Thank you, also, to my faithful readers. Every single read, every review means so much to me. To my awesome Beta and ARC readers, thank you so much! I couldn't be ready for publication without you. To my new critique partner, thank you for your comments and support. Last, but not least, I remain grateful to God for giving me the gift of words. It is such a blessing to me.

~ D.L.

Other Titles By This Author:

** The Jameson Collection: Rick*

** The Jameson Collection: Tammy*

** The Jameson Collection: Jack*

** A Jessip Ranch Romance: Mending Fences In Her Heart*

** A Jessip Ranch Romance: Tracing Hearts*

** Scooping The Pitcher*

** In The Heart Of Cheston*

Prologue

Everyone is entitled to secrets. Every family has them. Some secrets are innocent enough, while others are darker, more dangerous, even menacing. One can only hope, with the latter sort of secrets, that they can be contained, controlled, and prevented from touching what one loves most in the world. These sorts of secrets were plentiful in the Caprianno family, and they were known to have long-reaching arms.

Ten-year-old Nicky ran down the marbled floors of the main hallway in his family's estate. The oversized mahogany door to his father's study was ajar and he slowed to a stop, hearing a muffle of low voices coming from the gap. Not wanting to be discovered, Nicky softly shuffled his feet closer.

Salvador Caprianno, his father, was always kind to his wife and children, but he was a shark of a businessman. One day, he would pass the business to his son. Though Nicky was generally a welcome visitor in his father's office, there were a few partners, associates his father called them, that Nicky and his sister Marie knew barred them from entering.

Of all the visitors to the house, Nicky was most curious about these particular men. They wore dark suits and came in dark cars, never traveling alone, never being introduced to the Caprianno family. Nicky and Marie were always shooed from sight when they came to the house, often being instructed to play outside.

"After this last project we work on together, I want to be clear with my intentions. You all know that this buyout means that the Caprianno Corporation no longer has any ties to any future ventures." Salvador's voice was low but stern as a string of document folders made their way in rounds for each man at the table to sign. "With great respect to all of our associates, this deal serves as a clean finish to our shared ventures."

A man of generous build with thinning gray hair, wearing an expensive-looking black suit, nodded solemnly to him, offering a thick-fingered hand to Nicky's father. "It has been a pleasure doing business with the Caprianno family for so many years, but I understand your motives, Sal, and I do not blame you. That was a close call with your boy last year. Ga'forbid our children should come to be touched by the problems we've known in our businesses."

Nicky's brows tucked inward. What troubles had almost touched him that no one ever saw fit to mention? He couldn't recall getting into any scrapes. He could tell by the stone-faced expression on his father's face that something, some worry or concern, had taken hold of his thoughts in response to the man's comment.

"I have children of my own, now a first granddaughter. I hope to do the same for them as you are doing for yours, one day." The man went on. "I can only say this, that though we are no longer partners after this last venture, you will always have a friend in all who sit at this table today."

Salvador's eyes swept around at each man's bobbing head, though one of them looked slightly uncomfortable. Scotty Jansen adjusted the tight squeeze of the tie around neck. Sal's gaze stopped at the crack in the door. Tightly knitting his brows, he looked off to the side at Frankie, the tall man that stood in the corner. He jerked his head in toward the door. Gulping hard, knowing he'd been caught, Nicky took a couple of silent steps backward, as little prickles of heat poked at the back of his neck.

Giving a nod, Frankie walked to the door without so much as a peep. The door swung wide for his husky frame, then closed quietly behind him. Nicky angled a curious, wide-eyed look at him as his heavy footsteps made their way over to where he stood.

"Come on outside, pal." Frankie dropped an arm over the boy's shoulders and he led him down the hallway to a side door. "We'll play ball a while, while your pop finishes his business."

"Who are those guys?" Nicky's eyes shifted at his tall friend.

Frankie was a stocky man, about twenty-five, with a cleanshaven face and thick black hair. Nicky wasn't sure why, but he had come to understand, over the last few years, that he was often in Frankie's charge, especially if Nicky or his sister went out anywhere without their parents. He had also come to know that, though he knew Frankie to be kind and friendly, to the unfamiliar eye he might appear to be a forbidding sort of figure.

The man shook his head, sliding an over-sized mitt onto his hand, then tossed the ball to Nicky. "It ain't my place to discuss your father's business, pal, with nobody, not even you. If he wants you to know his business, he'll tell you himself."

"Pop usually lets me go into his office when other people are there." He shrugged. "How come he doesn't let me when those guys are here?"

"He usually lets you come in because he knows you wanna be like him. He knows you're gonna take over for him, someday. As for the rest, like I say, everybody's got things they wanna keep to themselves. Yeah?"

Nicky nodded, disappointed, but understanding what he'd been told. "You think Pop's ever gonna tell me about private stuff?"

Frankie nodded, squatting down and holding his gloved hand out in front of him. "Your pop's gonna tell you what he wants you to know, when he wants you to know it. He'll probably clue you in when you get a little older. A father wants better for his son than he has for himself. Your pop is trying to do better by you. That's all I'm gonna say about that."

Better? What did he mean by that? Nicky and Marie couldn't have asked for anything more than they had. They never wanted for anything. Truthfully, they were probably on the spoiled side. They had toys, books, clubs and sports, all sorts of travel and adventures, a massive home with horses and a pool. Frankie even drove them back and forth to an exclusive private school. That raised another thought in Nicky's mind.

"Yeah, but…" Nicky rolled the ball around and around in his hands, studying the scarred marks on the white leather. "How come Mama and Pop make you go everywhere with me and Marie?"

A laugh shook Frankie's broad barrel chest and a toothy grin spread wide at his mouth. His gloved hand fell to the grass from his catcher's position. "Now, what kind of a question is that? We're friends, ain't we, Nicky? You ain't sick of me, are ya?"

"No." He shrugged, wondering why no one would ever explain it to him. None of his friends appeared to have a *friend* like Frankie. "Pop says you're sort of like a big brother, that you're there to keep an eye on us."

"Right." He held his glove out again. "Okay, so that's settled. Now, throw the ball, kid."

They continued to hurl the baseball back and forth for about ten minutes, until Nicky suddenly stopped, looking up at the men walking toward the cars in the driveway. He threw his glove down into the grass and sprinted to stand next to Frankie. He angled a curious look up at him again, but only received another shake of his companion's head. If he wasn't going to crack, Nicky was just going to have to ask his father, straight out.

The thought of confronting his father was a little intimidating. Though Salvador was kind, everyone understood that he guarded his privacy fiercely. Nicky also knew that he'd already trespassed on it once that day. Recalling that fact, he shrunk down a little, his eyes warily observing the determined way his father started across the lawn toward them.

"Frankie, go get a drink in the house, huh?" Salvador's gaze remained firmly on his son.

"Sure thing, Sal. It is a little warm out here." Frankie slipped the glove from his hand, tucking it under his arm, and gave the boy a wink as he headed toward the house. "I'll be right inside."

Salvador squatted in front of his son, curling a hand over one of his thin shoulders. "Nicky, you know you aren't supposed to be in my business when my door is closed."

"It wasn't closed, Pop." Nicky shrugged, then swallowed hard against a lump that instantly formed when his father's gaze sharpened on him. He dropped his eyes to the ground and he let it his head bob. "Yeah, Pop. I know."

His father reached a hand, lifting his son's chin. "When two men are talking business, they look each other in the eye, out of respect and honesty. Understand?"

He nodded again. "Yes, sir."

"Good. You remember that." He sighed, patting a hand against the side of his son's face with a smile. "Ah, you're a good boy, Nicky. Now, what was it you wanted?"

Remembering what his father had said, he firmed his jaw and kept his eyes directly on his. "Who are those men that I never get to meet, and why can't Marie, or Mama, or I ever go in when they're here? And what trouble did I almost get into last year? Frankie says that someday I'll be running the business. Shouldn't I know what *all* the business is, then?"

"So many questions, Nicky."

Salvador studied his boy's face, admired the nerve he knew it must have taken him to ask such questions. His chest rose and fell evenly. If only he could explain to his satisfaction, without scaring him, why he had severed ties with men who called themselves his friends, why Frankie was always around, and why he had more secrets than would ever be safe for his son to know. The time for sharing some of them would eventually come, but not today.

"You will take over for me, Nicky, eventually. One day, you'll have something so precious to you that you'll understand why I have secrets to protect the things that are precious to me. One day, I promise, no more secrets, not from you." He shook his head. "Today isn't that day, though. It's not always good for a man to know so much. You have to trust me. Yeah? You just take my word for it that I have reasons for the things I do. You remember that Frankie is here to make sure no trouble *does* come to you. Okay?"

Nicky felt somewhat disappointed by the vague reply, but nodded. "Sure, Pop."

"Good boy." Salvador straightened his posture again, draping an arm across his son's shoulders, walking with him toward the house. "Very good boy."

Chapter One

On the corner of Grafton and Nineteenth Street, in Saint Adeline, Illinois, a medium-sized town not too far from Chicago, there stood a smallish Irish restaurant by the name of MacCarthaigh's. Nicholas Caprianno generally conducted business at favorite dining spots, when not in his large city office or the satellite office he kept on the outskirts of Chicago.

On this day, however, his previous meeting had detained him long enough that he didn't want to travel into the city for lunch. In the end, and as his previous point of business had directed him to Saint Adeline, he and his business advisor settled on trying the mom and pop-style establishment.

The restaurant buzzed with a mixture of murmured conversations at the tables around them, and occasional loud cheers traveled over from the bar. There was a total of fifteen tables and a long dining counter off to the side. The shift change had left them sitting with empty glasses for the last few minutes, but that didn't matter. The two men were too busy discussing important proposals to be bothered by their empty tumblers.

"Good." Nick flipped the cover of a folder closed and slid it onto a small stack next to him. "I think we can do better, though. Get a hold of their lawyers and counter with a four percent increase."

"Four?" His companion shook his head. "They'll never go for that."

"Trust me, Alf. All right, now, what else you got?" Nick took the next file that was extended to him. After scanning the header, he flicked a glance across to his companion's side of the table. "This is that same deal you brought me a couple of weeks ago. I thought we decided we weren't interested in pursuing it any further."

"When I went back to them, the head, Jansen, asked me for a private meeting. He… made a good case for another shot."

Nick only silently stared back at him. Alf, the broader-built man wearing a dark silk suit shrugged to him. He wiped a napkin over the mayonnaise that caught in his grayed mustache. The deepening wrinkles on his face showed him to be somewhere in his mid-sixties. He frowned, realizing that his boss wanted more explanation.

"It has the potential to be a good deal, Nick. I think it's worth another look."

"Jansen." Nick furrowed his brows slightly as he dug way back into his mind, back to a hazy familiarity buried in the cobwebs of the past. "Why does that name ring a bell?"

"Should ring a few. This is Crispen Jansen." Alf cleared his throat, flicking his eyes away from his boss' study. "Your pop had dealings with his old man, back in the day, Scotty Jansen."

"Back in the day, huh?" Nick's brows dipped lower. That phrase didn't inspire much confidence.

It was Alf's turn to stare back at the younger man in silence. Nick was just tipping thirty. His complexion had a light olive tone, and the smooth lines of his handsome face had been cleanly-shaved. Owning a savvy mind for business, an MBA from an ivy-league university, and having been trained in the operations of his family's business since he was young, Nick knew better than to sign anything without fully picking it apart first.

He ran a hand over the side of his carefully combed, thick black hair as he moved his dark-eye gaze over the document before him again. Viewing a few too-carefully phrased portions of the proposal in his hand, he pulled his lower lip between his perfect teeth, flipping back and forth through pages. After another minute or two, he drew his mouth into a firm pout and he slowly shook his head. Looking across the table at Alf, he mirrored the shrugging motion he'd been given.

"Nah, Alf. This isn't gonna fly." Nick cleared his throat, leaning back in his chair. "No go. Not this way. This Jansen guy wants to deal, he better come up with something a whole lot better than that. To be honest, I'm not so sure we even want to deal with him. I haven't heard much good about him, or the boys he has working for him."

"Come on, Nicky. How many times have people said the same about you? You know better than anybody that reputations only speak so much truth. Anyway, it looks okay, at least as a starting point for negotiation."

"I don't know." Nick shook his head, rubbing a hand back and forth over his mouth.

Alf's chest slumped and he shot a hard breath out when Nick folded his arms. "Listen, I started working for your grandfather when I was a kid. I was your pop's advisor for years. Now, I'm working for you, ain't I? You think I don't know the business? I talked to these fellas, myself, for cryin' out loud!"

"At the end of the day, it's my money I'm risking. And speaking of reputations, it's my reputation, and the reputation of the whole Caprianno family, we're playing with when we do a deal. If you want me to take another look at this guy, fine, but I'm going to want you to…" His eyes flicked up when a new waitress lifted his empty glass and replaced it with a fresh drink. She rattled off a quick apology about the wait, then moved off. "To, ah…"

Alf wrinkled a frustrated brow in response to his boss' sudden stammering tongue. He'd never known Nick to trip over his words before, or to be distracted when it came to business. Shifting a glance to follow Nick's watchful gaze, he observed her quickly and efficiently clearing tables around them, observed the light upward tug at one corner of Nick's mouth.

Her dark copper hair was tidily pulled back from her face, her curves trim and petite, but not unfeminine. Even her emerald green eyes appeared to smile when her lips curved at one customer or another, a pleasant laugh occasionally rising over the din. She appeared to be a few years under Nick, somewhere between Nick and his younger sister Marie. It wasn't a brotherly eye that Alf monitored from his boss, though.

The older of the pair leaned back in his seat, folding his arms across his thick chest. After a moment, the woman made her way back over to their table. Pen in hand over her order pad, she hadn't even looked up to notice Nick's captivated stare, or Alf's disgruntled frown.

"Can I get you anything else, guys?"

Glancing to another table where a patron had lifted a finger to get her attention, she nodded with a wink, in signal that he would be next. Turning back to Nick and Alf, she finally lifted her eyes to the younger of the two men. She felt her face flush slightly because of his intense gaze. He was one of those men that made a woman want to sigh, just because he was there, but she held back.

"Ah… Is that going to be it for you today?" Her thumb clicked and unclicked the pen in her hand a couple of times. "Dessert, or another appetizer?"

"Nah, that's it. We got business." Alf grumbled. "Just leave the ticket and shove off, doll."

At that, she flicked a hot glare at the older man. Ripping the sheet from her pad, she extended the page to Nick's quietly outstretched hand without shifting her gaze again. She tapped the nail of her right index finger against her acrylic name badge.

"It's Cathlene, not doll." She corrected sternly. "My head isn't stuffed with cotton."

"Yeah, whatever." Alf waved a hand off at her as she started away from the table again. "I'm just saying, I think it'd be a mistake to blow this deal off before we have time to really check it out. Give me time to work with these boys. This Jansen kid might not have the best reputation, at the moment, but once upon a time… Nick? Nicky? What are you doing?"

Nick signaled to the hot-tempered redhead again, still not having taken his eyes off of her. Though he'd first been captivated by her remarkably attractive looks, she'd further snared his interest with her snappy response to Alf. Something fascinated him about the way she'd flashed such a sharp look, lashing her words at a man that intimidated most people.

"I'm ordering dessert." Nick answered distractedly. "What do you think?"

"Dessert?" Alf puffed a heavy breath and rolled his eyes. "I'm talking about the return interest on a two-million-dollar investment of *this* pie, and he wants to hear the dessert specials from some saucy little fire bunny. You sure you know what you're really trying to order, Nick? I don't think what you're looking at is on the menu."

Approaching them, she abruptly reached to take the check from Nick's hand. "Mistake on your bill? Happens between shift changes, sometimes, especially with a new kid. If you'll just hand it back, I'll-"

"No, no. The ticket's fine." Nick shook his head, a smile etching decidedly onto his mouth in response to the terse inflection of her voice. "I just thought I'd like to have something sweet, after all. Give me a run-down, *Cathlene*?"

"Something sweet." She cocked her head slightly, pinning a no-nonsense stare on him. "Sure."

She lifted a brow to him, uncertain of whether he was attempting to come on to her, or to make her the butt of some unspoken joke between the two men. Perhaps both.

Never shrinking from a challenge, she folded her arms, continuing to stare directly back at him as she prepared to rattle off the options.

"Two kinds of pie today, apple and cherry, scoop of ice cream with either chocolate or caramel sauce, or MacCarthaigh's famous chocolate cake with whipped Irish Cream frosting."

Hearing the underlying fire in her voice, Nick grinned a little deeper. She clearly understood his motives, perhaps better even than he had himself. "If I asked pretty please, what would the odds be of getting a couple of cherries on top?"

"Cherries." She rolled her eyes at the obvious flirtation. When he gave a soft, harmless laugh, she found herself unable to suppress her own smile. "Cherries on top of what, charmer?"

"Forget the cake, Nick!" Alf pounded an impatient fist on the tabletop, making the dishware rattle. His action elicited another heated flash from her eyes, quickly dissolving the curve Nick had drawn from her lips. "We got business to finish, here."

"I'll, ah…" Nick exchanged the dark look he'd leveled on Alf with a softer one for her. "I'll take the cake to go."

"I'll box it up. It'll just be a minute." She nodded as she started away, maintaining the sharp expression she held on his companion. "I don't want to hold *you* up."

Alf slanted a frown back at Nick and grumbled something about her being a feisty little broad. "Can we get through the rest of this, and then you can go romance the skirt?"

Cate rounded the bar, sliding a small takeout box in front of her brother, Shayne. "Do me a favor, throw a couple cherries on that, will you?"

"Cherries?" He squinted as if he hadn't heard correctly, scratching the tip of a finger at the manicured edge of his red-blonde beard. "On the cake? This cake? Gran's Irish Cream chocolate cake? You sure about-"

"Ugh, just scoot over. I'll do it myself." She reached around him, throwing a few cherries into the box with a pair of ice tongs. She nudged him again. "Hey, Shayne. Those two at the table over there, the old goat and the nice-looking one. Who are they? You know? I don't think I've seen them in here before."

He slid a tall pint of dark stout in front of a man a couple of stools over from where they stood and cast a glance in the direction she'd indicated. Giving a short laugh he shook his head. "You can't be serious. You been living under a rock?"

"What?" She shrugged. "Who are they?"

"Those are not guys you want to mess with, Cate." He warned, lowering his voice, observing the interest she scanned the younger man with. "That's Nicholas Caprianno and Alfonse Giuseppe. Caprianno owns most of this street. Forget that. He just made a deal to buy most of this block, and a good chunk of other real estate around town, too. He also has holdings in Chicago and its surrounding area. He's got his finger in pies all over the place. Giuseppe is one of his, ah, *associates*."

"Associates?" Bewildered, she turned toward him, lowering her voice a little. "What do you mean? Why do you say it like that? *Associates*."

"Let's just say, guys like Nick Caprianno do lots of deals, and I don't want to know anything about any of them, or the people involved in them. I just want to serve them and get them out of here." Lines of disapproval drew between his brows in response to the smile on her lips when Nick glanced in their direction. "Don't even think it, Cate."

"Don't think what?" She rolled her eyes, unwilling to admit that Caprianno had, indeed, managed to capture her attention. "I'm sure they're both harmless, Shayne. Your problem is that you watch too many movies."

He nodded, wagging the bossy finger of an older brother at her. "And maybe you don't watch enough of them."

Nick blotted a napkin over a water spot on his silk tie. "That finally it?"

"Not quite. What do I tell Jansen about his offer?" Alf shuffled the portfolio folders into a pile and slipped them under one arm. "He's gonna want to know what's holding up your decision."

"Well, at the moment, you are." Nick leaned an elbow on the table, flicking his brows indifferently as he replied. "The idea of renewing any connections to the old days isn't necessarily something I'm anxious to do. I don't want there to be any question when it comes to our business ethics. I want a whole lot more homework done on him, and his people, before I make any final decisions. Just tell him I want more time to think it over."

Alf pulled his lips to a loose pucker, furrowing his overly-thick brows, and he nodded. He wished things had run smoother. "I'll let him know your concerns. We might be able to work out some kind of middle-"

"Who you working for, this Jansen guy, or me?" Nick shook his head, his voice growing slightly louder. "You don't tell anybody anything about my business, or about my thoughts on this. You tell him I haven't decided, if you want, but that's all he needs to know. That's it. Understand? He's wanting a favor from me, not the other way around. I couldn't care less if he feels like we're leaving him hanging. He needs somebody to hold his hand, he's in the wrong business."

"All right." Alf nodded, lifting his heavy frame from the chair with a light groan. "Just don't wait too long. You might want to simmer that hot temper a little. Even if you decide not to go ahead with it, he isn't the sort of guy you want to insult."

"Neither am I." Nick tilted a stern look up at his friend. "You can tell him that, too. I'm not getting hooked up with some small-time hood, looking to break into a larger bracket of operations. I don't intend to be anyone's free ride."

"Okay, Nicky, okay." He nodded, patting the side of Nick's face in a paternal gesture. "I'm just trying to help. You know I got your back, yeah? We good?"

"Yeah." He nodded with a calmer expression. Feeling the tightness in his jaw beginning to relax, he began to lightly smile. "Yeah, we're good."

"All right. Good." Alf stepped back, giving a sideways glance as Cate started toward them again, then chuckled, flipping his brows at his friend. "You got your eye on something, though, don't ya?"

Nick's lips loosened into a more pleasant smile. "Get out of here, or I'll never get anywhere. You set her on edge."

Alf grinned back, pushing in his chair. "Pay attention to that red hair. It's probably a fair warning about her temper. I'll bet she's got a hot one."

"So do you. Hasn't stopped me from liking you, all these years, has it?" Nick's quick laughter was telling of their relationship. Though no blood relation, Alf had acted as a sort of guiding force for as long as he could remember. "Well?"

"No, it hasn't stopped you from liking me." Alf shook his head. He squinted, silently considering the deal again. "What is it about her?"

"I don't know." He looked down at the table, still unable to control the upward turn of his lips. "Something tells me it's worth finding out, though."

"I know. You feel it inside, right? Ha! You and that gut of yours. You crack me up with that, kid." He chuckled. "Yeah, okay. Well, I'll go talk to this guy and check back in with you at the office tonight. Have fun, kid."

Cate strode up to the table, placing the box on the tabletop. She flattened a palm next to the cake, watching Alf go out the door, then turned her attention to the man smiling up at her. "Your friend better watch his blood pressure. I'm not up to date on my CPR."

"I'll tell him." Nick gave a light chuckle, pulling the money for the tab from his wallet, along with a generous tip. Yeah, he liked her spunky presence. "Can I ask you something?"

She shrugged, reflecting the curve of his lips. "Can I stop you?"

His chuckle gave way to a heartier laugh as he replaced his billfold into the inner pocket of his coat and stood. "You, ah… You work this shift, usually?"

"Monday through Wednesday and again Saturday. Thursday and Friday I work the dinner shift, and Sunday's I have off. Why? You planning to request me for your server whenever you're doing a business lunch? I only see to certain tables, you know."

"I guess I'll have to be careful about where I sit. Would you mind?" He flashed a flirtatious grin, leaning just a little toward her as he did so. "I'll be doing a lot more business in this neighborhood, as it happens. Might be nice to see a friendly face."

"Free country." She shrugged, doing her best to keep the pink from darkening too much in her cheeks. Oh, his cologne smelled divine, his grin and his close proximity tempting her pulse slightly faster. "You can conduct business anywhere you please, so long as you aren't just table hogging."

"Good to know." He nodded, pulling a set of keys from his pocket and bouncing them a couple of times in his hand. He pushed his chair in and lifted the to-go box for a curious whiff. "Mmm. Very good to know."

"So, Mr. Caprianno…" A warm, tingling sensation painted the apples of her cheeks when his deep brown eyes suddenly flicked onto hers again. "I guess I should expect to see you again soon?"

"Soon, yeah." He gave a quick laugh, nodding, knowing that he hadn't mentioned his name and that he'd paid the bill in cash. The appealing idea that she'd asked someone about him forced the corners of his mouth to lift a little higher. "I'll see you, Cathlene."

"Oh, um… Cate." She gave a quiet laugh and shrugged. "Cate's fine."

"I'll tell Alf." He paused, lightly nipping the edge of his lower lip between his teeth.

"*He* can call me Cathlene." She gave a curt nod.

As he passed her, she tucked the cash from the table into her apron and returned his amused smile. As she began clearing the dishes, her gaze followed him all the way out the door. She giggled softly in response to the warm, enticing grin he cut back at her from the sidewalk.

Shayne stomped up behind her, his voice low in her ear. "What did I tell you about that guy. Are you crazy flirting with him, that way?"

"I wasn't flirting."

"*Ohh, call me Cate.*" He mimicked her higher pitch, in a grating way that only an older brother could manage.

"Oh, wind your neck in, Shayne." She tweezed the water glasses between her fingers and started past him. "He was just being friendly, and so was I, same as I would be with any other customer."

"I don't often see you smile like *that* at other customers." He shook his head, following her back behind the bar as she discarded the dirty dishes into a bin, and he thrust a bossy finger at her. "You need to be more careful who you're flirting with."

"You know, the older you get, the more paranoid you get." She rolled her eyes and washed her hands before filling a couple of pints for a table near the window. "You're my older brother and a co-owner, not my keeper, not my boss."

"And still, you know I'm usually right." He dropped his knuckles onto his hips as he watched her walk away.

"You'd like to think so." She grumbled, stalking off. "There's an awful lot of room for interpretation in that word, *usually*."

She placed the two glasses onto the table that had ordered them, smiling deeply at them as she took their lunch choices. To prove her point, she laughed and swiped a hand at the shoulder of one of the men. Turning, she beamed back at her brother. She would smile and flirt with anyone she saw fit. She had never been a woman to be told what to do, and she wasn't about to change that for, or because of, anyone. Shayne only sighed, shaking his head.

Chapter Two

Cate placed the thick white plate down on the top of the lunch counter and slid onto her stool. Her eyes had been too preoccupied by the contents of her cellphone screen to notice much else around her.

Being at the restaurant five days a week, she counted her breaks as sacrosanct, even unpinning her name tag a lot of times so that she wouldn't be bothered. The regulars, of course, knew that she was one of the family who owned the restaurant. As the regulars had become more like family to the MacCarthaighs, though, they didn't generally bother Cate or Shayne when they finally had a moment to sit.

"I see you're taking your break, right on time." Smiling over the rim of his coffee cup, Nick slanted a look in her direction.

"Yeah, I guess I'm pretty… predictable." She turned her head to the side, looking a couple stools down from where she sat. She shouldn't have been too surprised to see him sitting there, but it surprised her nonetheless. "Ah. So, my lunch date returns. You really *are* getting to be one of the regulars around here."

"I guess I am." Giving a soft laugh, Nick stood, sliding his dessert plate and cup to the place next to her. "So long as we're already talking, I didn't figure you'd mind if I joined you."

"Wow. That was smoothly executed." She shook her head with a light giggle. "I was beginning to think I wasn't going to see you today."

"Yeah, I, ah… I guess I do usually sit at a table when I come in, don't I? And a little earlier." He shrugged, shifting his eyes away from hers with a rarely-given sheepish grin. By coming later, he knew he'd have more chance of a conversation with her. "It's just that I noticed you take your breaks about now, and that you sit at the counter when you do."

"Mmm, and you've been keeping tabs on me." She nodded, admiring the unfamiliar flicker of discomfort in his expression. "Actually, I don't like to hog customer tables, when we're busy."

"You're in here a lot." He observed. "Like, every time I come in."

"Mm-hmm. Funny, I was just about to say the same thing to you." She smiled back with another soft laugh. "What can I say? When it's a family-run restaurant, and your parents semi-retire, you're responsible for picking up the slack."

"Ah, family business." He nodded, as if he hadn't already asked around about her. "Me, too."

"Yeah, I think I heard that somewhere." She smiled at the underlying uneasiness that peeked from his eyes when she'd said that. "MacCarthaigh's has had a steady stream of business since 1954. I was conscripted into service when I was fourteen. Now, I guess you could say I'm one of the engines that keeps the machine working. What's your excuse for being in here all the time? You have to be getting sick of the same thing for lunch every day, for the last two weeks."

"Well, I don't always come in for lunch." He flicked a look down between them, though he couldn't quite fully conceal the grin she'd brought to his mouth. "Sometimes I come in for breakfast, or haven't you noticed?"

"Come to mention it, I have noticed a fairly regular visit on the days I pull a morning shift." She nodded, then jerked her head in the direction of the bar. "So has Shayne, by the way."

"Shayne." He cleared his throat, the curve at his lips straightening a little. "Right, the ah, extremely suspicious older brother."

"Mmm. Accurate, but let's go with cautious. Sounds a little less intrusive. He means well, especially when a man appears to be mirroring my schedule." Laying an arm across the countertop, she gave a short laugh and cocked a bewildered expression in his direction. "How did you know he's my brother, anyway? I don't think I've ever said."

"Oh, I must've heard somebody mention it." He cleared his throat, pushing the cherries around the plate, then shrugged and dropped his fork again. "Anyway, I'm all right with suspicious older brothers, as it happens. I have a lot of respect for them. I'm one, myself."

"Are you?" She nodded, flicking one of her perfectly-shaped brows as she reached for her glass. "Your sister has my sympathy. I assume it's a sister. Brothers don't tend to bug one another in the same way."

"A sister, yes. Marie. I'll have to remember to pass your condolences along to her." He laughed, understanding the wary eye Shayne held on him, more than she could possibly realize. "She's in grad school, but I'd probably still be giving any guy sitting with her the same look he's got pinned on me. You can tell him he doesn't have anything to worry about from me, though."

"Ha! Wanna watch me try it?" She laughed again, shaking her head. "Would you really believe that if any guy hanging around your sister said as much?"

He considered her question for a second. Creasing the space between his brows, he scrunched his nose a little and shook his head. "Nah. Not for a minute."

"Yeah. Didn't think so." Her mouth edged up higher at the corners. "Neither would Shayne. Think I'll just keep your tidings of good will between the two of us, for the time being."

"Probably best." His chest vibrated lightly with amusement and he drew an inconspicuously deep breath. "So, listen… Not that it isn't nice seeing you in here, but I was thinking that, maybe sometime we could-"

"No." She'd sobered quickly and shook her head. "I mean, thanks, and no offense, but I don't think so."

"Oh. Okay." He slouched back, confusion painting itself onto his face. It was almost as if someone had flipped a switch within her. Attempting to draw out her smile again, he gave a soft laugh. "Mind if I at least ask why? Is it Alf? I know you two didn't exactly hit it off, but he doesn't go everywhere I do."

With a soft curve resurfacing at one corner of her mouth, she settled her eyes back on him again. "You're easy to talk to, and you seem like a really nice man, Nick, but…"

"I *seem* like a nice man. Ouch. 'Seem' being the operative word, in there? I guess that means you've heard some things, huh?" The grin from seconds before was now devoid from his lips, and he nodded. "I don't suppose it would help any to say that you shouldn't believe everything you hear? Books and covers, and all that."

"It's true that I like to make up my own mind about things, but… Well, there's an awful lot written on your cover, Nick. Some things that are pretty hard to ignore." She shrugged. "It would make Shayne crazy, anyway. You're an older brother. I'm sure you get that."

"I do." He nodded again. "I also know that Marie wouldn't give my anxiety a second thought before she did exactly what she wanted… if she wanted to."

"Sounds like your sister and I have a lot in common." She slanted her gaze away from the handsome grin that had returned to entice her. "I really do have some doubts of my own, this time. In this particular case, I'm not the best at turning a deaf ear to what I've heard. I'm sorry if that sounds offensive."

"Not offensive. Maybe just a little misinformed. I guess that's what you'd expect me to say, though, huh?" He sighed, genuinely disappointed. Shifting a look from where he drummed the fingers of his right hand on the counter back to her, a soft curve peeked back onto his lips. "Mind if I keep coming in? Maybe you'll eventually change your mind. Might even hear a few good things, somewhere in there, too."

A short laugh quietly escaped her and she nodded gently. "I might hear some good things, but I don't know that they'd be enough to change my mind."

"Okay." He took a second to run through his options. "I obviously noticed you take your breaks at the same times, each shift. Maybe we could just talk some more. Give you a chance to make up your own mind, since you say you like to."

"Oh, boy. You don't often take no for an answer, do you?"

"Not when I can help it. Not when I think it's worth it." Keeping her in his sights, his eyes focused more deeply, convincingly on hers. Her hesitation to shoot him down made her appear less than settled on the decision she'd made. "So, would you mind?"

"I told you before, it's a free country." She felt her own smile slowly returning with the warmth of his gaze softening something within her. "All right, truth. I've enjoyed our banter today, but I'm going to feel really bad if I end up giving you the wrong idea. I really don't think I'm going to change my mind."

"The wrong idea?" He laughed. "I think I'm bright enough to figure out if you definitely make up your mind about me, one way or another. I just don't want you to make up your mind before you have all the facts."

She rested her head against the curl of her hand, her eyes glancing away from his amused study of them. "I didn't mean to imply that you weren't bright enough to recognize… You are determined, though."

"I was only kidding, Cate. Determination, that helps with *my* line of business." He reached to stroke his finger over the hand she had rested on the counter between them. "I knew what you meant."

"I better get back to work." Catching the heated, watchful stare from her brother, she withdrew her hand. Her skin continued to tingle from Nick's warm touch. She'd only taken a step or two away from him when she felt the urge to turn back, though she kept her voice quiet as she spoke. "Nick… I'm not saying yes, or even that I'll think about saying yes, but… I will say that I won't mind if you want to keep coming in."

"Yeah?" He nodded, letting the hint of a laugh pass from his lips. There it was, the open door he was hoping for. "Okay, good."

"Yeah, good. Good." She patted the heel of her hand on the back of a chair, smiling with a pleasant blush at her cheek. "Oh, and, I do take my breaks at the same times, each shift. But, ah, bring something to work on when you come in. Less conspicuous, that way."

"I can do that." He laughed softly, giving her a last nod.

He watched her walk away, grinning deeply at the way she'd sneaked a glance back at him, once or twice. It would take some time. It would take patience and a whole lot of convincing, but he didn't mind the wait or the effort. She was worth every ounce of whatever it cost him. He couldn't say why, but he just felt it was right, just as he did when a business deal was going to work out. It was something in his gut, the intuition Alf had teased him about.

Chapter Three

Cate ambled through the Saturday morning farmer's market by herself. Her light-wash jean jacket was zipped snugly, her thin green scarf wound lightly around her neck. She'd misplaced her gloves, again. Her fingers would've been icy-cold, had it not been for the latte she'd picked up in her favorite little shop just off the square. As it was, with her jacket and scarf, and her favorite pair of jeans, the coffee made the chill in the air bearable.

She winced a little, as she made her way up to one of the booths. The farmer's market was one of her favorite things about living in Saint Adeline. She wasn't about to let an unfortunate, throbby ankle stop her from her weekly tradition, especially as the market would be closing down in a few weeks for winter. Still, she made a light grimace. She probably should've worn different shoes. Glancing down at her foot with a frown, she hadn't noticed where she was walking, and bumped into a solid figure in a dark overcoat. They both stumbled, but neither fell.

"Oh, I'm so sorr…" Her eyes clapped onto the grin belonging to the ill-fated recipient of her clumsiness. "Nick?"

"Cate." He laughed softly at her surprise, enjoying the shock that held her mouth open for a few seconds. He continued to hold onto her as she balanced herself a little better. "Hey, why don't you look where you're going, lady?"

"I'm sorry." Her laughter came easily at the tone of his playful scolding. "I guess it isn't really the best idea to walk around a public place, staring down at your feet. If I was going to make someone my victim, I suppose I should be glad it turned out to be you. At least, I'm fairly sure you won't be too angry."

"Not at all, actually. I sort of enjoyed the run-in."

He let his hands slip from her arms as she slid a step back from him, an awkward smile being aimed back at him for the familiarity, and for the comment. He wasn't about to admit to her that he'd overheard her plans and that their meeting had been less fortuitous than she recognized. His glance shifted around the groups of faces in the crowd surrounding them.

"You here alone, too?" As if he didn't already know the answer to his question.

"Yeah. It's sort of my thing. It's the quiet before the chaos of my Saturday afternoon shift." She nodded, twisting her brows a little when she noticed the dribble of coffee down the brushed wool lapel of his overcoat. "Sorry about that. I know it's a pain in the butt to get coffee stains out. If you want to have it dry-cleaned, I'd be happy to-"

"Nah." He shrugged, the curve still solidly on his lips. "Don't worry about it. If I had a dime for all the times that I've spilled coffee on myself at work, I'd be a rich guy."

She snorted a laugh in response to his statement, the arch of her brow creeping a little higher. "If I remember correctly, you do have quite a few dimes, Nick."

"Yeah, well, what can I say? I've spilled a lot of coffee." He laughed again, rubbing the back of his neck. "Don't worry about the coat. I have interests in a dry-cleaning front, just down from my Chicago office."

"A front?" She edged a step back.

"Not that kind of front, Cate." His chest shook lightly and he cut an amused glance back at her. "I meant a storefront. You know, strip malls. That kind of thing."

"Ah, right." She blushed lightly, cutting her eyes away from him. "Well, I guess I should-"

"Join me?" He extended his arm out to her. "Might as well, right? Be kind of weird to pretend we're surprised every time we bumped into each other now."

She flicked a look down at the offering, a soft laugh escaping her as she took it with a nod. "I've learned my lesson. Pay attention. I think I can safely promise not to run into you again."

"Pity. It was a pretty pleasant experience, as those things go." Probably best not to mention that he'd actually stepped into her path when he'd noticed that she was distracted. His smile softened and he drew his brows when she looked down again. "Hey, what's so fascinating about your feet, anyway?"

She let her head fall back with a disgusted growl. "Well, Shayne would have you believe that I was just born clumsy, but the truth is, I jammed my ankle leaving the restaurant, the other night. The sidewalk is broken and buckling a couple of squares down from the front door. Technically, it's the city's responsibility. It's just on the edge of the corner of our building, though. They claim it's on our property, so it's our problem. They've been giving us the runaround about it for months. I'm just glad it was me."

"Glad it was you?" His brows pulled further in. "Why would you say that? Should we sit down somewhere?"

"No. I'm fine, just a little embarrassed, and a lot mad." She rolled her eyes, laughing at the way he'd immediately begun to scan the area for an available bench. On Saturday mornings, there were never any empty benches. "If it wasn't my ankle, it might have been a patron's. Since the responsibility of the section of the sidewalk is up in the air, it could mean a lawsuit for MacCarthaigh's. Shayne coned it off after this happened, but we'll probably just end up fixing it to save the hassle."

"Let the city get away with that?" He shook his head. "I'm surprised you, of all people, would cave without a fight. Doesn't really seem to fit your temperament."

"Are you implying that I'm stubborn?" She narrowed her eyes slightly. When his mouth poised to speak, but no sound came out, she puckered her lips to keep them from budding into a grin. "Hmm. Lucky for you, I happen to consider stubbornness positive."

"I'm definitely one person you don't have to explain stubbornness to."

"In any case, it would probably be better, and safer, if we just saved the hassle and had the stupid sidewalk fixed."

His expression shadowed in reflection of the thoughts tumbling around his head. He'd managed to paint a passable smile back onto his mouth when he noticed her careful study of him, though, and he gestured to her foot. "You sure you don't want to stop somewhere?"

"Nah." She shook her head, giggling quietly as she considered his question. "I choose to not give in to it. Like I say, I do consider stubbornness an attribute, not a failing."

"I'm not sure that ankles really understand attributes." His smile strengthened in response to her reply. "Attribute, or not, you're not going to be happy if that swells up on you. Come on. Just a quick stop."

"I also don't do well being told what to do." She bobbled her head, shooting him defiant grin. "You may as well put that bossy tone away, Mr. Caprianno. I can promise *you*, it'll be of no assistance to you when it comes to me."

The corners of his mouth tugged up harder and he nodded, walking on with her, though a little more slowly than they'd begun. "So, what brought you to this thing? Alone, I notice."

"Yes, alone." She laughed again. "You're alone, too. I like wandering around the market, especially on crisp days. The smells, the sounds, everything is intensified. Just, stop for a second. Close your eyes and breathe deep. You'll see what I mean."

Growing self-conscious in the crowd, he grinned wider and stared at her. She'd stopped right in the middle of the walking traffic to demonstrate her point. The mid-morning sunlight reflected off of the deep ginger tone of her hair, giving it a fiery glow against her porcelain skin. The apples of her cheeks and the tip of her nose had taken on a rosy hue in response to the nip of the air around them.

"Cate, we're right in the middle of things." He chuckled, attempting to guide her off to one side.

She tugged her brows in and huffed a breath, slivers of green cutting toward him from under the slight lift of her lashes. "You're not playing along, Nick. Try not being the boss, for just a minute."

Feeling a little silly, he gave in, closing his eyes. "All right, now what? What am I supposed to be doing?"

"Take a deep, saturating breath, and listen." She let the strong inhalation slowly leave her lungs again with a sense of satisfaction. "What do you smell? What do you hear?"

"I hear traffic." He drew a deep breath in through his nose, nearly chuckling when he heard her sharp exhalation and felt her chest slump next to his. "And I smell the coffee on my coat."

"Nick! Come on!" She felt a smile breaking over her lips again. "Fireplaces, popcorn balls, salted caramel, and coffee from vendors all along the way. You can hear the kids and all of the chatter about the drop in temperature."

"Yeah, okay." He nodded, cheating as he peeked a glance over at her again, admiring her all the more.

"There's popcorn and people talking about the cold weather. So?"

She laughed, opening her eyes to look back at him again. "*Fall*, Nick! It's not quite here, but it's just around the corner. Won't be much longer before kids are tramping down the sidewalks begging for candy." Noting the intense way his eyes had fixed on hers, she took a slight step back. "It's just one more reason to make sure that sidewalk gets fixed. We always have neighborhood kids pop in."

He quietly observed her as they began to walk along again, appreciating her on a deeper level than he had before. She was beautiful, intelligent. He loved the flare of her temper and her fiery spirit. He liked that she didn't appear to be at all intimidated by someone like grumpy old Alf. He appreciated that she hadn't been fully put off by the gossip surrounding his reputation. Here, though, in this place, he'd managed to get a closer look at her, at who *she* was.

Family was clearly important to her, as it was to him. She was every bit as strong-willed as he was, and she obviously wasn't interested in changing that fact any more than he was. He enjoyed her pert opinions and the way she'd scolded him into following her lead in enjoying the sights and sounds around them. It had been a long while since he'd taken the time to appreciate the slower pace of anything. It had been even longer since he'd let anyone boss him around.

"Oh, aren't those lovely?" She slipped free of his arm when they'd reached a floral booth. Her smile shifted toward the older man behind the table. "Mr. Donatello, you always have the most beautiful mums. You know I can't ever resist them. I think you purposely put them on the corner of your stall at the beginning of every autumn, knowing you're going to reign me in. I think I'll take a few bunches for the tables."

"Well, you can't start into fall without a good, healthy bunch of chrysanthemums." Though he nodded out of politeness, the vendor's laughter faded out a little when he recognized the man standing next to his favorite customer.

"Got what you want?" Nick watched as she gathered bouquets of deep burgundy, golden yellow, and butterscotch orange. He held a few bills out to the man when she'd finished making her selection, earning himself a surprised expression and the start of a protest from her. "Consider it a thank you for keeping me company."

Her eyes swept back over to the flower vendor and she offered him a smile. "Thank you, Mr. Donatello. These will look lovely on the tables."

"You have a wonderful day, dear." The older man nodded, keeping a careful eye on her companion as they started away from his booth.

Cate ran the tips of her fingers over the velvety petals. "That was thoughtful of you, but it wasn't necessary. I seriously doubt you were in need of company."

"I'm also not likely to turn down yours." He smiled with a shrug when she flicked a glance at him. "Anyway, I'm not too familiar with this part of Saint Adeline yet. I might've gotten lost or found myself in a precarious situation."

"Something tells me you could've taken care of yourself, just fine." She snickered at the too-serious expression he'd teased her with, then nudged his shoulder with hers. Stopping for a bag of caramel corn, she popped a piece into her mouth and walked on with him. "All right. So, what are you really doing here?"

He rocked his head lightly from side to side, stealing one of the sugary puffs from her red and white striped bag. He could tell, by the pointed expression she held on him, that she was wise to his motives.

"Okay, I confess. I might have overheard you talking about the street market with someone in MacCarthaigh's, the other day. Sounded interesting, so I thought I'd come check it out. Free country, and all that."

"Uh-huh. It is." She nodded, smirking back at him. "Did you also happen to overhear what time I was planning to be here?"

"No." He gave a sheepish chuckle, shaking his head before he admitted what came next. "I did, however, guess that you'd be at MacCarthaigh's later for your regular shift, so you'd have to be here early. I figured, if I walked around long enough…"

"That you'd run into me? So, it wasn't altogether a surprise when I bumped into you?" She rewarded him with another soft giggle, nodding. "Well, as nice as this impromptu meet-up has been, I really do have to get going."

He nodded. "Walk you back to your car?"

She shook her head. "No, thanks. I just live around the corner."

"Walk you home, then?" He shrugged, still grinning. "Safety, and whatnot?"

"I think I'll manage without an escort, thanks. It really isn't far. Daylight. Lots of people." She snickered gently, offering him a last sample of her caramel corn. "And, before you suggest a piggie back, my ankle will make the trip, just fine."

"I guess, I'll see you around, then." One corner of his smile stretched a little higher.

"Mm-hmm, and apparently, it could be anywhere. I'd better watch my step." She nodded, starting away from him with a long roll of laughter. "Bye, Nicky."

As she made her way down the sidewalk, he watched attentively, the curve never fully clearing from his lips. He'd heard, and appreciated, the way she was beginning to use his name less and less formally, and the way she'd begun to grow more playful with him. He enjoyed the way they were together.

Once she'd rounded the corner, he stole a glance down at his wrist watch, groaning. He was going to have to call Alf to push some of his appointments back. Letting his eyes move back to the direction she'd gone, he felt a warm sensation settling into his chest. The morning had been worth any inconvenience.

Chapter Four

Friday nights were particularly crammed, more so than the typical night at MacCarthaigh's. On Friday nights, a lot of the locals gathered at the bar to watch boxing on the televisions, while families and dates generally took up the dining area. One of the larger tables in the room had recently become a regular booking, always filled, always a large tab, always seen to only by Cate.

"No." Nick shook his head vehemently to whatever had been suggested. He slammed an elbow on the tabletop, aiming a finger at the man across from him. "You go back there, and you tell them that I'm not playing games with them! They either take this negotiation seriously, or the deal's off the table altogether. You can also let them know that the offer has been rescinded by another two percent for the hassle, and that's still a better deal than anyone else is going to offer them."

"Okay, Nick, okay." The man seemed to sink back into his seat, shoving the folder back into his briefcase as quickly as possible. "You're right. It ain't ready to sign yet. We ain't nobody's patsy."

"That's right. It's business, not favors." Nick gave a hard nod. "Now, what about this Jansen thing Alf keeps droning on about?"

Cate watched him from the bar, the cap of her pen between her teeth as she admired the concentration on his face. So firm, so commanding. Unwaveringly handsome, even when he frowned. If she hadn't been so engrossed by the gathering, she might have noticed Shayne's hip leaned against the bar next to her, his arms folded, scrutinizing her with caution.

"You wanna go pull up a chair, maybe?" He grouched, sliding a tray of drinks over to her. "I'm sure your boyfriend wouldn't mind if you just helped yourself to his lap."

"Don't be such a butt." She dropped her arm slack at her side, her order pen hanging loosely from the tips of her fingers. "He isn't my boyfriend. Nicky and I are just… friendly when he comes in."

"Nicky? Yeah, well, he's been *in* almost every day for the last eight weeks."

"Eight weeks? Really?" She poked him in the ribs. "I can't believe you've actually been keeping track. Don't you have anything better to do?"

"He's here whenever you're in, I notice." He grumbled, slicing another thin glare across the room when Nick looked up and caught her eye. "Get that tray to table eight."

"Yes, sir!" She saluted her brother, shoving him with her hip as she moved off.

Nick's concentration broke off from the group when she passed so near to his chair. He glanced to the side at her, not seeming to register any of the conversation around him. Grinning, he leaned back in his seat when she walked by again and flicked a quick wink in his direction. Now, if he could only be sure that it had been for his benefit, and not for her brother's.

"So, Nicky, what do you think?" Louis, the man to his right chuckled heartily, bumping elbows with him.

"Ah…" A mystified expression flashed back from Nick's face. "What was that? I think I might've missed…"

"Hey, fellas, I think his mind is somewhere else, tonight." Louis snickered again. "Something screwy about this place, I don't know. Always seems to make him a little distracted, huh?"

"All right, Louis, all right." Nick cleared his throat, adjusting the tie at his neck. "What else have you found out about the company dealings? I don't mean what his jerks are trying to pass off on paper. Something doesn't feel right with Jansen. I can smell it. If there's anything going on, I wanna know."

"We're still working on it, boss." Tony, a rail-thin man with silver hair muttered from Nick's left. "I don't know, though. You said that's why Alf is with them again tonight. He keeps saying he's checked them out. He seems to think it's legit enough to sign."

"Alf's the only reason I'm even still looking at this. When he throws out two million dollars, he can sign up with the girl scouts, for all I care. How many times do I have to say it? While it's my money and my name, I don't sign until *I'm* sure it's…" He trailed off again when Cate stepped next to him and dropped a hand over his shoulder.

"You guys want anything else? Dessert for the table? Louis, refill on your drink?" Smiling pleasantly at the courteous refusals of the men, she let her gaze drop to Nick. "Nicky, some chocolate cake? Just opened a whole new jar of maraschino cherries."

Laughing gently, he shook his head. "Not tonight, Cate. Thanks."

"All right." Making a final check with the others, she let her fingers slip from the shoulder of his dark suit jacket and started away. "Just let me know if you need anything."

Nick stared after her. As he watched her interactions with male patrons at another table, the upward tug at the corners of his lips slipped a bit. His heart began knocking a little harder against his ribs when she drew a hand to her chest, her head falling lightly back with a laugh in response to something that was said. Hearing the chuckles rising from his own table again, Nick shifted his gaze back down at his papers.

"Sorry. Where were we? Oh, right. I want more on Crispen Jansen. I don't care if you think you've found everything. I want you to look again."

The muscle along Nick's jaw rippled softly as his eyes strayed again from the open folder, over to where she skillfully side-slipped the attempted embrace of an intoxicated bar guest. Though the need for it irritated Nick, she appeared to be good at taking care of herself. The sharp inward draw of his brows softened as he observed Shayne helping the man to the front of the house where a cab waited.

Nick finally gave up the attempt to shake the distraction from his thoughts. "Okay, that's all for tonight, fellas. You get the idea. You know what I want."

"All right, Nick." Louis shook his hand as he stood to leave. "I'll see what else we can find out about Jansen and his boys."

"Thanks, Louis. Tony, go ahead with the counter on the New York deal and let me know what they come back with. Better yet, have our contact call the office when they get closer to making up their minds." He shook the hands of the other men and they all began to clear off. "Goodnight, guys. Thanks."

Making his way back behind the counter again, Shayne shook his head. "Well, there they go. Younger ones, older ones, looking like a table full of pallbearers. All wearing expensive suits as if they were cheap uniforms. You know, it surprises me that they don't ask for a dark corner when they come in, something away from the windows."

"Oh, pipe down!" Cate snapped, pulling her orders from the pick-up window. "What do you care where they sit? They run up a good-sized tab every time they come in, and they've never once caused any trouble. I really think most of what you assume is going on with Nick Caprianno is all in your own head."

"I care because of the way that goon looks at you, and because of the way you two laugh and talk whenever he's in here. It's that space around 'most' that has me worried. You're a smart woman, Cate. Don't be dumb about this. Men like Nicholas Caprianno attract trouble. Period. It's in their nature."

"You mean, how being overly suspicious is in your nature?" She dropped the orders onto a tray and slipped past him with a thin glare.

"Just doesn't think." Shayne huffed another breath as he filled an order at the bar. Those two were getting entirely too familiar for his liking. Leaning forward, he looked up at the man who reached for the glass. "You got a sister?"

"Uh, no." The confused patron twisted a look over his shoulder at the object of his bartender's dismay. "Two brothers."

Shayne nodded, flipping his white bar towel over one shoulder. "Lucky you."

Nick snagged the fingers of one of her hands after she delivered an order to a nearby table. "Cate, I hope we didn't bother you too much tonight. Your brother looks a little more antsy than usual."

"Believe me, Shayne is disturbed enough on his own. You guys were fine. You're always welcome here, Nicky." She smiled, letting her hand slip from the warm tingling sensation his touch evoked, then allowed the empty tray to hang at her side. "Are you taking off?"

"Yeah." He grinned softly, noticing the slightly quicker pace of her breaths. "Nice having someplace other than an office to hold meetings. After a while, the walls at work start to close in, you know?"

"Ha! Do I ever." She dropped a hip against the table his party had just vacated. "My shift ends in five minutes, though. Shayne's turn to close."

Nick dipped his brows at the news. He turned to look at the inky sky through the windows, then turned back to face her again. "You're going to leave by yourself? It's pretty late. Pretty dark."

"Well, that happens at nighttime. Sort of a cyclical thing, bright in the day, dark at night. You're usually gone by the time I leave, or I'm sure you would've noticed before. Anyway, the rain stopped, so I won't even have to make a run for my car. I'll be fine. Always am."

"Someone should walk you out." He muttered.

"I don't need anyone to walk me out."

"Oh, tough girl, huh?" He grinned.

"That's right. Night, Nicky." She patted a hand against the front of his dress shirt and started toward the kitchen to clock out. Noticing him only a step or two behind her, she shook her head. "I sure hope you're not going to start on a protective kick. I'll tell you the same thing I tell Shayne. I can take care of myself, just fine."

He stopped walking when she looked back at him. "I guess I'll see you later."

"Right, tomorrow." She laughed, watching the grin on his lips deepen more naturally before she pushed the private service door open. "Goodnight, Nicky."

He stopped at the register near the door. It was used for the evening crowd. Easier than picking up the tabs at each table when they were busy. After signing the receipt, he pushed through the exit, glancing back through the glass door one more time.

Cate pecked Shayne on the cheek and jingled her keys in front of him, taunting him. They took turns closing on Fridays, though Shayne generally busied himself in the back office when it was her turn so that he could walk her to her car. Like Nick, the thought always set him on edge when she left alone. He knew that sometimes the parking near the restaurant was already full by the time she got there.

"Night, Janet." She waved to the girl at the register and stepped out into the nippy draft of night air. Once on the sidewalk, she tilted her head back, closing her eyes, and sucked a deep breath through her nose. "Hello, fall."

"It is a good time of year, isn't it?" Nick spoke from where he was leaned against the side of the building. He laughed, holding his palms out between them when she jolted in surprise. "Easy. It's just me."

"Nicky!" She stepped forward, taking a swipe at his shoulder. "You scared the living daylights out of me! What are you still doing out here? I thought you left."

He shrugged. "Figured I'd walk you to your car."

She gave a quick laugh, then slowly reached to take the arm he offered her. "All right, fine. But I doubt *you* walking me would make Shayne feel any better."

"He really is pretty dead set against me, isn't he? He looks like he'd about like to eat me alive, most times when I'm in. Where are you parked?"

"Down that way, and around the corner. There's an empty lot I stop at when the parking on the main street is full." She clicked her tongue and rolled her eyes, rocking her head away from the scolding expression he aimed down at her. "Don't you start. I hear enough from him about it."

"Do you have to do this often? Walk in the dark, I mean."

"It's not so dark. There are streetlamps the whole way there. Besides, it isn't as if I have to worry about twisting my ankle anymore. The city finally came out and fixed the sidewalk."

"I thought I saw that." He gave a nonchalant nod, careful not shift his eyes in her direction. "It was past due."

"It was. Funny. We've never really discussed it since it happened, but there was a crew out there working that very afternoon. Just like that. They seemed to be pretty concerned that it was done with the utmost speed and care. After all that time and all that fight. I wonder what could've lit a fire under them, that way… or who."

"Huh. Mystery." He cleared his throat. "So, how's your ankle? I haven't noticed you favoring it, lately."

"Nicky." She compressed the knowing grin on her lips. "It was you, wasn't it?"

"What was me?" He couldn't help but laugh when he noticed the grin on her lips curving with such deep satisfaction. "What?"

"The city. The sidewalk. I know I don't have the kind of connections to make people move that fast. Goodness knows Shayne tried for the longest time. It was you, wasn't it?"

"It was a hazard to public safety. I might have had access to a phone number that you and Shayne didn't, that's all. They just needed to be persuaded that they were in the wrong."

"Persuaded. Right." She nodded, feeling her smile twist awkwardly. "Might not mention that to Shayne."

"I had my lawyers call the city, Cate." He twitched his lips playfully upward. "I didn't send anyone fish in the mail."

"Nicky." She gave an amused snicker. "Well, thank you. It really is a load off."

"It wasn't any trouble. See, I can be pretty useful to have around." Contemplating the long trek they were still making, he sobered his smile. "Listen, the sidewalk aside, this is still a pretty long way for you to go on your own."

"I am perfectly fine, and I refuse to listen to any statement to the contrary. Stubborn, remember?" She hugged his arm fondly closer when his expression rumpled at her. "Anyway, I seem to have a bodyguard tonight. Don't I?"

"Bodyguard? You know, that's not a bad idea. I should talk to your brother about security. I have connections with a security firm."

"I don't doubt that." She snorted at that thought. "But, please. Do talk to Shayne, and make sure to give me advance warning. I want to make sure I'm standing somewhere nearby with a bag of popcorn while you try and give him advice."

"Really. They could walk you to your car at night, especially if you have to keep parking this far out. How much farther is it, by the way? We're gonna be in Timbuktu, pretty soon."

"That's it, there." She pointed to a sensible charcoal sedan a little farther off. "You don't have to walk me the rest of the way if you're too tired from your meeting. I'm not afraid to be on my own. I told you, I do it all the time."

"Oh, like that's supposed to make me feel any better?" He angled a smile down at her as they trudged on. "My meeting was fine. Just one problem child in the mix. One that keeps trying to rear its ugly head."

"You did look pretty intense a couple of times. Are you… I mean, is everything okay?"

"Okay?" He shrugged. "When you're dealing with a two-million-dollar investment, you want to be sure of who you're getting into bed with. I'm not convinced this is the right move to make."

She stopped short, nearly tripping over her own feet. "Two million dollars? As in… two *million*?"

"Yeah, two million." He laughed, a curve shadowing his lips again. "Sometimes it's more, sometimes less. I play high stakes in my business."

"That's just *one* deal?" She shook her head, her brows tugging inward. "I thought Shayne was making it all up to shake you loose from me, but…"

"Just because some of what you hear about me is the truth doesn't mean it's *all* gospel, Cate. I wish you'd believe that. Remember, you like to make up your own mind."

"I do, and I am." She recovered quickly enough, at least outwardly, and granted him a nod. "So, what was the problem? Something specific, wasn't it?"

"Yeah, it was. It is." He let out a long sigh, watching as she fished the keys from her purse. "The guy, the big guy you butt heads with occasionally, Alf, he keeps telling me that this deal, these guys, that they're okay."

"But you don't think they are?"

"I'm not sure what to think. Alf says it's good, but... I don't know."

"This Alf character," she frowned at the mention of him, "you always listen to what he says?"

"Mostly. Advice is what I pay him for, but more than that, Alf is... It's complicated."

"I see." Taking a few steps toward him again, she leaned against the front fender, studying that same troubled look on his face that she'd noticed before. "Nicky, would you let me make an observation, even though it's none of my business?"

"I guess I've bugged you enough in the last couple of months that you're entitled."

"Okay." She laughed, her eyes remaining fixed on his. "When it comes to your sister, do you trust your gut? The guys she dates, and such. It sounds like you do."

"Yeah, sure I do, mostly." He nodded, confused by her question. "What's Marie got to do with my business deal, though?"

"Just a minute." She held a hand up to him with a smile. "Your friends, Alf aside for the moment. Do you trust your gut when it comes to them?"

His brows drew in a little further, but he bobbed his head again. "In my business, you get into trouble if you can't trust the people around you."

"Well, what about me? Do you trust yourself when it comes to me?"

"Ah…" He gave a quick laugh, hoping she wasn't going to ask him to elaborate too much on his thoughts regarding that one. "Where are we going with this?"

"This deal is obviously tying you up in knots." She tilted a concerned look at him. "You're a successful man in your own right, in business, and as a person in general. You didn't get that way by accident, Nicky."

"No."

"Well then, if something is telling you to walk away from these guys, ignoring the instincts you trust in every other area of your life would be pretty foolish."

"Foolish." Nick pressed his lips firmly together and stared back as he processed her summation.

"That isn't to say that *you're* foolish. Far from it. I just think…" Seeing more trouble in his expression than before, she gave a soft groan and winced. "Oh, Nicky, I'm sorry."

"For what?"

"For whatever I said to bring that look to your face. I didn't mean to bully you about this. People are always telling me I offer my opinions too bluntly, and often unsolicited."

He curved his mouth softly to one side. "I'm not mad, Cate."

"Maybe not, but…"

"Don't apologize. Not to me." He shook his head as he looked at the discomfort reflecting back at him from her lovely face. "You gave me a lot to think about. That's all."

She laughed gently. "Is that a good thing?"

"It's not necessarily a bad thing. You actually made a perfect analysis of what I've been feeling for a while. I just didn't have anyone to say it to, or anyone willing to say it to me. I appreciate that."

"Then, take this for what it's worth. You're a strong man, Nicky. I don't mean just your looks or your physical characteristics. It's not even something that comes from just an image or a reputation."

"Reputation?" He went visibly rigid and took a step back.

"Yes, a reputation, *your* reputation." She reached for his hands, tugging him back toward her with a laugh. "There *are* a lot of stories floating around about your family and your business. I try to ignore as many as I can, honestly. Because whether or not they're true, the Nick Caprianno I'm getting to know, for myself..."

He sucked in a slow breath, slightly on edge for what she would say. "Go on. What do you think?"

"I think you're tough when you need to be. I also think you're a man who could probably be just as tender, in contrast, if the situation called for it."

His smile hinted a return, pleased that in spite of all the rumors, she really did appear to be taking the time to make up her own mind. "I might have a softer side, buried deep down."

"You do. Because you do, I can see why you might find it difficult to keep personal feelings, even a sense of loyalty, from overshadowing areas you'd rather keep separate."

Continuing to hold her hands, he fixed his gaze fully on hers again, pleased, yet still a little stunned by her acuity. "So, what would you recommend to a guy in that situation, if the lines between his business and personal ties started to blur?"

"I would say to keep your friendship, but go with your gut. I think it's a mistake to ignore such… strong feelings."

He took a step nearer to her again, incapable of maintaining distance. "You get them, too, Cate? Strong feelings."

She swallowed lightly, staring up at him, her heart fluttering in her chest. "Sometimes."

The expression he aimed at her intensified, forcing her to hold her breath for an instant. With just one steady glance from Nick Caprianno's sultry, dark eyes, Cate felt a tingle sweep over her skin. She let her eyes drift along his strong jaw, down his neck. Even without speaking another word in that deep, persuasive tone of his, he'd nearly coaxed a sigh from her lips. Though she wouldn't admit to it, the more time she spent with him, the more her mind wandered down all sorts of tempting rabbit trails.

"You're studying me, Cate. Have me figured out yet?" He unintentionally leaned a little nearer to her. "I hope that means you're starting to see a guy you can't resist much longer."

She passed him an embarrassed smile and glanced away, finally slipping her hands free of his. Could he read thoughts, too, or was she just that transparent? Realizing the potentially dangerous accuracy of his statement, she stopped herself from replying too quickly, taking a few seconds to get her train of thought back on track.

"Cate?" He noticed the blush at her cheeks.

She managed a noncommittal smile. "Can I give you a ride back to your car?"

He shook his head, reaching around her to open the car door. "No, thanks."

It was unclear if it was the warmth of his skin, or if it was his closeness that caused his cologne to tempt her senses, but it did. "You sure? I feel kind of bad, you walking me all this way, and then-"

She stopped short, her breath gently catching when he unexpectedly stepped in toward her. Unable to resist the urge, he brushed a single light kiss against her cheek. Hearing the quiet exhalation of her breath next to his ear, his pulse quickened. As he began to edge back from her again, he noticed the slow, drowsy blink of her lashes. He'd never been made weak by such a simple, innocent reaction.

Hesitating, he nearly brushed her lips, too. He could almost swear that she'd leaned in for it. The prospect hinted a faint smile at the corners of his mouth. He longed for more, but knew there wouldn't be, not unless she let herself change her mind about them. Running the tip of a finger along her jawline, he stepped away before he acted on impulse.

"Goodnight, Cate."

Somewhat dizzy, she lowered into the driver's seat, thankful for its support. "Goodnight, Nicky."

Feeling her face burning brightly, her eyes remained on his as he closed her door and waited for her to start the car. She lifted a hand to the window, smiling softly when his fingertips pressed lightly against the glass to meet hers. Her heart held the steady, quick pace that she'd felt ever since he'd placed that kiss so gently on her skin.

His hand slipped from the glass and he started down the street. She felt stunned, almost unable to move, let alone drive. After a few times of him glancing behind at her, obviously waiting for her to take off, she put the car into gear. Nearly breathless for what he had undeniably made her desire from him, she felt a shudder run the length of her body as she drove past him.

Chapter Five

Alf leaned over the open files on Nick's desk, his cellphone held to one ear as he waited for news on the New York deal. Rocking in his leather office chair, Nick slouched back, rubbing a hand back and forth over his mouth. Buying into a business was never as straightforward as it seemed, no matter what condition the business was in, no matter how much work had gone into the deal. They'd been working on a couple of deals with contacts in New York, for a while.

"All right, Cameron. All right. Good boy. That's good to hear." Alf's lips pulled back to reveal a toothy grin. "Nah, we aren't quite there, but that's more along the lines of what we were thinking. We'll be in contact after I talk it over with Mr. Caprianno. Mm-hmm. Thanks again for getting back to us. All right. Yeah. Bye."

"So?" Nick leaned forward, looking up at his advisor. "It's just what I said, isn't it?"

"Yes, you're a very smart guy, Nick. No news there." Alf sighed with a tired laugh. "You're the one that said Rothberg was about to cave. I'd say, if you go in with your new offer, you'll be where you want by the end of the week."

"Yeah! That's how it's done!" Nick leapt from his chair, cracking a sharp five against Alf's open palm. "Perfect! All right, so, I'll head to New York to get things tidied up and we'll be into that one at a ten percent higher return than they were willing to offer in the beginning. I think I'd better head out, first thing, though. I don't want to give those boys a chance to change their minds."

"Yeah, you better not." Alf popped a couple of antacids into his mouth. "You romanced them, played hard nose, and waited them out, all in the last three months. I shouldn't be surprised it panned out. I tell you what, kid, you could sell toys to Santa Clause."

"Yeah, yeah." Nick grinned cockily, shrugging. "So, I'll go in and make a play for thirty percent, then take the twenty-five they'll counter with, which is what I wanted in the first place."

Alf picked up his pen, twisting it closed, then tucked it into his pocket as he gave him a side-eyed glance. "You think you'll get the full twenty-five?"

"I'll bet you five bucks." Nick tugged his grin a little higher up.

"Nah." Alf shook his head with a low chuckle. "We ain't into the gambling racket, no more."

"Right." Nick's chest shook lightly. "Well, bet or not, they'll get their investment, I'll get my return, and we'll both make a whole lot of money. Bam."

"All right, kid, all right." He nodded, rubbing a hand over the fire in his gut. "You win."

Nick shuffled some papers into a pile on the corner of his desk, his glance cutting over at his friend a few times. He'd noticed him peeling the paper back on a roll of antacids. "Hey, Alf, what's with the pills? You know those things aren't candy, right? You okay? Can't handle a game of fastball anymore?"

"Nah. Nadine keeps trying to spice up her lasagna recipe. I keep telling her," he gestured his hands between them for emphasis, "Nadine, what, are you trying to burn a hole in my gut, after all these years? She says she's just trying to keep the spice in life. I don't know. I think she's trying to kill me, or something. She said, if she was gonna kill me, she'd just bust my skull in."

"Maybe because you been stringing her along for the last twenty-five years, or so." Nick dropped back down into his chair with a mocking grin. "Why don't you just marry her and let her make an honest man out of you, already? She's been like another aunt to me, my whole life!"

"I don't want her to think she's the boss, that's why." He shrugged, chuckling deeply. "All right, I don't want her to *know* she's the boss. Anyway, why bother now? First, her old man didn't want her chained to a bum, like me. Then, we figured, what's the point, huh? What are we gonna do, at our age? Start a family?"

Nick's chest shook with laughter and he shrugged. "Well, there's no saying it's too late for *everything*, you know."

"Nah." Alf shook his head again. "Maybe if I was your age again. Eh, me and Nadine, we enjoy each other's company. That's enough."

"All right." Nick angled an ill-behaved expression up at him. "If you say so."

"I do." He flipped through a couple more files in his hand, pausing over the Jansen folder, then glanced Nick's way again. "Listen, kid, since you're such a rock star tonight, you're in such a good mood, why don't we talk about this one? They've come up another percent from their last offer."

"A whole percent? They want me to invest two million dollars, and they're going to come up a whole percent? Gee. Pinch me." The curve at Nick's lips began to slip when Alf scrunched his mouth to one side, and he shook his head. "Nah. Why spoil a fresh victory with yesterday's garbage? Anyway, I gotta call Jake and tell him to get the plane ready."

"Okay." He shoved the files down into his briefcase and snapped it closed. "You'll be gone, what, a couple days? You gonna go see that bossy little broad you're becoming so obsessed with, before you go?"

"No." The remnants of Nick's smile dissolved quickly, and he dipped his brows. He'd gone over his last few minutes with her about a million and one times, since he'd left her. "No, I don't think so."

"Things starting to fizzle out already, huh?"

Nick loosened the tie at his neck. Although he found himself thinking about Cate constantly, he'd skipped the restaurant for meetings in the city over the last couple of days. It wasn't that he hadn't wanted to see her. More that, her spot-on view of him made him consider other aspects of himself. She was right. He trusted his gut in most areas of his life, so it didn't make sense for him to second-guess himself with the Jansen deal.

He knew part of his dithering was down to Alf's continued insistence. He trusted him. He relied on him. Still, something wasn't sitting right when it came to that deal, and he'd never taken kindly to feeling as if he was being handled. He wasn't sure he was ready to take too close a look at what bothered him yet. He did miss his daily run-ins with her, though. Alf's summation of Nick's obsession struck with nearly pinpoint accuracy. Some space, some time apart might be beneficial to them both.

"I need to get this New York deal tied up. I can't afford any distractions until I do. I'll check in with her when I get back." He flipped his schedule open. "Hey, I'm gonna stop by a couple of our other partners in Jersey, as long as I'll be so close. Probably be gone a week, or so. If there's something here that can't wait until I get back, run it past Pop."

Alf's eyes flicked up in surprise. He'd noticed the silent change in him when Cate had come up, not just in Nick, but in the way Nick was with him. Something in the way he insisted that he check in with Sal while he was gone. Alf hoped it wasn't an indication that this girl would be trouble.

"All right, Nick. You take some time. You've earned it. Plenty of time to romance the redhead when you get back. You taking Frankie with you?"

"Nah. Tony can come. He can visit his daughter while we're in New York. I've got something else for to keep Frankie busy." Cautious to keep his plans close to his chest, Nick shook his head. "You keep the fort down, while I'm gone, all right?"

"Come on, you gotta ask?" Relieved by the question, Alf waved him off. "Forget about it. You just go get that deal signed."

"You know it." As Nick's thoughts slipped off toward MacCarthaigh's again, he looked up, just before Alf had a chance to leave. "Hey, is Frankie still out there? I need to talk to him."

"Yeah. Hey, Frankie! The boss wants ya." Alf turned back from peeking around the corner. "Bye, kid. Have a good trip, huh?"

Plagued by the thought of the file in his briefcase, the one that seemed to have a heartbeat and a voice that breathed constantly in his ear, Alf unwrapped another antacid from his pocket and popped it into his mouth. If Nadine's cooking didn't kill him, riding both sides of the fence on the Jansen deal just might. He'd like to tell Jansen where he could shove his proposal, but that could prove dangerous for him.

Leaving the branch office of the Caprianno Corporation, Alf tugged his coat collar up against the increasingly chilly breeze. Nick preferred to work in the smaller building, rather than the big one in the city. He grumbled to himself, a little peevish about being one of the last to leave again. For thirty-seven years, he'd been one of the last ones to leave at night, come rain, sun, or snow.

Though the days were still balmy, nights were getting colder already, and the wind and moisture of the last couple days didn't help any. Water from the puddles splashed and splattered over the shiny leather tops of his black oxfords as he walked down the glossy parking lot.

Just as he lifted his fingers to the handle of the driver's door, a pair of headlights flicked over the dark charcoal paint of his Cadillac. He tugged the door open and tossed his briefcase onto the seat, then turned to see who had pulled in. A black sedan had stopped directly behind him, blocking any retreat. Recognizing the two men that got out of the car, he closed his door and swallowed hard.

"You crazy showing up here, like this?" Alf glanced quickly from side to side, then up at the second-story security camera that was aimed at the parking area. "Nick would blow his top if he knew you were crashing his place of business. There's nothing I can do if he thinks you're getting pushy. He don't respond to bully tactics all that well."

"Relax, Alf." One of the men, a tall, gangly creature of about thirty, wearing a pair of dark slacks and a gray coat that swamped his frame, grinned at him. "We were just in the neighborhood. Mr. Jansen wanted us to do a progress check, see if there was anything we could do to ease your boss' mind about the deal."

"You want to kill it, Alex?" Alf barked quietly. "You want to muck everything up? Tell Crispen that if he pushes too hard, the whole thing'll end up in the crapper, and we'll *all* lose out."

"Oh, Alf. Alfonse, my friend." Alex sucked a sharp breath through his teeth and he shook his head. "Mr. Jansen wouldn't be happy to hear that. Maybe you should phrase your message a little better."

Alf pulled up the corner of his mouth, snarling lightly at the younger man. "Listen, you disrespectful little punk. I was leaning on heavier guys than Crispen Jansen before you were around to hang on your mama's apron strings. *You* don't advise *me* how to phrase my messages. You got it?"

"Whoa, whoa." Alex shook his head, holding his palms between them as he feigned an amused laugh. "I think you're missing the point, *Mr. Giuseppe*."

Alf leaned against his car, folding his arms across his broad frame. "You got a point, make it quick, junior."

"I'm just trying to do you a favor." He laughed again, though there was a mean edge to it. "I know how long you been in the game, Alf, so does Mr. Jansen. Keeping your nose clean for so long, your arms don't stretch near as far as they used to. And they used to reach some… pretty grubby places, from what I understand. Didn't they? So, again, you wanna rephrase your message to Mr. Jansen?"

Alf shoved down the fireball of a knot in the pit of his stomach, doing his best not to let his nerves show in his expression. The kid was a cheap hood. In Alf's hay day, he'd have mopped the floor with him, or possibly worse, for even a hint of insult to his boss.

Now, though, Alex was right. Alf was getting older, he wasn't as spry as he once was, and he'd been walking the straight and narrow for too long for his threats to be taken seriously by such a group of men. He'd learned enjoy comfort, had relied too much on the safety of caution in his later years. It was the wrong point in his life to have to worry about the sins of his past catching up with him. Crispen Jansen knew enough about him to bring the world crashing down around his ears, if he wanted to make it happen.

"All right, Alex. I'll rephrase, make it crystal for you."

Older or not, less agile or not, Alf still had four inches and a good fifty pounds on that worm. He intended to use every ounce of advantage he had. His feet shuffled a couple of steps toward him, his forehead creasing with a dark expression.

"You tell Crispen that I'll talk to my boss again in a few days. I've known Nick since he was born, and I know his temperament. He don't like nobody leaning on him, especially nobody that wants something from him. That sound good enough for you?"

Alex edged back a step or two, chuckling against the intimidating glare of the older man. "Yeah, Alf. Yeah, I'll tell him that."

"Good." Alf jerked his head in the direction of the car, shooting another thin squint at the other man, the one who had silently remained by the driver's door. "Now, you and your babysitter get out of here before somebody sees you."

Alf witnessed the insulted anger wrenching up in Alex's face, in the tightening of his jaw and the thin press of his pouty lips. Oh, that little terrier would love to take a bite out of him, but Alf also knew he wasn't as confident against him as he let on. However much older he was than Alex, Alf's reputation, the things he'd seen and done, far outweighed anything that snotty little pup would ever know.

"We'll see you around, Alf." Alex nodded, getting back into his side of the car. "Hopefully you'll have better news for us next time. I'd hate to think we weren't gonna be friends, no more."

"Get out of here, you're breaking my heart." Alf smirked back at him. He still had it. "Next time, maybe you boys should make an appointment."

"Next time, maybe I won't offer you any favors." Alex sniped back.

"Yeah." Alf waved him off with a scoff. "I'm shaking in my boots, kid."

Alex slammed his door closed, thrusting a thumb at the driveway exit. "Let's get out of here, Bobby."

Alf kept his steely-eyed gaze on them the whole way to their turn at the corner. After he got into his car, however, he felt the exacting toll of the altercation weighing down on him. A tight pressure filled his chest and he heaved a few heavy breaths. Thumping his head against the seat rest, he swallowed down his anxiety.

Chapter Six

Cate slumped onto a green paisley cushion of her grandmother's couch. The MacCarthaigh's always spent Sunday evenings together. The family dinners were a tradition long before Cate and Shayne were born. Usually, it was nice. Cate wasn't in a great mood that night, though. Shayne's wife, Bethany, bobbled their ginger-haired six-month-old on one knee. The drooling baby gnawed her raw gums against her mother's finger.

"What's the matter?" Bethany appraised the oddly peevish expression on her sister-in-law's face. "You're never this quiet, or this out of sorts."

"Who says I'm out of sorts?" She flicked a look over at her, wincing as she heard the snappy tone of the words as they left her mouth. "I'm sorry. I guess I have been a little bothered for a few days. It's just a… friend. I thought he was a friend, anyway. I haven't seen or heard from him in a while."

"Why don't you give him a call?" Bethany shrugged, jostling the babbling baby on her knee.

"I'm not sure if he'd want me to. I said something to him a little while ago. You know how I can be. I'm wondering if we're on the outs and I just don't know it. Think I might have really messed something up, there."

"Well, it's kind of a childish way to behave, for a grown man, if that's really what happened. Maybe he's just busy." She shifted the baby to her shoulder, patting her back softly. "Did he say he was upset with you?"

"No." Cate angled her head a little to one side, smiling softly as she recalled the gentle brush of Nick's lips on her cheek. "Actually, he told me not to apologize. I guess that's why I'm so confused that he'd just disappear. Maybe we just weren't quite as friendly as I thought."

"Oh." Bethany giggled softly, spying the upward turn of Cate's lips. "Just how friendly were you getting to be?"

"Friendly enough to be confused by him disappearing, this way." No. That wasn't entirely true. The smile on her lips began to fade. The thought had occurred to her that perhaps he'd finally just grown tired of waiting on her. "I don't know."

"What goes on here?" Shayne snagged the baby from his wife, blowing a long raspberry against his daughter's tummy and making her giggle. Sobering when he read the sympathy on Bethany's face, he shifted his eyes to make a study of his sister. "You two look like you're planning a wake."

"No. Some guy friend of Cate's up and vanished." She pinched her brows inward when her sister-in-law's eyes widened and she shook her head to her. "Ah, no. I mean… *I* had a friend disappear?"

Cate blew out a long breath, then leaned forward, patting her on the hand. "Thanks, Bethany. I got it from here."

Shayne laughed heartily. "You know, a comforting thing about being married to a woman like my Beth is that she's a terrible liar. I'll never have to worry about her trying to pull a fast one over on me."

"Very funny." Bethany reached a hand over to him, lovingly combing her fingers through the back of his red-blonde hair. "Not very helpful, but funny."

"I don't know how helpful I want to be." Shayne sighed, settling his eyes back on his sister's. "If this is about who I think it is, I don't care who or what caused it, I'm just glad he's finally gone."

Bethany's mouth dropped open as she stared at him. "Shayne MacCarthaigh! What a thing to say."

He gave a dismissive shrug and went on. "It's about time, too, I'd say. He and his cronies setting up at the tables a couple times a week, him coming in to flirt with Cate every day. MacCarthaigh's already has its own atmosphere, without him bringing his version in with him."

"Oh, shut up, Shayne!" Cate scowled darkly, chucking an ugly gold tasseled throw pillow at him.

"What's all this squabble about? I want my part in it." Their grandmother lowered into her chair, her gaze scanning her suddenly tight-lipped grandchildren carefully. "Quick, now, I want to hear all about all of your shenanigans before your parents finish fixing the coffees and interrupt us."

Maureen MacCarthaigh had once been a vivacious, hot-tempered Irish girl with flaming red hair and opinions as loud and as pert as any person ever put on the earth. Now, she had become like many other elders in the neighborhood. She kept more to her home, not to say that either her opinions or her temper had been balanced by time. Though her appearance had changed to a frailer, bottled red version of her former self, her mind was as sharp as a tack, and she was as feisty as ever.

Cate folded her arms sulkily, cutting a warning look over at her brother. "It was nothing, Gran. Shayne's just butting in where he shouldn't, as usual."

"Butt in, nothing!" He bobbled his head sarcastically. "Bethany said-"

"Nope!" His wife flicked a sharp expression in his direction, reaching to give the baby her pacifier. "I've already said too much. I'll thank you to leave me out of this hornet's nest."

"Ah, tut, tut." Maureen shook her finger at the angry scowl Cate maintained on her brother. "You know what your granddad used to say about brothers, rest his soul. A brother is-"

"A gift from heaven, sent to guard his sister from harm and to preserve her honor from fallen ways." Cate rolled her eyes. "I know. I know. Granddad was also known to hold his share of stout while he railed against whatever cause he was upset with at the time. Let's not forget that."

Maureen shrugged. "Well, now, that's true. That's true. To tell you the truth, I used to be convinced he made most of what he said up just to try and reign me in, as if he ever could. I'm no more convinced by his prattle now. So, now, Shayne, you leave your sister be. I'm sure whatever it is, Cate knows her own mind. She's a smart girl."

"I thought so." Shayne gave a deep nod, grinning smugly. "What if I told you she's got a thing for Nicholas Caprianno? She's had him hanging around downstairs with his cronies for weeks. You still want me to leave it be?"

"Nicholas Capri..." Maureen paled, her body thumping back into her seat just as she'd begun to rise from it. Widening her eyes, her brows arched with a heightened alarm. "A hood? Downstairs? In MacCarthaigh's?"

Coming to Nick's defense, Cate glared at Shayne. "Nicky isn't a hood! He's very thoughtful, and he's flattering..."

Shayne snorted a laugh. "Well, then. I guess that makes him fine."

"And we've never once had any trouble from him or his friends!" She shot back. "They rack up sizable bills when they come in. I haven't noticed you complaining about those! Besides, there's nothing written in stone that whoever I'm interested in has to be an Irishman, either!"

Maureen's voice became a little cross. "Well, no, dear heart, but it certainly couldn't hurt for him to be one. How in the world does a girl by the name of Cathlene Rose MacCarthaigh become interested in a man like Nicholas Caprianno? Oh, he's got money, to be sure, but how did they come about it?"

"He's brilliant at business." Cate insisted, tilting her chin up.

"And what kind of business, do you suppose? Hmm? Haven't you heard all the stories?" Maureen gave a whoosh of breath and shook her head. "Why, your great granddad, rest him, told me tales about Santino Caprianno that would make your hair curl into ringlets! He ran quite the operation all around here when your granddad was just a boy."

"Well, Nicky's not like that. I can tell."

"Oh, my darling girl, those Italian men, they're charmers, I'll give you that. But you'd do well to keep your head square on your shoulders and just pass him by altogether." Her grandmother gave a curt nod, the wrinkles at her lips deepening as she pursed them tightly. "If he's gone, so much the better for you. You take my word for it."

Shayne gave a deep nod. "MacCarthaigh's has managed to stay afloat all these years without the likes of Caprianno money, and we'll do just fine without it again.

"Enough!" Cate's voice rose sharply. She snatched her coat and scarf from the piano bench and stood. "Everyone in this family would do well to keep their opinions on the subject of *any* men in my life to themselves."

As she entered the room with a tray of coffees, Sylvia MacCarthaigh sent her daughter a surprised look. "Where are you going in such a huff, Cate?"

"I'm sorry, Mom. I'm not staying for coffee." She leaned over, brushing her mother's cheek with a kiss. "I'll call you in the morning."

Shayne caught her eye. "Yeah, well, don't forget, it's your turn to open tomorrow."

"Have I ever missed a shift? Honestly, Shayne, I have poured just as much time and sweat into that place as you have!" Stomping toward her grandmother, Cate bent to peck a terse kiss to her cheek, then crossed the room, slamming the door as she went out.

Daniel, Cate and Shayne's father, came out of the kitchen just in time to see the back of his daughter disappear behind the door. "Well, where's she gone?"

Cate's feet scurried down the access steps to the empty restaurant. She paused at Nick's usual table on her way to the door. She let her fingers run along the back of his chair, then curled them, white-knuckled, over it. *His* chair. Funny how she had started to think of it as his, he'd been in so often.

"Well, Cathlene MacCarthaigh, you shoved your blunt Irish opinions at him, told him you would only be friendly with him." She scolded herself, stamping her foot. "What difference is it to him if he moves on? It's only yourself you've got to blame if he has."

After another moment of deliberations, she plunked her purse down onto the table, thinking over Bethany's suggestion. Beginning to dig through her bag, she searched for the business card Nick had once given her, in case she ever needed anything. Nearly dialing the number at the bottom of the small rectangle cardstock, she gave a small laugh and sniffed.

What was she thinking, nearly calling Nick to find out why he hadn't been in to MacCarthaigh's, or at the very least, why he'd just vanished without so much as a word? She shook her head, stuffing the card back into her purse and went for the door. It was none of her business what he was doing or where he was. She wasn't entitled to any sort of explanation, nor might he be willing to give one.

Chapter Seven

It had taken a couple of days for Cate and Shayne to speak and work together again without little snipes, here and there. That was if they spoke, at all. MacCarthaighs had hot tempers and stubborn streaks a mile long, but their hearts always won out in the end. Still, neither of them was willing to apologize for their argument. They were good people, but they were far from sainthood.

What good would it have done her to fall out with her brother over Nick's absence, anyway? What right did she have to feel such a sharp sting over it? She did feel it, nevertheless. Shayne could sense it, and decided it best to keep his thoughts to himself, for once. No point in salting an open wound. He was convinced he knew the way it would turn out all along, with a stirring of trouble and then a sudden sever of ties.

Cate looked to where her brother stood, taking a call from one of their suppliers from the other side of the bar. She stretched forward, giving him a quick peck on the cheek as she dropped her apron onto the glossy top. "I am out of here. I'm so tired tonight. I can hardly stand myself, let alone you."

"You didn't park far out again, did you?" His laughter had turned into an anxious reply when she tugged on her coat and flicked a silent glance at him. He recalled how busy the street had been when she'd gotten there. He held a hand over the receiver. "Well, wait a minute and I'll walk you to your car. This won't take long."

"Ugh, Shayne." She rolled her eyes, shadowboxing the air between them. It was easier to be silly than to recall the last time someone had insisted on walking her to her car, namely Nick. "You know I have the fighting MacCarthaigh spirit. Nobody would dare bother me."

He shook his head. "All the same-"

"All the same, I'll do as I please, just as I always have. No amount of fussing or insisting from you is about to change that." She started out the door, calling back to him. "See you in the morning!"

She pulled her coat tighter around herself, cinching the belt against the chilled wind. Nearly a moonless night, there wasn't much light. A couple of the streetlamps down the side street had been broken by neighborhood kids earlier in the week and still hadn't been replaced by the city.

Although she didn't want to admit that Shayne was right about her walking to her car, she felt an anxious shiver crawl up her spine. Something felt different. Probably just the missing lights. She'd already started out the door when Shayne triggered the memory that she'd had to park near the vacant lot around the corner again.

Her eyes shifted around the dimly-lit sidewalks. She gulped hard as she passed a parked black sedan with dark tinted back windows. It sat on the corner between the restaurant and the side street.

A large man sat behind the wheel, motionless aside from his breathing. Though he didn't appear to so much as glance up as she went by, she did notice his eyes shift into the side mirror, and her feet sprung to a quicker step. She was sure she'd seen that car before.

Having found herself preoccupied by the man in the car, she didn't have the chance to notice a tall, wiry figure in the shadow of an alleyway. He'd noticed her, though. Small, he surmised. Pretty. Purse would be an easy grab, and maybe a car, too. It was a cold night, and late. He swept his eyes back and forth down the street, not seeing anyone else, and he stepped onto the asphalt behind her.

"Hey, lady." He sucked a long, last drag on the cigarette between his teeth and flicked it to the pavement. He painted as friendly a curve onto his mouth as he could manage, approaching her quickly. "You got a few bucks?"

"No. I'm sorry." She nearly jumped, gasping with surprise in response to the unexpected company. She half considered running back to the restaurant, but she'd have to pass him to get there.

"A dollar? Just a dollar?" He stepped up his pace, grinning harder at the way she hurried along. He flung a thumb at the darkened alleyway, knowing most people were suckers for animals. "I gotta get some food for my dog. Anything you can spare."

"I don't carry cash on me." She flashed a glance at the passage, though she kept moving. No dog. She attempted to keep her voice strong. "You need to back off."

She fumbled with her keys, her heart pounding in her ears. Why hadn't she just waited for Shayne to walk her? The neighborhood was safe enough during the day, but she couldn't deny that it had gone down enough since she was a kid, that it wasn't smart to walk alone on deserted streets at night. He was always on about the recent crime wave.

Shayne was right about it. Nick had been right, too. Everyone had been right, only she'd been too bullheaded to heed the warnings. She was generally too stubborn to listen to warnings. She started to uncap the pepper spray she kept clipped to her keychain when he snatched the keys from her hand.

"No. You don't want to do that." He slammed his hand against the door just as she opened it, trapping her between himself and the car. "That ain't very nice."

"I told you, I don't carry cash." She swallowed hard, aiming a defiant glare over her shoulder at him. "Listen, take my purse, my car, my phone. I don't care, but know that if you try anything else, I will scream bloody murder and draw every eye from every window down to this lot."

"Oh, feisty." He laughed, letting his eyes slither over the length of her, pausing at various points of interest to him. Looking back up at her, he shook his head. "Yelling like that wouldn't be a very good idea."

"Well, I've never been one to do what I was told!" He'd moved just enough that she slammed her elbow into his gut, then gave him a hard shove away. "I am also not the type to give in quietly."

"Big mistake." Rubbing a hand over his middle, he snarled, slivering a glare back at her, and took a step toward her again. "Big."

The squeal of rubber against blacktop caught the attention of them both, their glances shooting over to where the black sedan whipped a sharp U-turn and barreled toward them. Screeching to a stop, the tall, broad figure stepped out from the driver's seat.

The thug stumbled back a step, in surprise, but angled an angry look up at him. "Move on, pal. I saw her first. This don't concern you."

The burly man merely tilted his head to one side, audibly cracking his neck. He adjusted the tension in his shoulders, stretching his frame to make his already large silhouette appear that much more intimidating. "Nah. I think *you* better move on."

The would-be mugger shifted a look from his prize, back to the man, irate at the thought of losing what he wanted. He gave a shout and lunged forward, barreling toward the man from the car. Being surprisingly calm and collected, though, the larger man swayed out of the way of the wild-flying fist. He returned the swing with an expert club of his own.

"Aw, man! I think you broke my nose!" The mugger drew a hand to his face. Seeing blood covering his fingers, he stumbled back, eyes squinted and watering. Giving her one last glance when the big fellow stepped closer to him, he threw her keys to the ground and turned, running back across the street and into the dark alleyway. "Man, forget this!"

Unsure of his motives, Cate slid a foot back, putting more space between herself and the man from the car. She made a cautious study of him, her chest rising and falling quickly. "What do you want?"

"I don't want anything." He shook his head, bending to pick up the keys that the mugger had dropped, then held them out to her. "You really should be more careful, Miss MacCarthaigh."

"MacCarthaigh? I don't understand. How do you…" She reached a trembling hand out to take the keys from him. "Do you know my brother? Are you a friend of Shayne's?"

"No, ma'am. I seen you around, that's all." He shook his head and took a wide stance with his hands folded in front of him. Aiming a forbidding expression back and forth to both sides of the street around them, he gestured to her car. "I'll wait to leave 'til you get going."

She swallowed hard, feeling her heartbeat beginning to slow down a bit. She squinted her eyes. "Wait. You look familiar. I've seen you at the restaurant a few times, haven't I? And around the neighborhood, all week this week, right?"

Though he remained silent, she could see another slight adjustment he made of his neck. Hmm. Discomfort. What had she caught him up in? He did look familiar. She knew she'd seen him at a back table of the restaurant before, and a few other places, generally on her later nights. Now he shows up like a guardian angel, or a bodyguard? As a thought occurred to her, she drew her eyebrows sharply in. A bodyguard.

"I want to see Nick." She pressed her lips thinly together, holding a palm up to him when he started to deny knowing what she was talking about. "I said, I want to see Nicholas Caprianno. Is he in there? Is he in the back of the car?"

"No ma'am. Nicky ain't-" Letting his chest drop with a huge exhalation of restricted breath, he turned, walking to his car, and opened the back door. He must be losing his touch. If he hadn't been busted before, he'd just given himself away. "All right, but I'd lock my door before we go, if I was you."

Flaring her nostrils a bit, she gave a sharp nod. Well. That answered that question. She clicked the button on her key fob and slid onto the plush leather cushion of the back seat. Pulling her cellphone from her purse, she sent a text to Shayne, letting him know that she was out with a friend, in case he saw her car on his way home and worried.

As they drove along, Cate kept watch on the front seat. She sharpened her hearing to eavesdrop snippets of murmured conversation as the driver spoke lowly into his phone. She occasionally caught a glimpse of him in the rearview mirror, though he generally flicked his glance back to the road when they made eye contact. He looked beefy and forbidding, like one of the characters from one of Shayne's movies.

After about twenty minutes, the car pulled through a set of iron gates, down the long gravel driveway of a large estate home. Under a massive stone porte-cochere, the ride came to a stop, and he walked around to open her door. She stepped out, shifting her eyes at her surroundings. She tried to conceal the apprehensive breath she took. What had she gotten herself into?

She flicked a brow at him as he opened the oversized wrought iron front door for her. "I might as well have a name, if you're going to go around saving my neck."

"You can call me Frankie." He closed the door, leading her across a wide marble foyer to a pair of mahogany French doors. "Excuse me for me a second, Miss MacCarthaigh."

"If I'm going to call you Frankie, you might as well call me Cate." She shrugged when the look he cut her slowly morphed into a smile. "We're old friends, now, right?"

"Yeah, right." His mouth stretched to an amused half-grin. "Excuse me."

He slipped behind the doors, leaving her to gape at the immense house. A sparkling chandelier hung overhead, next to a wide, curved staircase. Photos were carefully placed on tabletops, and museum quality paintings hung on the walls.

"Go ahead, *Cate*." Frankie stood with the door held open for her. He gave her a quick wink as she passed him. "Nicky's right in there. He's just finishing a call."

"Thanks, Frankie." Her tension eased a little with the aid of the friendly gesture.

Chapter Eight

"Didn't I tell you, I knew what I was talking about? Yeah? Well, then, next time, take my word for it. Make sure when you call them, you… Tony, I'm gonna have to let you go. We'll talk more tomorrow."

When Nick saw her come into the room, he lifted himself from the seat of a high-backed chair. He slid his thumb over the screen to disconnect his call and placed his cell phone carefully on the top of a side table. He cast a wary eye on her livid expression. He could tell by the tight press of her lips, the defiant way she was staring back at him, that he was in trouble.

"Frankie told me what happened." He took a couple of steps toward her, though he maintained plenty of distance between them. He tucked his hands into the pockets of his dark suit trousers and adjusted his neck. She looked as if she was about to eat him alive. "Are you okay?"

"Am I okay?" She demanded. Her voice was surprisingly loud as it echoed against the high coffered ceiling of the room. "I guess that all depends on the context of the question. Am I okay because of the mugger, or am I okay that I just found out you've been essentially paying someone to stalk me?"

"Ah… Thanks, Frankie. I'll let you know when we're done... if you don't hear for yourself." Nick nodded, waiting until the door was closed so that it was just the two of them. "I wasn't having you followed, Cate."

"Really? You really want to start this with a boldface lie?" She shook her head, her arms folding tightly in front of herself. "I know I've seen Frankie, and probably a few others hanging around, now that I think of it, not that *you've* been one of them."

"I know I haven't been around, but I had a good reason-"

"And, what would you call it, if not being stalked, or *followed*? What? Have you been having them report back to you about me? Who I'm with, what I'm doing? Is that your idea of-"

"I swear, I never once asked what you were doing or who you were with." He held his palms up between them and pressed his eyes closed. "I only asked that they made sure you were safe doing whatever it was."

"Well, it was a huge invasion of privacy!" She clapped back.

"It may seem that way, but I had to go out of town for a few days, and I just felt more comfortable having someone keep an eye out *for* you while I was gone, not *on* you."

"What am I, a yorkie? I need a sitter? Nobody asked you to take that on yourself, Nick!"

She was unsure of whether the jumble of nerves in her gut stemmed from the near mugging, or the realization that she'd been followed for over a week. It could've just that he was back and standing right in front of her. Maybe it was an even split between the three.

In any case, she was angry with herself for feeling some sense of relief at seeing him again, regardless of the circumstance. Whatever his intent, she was still genuinely furious with him. Her hands were still slightly trembling from the earlier altercation. She took a step toward him.

"Do you have any idea how unnerving all of this is for me? You try to tell me that I have nothing to worry about with you, but you sound like a stalker! I don't care how much money you have, or how sinfully good-looking you are! However you meant it, it was still next door to stalking!"

"I'm sorry. I swear, that was not my intention." He assured her, then took a few steps nearer to her, almost making the mistake of allowing himself to smile. Judging by the smoldering look in her eye, that could've been a deadly misstep. "I was worried about you… justifiably, as it turns out."

"Justifiably?"

"Maybe I didn't have the right to do what I did, and maybe it's because of what I do and what I've seen that I have a reason to be more cautious when it comes to people I care about, but I can't help that."

"I am not another deal for you to manage, Nick!" She nodded, still fuming. "How many other women do you have this arrangement with? Does Frankie follow them all around for you, or do you have a different protector for each of us?"

"This is definitely a first for me." He did smile, then, laughing at her summation. A quick flash from her blazing eyes sobered him again. "All right. I'm not saying you don't have the right to be miffed with me, but-"

"Miffed! I can think of a lot more colorful ways of describing the way I'm feeling, right now, Nicholas Caprianno! Violated, for one. Incensed. Resentful, for another!"

"Yeah." He nodded, rubbing the back of his neck with a soft grin. "Yeah, I can see that. You don't exactly keep your cards all that close to your chest, do you?"

"You seem to be a master at keeping things to yourself!" She countered, then hesitated slightly. "I thought… Where have you even been all this time?"

"New York. I had business to work on there, and some holdings to check on in Jersey."

"It never occurred to you to mention that? I mean, I guess you didn't have any obligation to, but-" She huffed a frustrated breath at him. "You showed up every day, talked to me, flirted with me, let me get used to you being there.

Then you just disappeared, without a word? Who does that?"

"I'm sorry. You're right." He lifted a side chair between them, as lion tamer might going into the ring when she took a couple of angry steps inward. "Easy. I don't want to get blood on the carpet. Let's at least go outside, if you're gonna beat the crap out of me."

"I will not let you make this into a game!" She looked at him, at the conjured expression of fear on his face, and couldn't resist a quick snicker. Annoyed with herself for the escaped show of amusement, she aimed a warning finger back at him. "Stop it, Nicky! Will you put the chair down?"

At her request, he place it back onto the ground and nodded, chuckling lowly in his chest. "I know it's not a game. I know, and I'm sorry if it felt like I was sending mixed signals."

"Well, what *were* you doing? Just playing with me. After this, I deserve an answer, don't you think?"

Just playing? Hardly. In spite of her scolding, he'd like to gather her up in his arms and sink a kiss deeply onto those frustrated lips of hers. He'd thought about it often enough while he'd been gone. Even from such a distance, Cate was a relentless distraction to him.

"All right. Listen, Nicky, I enjoyed when you came into MacCarthaigh's. If I'm honest, I'd even started looking forward to it. I enjoyed talking with you… being with you, but…" Feeling a wave of vulnerability, she hardened her expression. "Will you say something?"

He nodded. "I wanted to give us both time."

"Time." She pulled her brows inward, shaking her head. "Time for what?"

"Time for us both to see how we felt apart, to really decide how we felt about each other. You already told me what you think of me, Cate. Now, I want to know how you feel about me."

She looked away, shaking her head. "I can't."

"Can't, or won't? Because, the way I see it, that distinction makes all the difference in the world in a situation like this."

"I…" She let a slow breath pass between her lips when he stepped closer. "I'm not sure."

"Yes, you are."

His gaze remained firmly on her. He noted the hesitation as she formulated a more complete answer. Experience told him that she would be honest with him. Taking another few steps closer to her, he measured her breathing and any changes in facial expression.

"You still think of us as just friends. You enjoy the company, the flirting, the banter, but that's all there is to it. Is that what you were going to say, Cate?"

"I think…" She didn't want to admit how crushed she'd been when he suddenly quit coming around. "I'm not sure how wise it would be for me to say how I feel about you."

He angled his head to hold her gaze, drawing so close to her that he could feel an exchange of heat between them. Maybe the period of silence *had* served its purpose. It had forced him to make up his mind about them, and it appeared to have done the same for her. She was hesitant to admit it, but he would show her it was safe to trust it, safe to trust him.

"I think you know we're more than just friends. Maybe… you even missed *me* a little?" Cautiously lifting a hand, he brushed his thumb over her cheek. His smile deepened when her eyes fluttered closed in response to the gesture. Bowing his head slightly, he lowered her voice to a near whisper. "Did you miss me, too, Cate?"

Too. The admission tugged at her heart. Standing so near as he was, the spicy notes of his cologne once more tempted her senses. It made her a little dizzy and it coaxed honesty into her silent reply. The faint nod she gave caused one corner of his mouth to tug softly up, and he closed the small gap that was left between them. Lowering his lips to meet hers, he stole the faintest hint of a kiss.

The brief indulgence was enough to convince him that he wanted more, so much more. Cate's perfect lips had been tempting him for weeks. The sensation of finally feeling the warm softness of them against his stoked a fire in the pit of his gut. If he wasn't a man with such impeccable control, he might just have gobbled her up, right then and there.

"You belong in my arms, Cate." His tone was low, seductively spoken. "Tell me you know you do."

"Nicky, this isn't fair." A weakened sigh escaped her and she shook her head. She lifted a hand to push him back, but it dropped limp against his shirt. "I'm mad at you."

"I can tell you *want* to be mad at me. Why don't we start with the feelings you think you shouldn't admit?" He laughed softly, his lips murmuring just barely above hers, enticing them as he went on. "After that, I'll explain why you should."

Fighting against the urge to give in, she took a step back. The safer space between them allowed her to look directly into his eyes. It wouldn't do any good to try and deny her feelings. She'd clearly already given herself away.

"I *am* attracted to you, Nicky. But before things have the chance to get carried away between us, I need to know who I'm getting involved with. I'm sorry if that sounds harsh."

"Apologies again. I told you, I appreciate your honesty." To be sure of keeping his hands to himself, he lightly folded his arms across his chest. "Are you asking if my business dealings aren't quite up to the legal side of the law, Cate?"

She felt a nervous flutter in the pit of her stomach, but managed a soft nod. "You may say it's none of my business, but under the circumstances, it is a legitimate concern for me."

"I agree. You're honest with me. I'll be honest with you. Can we at least go sit while I explain? Please?"

Lightly resting his fingertips against the small of her back, he guided her across the room. They lowered onto a plushly upholstered couch, sitting next to one another. He could see the anxiety displayed in the tilt of her eyebrows. She must've been sure that Shayne was right in all that he'd said about him.

"You aren't entirely wrong about my family, Cate. My great, great grandfather immigrated from Italy when he was a small boy. His family wasn't anything special. Not broke, but no money to speak of. Prohibition came along, and that changed, for reasons you can guess. It changed things for a lot of people."

"By people, you mean bootleggers." She shrugged when he angled a cautious expression at her. "One of the selling points of MacCarthaigh's is the bar, Nicky. I'm not going Prohibition Sally on you."

"Yeah, bootleggers." He nodded, drawing one corner of his smile higher. "He passed things on to my great grandfather, from there. Some of his business dealings also weren't what you would consider quite above board, either."

"Okay." She nodded. "More recently?"

"When my grandfather took over the family businesses, he began to invest the money into corporations, television, real-estate, oil. You name it, at one time or another we probably had our finger in the pie. Not all of them legal."

"And your father?" She arched a brow at him. "*You?*"

"When Pop retired, two years ago, I took over a hundred percent. Before that, I worked under him, learning every facet of the current business, working to maintain things on the level we presently sit at. It was him that wanted to make the whole thing completely legitimate."

"Admirable. I can imagine that wouldn't have been an easy undertaking." She felt the worst of her tension beginning to loosen. "Did it work?"

"Yeah. It was risky and time consuming. It didn't all happen overnight, but it was worth it. By the time I was ten, the whole thing was completely legal. Before that, I honestly can't vouch for every connection, every deal. To this day, I don't even know them all. Makes no difference, since there's no longer any ties to the past. My father told me what I needed to know to run the corporation, as it stands."

"So," she hesitated slightly, "you're saying that the stories, the reputation about you and your father, it's talk."

"Basically, yeah. I mean, Pop and I have made some shrewd deals, over the years, but nothing underhanded. There hasn't been a sketchy deal done since I was a kid. I don't share my business with anyone else because of the value of what I do, not because any of it is illegal. I will show you anything you want to see, right now. Anything."

"I recognize that that's no small offer for you to make. Even if I wanted to, though, I wouldn't have a clue what to ask." She folded her arms, still not thoroughly convinced yet. "If there's nothing shady going on, then why not just refute what people say about you and your family?"

"I can't exactly dismiss what's partially true, but they're talking history, not me. Now, what else you got?"

"Why all the security? Is it the money, the reputation? The whole idea of having a Frankie is a downright foreign concept to me, and the need for one is more than a little unnerving."

"Just because I have a Frankie doesn't mean I'm necessarily going to need to use him. You do have to be a little more cautious when people know you have the kind of bottom line on your bank statement that my family does. On the other hand, you're not toting my kind of money, and *you* still ended up benefitting from his service."

"You can't honestly be claiming that your money doesn't have any bearing here."

"Not just the money, no. The average guy in my wealth bracket runs to the store, goes to the movies, dates, and whatever else without much, or any security, at all. Nobody probably even knows he has money unless he says so. No problem. My circumstances are a little different, though. Everybody knows the Caprianno name, and the reputation that goes with it."

"Mmm, yes." Her brows flicked up. "My brother certainly seems to."

"Yeah, well, it's my money, in combination with my family name that does tend to make me more of a commodity."

"And me being attached to you could make me one, right? Yet, knowing that it could be a concern, you chose to draw me into a need for it by coming to see me every day." She pulled back when he reached for her. "Honesty, Nick, or I walk out that door, right now."

"Nobody else knows the way I feel about you. I mean, Frankie, my guys probably, but," he shook his head, "nobody else knows why I go in there. There's lots of places I hold business meetings, lots of places I count as my favorites."

"Then, what was the idea of Frankie following me? Much as I wouldn't hesitate to call him my guardian angel, tonight, he didn't just drop from the sky!"

"I swear to you, the only reason I did it was because… I care about you. You're a strong woman, Cate, and independent woman. While I respect that about you, I also know that isn't always the best area to be alone after dark. After that last night, when I walked you, it was driving me crazy just thinking about it."

She shifted a little in her seat, then, her tight-jawed expression relaxing a bit more. She couldn't say he was wrong about her sacrificing safety for the sake of stubborn pride, from time to time. Thinking about what Frankie had done for her, realizing what could've happened if he hadn't been there, her remaining anger began to wane. While she didn't necessarily agree with Nick's decision, she at least understood his motives a bit better.

"Shayne says men like you attract trouble naturally."

"I respect your brother, Cate. I do. At this point, I hope you can see he isn't an expert on me, though." He smiled. "You're right, in a sense, when you say that being with me could make you more of a commodity. Then again, I have my own concerns about your safety, regardless. Tonight was proof of that."

"What happened tonight was a fluke. Nothing like that has ever happened before and it isn't likely to happen again."

"Stubbornness isn't always a virtue."

"It isn't always a weakness."

His chest slumped and he nearly laughed. "Either way, I would really feel better if you let Frankie keep an eye out *for* you, if we're going to be together. With the precautions I take, in some ways, you'd actually be *safer* than the average person."

"Safer. I see. At what loss of privacy, I wonder." She nodded, squaring her shoulders and edging back from him a little. While she believed his explanation, she wasn't quite sure how she felt about it.

"Hey." Pulling her hands to his lips, he pressed a light kiss to her fingers, fixing his eyes fully on hers. "Don't box up, like that. Talk to me."

"I'm just thinking, Nick. I suppose I'm allowed to do that much on my own." Her voice was slightly cross, her brows twitching softly inward. "This is a lot to take in for someone who isn't used to it. There's a lot to consider."

"I know that. While you're thinking, though, I want you to consider something else. The idea might be new to you, but it's not new to me. I know what I'm doing. I will not let anything bad happen to you. Frankie, or no Frankie, security team, or not. I will keep you safe. That's a promise."

"A promise." She shifted a look over to the fireplace as she continued to mull what he'd said. "What if something happens out of your control? No one can control everything, Nicky."

"Maybe not, but it's been my experience that the best things are generally the things worth taking risks for."

"We aren't talking about investing in a deal, Nick."

"We're not. We're talking about investing in each other. There's no way of proving it to you, so you're just going to have to decide whether or not you believe me when I say that you're safe with me." He reached a hand to gently turn her face back to him again. "Do you think you can do that?"

"I…" She thought for a second, her reservations growing dimmer with his gaze so warmly and sincerely fixed on her. "I want to."

"Good." His chest shook with a soft laugh, and he nodded, grinning that enticing grin of his again as he leaned toward her. "We'll work on it."

"Just a minute." She slipped a hand against his chest and angled back from him. "I *can* see you were just doing what you thought was the right thing, in your own bumbling way, but because I am who I am, we need to find a compromise."

He drew the corner of his mouth up and nodded. "I might be willing to enter into negotiations."

"If I promise to be more careful, to park a little closer, if I can, then you call off my babysitter." She turned her face away from him, holding a hand up to the start of his protest. "Ah-ah! Much as I like Frankie, that's the deal."

"In business, it's rarely a good idea to accept a first offer. You can almost always do better. So, what are you gonna do if I refuse to accept your terms?" He gave a soft chuckle and shrugged when she lifted a brow to him. "Like you keep saying, it's a free country. Frankie can go anywhere he pleases."

"You aren't going to refuse this offer." She tilted her chin at a haughty angle. "If you refuse, I'll… I'll think of something."

"Oh, that's a threat?" He laughed deeper, full amusement lighting up his expression. "I think I'll take my chances."

"You could, but it's probably in your best interest not to underestimate me. I do have a counter." She felt herself finally beginning to smile again, the smile he usually managed to draw from her, and she leaned forward a little, smoothing a hand down the front of his tie. "Frankie doesn't hang around anymore, unless it's a night I work late. If it'll really make you feel better, and because he's already saved my neck once, I'll let him walk me to my car, those times."

He shook his head, edging closer to her. "Your counteroffer needs work, but I'm not quite ready to leave the table."

"Why doesn't it work? It sounds more than reasonable to me."

"Too broadly set, too many loopholes for both of us." Another laugh shook his chest and he lifted a hand, tracing the side of her face with his finger.

"For instance?" She nuzzled against his touch, welcoming the tingles that followed.

"For one thing, Frankie is always somewhere close by when I go out on a date." He stretched forward, closing what little space was left between them. His gazed moved down to her lips, wanting them again. "Who wins when we go out?"

"I win by default."

"Huh-uh." He shook his head, grinning harder at the almost breathless way her words had come out. "Like I said, needs some work."

When she curled a hand over one of his shoulders and lightly tugged him forward, his arms automatically slipped around her. Her breath was hot, soft, teasing mercilessly at his lips. As he allowed himself to sample them again, her eyes drifted closed. The long draw of her breath in response to him caused him to deepen the kiss that he'd initially kept light.

"Nicky…" Her fingertips pressed firmly against the crisp fabric of his shirt, her heart drumming in her ears as she eased her lips back from his again. "Oh, you are awfully pleased with yourself, aren't you?"

"I'm pretty pleased, at the moment, yeah." He laughed softly, craving another quick taste of her lips. "Why? You want to file a complaint?"

"No." As he began to trace his lips along her jaw, over her throat, her eyes rolled back and she pressed them closed again. Determined to regain her control, she swallowed hard and scooted back a little. "I suppose that that look of yours stems from being used to getting what you want."

Enjoying her saucy expression, he bobbed his head lightly in response. "It might be."

"Well, if you have your eye on me, you'll have to get used to the idea that not everything will come so easily to you as your business appears to."

"Oh, will I?" He drew one of his dark brows up at her and leaned forward, whispering lowly into her ear. "Whose benefit was that speech for?"

She held her breath for a second as he began sweeping tender kisses down her neck again. "Both of us."

He laughed, gently easing her into his arms, pleased that she allowed him to. Gratified that his patience had been rewarded, he lowered another burning kiss to her lips. They continued on with their conversation, speaking flirtatious nonsense between smaller kisses and nuzzles, his handsome grin occasionally growing deeper.

"When you got here, you said you had several concerns?" He pondered groggily. "We may as well get them out now, so we can focus on… more important things."

Other concerns. Other concerns. She attempted to formulate her thoughts into cohesive sentences before she spoke them. Not as easily done as she might have wished. Good grief, she'd settle for just one clear line of thinking. She slipped a hand over the hard thumping of his heart when a thought finally came to her.

"Alf."

"Alf?" Chuckling deeply, his lips vibrated against her throat as he continued to caress it with adoration. "You want to talk about Alf? Now? Come on, Cate."

"You asked if I had any other concerns." She drew back from his grasp. "Nicky, seriously, is Alf, you know… okay?"

"Okay?" He groaned when she refused the reach he made for her. Still breathing quickly, he dropped an arm over the back of the couch, twirling a lock of her fiery hair between his fingers. "What do you mean by that?"

"You know exactly what I mean." She flicked a brow at the frown that began to shadow his face. "Is he?"

Withdrawing his arm, he also began to scoot back a little. "Cate, Alf has been like one of the family, as long as I can remember. He came in at the tale-end with my grandfather, worked with my father for years. I rely on his advice for a reason. He knows the business inside and out, every bit as much as I do, maybe more."

"I'm not suggesting he isn't important to you. I can see that he is. That wasn't what I asked."

"Well, what?" He folded his arms. "So, he wasn't always as squeaky clean as he is now, but I told you, everyone and everything associated with the business is on the up and up, now."

"And that includes Alf?"

"Yeah. Yeah, that includes Alf."

"You're sure?"

"I'm… I'm sure." He shook his head when she flicked her brows and looked off to the side, apparently unconvinced because of his hesitation. "What?"

"I just…" She studied a framed photograph of him with Alf and another man, she assumed his father. "I don't get a good feeling from him."

"Do you get a good feeling from me?" His brows turned downward.

"Considerably more than I let on before." She lifted a hand to check how smudged her lipstick might be. "I think that much should be obvious."

"Then, trust me." He relaxed his arms from the tightly clamped way he'd been holding them when she stared back at him and gave an abrupt nod. Reaching forward, he caught her fingers in his when she suddenly stood. "Whoa, wait a sec. Where are you going?"

"I'm going home." She shook her head. "I think we'd better call it a night."

"Call it a night? Now?" He lifted himself to his feet. "Why?"

"Nicky, you can't ask me if I have any concerns and then jump all over me when I voice them. It feels like a trap, or a test. Either you want to know, or you don't, but either way, I still have them." She folded her arms against herself, a barrier between them, and looked down with a shake of her head. "I know me. Whatever I feel for you, I have to be able to speak my mind."

"You're right. You're right. I'm sorry. I like that you aren't afraid to step on my toes, Cate. I like that you aren't afraid to speak your mind with me, loudly even." He stepped in, reaching to tuck a lock of hair behind her ear with a renewed gentleness. "You aren't really going, are you?"

"I don't know. I suppose it depends on how much you really meant that." She looked up, quirking an inquisitive brow at him.

"I realize we aren't always going to agree on everything." Lowering down to the cushion, he tugged her gently onto his lap. "I like that you know your own mind, and that you don't sugarcoat what comes out, not even for me. You might be right about me being used to getting my way, but I don't want to change you, ever, not even when I do get upset."

"Well, then, I think you may have settled your interest on the right woman, after all." Her smile returned. "I'm definitely not shy about speaking my mind."

"I'm glad." He chuckled, edging his lips toward hers again. "So, I'm curious. Does this count as a first fight? Because, it really wasn't so bad."

"Oh, Nicky." Her head fell back, a sharp burst of amusement rolling from her mouth. "I'm full of hot Irish blood and you're full of Italian passion. I don't think either of us has a clue what sorts of fights we have in store."

"Yeah, maybe." He nodded, admiring the glow that had come to her complexion, then stole a quick kiss from her when she looked back at him again. "I'm curious how that's gonna translate to the making up part, though. Could be pretty interesting."

"Could be pretty volatile. More likely, too. I have a hot temper, and I'm not likely to forget an argument just because you flirt with me, however well you do it. I've been known to stay mad for days."

"Days, huh?" He squinted to the challenge and nodded, then began to murmur his next words against her lips. "I'll have to see what I can do about shortening that timeframe. I don't think I'd want to spend that much time away from you."

"I'm not likely to be all that approachable, if we've been arguing. My temper doesn't just shut off like a hot and cold tap." She gripped his tie firmly, the curve of her mouth drawing wide. "Still think you're prepared for a challenge, like me?"

"I thrive on challenge. The bigger, the better."

"Then, you really do have your work cut out for you."

"Come here." He laughed, angling for her lips again, tucking his arms fully around her. "I like to study my challenges before I fully commit to a task."

Letting the kiss that followed their short argument stretch on, they'd both begun to lose track of time. Cate melted into his embrace, swiftly losing sight of the worries that had originally kept her from him.

After weeks of imagining what it would be like to hold her so closely, Nick's desire for her consumed him. He'd wanted and waited for so long, he thought he might find himself in danger of always giving in to anything she might ever ask or demand of him. It was a completely foreign sensation to him, the sensation of being powerless and under someone else's control. More often than not, it had been his experience that he called the shots in most situations. Now, he felt as if she definitely had him right where she wanted him.

"Hey, Nicky! Everybody still alive in there?" Frankie's muffled voice snickered from behind the heavy door. "Nicky! Okay if we come in?"

If either Nick or Cate had heard him, they hadn't paid any attention. The heavy pounding on the door that followed did manage to draw her into the moment, though. Frankie called out again, a bit more serious than he had before, asking if everything was all right. He wasn't used to not getting a response from his boss.

"Nicky." She laughed, pushing him back when he started to follow her retreat from his arms. "Nicky, you better answer Frankie before he beats down the door. I've seen him in action. It wouldn't take much effort."

He gave a peevish squint over his shoulder, but then began to laugh. "Yeah! Come on in, Frankie!" He looked back at her, grinning deeply. "To be continued?"

"To be continued." She reached forward as the door opened, combing her fingers through his black hair. "Definitely."

"Hey, Nicky, Alf is in the foyer. You want I should let him in? He says he's got something to tell you about that deal you two been working on, only I told him you were a little… preoccupied."

"You mean the deal he's been trying to get me to work on. Yeah, it's fine." Nick lifted himself from the sofa, tugging her up with him. Slipping his arms around her waist, he dipped his head to press a quick kiss to her lips. "I'd drive you, myself, but I don't know how long this is going to take. How about if I have Frankie take you back to your car and follow you home?"

"He doesn't have to follow me home." She shook her head, adjusting his loosened tie before tucking her arms between the two of them. "I don't think that guy is waiting around for me to come back, especially after the jab Frankie gave his nose."

"Hey, that was a pretty good shot you gave him, yourself." Frankie rested a hand over his heart. "Seeing you home would be my pleasure."

Nick tilted a determined look down at her. "You know, we're going to have finish our negotiations for Frankie's custody agreement, too. Another thing to be continued?"

"Mmm. Another thing." She laughed, stretching up on her toes to kiss the determined tightness in his jaw. "Maybe we can fight about it Saturday night, after I get off work?"

"Yeah?" The grin that returned deeply on his lips lowered to hers one last time, melting with them for a few long seconds. "I'll have Frankie pick you up, okay? Call you in the morning?"

She nodded, stepping away from him, smiling at the way he held her fingers until they slipped free at a distance. "Goodnight, Nicky."

Alf puffed up, narrowing his eyes just slightly as he passed her. He could tell she didn't care much for him, didn't trust him. She held her gaze just as sharply to his. What Nick saw in that hot-headed woman was beyond him, but he appeared to be fully smitten with her. Alf only hoped she wouldn't find a way to muck things up. He still needed Nick on his side.

#

They rode quietly all the way back to where Cate's car was parked. Frankie glanced into the rearview mirror a few times, smiling at the satisfied and dreamy curve on her lips. Nick didn't slow down very often, and it had been a long time since Frankie had seen such a genuinely happy expression on his face, too. Glancing at her in the mirror,

Frankie gave a light nod. He definitely approved the choice.

"So, Saturday night, I'll pick you up around seven, take you over to Nicky's place, yeah?" He peeked back at her again with a nod. "You'll love Nicky's place."

"Wasn't that where we were?" She drew her brows in, leaning forward and resting her cheek against the back of his seat.

"That place? Nah. Nicky calls it the mausoleum." He gave a good-humored chuckle to that thought and shook his head. "That's just the family's home base. Nick and Marie grew up there. He just stops there to check in when he gets back into town. Keeps a lot of his business papers in the safe."

"I see."

"He's got a loft just outside the city. It ain't too far from here, little more than halfway to Chicago from Saint Adeline. It's a lot more his style. A lot more comfortable than that drafty old barn of a place. Of course, my father always said no place was truly home without a woman's touch."

She felt her cheeks glowing pink in response to his hint. "I'm sure Nicky already has his place exactly the way he likes it."

"He'll like it better with you in it, trust me." He pulled to a stop next to her car. "Here we are."

He opened his door and got out, moving to open hers for her. With a grateful smile, she walked to her car. It gave a cheerful chirp when she clicked the button and she turned back to look at her protector again. He stood at attention, scanning his eyes along the streets, his build stretched as broad as it would allow. He really was a loveable bulldog.

"Oh, Frankie," she stretched to drape her arms around his neck and gave him a big hug, brushing his cheek with a kiss, "thank you for being my guardian angel, tonight."

"I been called a lot of things over the years, but angel ain't never been one of them." He did his best not to let the color rise in his face, but he couldn't quite suppress the curve that came to his lips. He gave her a light shrug when she stepped back again. "Anytime."

Chapter Nine

Alf had driven fifteen minutes out of his way to stop at Crispen Jansen's office on the outskirts of lower downtown Chicago. He shifted his eyes left and right in the parking garage around the corner. The alarm of his dark sedan gave a chirp as he pressed of the key fob. It had been a good number of years since he'd conducted business on behalf of the Caprianno family in such a place, since Nick was just a little squirt.

After walking down a short section of broken sidewalk, he passed into the lobby of a small business structure. It was dingy and cramped, smelling of cheap floor wax. Yellowish incandescent lighting lit the way to the door at the far end of a narrow hallway. Claustrophobic, he thought.

He sure didn't miss this part of his former life. He did sometimes miss the way of handling things in the old days, though. Then, situations were handled the hard way between two men, not dancing around the way he had been with Crispen Jansen. Thirty-five years earlier, thirty even, he would have put an end to this nonsense himself.

He came to a stop in front of the dark wooden door at the end. Stenciled lettering on the opaque glass window bore Jansen's name. With a grimace, he glanced back down the hallway again and shook his head. What a dump.

Pulling the door open, he moved to a small secretary's station. Placing his hand over his tie to keep it in place, he leaned forward, keeping his voice low as he spoke to the girl behind the desk. She nodded and pointed to an empty chair in the waiting area.

Upon sitting, he glanced at the seats next to him. Two unsavory-looking men stopped talking, scrutinizing him as if they were measuring him up for something. The one with ratty mouse-brown hair had jittery hands and deep sunken eyes. The other was wafe-thin and his skin appeared pasty against the darkness of his unkempt hair. Typical Jansen style, Alf thought. The whole operation appeared to be jammed with dollar a dozen thugs, not worth mentioning in any enterprise other than one such as this.

"Mr. Giuseppe," the secretary looked up, "Mr. Jansen will see you now."

"Thanks, sweetheart." Alf lifted his frame from the chair and made his way over to the private door.

His gaze locked darkly onto Crispen's when he entered the room. Finishing up a phone call, Jansen motioned to the chair just opposite of his. Alf lowered onto the seat, looking back and forth between the two goons that flanked either side of their boss' chair, and he laughed, shaking his head again. Alex looked about as intimidating to him as a gawky bean rail. The other, Bobby, was slightly taller but much more thickly framed. He was the silent, stern type, but still, the thought of him didn't bother Alf too much. Anyway, he was used to them.

Jansen's inner office was night and day different from the rest of the building. It was lavishly decorated. Some of the furnishings, Alf was sure, were more than likely hot. There was no way a small-time operation like Crispen's could afford the antique rugs, leather seating, or the genuine tiffany lamps that were placed on each corner of the too-large mahogany desk. Still, maybe he could. Small-time thugs had a way of finding cash when they wanted it, no matter the means of accessing it. Crispen had already proved his resourcefulness, coercing Alf into business by means of the blackmail he loomed over his head.

"I don't care, Malone. Just do it." Crispen slammed his receiver down onto the hook and shifted his attention over to Alf. "Alfonse, my friend. I hope you brought me better news than you've been giving me over the phone."

Alf's eyes swept back and forth between the two standing men and he jerked his head in gesture to them. "Get rid of Laurel and Hardy and we'll talk. I'm not discussing Mr. Caprianno's business in front of those two clowns."

Crispen laughed, holding a hand up to the skinny man on his right when he started to wind up. "Bobby, Alex, go take a walk. This won't take long."

True to his word, Alf didn't open his mouth again until the two men were on the other side of the door. "What do you keep those two around for, anyway? Atmosphere? They kind of stink the place up, don't they?"

Crispen's wily grin curved higher. "They serve their purpose, when the need arises."

"Yeah, maybe if they had half a brain between the two of them." Pulling the file from his briefcase, Alf slid it over to the other side of the desk and shook his head. "Nick ain't going for it. Not while it still looks like this."

Crispen's smile began to narrow at the corners as he leaned over the papers. "What's the problem now? I thought you said you were going to get this done? It's starting to feel like you're dragging your feet, Alf. I thought we were going to be friends."

"I said I'd do what I could." He shook his head, his brows pulled sharply in. "Whatever business we have, I ain't leaving Nick unprotected. He ain't gonna sign it until he is."

Crispen silently closed the folder, his gaze pinning on the man across the desk from him. He sat for a few seconds, his fingers drumming over the file, and he finally sucked in a long breath. Standing, he went over to the window, his back to Alf as he looked out. Caprianno was going to sign, no matter what. He would only be patient for so much longer before he stopped letting the old-timer think he had as much power as he did, and instead did things his own way.

"What's it going to take, Alf?" He twisted his frame, looking over his shoulder. "What is it he wants to hear?"

Alf slumped back in his chair and linked his fingers over his stomach. "Nick wants to be sure this is an honest enterprise to be associated with. He wants to be sure it stays that way. You don't exactly have the best street credibility. Don't really look like you're doing much to change that image, either, not with those two hanging around. You and your boys have been involved in some pretty shady dealings."

"No convictions. No ties to me." Crispen threw his arms out to the sides, offering an innocent shrug. "Can I help it if the cops got it out for us? Now, what some of my associates have been linked to, I can't say. I can't be responsible for what other people do, am I right?"

"Nick don't see it that way. He makes it a point to know what everybody who works for him is into, and everyone they work with, too." He adjusted his position in the chair more comfortably. "Aside from that, you and I both know the return percentage you're offering his investment is an insult. It was all I could do to keep him from laughing that file right into the paper shredder when he looked at it, this last time."

"Oh, really?" Crispen's complexion darkened in response to the reply. "The Caprianno family wants to be sure they get a fair deal? Like the one they dealt my old man?"

"Nah. You forget. I was there when that partnership was dissolved, right there in the room. There wasn't nothing underhanded about it. Sal and your old man parted ways with a handshake and no hard feelings, just like he did with the others."

"That's a rosy spin. My father didn't have a choice. Never mind what it did to him. Never mind what it meant for *his* business." Folding his arms tightly, he looked away, running his tongue back and forth along his teeth as he considered his next move. "All right, Alf. I'll make a few changes. A *few*! Then, you're going to take that proposal back to *Mr. Caprianno*, and you're going to make sure he signs it."

"Hey, I can't make any promises."

"I'm starting to lose faith in you, Alf, and believe me… that wouldn't be a good thing."

"I'll talk to Nick again. I won't do it for another week, or so. Maybe even a couple. Any sooner, he's gonna just shove it off his desk. I promise you that."

"No, he won't, Alf." Crispen dropped his palms over the top of his desk, leaning forward with a cruel sneer. "You're not gonna let him. I told you, when my father was dying, he did a lot of talking. I found a lot of interesting things in his papers, things to do with your earlier involvement with the Caprianno family."

"I'm sure, but-"

"Something also tells me that Nicky boy doesn't know *everything* about all the skeletons in his consulente's closet. He wouldn't be too pleased to find out you're riding both sides of the fence on this deal, either."

Alf did his best not to allow the hard swallow of his throat to be too conspicuous. Alone in the room, as they were, what he wouldn't have given to allow himself to be his old self for just five minutes. He had to clean up this mess, so that it would never bother him again, and so it would never even chance touching Nick.

Now that he'd gotten Nick involved with the whole thing, he knew it would reflect badly on his boss, even if he did let himself teach Jansen an old-school lesson. As it was, Crispen knew he had him exactly where he wanted him with his blackmail.

"I'll see what he says." Alf nodded. "No matter what you think you got on me, I can't make any guarantees. Nick listens to me, but he's his own man. He's not gonna miss much, either, so trying to pull a fast one on him ain't gonna work. He's a lot smarter than… well, other fellas I know."

"All right." Crispen's grin peeled back meanly over his teeth. "Then, I guess we'll stay friends… for now."

"Goodie." Alf picked up his briefcase again and lifted himself from the chair. He pulled the cell phone from his pocket when it began to ring, allowing his eyes to glance at the screen. With a hesitant inward groan, he lifted it to his ear. "Hey. Nah, I can't talk. Yeah, yeah. Don't worry, Romeo. I'll call you back before she gets there. I wouldn't want to interrupt again. Give me a minute, yeah? Yeah, okay."

"Was that our boy? So, he's finally settling down, huh? Didn't think Caprianno had it in him with that 'all work and no play' reputation of his. Who is she?"

Alf tapped a finger against his temple, shaking his head. "You know. Ain't that a kick? Must've just slipped out of my head."

"Right." Crispen grinned broadly when Alf scowled and dropped his cell back into his pocket. "Well, give him my best."

Alf lowered his eyes to the hand that was extended across the desk toward him and he laughed. "I'll be in touch, kid."

Crispen gritted down hard on his teeth at the insulting slight and lowered his hand again. "You count on it, Alf. You count on it."

Giving him a crooked smirk in receipt for the statement, Alf slipped out the door past Alex and Bobby, and headed for the parking garage. The two cronies moved into the room and took the seats across from Crispen. He was leaning back in his chair, a deep grin on his face.

"I got some homework for you boys." Beginning to swivel side to side, he rubbed a hand over his mouth and laughed. "Nick Caprianno's got a girl. Don't do anything. Just find out about her. *Everything* about her. I think I may just have found our missing piece of leverage."

#

Alf thumped himself down into the leather seat of his car, flipped a hand over the warming dial, and hit the call button on his hands-free screen. "Hey, Nicky. Sorry about that."

Nick heard the echoed screech of tires on concrete and laughed, stirring the sauce on his stove. "Where are you, anyway? You should've been done with that meeting in the downtown office an hour ago."

"I was." He cleared his throat, his heart thudding a little heavier in his ears. "I was meeting with Crispen Jansen."

"Jansen?" Nick frowned, turning down the burner and leaning a hip against his countertop. "Why?"

"I figured, so long as I was in the area, I'd talk to him in person. It wasn't too far out of my way." He swallowed against the lie. "I thought I might get through to him that he needs to be more serious when he's dealing with us. I told him that percentage he offered was a joke."

"It was." Nick nodded, thinking the whole situation over carefully. "What did he say?"

"He said he'd work on it. I think I finally got through to him that we're done playing games. It's time to get serious." He reached a hand out of the window, handing cash to the parking attendant, and took his receipt. The silence on the other end of the call made him slightly apprehensive. "Nick?"

"I'm here. Just don't give too much to them. They don't need to know where our heads are. It's gonna take a lot of proof and convincing before I edge any closer to a yes than I am now. I'm still not even sure it's worth it."

"I told him that."

Nick folded his arms, glancing again at the clock. "Why didn't you say you were going there? If it's really that important to you, I could've met you in the city. We could've had them in our office, on our turf, made it a meeting with both of us."

A light mist dewed on Alf's forehead. "Ah, don't worry about it, Nicky. I found us this deal, let me worry about hammering out any details. These boys are a little rough around the edges, but I can handle it on my own."

Nick remained quiet for a second or two, then nodded. "Yeah, well, don't let them talk you into anything."

"Come on, Nick. You know better than that." Alf swallowed against that hard lump again and smiled weakly, attempting to draw nonchalance into his voice. "I ever steered you wrong? Huh?"

"I guess not." Nick tapped the spoon on the edge of the saucepan and placed it carefully down on the rest again. Something with the whole situation didn't smell right. "Night, Alf."

"You wanna go over the meeting at the downtown office?" He pulled off to the side of the road, feeling a little too anxious to focus.

"No. We'll get into all that it in the morning. Cate's gonna be here soon. I don't have time."

"All right, kid." Alf laughed. "Have fun."

Nick disconnected the call, looking down at the phone in his hand for a long few seconds. Something was off with Alf. He could feel it. Maybe the stress really was starting to eat at him too much. Surely it couldn't be anything more than that. Alf had been looking out for him since day one. With a discomforted feeling in the pit of his gut, Nick turned back toward the stove and stirred the contents of the pot again.

From where Alf remained parked at the side of the road, he rummaged around in the center console of his car. He pulled out a half-eaten roll of antacids. Chucking two or three into his mouth, he closed his eyes, grinding the chalky tablets between his teeth. After another moment, he put the car back into drive and headed for home.

Chapter Ten

Though the rainy night could have caused delays, Frankie was good to his word, picking Cate up at the exact hour he was to appear on Saturday night. She chatted with him a little, here and there, not about anything in particular. It was a much shorter ride to Nick's than she anticipated, but traffic had been light. As much as she found herself liking Frankie, it still felt odd to be picked up by a driver, let alone a man she knew to be a bodyguard. Cate stepped out of the car and under Frankie's opened umbrella when he'd pulled her door open for her.

"So, Nicky's sister, Marie... What does she think of having a security detail following her around everywhere? I assume she does, too."

"Mm-hmm. Sometimes." His large chest shook and he gave her his arm as they made their way up to the building. "She don't like it no more than you do. Even though she and Nicky don't really know no different, they still don't exactly see eye to eye on it. It's the way they was raised from the time they was born. I guess it just don't bother Nicky as much as it does Marie."

"Hmm." She angled a sideways grin at him. "Something tells me that Nicky has a lot more say-so than she does on the matter."

She nodded when Frankie only smiled. It was becoming more apparent that Nick not only ran the business, but had stepped up as a sort of co-head of the family.

She gave the brick building before her a quick study. Considering the age of the surrounding area, she guessed that Nick had sunk a pretty penny into refurbishment, but had managed to maintain the authentic vibe of the neighborhood. Her glance shifted around. There were other businesses, but Nick's building was the largest by far, and she didn't see any houses on that street. *Caprianno Corporation* was printed in large, bold letters above the oversized glass doors.

"I thought we were going to Nicky's place." She quirked her brows upward. "Was there a change in plans? Did he have to work late, or something?"

"Oh, this?" Frankie's barrel chest shook again and he pressed his thumb to the door's fingerprint recognition pad. "Nicky works on the lower floor, but he's got an apartment above the office."

"Ah. My grandparents lived above the restaurant for years. My mom tried to get Gran to move in with them when my grandfather passed, but she refused to budge."

"That a fact? I know some people don't think it's right, Nicky living above the business. Most guys need a break from it all, once in a while, a separation between business and home, but not Nick." He shrugged walking up a flight of stairs with her. "But, what do I know, huh?"

They walked down a short hallway at the top and he lifted a fist to club the door. "Hey, Nicky! Nicky, open up, will ya?"

She could hear footsteps briskly nearing the other side, and the door was pulled open. A rush of tingles skittered over her flesh when Nick aimed that handsome grin of his at her, then leaned to brush her cheek with a kiss.

"How was the rain situation with the drive?" Nick questioned her escort as she passed into the entryway.

"Wet." Frankie gave a deep-chested chuckle and shook some drizzle from his black polyester rainslicker for effect.

"You gonna be next door?"

"Well, I ain't gonna stick around here and watch the two of you play footsie all night." Frankie laughed, shaking his head, then cleared his throat when he noticed the bright flush that rose in her cheeks. "Sorry, sweetheart."

"Yeah, yeah. Get out of here, you clown." Nick grinned, closing the door as Frankie started down the hallway. A light chuckle escaped Nick's lips when he saw the bewildered twist at the inner corners of her brows. "What's the matter?"

"Where's he really going?" She walked further into the apartment with him, turning as he reached to help her out of her coat.

"Next door, like he said. The guys have their own apartment over there. Security doesn't have to mean a loss of privacy. You didn't really think he was going to stick around?" He leaned forward, pressing his lips to the back of her shoulder. "I mean, if you really think you're going to need a protector, I can always call him back."

She curved her mouth into a smile as she turned to face him again. "We'll have to see how trustworthy you prove to be, first."

"Ah. Still on probation, huh?" He slipped his hands to the curves of her waist and lowered his lips down to the sassy grin she'd aimed back. "So, you wanna check the place out, or what?"

"Shall I just make myself at home, then?" She giggled softly.

"Go ahead. Get comfortable." He nodded, dipping his head to kiss her again, but falling short of his goal when she slipped back from his reach with a playful giggle.

Retaining the amusement in her smile, she pivoted from him, the heels of her black stilettos tapping softly over the satin-buffed wood floors. Lifting his brows with a smooth grin, he tucked his hand into his pockets and followed behind her. Taking it all in as she went, she meandered further through the space, glancing back at him in the reflections of windows and other reflective surfaces she passed.

The foyer led into a large open kitchen with red brick walls and shining appliances. A grand island was centered by a u-shape of marble countertops and long glass pendant lights. She cut a quick glance off to the side, noticing the simmering pot on the stove. The warming function had been set on the digital screen of the oven, as well. Nodding approval, she resumed her investigation.

She knew he was watching her, smiling at her as he followed silently along while she moved on to the main living area. It was separated from the kitchen by a dining table that fit the space, but was really too large for a bachelor alone. Trailing a hand along the back of one of the dark dining chairs as she passed it, she kept a slow and steady pace, hearing his quiet footsteps, just behind.

Her eyes moved up and down the walls, over the bookcases and furniture. The décor was a bit sparce for her liking, but his book selection looked to be more than adequate. A television was hung above a large gas fireplace that steadily flickered at the far end of the apartment. The chimney, which ran to the ceiling appeared to be a dark gray slate. The adjacent wall was made up almost completely of large paned windows that stretched from floor to ceiling, and a sliding glass door that led to a small balcony patio.

Feeling the whisper of a kiss on the back of her shoulder when she stopped to look down at an antique turntable, the apparent source of the lovely, snowy-sounding notes of music, she looked to the side at him. At the lifting of gooseflesh where his fingers skated softly down her arm, she resumed her tour just before his lips could reach hers.

He grinned after her, his heartbeat pulsing stronger in response to the coy game of cat and mouse she was leading him on. It only made him want her more, increasing the pleasant balance of tension that existed between them. He had a feeling, by the saucy upward lift of her luscious lips, that she knew exactly what she was doing to him, and that she was taking pleasure in it.

Resting a hand over the back of the stiff, dark leather couch, she gave the equally uncomfortable-looking leather and chrome chairs a thin glare. After shifting a study over to the black metal stairs that led to what she assumed was his bedroom, she turned to look at him again.

She tugged the arch of one of her brows up at him with a small laugh. His eyes had to be lifted to meet hers, forcing him to abandon his preoccupation with the back of her black dress and the shapely legs below its hemline. Caught. It wasn't the first time, though generally he appeared more embarrassed than he presently was. He no longer gave the impression of being bothered by her catching him. Instead, the pleasure in his expression only grew stronger.

"So, what's the consensus?" He shrugged when she'd only nodded and then bobbled her head lightly from side to side. Giving a short laugh, he mimicked her gesture, then reached to a small beverage cart to pour two glasses of champagne. "What's that supposed to mean? Am I gonna have to move, or what?"

"Not if you like it. It's your loft, after all."

She stepped forward, reaching to take the glass he held out to her, angling her head when he started to pull it back with a questioning tilt of his dark brows. Stretching farther, she took the glass and slowly lifted it to her lips for a quick sip.

"It's nice… in a masculine sort of way. Industrial."

"Ah, okay." His laughter returned and he took a sip from his own glass. "Not fond of lofts, I take it? Ceiling too tall? Too many windows?"

"No. Lofts are fine. I love the window wall. Industrial doesn't even bother me… to a point."

She walked past him, back toward the kitchen. Placing her flute on the countertop, she stepped into the heart of the room to peek in and see what the oven was keeping warm. Tsking her tongue against her teeth, she shook her head.

"Braciole? Really? Nicky, Nicky. All that garlic. Should make for an uneventful evening, later on."

"I guess that means no lingering goodnight kisses, huh?" He placed his glass next to hers, then crossed over to where she stood. "You wouldn't really let a little garlic stop you? Thought you were braver than that."

"You never know. I might be."

She laughed softly, tugging him closer by the collar of his crisp gray dress shirt. Fiddling with his tie for a few seconds, she loosened the knot until it hung lifelessly down either side of his chest. Flicking a finger to undo his top button, she gave a nod, her eyes settling on the amused curve at his lips.

"Better. You know, if you wanted me to feel at home, you should have probably looked a little less like you were going to a business meeting right after."

The smooth grin he wore edged toward hers and he drew her the rest of the way to him. His fingers rested lightly at her neck as his other hand found a home at her hip, then slipped to the small of her back. There was that connection, with her feeling all warm and soft in his arms. His lips greedily preoccupied hers, not satisfied until he heard the contented sigh she softly made and felt her melt against him.

He'd waited nearly all week to hold her again. It had been her idea that he shouldn't show up so often to the restaurant, in case Shayne's hot temper decided to boil over. Although, he'd countered that Shayne may as well get used to seeing them together as a couple, he'd respected her wishes.

He had, at the very least, managed to talk her into sharing one coffee break, midweek. It wasn't as if he was exactly free to be so near to her then, as he was now, though, not with Shayne watching like a forbidding gargoyle from the bar. She'd offered him a quick kiss when he left, but not like this one. This one stretched on, and delved so passionately deep that it made his thoughts go pleasantly foggy.

"Ha! Son of a-" He yelped, jumping back from her, flipping his hand a few times.

He rattled off a few expletives in Italian. It made him feel better, and felt less offensive to his guest in another language. Having been so consumed by his pursuit of her, he'd lost sight of the fact that she'd been standing next to the stove… and the scalding pot on the front burner. His brows quirked up when he noticed her quietly snickering at him, and he stepped back in.

"Oh, is my pain funny to you?"

"Dinner and a show. Pulling out all the stops, huh?" She continued to laugh, resisting the reach he made for her again. "There's just one thing about the dinner."

Turning, she snatched a half apron from a hook and tied it around her waist, then kicked the tall shoes off of her feet. Though the wood floors were chilled, feeling the soles of her feet pressing against them gave her a warm feeling, cozy. For all of its flash, his kitchen was a homey space. She lifted a spoon in her hand and tasted the contents of the pot.

"Mmm." She shook her head. "That's what I thought. I'm going to have to tweak this a little."

"Now, what could an Irish girl possibly know about my Noni Gianna's minestrone soup?"

"More than you do, apparently."

His arms slid around her from behind and he shook his head. Bossy. He liked her in just her stocking feet. It put her at just the right level for him to nestle against her back and nuzzle her. Sweeping her hair to one side, he traced kisses down the satiny curve of her neck.

"It's perfect, as is, Cate." His words were warm in her ear and he smiled when she turned her head to the side for a quick brush of his lips. "You're crazy if you think you're gonna add anything to it."

"You're crazy if you think I'm not." She bobbled her head lightly and turned her attention back to the stove. "My best friend, growing up, was from a family just as Italian as yours. Stephania Russo. Drove my Gran nuts. Why can't you play with Cora O'Shea, Cathlene? I can only imagine what she'd say about me being alone here with you all night."

"All night, huh?" He lifted one of his brows when a blushed shade rose in her complexion. "That sounds promising."

"Well, maybe not *all* night." Looking away, she reached onto the spice shelf and added a dash of this and that, tasted again, and turned in the circle of his arms so that he could taste, too. "Go on. Don't be a spoil sport."

"Cate, I don't…" He frowned, unsure of whether he wanted to tackle her dismissal of his cooking abilities, or the grandmother's comment first.

"Don't you dare say you hate it until you've tried it, at least. That is exactly what it needed. Trust me." She insisted, then flung a high brow at him when he'd finally accepted the offering. "Well?"

"Huh. You know, Noni Gianna always left something out of her written recipes, like a secret she took to the grave. But that... What did you do? Ten years, I've been making this, and it's never come out right." He nodded, looking at the little jar on the shelf, then dropped his lips to hers again. "I would've never guessed. I guess we make a pretty good team."

"And, I was right?"

"Yeah." He laughed. "You were right."

"*I* am always right." She lifted the wooden spoon to wave at him in warning. "You'd just as well agree to that, now. Trust me, it'll save you a lot of grief later."

"Happy wife, happy life, right?" He chuckled, amused by the way her mouth fell open, obviously too stunned to reply. Turning, he walked with a cocky jaunt over to the countertop and hoisted himself up to sit. "What? We both know that's where this is going, don't we? Why beat around the bush about it?"

"Nicky, we've barely started dating."

"So what?" He shrugged.

She dropped the spoon on the rest with a clatter. Her stocking-clad feet swished against the floorboards as she stepped in front of him, measuring the sincerity hiding beneath the mischievous grin on his mouth.

"How can you possibly claim to know something like that, so soon?" She shook her head at the cocky expression he maintained. "I suppose, among all of your other talents, you're clairvoyant, too?"

"Maybe I am. I can feel it when something's right, like you said. Here. In my gut." He tapped his stomach, then reached into a chilled stoneware bowl and popped a blueberry into his mouth. "You feel it, too. You wouldn't have kicked off your shoes and made yourself at home in my kitchen, if you didn't. There's my tie and shirt button to consider, too. They didn't just undo themselves."

"If I was you, I wouldn't be so sure of myself." She dropped her hands onto the tops of her hips, angling her head a little to one side. "How do you know I wasn't just tired of walking around in those? Maybe my feet were sore. Maybe I just thought you looked uptight. Or, maybe I thought you meant it when you said-"

"All right, all right." He held his hands up between them, chuckling at the quick flash of temper from her. "Ti sento, amore mio."

She flicked a brow, her hands digging firmer at her hips. "That better not have been anything snotty."

"I said, I hear you, my love. We're going to have to work on your Italian… at least the dirty words." He gave another impish laugh, attempting and failing to maneuver for a kiss. "Okay, fine. Maybe your feet were tired, and maybe I looked uptight. Will you come here?"

"Hmm-mm. You were going to say something else."

He leaned forward again. "Maybe you were also imagining what it'd be like, ruling my kitchen, and just maybe, what it might be like to rule me… just a little bit."

"You are impossible." She shook her head, stepping from his reach.

"I might be impossible," he grinned deeper, snagging her before she could get too far, then leaned forward to peck a kiss onto the pout of her lips, "but I'm also not wrong."

"We already agreed-"

"Ah, ah." He shook his head. "You might always be right, but *I'm* not always going to be wrong. That's something else we might as well agree on now. Anyway, what's dating? Just each figuring out who the other one is and whether or not you'll drive each other crazy. I've been coming into the restaurant almost every day for the last couple of months. You met Frankie. He approves. The chemistry is… Well, it's practically signed and sealed."

"I suppose I have no say in the matter?" She slanted a testing gaze at him, waiting for his reply, her fists digging deeper against the waistband of the apron. "You may as well know, so long as you've got this in your head, that I'm not inclined to be what you would call a silent partner."

"Oh, I know that. I know. And, you've got at least two things to say about it." He slid from the countertop, curling her into his arms again. He enjoyed the way her soft curves felt against him. Grinning at the way her rigid frame had immediately gone slack in his embrace, he lowered his voice to a smooth and convincing whisper. "You still have to say yes, and I do."

"Nicky." She rolled her eyes, running her fingers through his black hair. "I suppose you made your mind up the second you laid eyes on me?"

"Pretty close. Told you. The gut." He tapped a hand over his stomach again. "You felt it, too. You just didn't see the significance as quickly as I did. It's why you gave me the cherries when I ordered the cake, that first day. I also noticed you never added it to the bill."

"I gave you a few lousy maraschino cherries and a complimentary dessert, and that told you that I wanted you?"

"It was an invitation to come back." He tilted his head back, his eyes looking down at her as he grinned satisfactorily at her silence. "Wasn't it?"

"It… I mean, I just… Ugh, Nicky." She pushed away, untying the apron and throwing it onto the counter in a wad, then walked to take up her champagne again. "I don't know why we're even arguing about this, or how we got onto it. It isn't as if this, whatever it is, is any sort of real proposal. No ring, no planning, no-"

"You want a ring?" He grasped a small velvet box from the shelf next to him and slid it across the counter to her. Leaning a hip against the cabinet, he folded his arms as he stared back at her with a satisfied expression on his face. "Go on. It's yours, anyway."

Chapter Eleven

Nick remained where he was, a cocky-wide grin spread over his mouth. She appeared to have been struck silent with shock. Though the expression on her face wouldn't have inspired a lot of confidence to a casual viewer, Nick had spent weeks observing her. He remained sure of himself, sure of her. Finally, she lifted her eyes from the box, flashing them onto him.

"What?" He laughed, shrugging. "So, we'll try it for fifty or sixty years and see if it works out."

She held her lips in a firm line and loudly smacked a palm against the counter, then jerked an accusatory finger in his direction. "That is not how you ask a woman to marry you, Nicholas Caprianno! Especially if you don't want her to think you're nuts!"

"I'm crazy, now?" He chuckled lowly.

"No." Her mouth pouted tightly, then she huffed a breath at him. "But if your gut was accurate, it would've given you a warning, or two, about how you do something like this. I still have so many concerns about us being together."

Sensing that she was actually beginning to grow angry, or that she wanted to appear to be, he knew he should've smoothed the strong curve from his lips. He couldn't quite manage it. Instead, he scooted nearer to her.

"That wasn't a *no*, Cate."

"I know it wasn't a no!" She shouted, leaving the unopened box on the counter, then stormed back into the living room. She thumped herself down into the corner of the hard couch. "And you have lousy taste in furniture!"

Taming down the broadest signs of amusement in his expression, he cleared his throat, snatching the box from the counter, and went to join her in the next room. He gently placed it on the glass-top coffee table and lowered onto the seat cushion next to her. He squished his lips together against the desire to smile when she flinched an annoyed glance at him.

"I think it's safe to say that I'm a little more attached to you than I am to the furniture, at this point. You can change it, if that's what's stopping you. You can change the whole apartment, for all I care. We don't even have to live here."

She twisted herself to face him, drawing her feet up with her onto the cold, firm cushion. "You have no idea what it's like being a normal person, do you, how normal people behave and act and what they have a right to expect?"

"Hey, I'm a normal person. Fairly normal, anyway." He shrugged, easing an elbow against the back of the couch, his temple resting against his loosely curled hand. "Is this about your grandmother and the Italian thing?"

"No." She rolled her eyes. "Gran isn't awful, Nicky, just stuck in her ways. She wants me to marry a nice, traditional Irish boy."

"Well, I'm a nice, traditional Italian boy." He shrugged again, laughing softly. "Is *that* your concern?"

"No. It's about most people not having whatever they want at their beck and call, or whenever they want it. I don't just snap my fingers and make something happen, but you seem to, and that…" She tilted her face away from his observation. "That's a little scary, Nicky."

"Scary?" He drew both of his arms down to fold over his chest. "I'm scary? Okay, my gut didn't really see that one coming, so you're gonna have to explain the logic to me."

"Not you, but your kind of money is scary, yes. At the very least, it's intimidating. The things that money can do and the consequences it can bring scare me, yes." She nodded deeply. "I know that no matter how hard you're trying to make tonight feel normal, just a guy cooking dinner for his girl at his apartment, there is a separate apartment, right next to this one, for a security team."

"Having money doesn't mean I'm not a normal person, Cate. That's kind of a harsh assessment." He frowned a little harder.

"That wasn't meant as an insult, Nicky, just an observation." She picked at her nails, shrugging. "I can't help it if it bothers me."

"Okay. I guess it's time we finished what we started with your concerns last time." He slipped his tie from around his neck and tossed it into a careless wad on the coffee table. Scooting forward, he took her hands in his. "I'm listening."

"Good. Because, it's not just security that bothers me."

"Come here. Please." He spread his arms open wide. A contented curve made its way across his lips when she only hesitated for another second, then adjusted to tuck herself into the embrace. "What else you got? Is *this* the part about the family?"

"No. Still your money. At least, another facet of it." Her eyes shifted up to his from where she'd rested her head on his shoulder. "There really is a lot of it."

"Yeah, there is. I can't do a whole lot about that." His chest shook against her. "We throw a lot at charities, but the stuff just keeps on multiplying. Sort of what it's meant to do."

"I'm serious." She sighed, stroking a hand down the side of his face. "People with money, your kind of money, do often think that they can have whatever they want. It's important to me that you know that my family and I have earned everything we have."

"You afraid I'm going to try and buy you out of your share of MacCarthaigh's?"

"I mean it. Whatever ends up happening between us, I don't want anything from you."

"Nothing?" He maneuvered for a kiss, sighing when she denied him.

"Nothing monetary. I expect you to know that you won't be able to just buy anything between the two of us."

"I respect you too much to have expected that, Cate. I can also see that you like working with your brother. I understand family. I'm not gonna try and make you give up something that makes you happy. You should know that anything I have, you'll have access to if we get married, though. I'm not having any mine and yours between us."

"Nicky-"

"No. I'm not bending on that one. Use it, don't use it. It'll be there, without question." His tone certainly didn't appear to leave any room for negotiation, his eyes leveling firmly on hers. "What else?"

"Here we're talking about marriage and money, and Shayne about hit the roof just because I told him we'd started seeing each other. He turned purple for a good five minutes before he started railing on about it."

"*Now* the family. Good. It brings me to one of *my* things. I want us to meet the families tomorrow." He shook his head when she instantly began to protest. "I mean it. Both of us, both families."

"I have Sunday dinner at Gran's tomorrow. I told you about that. With the whole family, Nicky. For someone as intelligent as you, that's a terrible idea. You'd be eaten alive! My grandmother is very old-school Irish. Irish in every sense of the word."

"Yeah, I got that. My family's old-school Italian, with a less than savory background, and my mom's a first generation Italian-American with a temper to match Shayne's. What's your point?"

"My point is that it would be like going to battle."

"I like to live dangerously." He laughed. "We should just have them both to one place and get it over. If MacCarthaigh's is better for you, we'll do it there. They're gonna have to get used to it, once we're married."

"You forget that I still haven't said yes."

"You still haven't said no, either." He shrugged, laughing softly. "We both know you wouldn't have a problem shouting 'no', loud and clear, if that was gonna be your answer."

She laughed, lifting a brow. "Are you always this pig-headed?"

"Determined." He corrected. "You have enough temper and stubbornness to balance me out, so it all works out fine. I have a feeling that you won't have any trouble keeping me in line."

She cut a sideways glance at him. "I can see we're pretty well matched on the stubbornness front, all right."

He nodded again, grinning deeper when he observed the way she couldn't quite manage to hold the stern expression on her face. Instead, it began to break into a slow smile. He lowered his lips, lingering with hers for a few seconds, and he slouched against the back of the couch again. He took pleasure in nuzzling the silky curve of her neck, his breaths drawing in the scent she wore there.

"Is there anything else worrying you about us, Cate?"

With her fingers curled tightly in the loosened collar of his shirt, she pressed her eyes tightly closed, brows flicking weakly. "Women, Nicky."

He slowly drew back, his gaze meeting hers again, observing the discomforted concern he found there. Her words, though few, had had such a decisively accusatory snap to them that it had broken his focus. He gave an amused laugh, earning the frustrated tilt of her brows in response.

"What? What about women?" His head dipped quickly again, pecking her lips with his before she had the chance to withdraw them. "What do you want to know?"

"When I told Shayne about us, he pointed out that… a man like you generally has a steady stream of women in his life. If we're actually going to consider something serious, really consider it, I think it's only right to tell you that I refuse to be one of many. It's not how I am."

"You could never be one of many, Cate. You are definitely a one-of-a-kind type of woman. A man only needs one woman in his life when she's like you."

"Nicky, stop. No flattery, no sweettalk." She grasped his chin between her fingers so that he couldn't go back to those delicious, distracting kisses. "I'm serious."

"So am I. Women aren't a problem. Up to now, I've had dates for parties and events, no girlfriends to speak of. If I have someone special, you, then, problem solved." He slipped free of her grasp and started back for his previous attentions to her neck. "That it?"

"So easy? Surely, there must have been-"

"There wasn't." He shook his head with another deep chuckle. "Ask anyone. Ask Frankie. You like him."

"I do." She nodded.

"Good. That's settled." He laughed softly against her ear. "Now, what's wrong with my furniture?"

"Absolutely nothing, if you like cold, hard, boxy couches and sharp cornered tables. Did you snag all this from one of your offices?" She tugged away, shaking her head as she swept another look around the room. "You'd really let me redo things, huh?"

"You could start tomorrow, if you wanted to. I don't care what you put in here, so long as I find you somewhere in the middle of it." He flicked a look at the box on the table. "Don't you even want at least a peek at it?"

She looked down when he reached to the table. With a conceding sigh, she took the offering. "All right, but this isn't a yes."

"So long as it isn't a no, you can take your time. I'm a pretty patient guy when it's important."

"I've noticed." She smiled. "Good things to those who wait, and all that?"

"Mm-hmm." He brushed her lips with a quick kiss. "Apparently so."

"Yeah, well, I…" She trailed off. Her mouth fell open when the hinge of the box made a soft creak on opening. She gaped at the ring, but flashed a glance back at the grin he wore. She snapped it closed again. "It's too big."

"I can have it sized, Cate." He chuckled. "I didn't exactly get it from a quarter machine."

"I meant the ring itself. The diamonds. My gran would say it's a knuckle duster, but what she'll really mean is that it's ostentatious and that I'm getting above myself. Besides, with something like that on my finger, I'd *have* to have Frankie standing guard. Maybe that's what you had in mind, all along."

"No, that wasn't what I had in mind when I picked it out, but I won't lie, the thought's a perk to me." When she still didn't smile, he nodded quietly. "Does that mean you don't like it? You can choose something else. I want you to be happy."

Observing the flicker of disappointment in his eye, she smiled. It was reassuring to know that he wasn't always so boldly confident, and the ring was gorgeous.

"I guess the least I could do would be to try it on." She shrugged. "Since you already have it."

"Yeah?" His mouth tugged up at the corners again. "Well, go ahead."

"Nicky," she leaned forward to kiss him, laughing softly against his lips, "I really thought Italian men had a better sense of romance than this. You're supposed to put it on for me."

"Is that how this is supposed to work? I thought that was only if you said yes, not if you were just trying it for size." He pulled the ring from its cushion and held it up between them. "If we go this route, I'm going to want to know what it means."

Chapter Twelve

While Crispen Jansen was far from being a patient man, he was good at plotting, planning, and waiting when he knew it would serve him well. He was a man of research where his enemies and conquests were concerned, though not in the same way that Nick Caprianno researched potential partners. Nick's discerning tendencies were due to the legalities of potential partners. Jansen's research was fueled by either vengeance or greed, whichever the situation called for.

Crispen sucked a long drag through the yellow-tinged filter of his cigarette and rocked back in his chair. "All right, boys. What gifts did you bring me?"

"We got plenty, Mr. Jansen." Alex's crooked teeth were exposed in a sneer as he laughed, dropping the file onto the desktop. "Artwork, too."

"Like an early Christmas, isn't it? You boys know how I like pretty pictures." Crispen grinned, rocking forward again to flip the folder open. His finger traced over the face in the photograph that was stapled to the front page. He nodded, with a flick of his brows, and expelled a colorful expletive. "Nicky boy does have good taste, doesn't he?"

"Yeah, she's pretty, ain't she?"

"Pretty? She's beautiful. More than that…" Crispen lifted the photo in his hands and rocked back in his chair again, fixing his eyes on the pleasant, oblivious expression on Cate's face. A malicious grin slithered over his lips as he studied her. "She is exactly what we've been waiting for."

"I knew you'd be pleased." Alex, delighted with himself, sat on the edge of Crispen's desk. He quickly stood again when his boss flashed a sharp glare at him. "It was easy as pie, Mr. Jansen. She works the same shifts every week. She goes to the farmer's market every Saturday morning. She lives and breathes by a clock. Lives alone. Wouldn't be a problem."

Crispen nodded, then flicked a brow up, looking back and forth between the two men. "How close is Caprianno?"

"Take a look at those next couple of pictures, boss." Alex leaned forward, doling photos out one at a time. "Here they are at the market thing."

"Sharing popcorn." Crispen chuckled. "Isn't that cute? What else?"

"This one, here, they're kissing. Not such a sissy kiss, either. You know what I mean?" Alex brayed a donkey-like laugh, then dropped the last photo down with a self-satisfied flourish. "And that, is about the biggest friendship ring I ever seen."

Crispen's grin grew dangerously broad, his eyes widening to take in the spoils of his victory. "So, little Nicky Caprianno is getting married, huh?"

Bobby finally spoke, his voice low and monotone. "She don't wear the bling much, but they're definitely engaged. Should we make a move before they have a chance to go ahead with it, boss? Might be more difficult, once she's under Caprianno's protection."

"Are you kidding? Look at that woman again and tell me you don't think she's already under Caprianno's protection. No. Let's not rush ourselves, boys. No sense in poking a beehive unnecessarily. What's she like?" Crispen angled a curious look at Bobby. "Tell me about…"

"Cathlene Rose MacCarthaigh." Alex released another laugh, elbowing Bobby before he had a chance to answer, his counterpart merely dusting a hand over his blazer. "People who know her call her Cate."

"Cate, huh?" Crispen let his gaze rove hungrily over the images. "Well, should we call her Cate, too, boys? I think we qualify as friends, don't we? Or, we very soon will. I have a feeling we're all going to be closer, in the very near future."

"She's got a hot temper." Alex leaned a hand against the desktop, grinning. "She don't like hearing no. She also don't like the word can't."

"Is that so?" Crispen nodded, admiring the red-hot glow of the sun's highlight on her hair. "Well, I don't think we really need to push things. If she's got an obstinate temperament, she won't be as willing as Caprianno would like her to be when it comes to letting him call the shots. We'll see what our friend Alf can do for us, first. If he doesn't come through, maybe *Cate* will."

"Alf ain't gonna do nothing to muck things up for us." Alex shook his head. "I seen him at the restaurant where she works. She was my waitress when I stopped in for lunch, one day."

"Oh, yeah?" Crispen wrinkled his brows as he fanned through the surveillance photos again. "How was that?"

"I sold him a song and dance, let him think we just happened into the place by chance. Told him we had other business in the neighborhood. He bought it hook, line, and sinker. The old putz should've been out of the game years ago."

"That's Caprianno's problem." Crispen reached across his desk, flicking his ash into a crystal tray. "Go on. What else happened?"

"She's got a nice voice. Smooth, like silk. Got a snap to it, though. She called this one joker out, while I was there, that was-"

"I don't care about her voice, you moron!" Crispen shouted. "What happened with Alf?"

Alex took a step back, swallowing down a lump of nervousness in response to the other man's flare of temper. "He just asked what I was doing there. At first, he thought we were there to keep an eye on him, or to try and talk to Caprianno on our own. He didn't have a clue we were there to check her out."

"Caprianno. Was he there? Did he see you? If you've crossed this, you idiot…" Jansen exploded, glaring violently back at his flunky.

"No, boss, no." Alex shook his head insistently. "Caprianno didn't see us there. He wasn't even there. Alf was there with Louis Tortoni. You know Louis. They were talking business. I could tell Alf didn't want Louis to know he knew us. He wouldn't even look at me while we talked."

"All right. All right, good." Jansen nodded, beginning to relax again. He sat quietly for another moment, his hand rubbing back and forth across the thin press of his lips as he considered his next step. At length, he looked from one man to the other and back again. "I want you boys to keep an eye on our attractive new friend. Don't make any waves. I don't want her or Caprianno on to us, not unless we need her."

"Sure, Mr. Jansen." Alex's nervous chortle was much less inspiring than the confidence he attempted to show. "Me and Bobby, we'll keep an eye on her."

"I don't want them wise to this, Alex!" He thumped an elbow on his desk, thrusting the point of an index finger at him. "I don't want this hand played until I say so. Now, get out of here."

"All right boss." Alex scrambled toward the door with a nod.

"Bobby!" Crispen called, just as the other man had reached the door.

"Yeah, Mr. Jansen." Bobby turned, closing the door behind him for a second, to ensure that their conversation was kept private. "You want something else?"

"Yeah." Crispen nodded flinging his hand in the direction of the waiting room. "Keep an eye on that idiot. Make sure he doesn't screw anything up."

"You got it, boss." He nodded, then turned to follow the other man out.

Crispen let his spine slump against the back of his desk chair again, quietly brooding, sucking the last bits of life from the white cigarette nub in his mouth. Bobby was quiet, but he sent him out with Alex for a reason. He would be able to keep that dolt in line.

He didn't count on saying a word about any of his plans to Caprianno unless and until the timing was right for *him*. Still, he stubbed out the butt in the crystal tray, grinning broadly as he reached for the phone on the corner of his desk. He didn't want Alf getting too comfortable.

"Alf." The hydraulic function of his chair expelled a wheeze of air in response to the readjustment of his weight. "How are things going, buddy?"

Alf sighed, rolling his eyes. Of all the times for him to call, Nick wasn't sitting five feet from him. "I can't talk, Nadine. Nick and I are in the middle of something. I'll call you back."

Crispen chuckled at the obvious cover Alf was attempting to spin in front of his boss. "Just, do me a favor, will you? When they make it public knowledge, tell Nicky boy I said… congratulations."

"What?" Feeling a fine mist dewing across his forehead, Alf drove his brows down hard, etching deeply creased lines into his expression. "Hello? Nadine, you there?"

Nick looked up from the papers on his desk, his own eyebrows tilting inward. "Alf? Something wrong?"

"Nah, Nick." He shook his head. "Nothing I can't handle. Nadine. She's, ah… she's still mad at me for being late last night."

Chapter Thirteen

Nick's foot bounced lightly on the scuffed oak floorboards as he continued to wait for Cate to reappear from her bedroom. She hadn't been quite ready, leaving him alone in the small main room of her apartment. Leaning back, he drew in the pleasant scent of cinnamon coffee and warm vanilla that he'd come to associate with her place. Down in the street below, the violinist who lived in her building played softly, as she said he did every night.

Generally, Nick and Cate met at his loft or went out. Though they'd made it a priority to continue being together at some point every day, he had only been to her apartment a couple of times. Being there allowed him to better understand the differences she'd been quick to point out between them. Still, he was confident he'd been successful in convincing her that none of that mattered. From the soft cushion where he sat, Nick let his eyes wander around the room.

Her couch was made for comfort. All of her furniture was plushy and soft. In contrast, his furniture was mainly just for a sleek appearance and was intentionally less relaxed, so that he could get work done without getting too tired. He knew he would have to cut back on his workaholic tendencies, once they were living together. Contemplating her redesign of his style, he could see the hazard such furniture as she preferred posed to him. Its comfort would force him to relax and nod off more easily.

Not just her living room, but the whole apartment was cozy and inviting, with candles and soft textures all around. It was tidy, small without feeling cramped. There was a large window next to the off-white loveseat where sheer ivory drapes swagged to reveal flower boxes with gold mums. The fuzzy throw blanket they'd cuddled under a few nights before was draped over one arm of the divan. With thoughtful use of accent colors and framed photos scattered about, her apartment was cheerful without being bright. It suited her, and he'd concluded that he would adapt to her tastes well.

Her footsteps kept a quick pace as she finally reappeared from the bedroom. She flicked a quick glance over to his smile and turned from him, toward a mirror on the wall. "I've felt like I was going to be sick every time I've thought about this today. Something like dropping a bomb and waiting for the fallout."

"Come on, Cate. We've pushed this off for two weeks. I don't think it's going to be all that bad. They already know we're together."

"They certainly do." She rolled her eyes as she thought of the chiding comments she'd received from her brother and grandmother in the past couple of weeks.

He rose from his seat and moved to step behind her. Slipping his hands onto the tops of her hips, he nuzzled the soft curve of her neck as she made a poor attempt at getting her small golden earring back onto the post. Cupping the side of his face with the fingers of her right hand, she laughed against the tickle of his lips on her skin.

"We just have to approach this like a business meeting." As he tried to convince her, he continued to trace along her neck and shoulder with his hot breath. "We don't give anything away until we're ready to. Just keep your poker face on and stick close to me."

"Nicky, you cannot approach every situation in life like a business meeting."

She turned in his arms, laughing softly as she accepted a light kiss from him. As she'd been too distracted to notice before, she finally let herself glance him over for the first time. He'd taken her suggestion of losing his tie and also worn a pair of jeans instead of a suit. It was the first time she'd seen him in them. Even paired with his crisp dress shirt, the style had given his appearance a sexy, more casual appeal. She tugged at his collar, unbuttoning the top button, and skimmed her fingertips against his skin.

"This is family, Nicky." She shook her head, smiling at the deep breath he took in response to her touch. "I don't know about the Capriannos, but he MacCarthaighs can smell fear. They're like bees."

"So, who's afraid? A little uncomfortable, maybe."

He pecked her lips again, his chest shaking lightly against hers. Apparently, *she* could sense fear, or at least the anxiety that indeed had the nerves under his skin tingling. Not many people could get a bead on him so well as she managed to. There were all sorts of things they were discovering about one another.

"Well, anyway, Frankie's gonna be there if things get too wild."

"Nicky!" She stepped back, swiping a hand at one of his shoulders for the joke. "You are terrible!"

"Yeah." He drew her back to him, the deep grin still etched on his face. "You love me anyway, though, right?"

"As if I had a choice. It appears that I can't help myself, even though my brother keeps telling me that I should know better."

"Oh, yeah?" The crease at the side of his mouth pulled in harder after she pressed a long, steamy kiss to his lips. With her confirmation, the prickling tingles of anxiety under his skin dissipated. "Just keep not being able to help yourself."

#

"Shayne looks about fit to be tied." Cate muttered, leaning toward Nick.

"He's not the only one." He lightly cleared his throat.

Looking back and forth between the disconcerted glances of his mother and her grandmother made them both feel slightly on edge. Thank goodness for the music that was piped in through the speakers, or the room would be filled with an unbearable silence. Neither family had ever endured such a quiet dinner.

"We'd just as well get it out of the way." Angling his frame toward her, Nick grinned, keeping his voice low. "It's not like waiting is going to change anything. It's this, or they find out after the fact. They know something's up, or we wouldn't have asked them all to be here together."

"I guess now is as good as any time. I still feel a little like there's fireworks going off in my gut." She snickered softly when he gave her hand a light squeeze. "Okay. Go ahead."

"If I could just get everyone's attention, for a minute." He stood, lifting his wine glass in one hand as he looked around the table. "First, I want to thank the MacCarthaighs for letting us join them here for dinner tonight. It means a lot to Cate and me to get to set aside this time together, with both families at one table. Family is really important us. We've been seeing each other for a little while, now, and-"

"A very little while." Shayne muttered, lifting a frothy pint to his lips.

"In any case," he looked down with a deep grin, meeting her eyes, and taking her hand in his, "Cate and I have decided to get married."

Any murmurs had been cut short. The uncomfortable silence that had presided over the evening resumed, though they both knew it wouldn't last long. Cate observed the red glow that tinged Shayne's face, Maureen obviously working at holding her tongue. There were also lots animated whispers shared between Nicky's mother and father. She shifted a glance to Frankie, who adjusted his tie, but sent her an encouraging wink.

"We realize," Nicky started in again when the muffled voices began growing louder, "that this might seem quick to everyone, but Cate and I are sure this is what we want to do. I have another meeting in New York coming up, so we'll spend a few days there, but we'll postpone any further honeymoon until summer."

Cate smiled. "Nicky has a few deals to complete in May. He thought we could spend some time in Italy, and then visit Ireland before we come back here."

"Out of the country just after tying up *business deals*." Shayne scoffed, shaking his head. "Now, I wonder why that doesn't sound too surprising. You're completely off your onion if you go through with this, Cate."

"Just what is that supposed to mean?" Nick's mother, Nicoletta, glared across the table.

"It means, I thought my sister had more brains than to get herself mixed up with a hood."

"Shayne!" Cate glared at her brother, her cheeks growing a shade near to the color of her deep ginger-auburn hair.

Nicoletta threw her arms up in the air, nearly shouting at Nick. "Questo è ridicolo!"

Cate leaned against him, keeping her voice low. "That one didn't sound good. How bad was it?"

A heavy sigh left his chest and he shook his head to her, drawing his thick brows down as he replied. "It's not ridiculous, Mama."

"This, Nicky? This is what you want to marry into? A family who thinks you're no more than a common criminal? *My* boy, a hood?" His mother began stringing long muttered sentences in Italian to her husband, only quieting when Sal silently lifted a calm hand to her. "Salvador, talk some sense to your son!"

"Just how soon are you planning on all this coming off, Nick? That New York trip is coming up pretty fast." Sal folded his arms, discontent tightening his face.

"That's right. Cate and I want it to just be family and close friends, and we don't see a point in putting it off, so we're setting it for next weekend. Anyone who can't find a way to make peace with it is more than welcome to abstain from attending." He stood firm, bracing himself for the immediate backlash that came, voices erupting into a loud jumble of incoherent noise.

"Next weekend!" Maureen stood, looking back and forth between them. "Never mind letting *any* of us get used to the idea, what will people think, rushing things this way? They'll say you *had* to get married, and that's why the hurry."

"I agree with Mrs. MacCarthaigh!" Nicoletta nodded. "Without such a rush, you may both come to your senses about this. There's no cause to start people to talking."

"I'd think the Caprianno family would be used to hearing people talk." Shayne muttered loudly to his wife, earning him a sharp glance from Frankie's loyal eye.

"All right, one," Cate answered back calmly, but firmly, "that was completely uncalled for, Shayne. Two, Nicky and I don't care what people think. *You* know that well enough about me, Gran. And respectfully, Mrs. Caprianno, Nicky and I are thinking perfectly clearly, right now."

Nick slanted his eyes down at his sister, who sat beaming brightly up at him. "Yeah, so what's wrong with you?"

Marie shrugged. "Nothing. I'm just glad it's not me setting everyone up in arms, for a change. Nice to just be an observer, for once."

"I'd like to say something." Sylvia quietly stood. Her eyes were glossed with emotion, though her voice remained strong. "I can't speak for Nick, of course, nor would I try to. I do know my daughter, though. She wouldn't jump without consideration. I trust her judgement. So, Nick, Cate, for what it's worth, you have *my* blessing and my sincere wishes for your lifelong happiness together."

"Thank you, Mom." Cate's voice thickened with gratitude.

The table grew quiet again as all who sat around it worked through the brief speech Sylvia had given. It was clear that Nick and Cate were unbending with their decision, that they would go on with, or without the blessings of either family.

Her father rose halfway from his chair, nodding to them, then resumed his seat position again. "You've got mine, too, Caty girl."

"Mama? Pop?" Nick folded his arms, staring expectantly at his parents.

Nicoletta rocked irritably in her seat. "How can you ask us to support you marrying into a family that thinks you're-"

"I'm not. I'll have to earn the MacCarthaigh's trust, just like Cate's willing to work for yours. Can you at least come to terms with that?"

"Ah, Nicky!" Nicoletta muttered something irritably under her breath, to which her son replied in the same tongue, and she looked back up at him with a huff, then wagged a finger at Shayne. "Fine! But my son is *not* a hood!"

"Pop?" Nick lifted a brow.

The older man gave a curmudgeon's nod. "You're a grown man, Nicky. You know your mind."

"Shayne? Gran?" Cate folded her arms, mirroring her fiancé. "He's right. We're doing this, either way."

"Then what difference does it make what we think?" Shayne fired back.

"Your view won't change my mind, but I'd like to know you're still on my side."

Her brother sat stewing for another few seconds, then shook his head. "I won't pretend that I like this, or even that I support the idea of it. But... I'll be here for *you*, whatever comes."

She nodded at the bitter, backward agreement. "Gran?"

"I still say it's a mistake to rush into it," Maureen sighed, "but I'll be there, just the same."

Sitting back down, Nick winced as Cate squeezed his hand so tightly that her engagement ring cut into his fingers a little. "You aren't having second thoughts, after all that, are you?"

"No, but I'm glad it's done, just the same." She smiled, leaning to accept the quick kiss he offered her. Hearing the words 'knuckle duster' and 'awfully quick' muttered from the other end of the table, she groaned. "Did I tell you?"

"I don't care. I'm just glad you'll finally be wearing it around. It's a ring that's meant to be seen."

"It's a ring that's meant to get me mugged." She laughed, smoothing a hand down the side of his face. "Oh, Nicky, I do love you."

"I love you, too. In fact, I don't want any mistake in the fact that you're off the market." His smile tugged playfully upward. "That's why the rock."

She pressed her lips lightly to his. "Mission accomplished.

Chapter Fourteen

In the end, Cate and Nick opted for a civil ceremony and then a light reception of close family and a few friends at the Caprianno's family estate. Ready to leave for their honeymoon, Cate had changed and was waiting for Nick in the foyer. Alf had snagged Nick's sleeve just as he was on his way up the stairs, so Nick told her he'd meet her after he changed.

Alf huffed a heavy groaning breath, flipping through the file he'd laid out on the dresser top. "Come on, huh, Casanova? Finish going over this with me and you can get going on your honeymoon."

"I don't want to mess with any of that garbage. I promised Cate, no business today. I already have that meeting to go to tomorrow morning." Nick grouched, zipping his jeans and started on his shirt buttons, making sure to skip the button at the top of the placket, knowing it was her preference. "Anyway, this isn't our real honeymoon. It's just a quick few days, and we'll be back Wednesday night. She's calling it our 'minimoon'."

"Yeah, yeah, whatever." He rotated the folder to face his boss, shoving it to the corner of the dresser while Nick checked his appearance in the full-length mirror. "Just take a quick look before you go. I think we're getting closer to finding some wiggle room with these boys."

Nick slicked his fingers through his hair a couple of times. "What boys?"

"Jansen and his guys. They've come a long way with negotiations. If you want to just sign it, and be done, I'll work out any last kinks while you're gone, so you don't have to deal with it anymore."

"Sign a deal that's still in negotiations? Who are you talking to, Alf? Come on. My father would knock me into next week if I did that, and we both know it."

Nick sighed, glancing off to the side at the papers while he loaded his wallet into the back pocket of his jeans, then reached for his shoulder holster. His eyes moved over the words on the document as he checked his gun and then put it on.

"I wish I knew what had you so sold on this stupid thing. I just don't see it. It's a lot more headache than it is a use to us."

"I told you. I knew his old man. I wanna help the kid out." Alf shrugged, continuing to conceal the full truth. "I told him I'd do what I could to help him bring his business to a legitimate footing, like Sal did for you."

Nick snatched the folder up between his fingers and drew his brows in as he flicked through the contract proposal, focusing on one section in particular. He scanned over the fine print, his lips moving softly as he read quietly under his breath. A crooked grin came to his mouth and then he burst out with a deep chuckle, tossing the folder back down with a smack of finality.

"This is a joke, right? I mean, have you even looked at it? You cook this up as a parting gag, or what?" He shook his head again and slipped his black leather jacket on to conceal the firearm. "You gone soft in your old age? This guy's playing you, Alf. You can tell him I said no dice."

Alf adjusted the discomfort from his shoulders and shrugged. "Ah, come on, Nick. That offer's no small thing for an operation his size. He's willing to cut you in-"

"He's willing to cut me in?" He laughed. "You and Pop always said business is business. You're talking pretty big favors for this guy. What? Does he have some dirt on you, or something?"

"What?" Alf felt his palms beginning to perspire in response to the unknown sincerity of Nick's joke. "Listen, I know the return is small beans compared to what we usually deal in, but you've done deals for less."

"All right. Then, maybe I just don't like these boys." He shook his head as he started for the door. "You think Jansen's such a great guy, he wants to be legit, you go ahead and read that fine print again."

"What print, where?"

"The liabilities clause." Nick flicked a finger at the page. "That's in legalese, of course, but the bottom line is, if anything crooked goes on to do with this partnership, we could be left holding the bag, while Jansen comes off smelling like a rose. It's a small section, but it's there. I'm surprised it got past you."

"Where did you see that?" Alf looked over the document again, pretending it was news to him. He'd more or less just wanted Nick to sign and then just hoped he'd never get bitten by the clause.

"I hope you're not starting to slip, you old badger." He grinned, teasing his friend. "You know, you gotta wonder why such an *upstanding* businessman, like Crispen Jansen, would see a need for that kind of disclaimer, and why he'd try to bury it in all that jargon."

"If that's all it is, we'll get him to work on the jargon."

"Nah. I know you want to help the guy, but this isn't a good fit. Just kill it. I'm sick of wasting my time with this guy. We got too many other irons in the fire to fool with it any longer."

"But, Nick," he followed after him down the stairs to the foyer where Cate was waiting, chatting with their parents, "this still has a chance of being a good-"

"I said, kill it!" Nick snapped, turning back to him. "That's it. I'm done playing with this joker. I'm done with anyone, *anyone* trying to shove it down my throat! Just, cut him loose, already. You got it?"

"Yeah, Nick." He nodded, swallowing hard in response to the sharp lash of his words, a prickling sensation burning down the back of his neck as he thought of breaking the news to Crispen. "I got it. It's dead. Forget about it. Go on your trip and have a good time. We'll talk when you get back."

Nick's chest collapsed and he curled a hand over each of Alf's shoulders, looking him in the eye. "I'm sorry I lost it on you. I know you look out for me. You always have. Always looking for a new deal. I just don't think this is it. We good?"

"Yeah, sure, kid. We're good." His glance cut away from the intense look Nick held on him. "We're good, kid. Now, get out of here. That spicy-tempered bride of yours already don't like me. She's really gonna have it in for me, if you don't get going."

"Alf..." Nick hesitated. Something about him not fully meeting his eyes struck him the wrong way, almost as if there was something in them that he didn't want Nick to see. "Yeah, okay. We'll talk when I get back."

Cate took his arm when he reached the bottom step. "Finally. What took you so long? I thought you said no business today."

"I know. I'm sorry."

The smile she angled up at him faded a little when she noticed the distracted way he glanced over his shoulder, at the way the features of his handsome face were drawn into a pensive expression, almost apprehensive.

"Nicky? Is everything okay?"

"Is everything okay?"

He hoped everything was okay. He forced the nagging sensation down, not wanting to put a damper on the start of their time together, and he bowed his head to kiss her. There would be time to dig into his concerns later.

Right now, he more than welcomed the distraction she offered.

"What could possibly be wrong when I'm with my beautiful wife?"

Cate stopped at the car, too preoccupied by the discomfort he was clearly fighting to pay much attention to their send-off. She looked directly into his eyes to study them. "Nicky, if there's something wrong-"

"Nah. It's nothing. Just some business headaches. Nothing that can't wait." He smiled deeper and pressed another kiss to her lips as their parents threw birdseed at them. "I really promise, this time. No more business today."

Her eyes flicked back to where Alf stood grim-faced at the door, but she nodded in response to him. "If you're sure."

Tony lit a cigarette, lifting his eyes to the darkening sky above them, nodding to the parents as they all went past him into the house. "You going home?"

Alf smoothed the sides of his hair down with the palms of his hands, doing his utmost to calm the racing nerves inside of him. "I got a business call to make for Nick, then I'll head out."

"Can you believe that kid?" Tony shook his head. "He ain't gone nowhere without one of us since I can remember. Now, he's going off for almost a week in New York with no one to look out for him. Kid thinks he's invincible, now."

"Nick can take care of himself." At least, Alf hoped he could. Watching the car leave the long drive, he turned, going back into the house. Tony was right. He should've taken someone along, to be on the safe side. "I'll see you around."

His feet were slow, the leather soles of his shoes making only the softest scuffling noise against the marble floor of the hallway. He glanced from side to side, then slipped into the office, closing the heavy door behind him. Shaking his head, he moved to the desk, dropped down into the leather chair, and lifted the receiver into his hand. Another dose of prickling heat tingled down the back of his neck and sent the flash of a burning sensation over his ears.

"Alfonse Giuseppe for Crispen Jansen. Yeah, I'll wait. Do I got a choice, honey?" The slumped position he held in his seat quickly straightened and he twiddled his fingers anxiously over his tie. "Crispen, how's things?"

"Forget the niceties, Alf." Crispen held a lighter up to the cigarette between his lips and sucked in a long draw. "Did he come across, or not?"

"I talked to him before they left," he paused there, not quite able to press on without a deeper breath, "but Nick says it's still a no-go."

"You said you could make this happen!" Crispen rose to his feet, his voice loudly echoing into the lobby of his little office. "You didn't try hard enough! He should've been distracted today."

"I warned you that Nick's radar is never down. He's a smart guy. He's a chip off his old man's-"

"I'll just bet he's a carbon copy of his old man!" Crispen railed. "What problem does the golden boy have with the deal, now? Huh? Why won't he just sign it, instead of dragging it on? It's chump change to the Capriannos."

"Are you for real? Two million dollars ain't chump change to nobody. Nick's got a lot of cash because he's discriminating on how it gets invested and how it gets spent." He quieted for a second, almost hearing the anger in the silence on the other end of the line. "The fact is… Nick says he's ready to kill the deal, altogether."

Crispen's face began to glow a shade of molten burgundy. "Kill it?"

"Yeah." He tugged at the silk tie he'd worn to the wedding that now felt as if it was choking him. "Yeah, he saw that disclaimer section and-"

"Well, why'd you let him look at it that close?" He shouted. "I thought you said you could handle this! You wanted to me to give you the time and the space to work on him, your way. I'm starting to get the feeling you're not exactly putting in the effort you should be. But I promise you, my friend, one way or another, I will have my deal!"

"Relax. I'll think of something." Alf stretched his tie looser, letting it hang down the front of his shirt.

"Relax?" Crispen snarled. "If you're trying to cross me on this, you know what the consequences-"

"I know we have an understanding. I'm not welching on it. I just need you to give me time to work on him about it. Nick trusts me, all right?"

"So you keep saying. I'll give you until after Thanksgiving. After that, I make no promises, other than to swear to you that I *will* have that deal signed, with or without you. Now, do you think you can manage to make that work?"

"Yeah. Yeah, sure. I can make it work." Alf's forehead became creased into a strong frown when he heard a loud crash on the other end and then silence. "Crispen? Crispen?"

Alf pulled the disconnected receiver from his ear, drawing his fist against the nervous dew that lined his top lip. Filled with unease, he reached across the desk to hang up the phone. He slammed a fist down on the mahogany top in front of him and forced out a few breaths. Nick didn't know how right he was about that scuzball. They never should've gotten mixed up with the deal, in the first place. It was Alf's fault that they were.

He had to make it come through all right, somehow. He had to find a way to protect Nick, if he could, and still save his own neck. Men like Crispen Jansen were unforgiving, and their memories stretched miles long. He ran his fingers through his thick, silvering hair and blew out another quaking breath.

If Alf didn't do what Jansen demanded of him, it would cost him dearly. However, if he managed to sell Nick on the idea, and then Crispen or his cronies got into trouble, Nick could be in some very hot water. He'd just have to get him to sign, and then do whatever he could to try and protect him in the contract. What else was there to be done? Whatever it took, he had to get this deal made.

Chapter Fifteen

Nick rolled over in bed, his fingers crawling across the sheet for her. He pushed himself up onto his elbows and glanced to her side when he discovered the void. Rolling onto his back, he looked over at the window and began to sit up, grinning at the sight before him.

From where she sat, with her legs tucked into the corner of a large windowsill, her dark cherry hair was swept over one shoulder and his dress shirt, much too large for her, draped long and loose over her petite silhouette. The autumn morning light glowed against her, softening the already tender expression she aimed over her shoulder at him when she heard the rustle of covers.

Her feet slipped down to the floor of the hotel suite and moved, one in front of the other, toward him. He enjoyed the view, appreciating every seductive sway of her figure as she crossed the room. How had he gotten so lucky?

"Weren't you cold over there?" He grinned, looking up to where she now stood beside him, and he snatched her fingers in his.

"I couldn't sleep any longer." She shrugged, coyly glancing away from him with a flirtatious smile of her own. "Anyway, I figured you'd be willing to help me take the chill off when you woke up, but it's getting so late, now, with the time difference and everything- Nicky!"

A long, deep chuckle shook his chest when he'd bolted up and swiftly tugged her forward. Throwing his arms around her waist, he rolled her onto the place next to him. Leaning over her, the deepest of mischievous grins etched firmly onto his mouth, and he dipped his head slowly to kiss her. He only edged back slightly to look at her when she moved her fingertips to trace the side of his face.

"Didn't I tell you?" He laughed softly again, angling for another kiss. "I knew we were right together."

"Ah, yes. That famous gut instinct of yours." She snickered, then jammed a finger into his side, laughing harder when he jolted. "Didn't see that one coming, though, did you?"

"Hmm-mm." He shook his head, tucking her closer against him and went to work caressing her neck with a steady supply of kisses. "This any better?"

"I'd like to say yes, but you slept so late, you're going to miss your meeting, if we don't go shower and dress." She giggled, framing his face with both of her hands when he shifted to look at her again.

He threw his head back with a groan, squinting his eyes shut, and he flopped onto his back next to her. "Tell me again why I didn't set the meeting for later in the day?"

Giggling lightly, she moved to nestle her head against his chest as she looked up at him. "You said, eight o'clock, Chicago time, was late enough, because you never sleep past six-thirty. I guess you weren't counting on being married relaxing you so much."

"Yeah." He nodded, lifting his head a little to look back at her. "Or making me so tired."

"Nick!" She sat up, swiping at his shoulder.

"Ah, ah. Where are you going?" He chuckled loudly, catching her wrist to tug her back when she'd feigned annoyance and started to scoot away. "I'm just kidding, baby."

"Hmm." She scrunched her mouth to one side and tugged free of him, pecking his grin with her lips before she left. "Well, I'm not kidding when I say you're going to be late."

"So, what if I am?" He thumped against his pillow sulkily. "It doesn't matter. I'll phone and tell them I'm held up in traffic, or something. I'll just reset the time. It'll be fine. I know a guy in the office that can fix it for me."

"*You* know a guy? Really?" She snickered, aiming a mocking expression at him. "I would never have believed it."

"Yeah, yeah." He grinned, throwing a pillow at her.

"Well, whether you 'know a guy', or not, *I* know that you like to be punctual." She reached to the floor, grabbing the pillow, and threw it back at him. "I'm not coming back to bed, so you might as well get up."

"I'm sorry you're going to have to wait around for me to do this." He sat up, watching her disappear into the bathroom. "I'll try to wrap things up as quickly as I can. It's just going over some final documents and then signing a few contracts at the lawyer's office. I like to finalize deals in person."

"You said. I'm not angry, Nicky." Her voice garbled from brushing her teeth. "If I get too bored, I'll just wander around the city a little and meet you back at the-"

"No. Aside from you not knowing where you are, I don't want you wandering around alone. It's New York City, not the Saint Adeline farmer's market. What if something happened to you?"

"I've managed to keep myself alive and well all these years. I think I can handle one morning alone in Manhattan. I'll cross with the lights, and everything." She peeked back around the door frame, lifting her brows to the disagreeable frown rumpling his handsome face. "Fine. You win, but only because I don't want to argue."

"Thank you. It would be an awfully lousy waste of a morning like this." Relieved, he yawned, walking toward the bathroom, leaning against the wall as he watched her rinsing her mouth. "I promise, I'll make it up to you."

"You'll have plenty of time. I know we keep calling it a minimoon, but it's four days in a whole other city. We took a private plane to get here. I don't think I'll ever get used to that, by the way. This is a five-star hotel suite, and a vacation by anyone's standards but yours." She returned his smile, lifting a hand towel to gently blot against her lips. "I'll live, so long as I have you to myself, at least a little, when we get home."

"That's definitely the plan." He slipped his arms around her from behind, grinning over her shoulder into the mirror as he flicked his brows suggestively at her, causing her to her laugh. "Maybe when we get back you can get to work on giving the loft your touch, cozy it up."

He moved past her to dig his toothbrush from his brown leather toiletry bag. Loading the brush with toothpaste, he shoved it into his mouth and cut a glance over at the shower. His eyes made a longing, sweeping study of her, of those luscious legs and the too-big shirt. The sparkle of her wedding set glistened as she gripped the glass shower wall with her left hand and stretched to reach her right hand into the water.

They were going to have to play things by ear when they returned. He didn't want her driving back and forth to Saint Adeline for work every day, especially at night and when the weather turned bad. Much as she liked the loft, he knew she wasn't terribly thrilled at the prospect of living right above his office. It was already difficult enough to peel him away from work, as it was. Neither of them appeared to be in a rush to search for a family home of their own, though.

She turned from the shower, letting her hand fall from under the water with a frustrated sigh. "We must be on the smallest water heater any hotel ever installed. After all this time, it's still just barely warm."

"The suite has its own heater. Maybe I should call the desk." He rinsed his mouth and moved to feel it for himself. "It's getting there."

"Mmm. Kind of a waste of water to let it just run down the drain, like that." She straightened to look at him when he reached for a thick, white hotel towel. She shook her head, tapping the point of her index finger against her chest. "Wait just a second. I got up first, I turned on the shower, and *I* am going first. If anyone's going to hog whatever heat we finally get, it's going to be me."

"We'll both go first." He laughed, giving her an impish grin when she pursed her lips and arched a brow. "I'm only thinking of saving time and hot water. You did point out that we're running behind. It's a double bonus."

"Who do you think you're fooling? I feel pretty confident in saying that your plan would *not* be a time-saver, of any sort."

She rolled her eyes, not quite able to suppress the upward lift at the corners of her mouth when he went to work pressing warm kisses to the side of her neck again. They were never going to make it out of the room, let alone to his meeting. Much as she enjoyed the distraction he offered, her laughter tapered off when she happened to glance back into the bedroom.

"Nicky," she attempted to shift back from him a bit, "I want to ask you something."

"Now?" His deep laugh was muffled against her skin. "The water's finally getting hot. Who knows how long it'll last."

"Now." She nodded, feeling herself tense up a little. "Nicky, why did you bring that along?"

"Bring what?" He angled back, letting his eyes follow to where she was gazing at the gun and shoulder holster that were slung over the back of a chair. He laughed softly again. "Well, you wouldn't let me bring Frankie. It was a trade-off."

"Bring Frankie? Here? I thought you were kidding! That would've been ridiculous." She drew her arms up to fold between them. "Nick, stop."

"What?" His shoulder slumped against the tile edging of the shower, though he didn't fully let her go.

"When we left yesterday, something was bothering you. Something happened between you and Alf. Before you deny it, remember, I appreciate honesty every bit as much as you do. So, was whatever happened the reason why you felt the need to bring it along? Is that why you really won't let me wander around on my own during your meeting?"

"Cate, come on." His arms slackened around her when he felt her muscles go rigid, and he shook his head. "I know you and Alf got off to a rocky start, and he may be a little rougher around the edges than you'd like, but that doesn't necessarily make him a bad guy."

She flipped her brows when he said that. "I don't know that I'd necessarily set him in with the *good guys*, either."

Sighing, he let his hands fall from around her, drawing one hand to rub his eyes. "I told you, you can… trust him."

"I can… trust him? Do you?" At his hesitation, she dipped her brows inward and cocked her head to one side. "Do you really, Nicky? Because, I think something deep down is nagging you, too, a doubt when it comes to him."

"Like what?" He gave a disgruntled shrug. "What do you think he's hiding?"

"Something. I don't know. I saw your face when you came down the stairs with him yesterday. I could tell that something wasn't right. You think you're the only one who gets feelings in your gut when something's off?"

"I think, maybe we should be married longer than eighteen hours before you start telling me what *I* feel." He stepped to the side, reaching to shut the shower water off.

"Listen. You didn't want any of the guys to come along on this trip. Fine. I wasn't happy about it, but I let you have your way."

"You *let* me have my way?" She scowled, moving back into the bedroom. "Nice, Nick. Very nice. That doesn't sound controlling, at all."

"It's not controlling. I've lived a different life than you have. Maybe I do look at things differently because of the way things were when I was growing up. This is what I know, though. I know what works. I don't change you, and you don't try and change me. We were both very much in agreement on that."

"I didn't say anything about changing you, Nick. All I wanted to know was why you felt it necessary to bring a gun along on our honeymoon! Why are you so defensive about this?"

"You knew, for better or worse, I wanted the things and the people I cared about to be protected. You knew I took that seriously. If the guys aren't here, and my gun gives me the control I need, then that's the way it is."

"Control again." She nodded her head.

"Fine. Yes. But in this case, it doesn't mean that there's anything wrong." He flattened a hand over his chest. "It's for my own peace of mind. I made the decision to bring it, long before Alf and I talked yesterday, so we can drop that."

"I guess you're saying I need to butt out."

With a low huff of breath, his chest dropped and he scrubbed his hands over his face. "So much for not spending the morning arguing."

She held her jaw tightly, giving an abrupt nod when he looked back at her. "*You* knew, for better or worse, that I had opinions, and questions, and needs of my own. I never asked you to change, Nick, but you have to know that's not going to change for me either."

"I don't expect it to." He shot back. "You wanted to know about the gun. I'm explaining about the gun. You asked about Alf, and I told you. That's it. That's all there is to it."

"You *are* asking me to change! Maybe not so much asking as telling me." She leaned forward, angrily jamming her finger against her chest. "I have never had a bodyguard, and as much as I like Frankie, I don't intend to change that now. I've never felt so scared that I needed to take a gun with me on a vacation!"

"I never said I was scared." He countered, walking to join her in the room, then. "I said, I need to have the control over it, if a situation ever does present itself. It's not like people plan for things like that to happen."

"Nick, you are so incredibly cynical about people. Ugh!" She shook her head. "You promised me that there was no need for me to feel insecure about safety."

"You have no reason to be insecure about safety, because it's already handled! The precautions I take are why there's nothing to worry about." His tone was growing louder, along with hers. "You call it being cynical, if you want to, Cate. I call it being prepared."

"We are not going to agree on this." She folded her arms, looking out the window at the way the leafless branches of the trees below swayed in the chilled breeze.

"You act like I'm going to take random pot shots at people." When she still wouldn't look at him, a long breath eased slowly from his chest and he walked to her. Reaching forward, he rubbed his hands up and down her arms. "I'll probably never in my life use that gun anywhere but the firing range, but I feel better knowing that I have it. Can you understand that?"

"I understand your logic, Nick. I think I even understand why you feel that way. I also expect you to try and understand why I don't. I'm not going to like it, or even agree with it."

"I didn't say you had to like it."

"But I have no choice in it. You also did basically say that I had to like Alf. I won't promise to do that, either. I do have my own gut instincts to follow… and I don't trust him." She moved farther from his reach, then, starting back for the bathroom. "I'll shower alone, thanks."

He cut a glance to the side. "Cate-"

"You should probably make that call to the lawyer. I'm sure it'll be fine if you're late. No doubt, most people realize that you're used to getting your way."

He pivoted, watching the door close between them, hearing the angry click of the lock on the other side. Dropping onto the edge of the bed, he let himself fall back on the mattress. Hearing the water flick on, he gritted his teeth and shook his head. The morning had taken a sharp nosedive in comparison to the way it had started.

If he was being completely honest, with even himself, she wasn't wrong to think that there was something off-kilter with Alf. But Alf had been a trusted part of the family since before Nick was born. It was crazy to think there could be anything seriously wrong. So far as security went, they were just going to have to agree to disagree. He'd made her a promise, and he intended to keep it.

#

Nick smiled, firmly shaking the hands of his new partners as the group left the conference room. All involved were pleased with the deal they'd come to, the way Nick liked things to be with all new projects, if possible. As he let his hands slip from the last parting shake, he shifted a glance around at the empty chairs in the outer waiting area.

"Excuse me." He leaned over the receptionist's marble partition. "My wife. Where'd she go?"

"Oh, Mr. Caprianno, of course." The woman shuffled through a thick stack of notes and offered a slip of paper to him. "She left this for you about forty minutes ago."

He scanned over Cate's scrawled writing and his jaw rippled lightly. He lifted his eyes back up at the receptionist and he gave her a soft nod. "Thank you."

"Sure. You know where it is?" She gestured as she gave directions. "Just go out through the downstairs lobby, hang a right, down two blocks, and make another right. You'll see it. It has big red awnings."

As he entered the dining room of a restaurant, Nick took a few calming breaths in an attempt to cool his temper. He was just about to ask the seating hostess about her when he spied Cate across the room. She was talking to the waiter, a few shopping bags in the seat next to her. He walked stiffly over to the table and lowered into the seat across from hers, his gaze holding firmly on her.

"I ordered for you when I got your message." She thanked the waiter and then looked back at him, lifting her glass to her lips. "Did everything go the way you were wanting?"

"The meeting did." He gnawed the edge of his lower lip, nodding to her. "Thought we agreed to go out together after I was finished."

"Well, after almost two hours, I was getting bored." She flicked a brow, piercing him with a determined stare. "Did you really expect me to just sit on my hands indefinitely? You can only reread so many outdated issues of *People* so many times."

He shrugged out of his overcoat, dropping it over the back of his chair. Angling his head sharply, he began with a low voice. "I expected that you'd follow through with what we agreed on."

"I am not a porcelain doll, Nick. I refuse to live under glass, prevented from living like a normal person. I want you to love me, not to be my bodyguard. It's unnecessary."

"Unnecessary." He nodded, folding his arms. "You've been a Caprianno all of twenty-four hours, so I guess you know-"

"I know who I am, Nick. I thought, when you asked me to marry you, that you knew, too. Apparently, we both need to go back to school. I went shopping in Manhattan, with literally thousands of other people, in broad daylight. Not one person cared in the least who I was or what I was doing there."

"Why can't you just…" He let his head fall back with a quiet growl in his throat. It was obvious that he wasn't making any headway. It would take time. Reaching across the table, he took her hands in his and drew them to his lips. "I promise you, I am not trying to make you a bird in a cage. I just want to keep you safe, like I promised I would."

"And I refuse to let you be so afraid for my safety that you keep us from having a life." The well-meaning, albeit tenacious look in his eye, the love and concern she saw there, caused her to soften. "You won't keep me safe by keeping me in your pocket."

"I'm not trying… to keep you in my pocket." He let out a long sigh. "I'll make you a deal. You stick close to me while we're in New York, and I'll agree to keep things the way they were before, when we get home."

"Freedom, other than late nights when Frankie drives me home? And I won't see any cars parked across the street from MacCarthaigh's all day? Because, I mean it, Nicky. I won't live that way. I won't."

"Like before, and under special circumstances only." He pressed a kiss to the palm of her hand, feeling his smile tugging stronger at the corners. "Will that work for you?"

"It seems to be the only compromise we're going to come to." She stretched to smooth a hand down the side of his face, smiling when he snatched it and pressed a kiss to her palm. "Now, can we get back on friendlier terms?"

"Yeah. I think friendlier would be good." He shook his head. "I love you, you know."

"I know." She nodded. "I love you, too."

Chapter Sixteen

At the table, Sal studied his son's face as Nick sat there, watching Cate puttering around the kitchen with Nicoletta and Frankie. It had been a good birthday weekend for Sal. It was a relief to him that Nick appeared less uptight than he'd been in years. No one could deny the reason for the deep richness that filled his smile whenever Cate was near. It did Sal's heart good to see his son so happy.

"I'm glad we were wrong about her, Nicky." His father spoke in a low voice, smiling broader when his son began to laugh at the light-hearted exchange between the two women. "She's a good girl. She makes you happy?"

"She keeps me on my toes." Nick nodded, keeping his eyes fixed on her. There were times he felt he couldn't be any more contented. "Yeah. Yeah, we're happy, Pop."

"Good. That's important." Sal reached across the table, patting Nick's arm a couple of times. A deeper laugh shook his chest when the two women bumped shoulders, chuckling together at some light-hearted prank they'd pulled on Frankie. "She's won over your mama. That's not an easy thing to do."

"No." Nick shook his head, knowing how true that statement was. Nicoletta was a fiercely protective woman when it came to her family. Once she'd accepted someone, however, they were in. "She and Marie went Christmas shopping together yesterday. I'm not sure which one complained more about Frankie tagging along."

"Ah, then she's won your sister's approval, as well." Sal shifted a curious glance at him, then. "Her family. How are things going, there? We never talked how things went over Thanksgiving.”

“Eh.” Nick adjusted his position in the wooden dining chair, rocking his coffee cup in easy circles on the tabletop. “Her grandma’s coming around… *slowly*. I think she still measures Cate’s waist every time she hugs her, to see if we really were pulling a fast one when we got married. Her mom and dad are all right, and her sister-in-law. Shayne, though… Well, Shayne’s like Mama. It’s going to take some work.”

“He still doesn’t trust you.” Sal nodded, understanding. “Well, your Mama and I were married for a long time before your grandfather accepted me, sometime after you were born. Children will help with that.”

“Easy, now.” Nick chuckled, looking over at him with a grin. “Don’t get any ideas about grandchildren, just yet, Pop.”

“No rush, Nicky. There’s plenty of time.” Sal lifted his mug to his lips, enjoying the rich taste of the Irish coffee Cate had made for him. “Everything… *good*, there, too, though?”

“Pop! Come on, will ya?” Nick cleared his throat, feeling another laugh sneaking up on him. At the lift of his father’s brows, he did laugh, but nodded. “Yeah. Everything’s as it should be in that department. That’s all I’m gonna say about that.”

“Ah, well, good.” He nodded firmly. “This early time together, it’s good that you’re close while you build your life. Makes you stronger as you get used to one another. Enjoying one another, not that it’s all sunshine and roses, trust me.”

“No, I know.”

“The rough patches, they force you to lean in and protect one another, rely on one another. They aren’t easy, but they make you stronger, as long as you’re both fair.

Don't forget that and try to avoid arguments to keep the peace. They help to clear the air."

"Believe me," Nick laughed, "we clear the air real good, just fine, at least a couple times a week. And don't worry about Cate. She can hold her own."

Sal chuckled lowly in his chest. "Like Mama."

"Yeah. Hey, Pop, I wanted to talk to you about something." He glanced off to the side at Cate, then back over to his father, his expression sobering some. He lowered his voice to a more confidential level. "Can we stay here for a while?"

"The mausoleum?" Sal grinned at the quick laugh that sprang from his son. "You think I don't know what you've always called the house? Oh, I know this place is big, but it gave us enough space that the family was safe, and there was plenty of room for Frankie and the guys out in the guest house. You'll understand, one day."

Nick's gaze swept over to where Cate was again. "I understand now, Pop."

"So, what's wrong?" He dunked the edge of his cookie into the coffee. "I thought you liked your apartment. Your wife doesn't like it?"

"No, we both like it, you know, for now. Especially since she's kind of warmed it up. Eventually we want a family home, but… I just don't like the idea of her driving back and forth to the restaurant while the weather's bad. It's been bothering me ever since we came back from New York. This place is closer to MacCarthaigh's."

"Ah, yes." Sal's forehead creased as he considered how treacherous the roads between the edge of Chicago and Saint Adeline could get in the winter. "I see. Well, Mama and I are usually in the city, now, and Marie shares that little place near the college with her friend. You'd have the place to yourselves. You're welcome to stay here whenever you like, Nick. You know that."

"Thanks, Pop." Squinting lightly at her, he drew his mouth more to one side. He watched her moving back and forth. "Now, I just have to find a way to convince her. I have a feeling we're gonna 'clear the air' when I bring it up."

"Ah, she really does have a temper, huh?" Sal smiled over at the fiery glint of sun on his daughter-in-law's dark copper hair.

Nick cleared his throat, lowering his voice again as he replied. "I wasn't kidding. She really could give Mama a run for her money."

At that, Cate turned, dropping a hand onto the top of one of her hips. "Why do I get the feeling that ill-behaved laugh was at my expense?"

She arched a demanding brow at him. Though Nick smiled innocently enough when she walked over to him, she waved one of the biscotti his mother had been teaching her to make at him.

"Nicholas Caprianno, you'd just as well come clean with me. You know I'll have my way, in the end."

"Yeah, I know." He stretched forward, snatching an arm around her as he pulled her onto his lap. He jerked for the biscotti, nipping a bite before she had a chance to pull it away. "Mmm. Good."

"Don't think you can distract me with that grin of yours, either." She dropped the breakfast cookie onto his plate. Leaning against his chest, she curled a hand over one of his shoulders and feigned a severe look at him. She drew her brows downward and her bright lips pursed into a tight pucker. "You know, I'll only let you tread so far on it, so you'd just as well-"

He tightened his hold on her, stopping her words with the firm press of his lips. His heart warmed within him when he felt her fingers relax their grip and move to the side of his face. He grinned the same smoldering grin at her when she drew back, fully pleased with himself for the weakened state he'd left her in. The rosy tint on her cheeks in response to the snickers of his family only broadened the curve of his lips.

"What was that you were saying?" He slid a fingertip down the curve of her neck. "Something about being immune to my charms?"

"Nicky." Blushing darker, she began to pull away, shifting her eyes around the room at the amused onlookers. Her footsteps quickly tapped away from him.

"Oh, hey, Sal." Frankie attempted to smother the smile at his own lips as he spoke, hoping to give them a little privacy to finish their discussion. "I got something I wanna run past you."

"I'll bring the biscotti into the living room, if you two are going to be in there for a while." Nicoletta picked up one of the plates.

After they left, Cate turned, allowing her back to rest against the cold porcelain of the apron-front sink, her arms folded tightly at her chest, settling her eyes firmly on him. "Well, you certainly managed to clear the room quickly. I assume that's what you were going for."

"What's the matter?" Nick adjusted his neck at the wave of a red flag. When she turned from him again, without answering, he lifted himself from the chair and crossed the room to where she stood. His arms slid around her from behind, feeling the tension of her frame, and he rested his chin on her shoulder. "What?"

"Honestly. Right in front of everyone, like that." She shook her head, still embarrassed by the deep display of affection.

"Oh, no! We better be careful. They might get the idea we like each other." He laughed, sweeping tender kisses along the side of her neck. "If that kiss was enough to bring this on, I just guess it's a really good thing everyone got held up so late from getting here Friday night. They might've realized what we were doing upstairs to kill time. You don't think anyone might've suspected that we were-"

"Nick!" She blushed darker, scowling heavily at him. "Stop it."

"What? This is silly, Cate. We're still newlyweds. So, they know we're happy. I'm happy. You're happy, aren't you?" He laughed, lightly nipping the lobe of her ear. "We don't want them to think there's anything wrong, do we?"

"I think there's little chance of that, the way you're carrying on."

"Carrying on?" He snickered, leaning to nuzzle the side of her neck.

"Nicky, stop." She shook her head with a sharp huff of breath. "By the way, I don't think we don't need to be quite so free with our *happiness* when we go to Gran's, tonight."

"Oh, yeah?"

She gave a curt nod, washing up the dishes in the sink. "The MacCarthaighs aren't quite so liberal with their displays of affection in front of others."

"What others?" He shrugged when she turned in the circle of his arms and glared up at him, the tight pout of her lips renewing and making him want to kiss them again. "It's just Mama and Pop."

"And Frankie. Sometimes even Marie, or Tony, or Louis." She lifted a finger to him, pointing out that fact quickly. "A whole audience."

"The guys aren't an audience, Cate." He dipped his head, hovering his ill-behaved smile just over her lips. "Anyway, you think Frankie hasn't seen us kiss before, or Marie?"

"Maybe, but it occurred much less intentionally before." She shook her head, fighting herself rather unsuccessfully to stay firm with the warmth of his chest pressed softly against hers. "I can see we're going to have to find some sort of middle-ground somewhere."

"That's usually the way these things end with our arguments, and then we make up. I'm all right with middle-ground. So, what about right now?" He teased her lips with his, nearly touching them, but not quite. "Is this permissible? No witnesses. You allowed to show me you like me, now?"

"Nicky, you are incorrigible." She sighed, slumping feebly in his arms. The sultry breath he ghosted against her lips made her stretch a little on her toes to meet his.

With their lips warmly tangled, her frame went fully slack in the support of his embrace. Her sudsy fingertips crawled up the front of his sweater, tightly gripping the soft charcoal-shaded cashmere. She did absolutely adore him, and she did find him to be much more irresistible to her than she had been prepared to be. Until Nick, she'd never considered that any man could so easily force her anger to mellow.

"Oh, gross, Nick!" Marie made a gagging noise as she strode into the room for a cup of coffee. "Can't you do that somewhere else? People do eat in here."

Growling lowly in his throat when Cate flung the high arch of her brow at him and side-stepped his reach, he gave a soft laugh. The triumph of being right beamed brightly on her face, making him want to toss her over one shoulder to take her somewhere he could more privately paint a darker flush onto her cheeks.

"All right. Point taken about the perpetual audience around here, but to be fair, she's just my sister. Everything I've done since we were kids grosses her out."

"Oh, he's right. It's true. He was absolutely revolting when we were growing up." Marie nodded, stepping next to Cate as she filled her mug with strong coffee from the pot. "When he was in high school, he and his friends used to belch the alphabet at me. Bet he didn't share that little gem with you."

"Oh, Nicky!" Cate laughed, shaking her head at him, scrunching her nose in disgust. "Ew!"

Snapping a piece of biscotti between his teeth, he continued to laugh, shrugging at them both. "Probably still could, if I put some effort into it."

"That's okay!" Pinching her eyes tightly shut, Marie held a hand up to him before he could test his theory. "I'll take your word for it. No demonstrations required. I'd like to keep my breakfast down."

"Seconded." Cate laughed. "I know all about gross, though. I have an older brother, too, remember."

"Shayne ever make you eat a bug when he was mad at you?" Marie lifted both of her brows, aiming an accusatory finger at her brother. "That jerk did it. A cricket, when I was nine."

He shrugged again. "It was just a little one. Don't be such a baby."

"No, Shayne never did that to me. Force-feeding bugs was more down to me." Cate nodded her head when her husband began to laugh, thoroughly amused by the ornery streak in her past. "I did make *him* eat one, once. Believe it, or not, I was the one with the temper."

"You *were* the one?" Nick chuckled when she scoffed at the insult, her mouth dropping open as she snapped a towel at him. He pulled her back to him, stealing a quick kiss from the pout of her lips. "And, there it is."

"Are you guys going to be heading back to the city soon?" Marie was halfway to the table when a thought occurred to her. "We could meet up for dinner."

"Nah." He shook his head. "We still gotta go to the MacCarthaighs' for Sunday dinner. Another night. We'll probably head home from there. I wanna grab some things."

"Grab some things?" Cate looked up at him, pinning a bewildered stare on him. "For what? Nicky, you aren't leaving again already, are you?"

"No." He shook his head, easing out a breath in preparation for his plan. "I wanted to talk to you about the loft, though."

"Nicky." His mother popped her head around the corner. "Alf is in the office. He says he needs to talk some business over with you. He brought some papers to sign."

"Yeah, sure. Tell him I'll be there in a minute, will ya?" He felt Cate slump in his arms, catching the annoyed manner in which her eyes flicked away from his. Giving a sigh, he pressed a last kiss to the side of her neck. "I won't be long, this time. I promise."

"Mmm." She nodded, stepping away from him. "Promises, promises."

Marie took a few steps toward her when he'd given her another reassurance before leaving the room. "Something up with Alf?"

"I wouldn't be surprised if it was." Cate folded her arms, her expression pulled tight. "He could be better to your brother. Has Nicky ever mentioned anything to you about not trusting him?"

"Ha! Nicky, say something against Alf?" Marie snorted a laugh and shook her head. "No way. He and Frankie know as much about the business and the family as Nicky and Pop do, a lot more than I ever will. I better go get my stuff packed up."

Hmm. Cate turned and reached for the biscotti Nick hadn't finished, taking a bite as she considered what Marie had said. She didn't question Frankie in the least. Alf, though... He might know as much of the family business as Nick did, but she wasn't so sure that was such a wise practice. She secretly wondered how much *more* about the business he might know than her husband did.

Nick signed a few papers after quickly scanning through them. Standard. Taking up another packet that had been sneaked into the mix, he slowly lifted his eyes from the words he'd been reading over. "What's this one? I thought we agreed to kill the Jansen thing before I went to New York."

"We did. When I told Jansen your concerns, he came back with something I think you'd be happier with, as a last shot. Just, hear me out, Nicky." Alf lowered into the chair across from his. "His father, Scotty, was an all right guy, good to your Pop."

"Well, we wouldn't be dealing with Scotty." Nick countered, cinching his arms tightly against his chest.

"I know, but he was a friend to us. I think, if we could find a way to help his son out, Crispen would be grateful. He might even return the favor, somehow, down the road. That's the way things worked in the old days, one hand washed the other, yeah?"

"My hands are already clean, Alf. I'd like to keep it that way. The buzz about this guy is… less than inspiring. You know what I'm saying?" Nick rocked back in his desk chair, pulling his brows tightly inward. "We don't owe him anything, and I certainly don't want his kind of favors in return."

"I think you're making a mistake." Frustrated by the younger man's dismissive stubbornness, he squared up his jaw when the look in Nick's eyes flared. "I just don't think it would be wise to sever the connection quite yet."

"Scotty Jansen had business with our family a long time ago. There were no loose ends when Pop ended things with him. It was a tidy break. Crispen's old man might not have been a bad guy, but I've seen and heard enough about the son to know I don't want any part of him. You've seen what Tony and Louis dug up. You've seen what he's tried to sneak in on the proposals he's had drawn up for us. Nah."

"But, Nick, if you'd just-"

"No!" He straightened in his chair again, reaching for the documents, ripping them in half. "There! I did it, myself. It's done, over. I don't want to talk about it again. It's dead! We gotta go over it again, or are we clear, this time?"

"Yeah, okay. We're clear." A queasy sensation filled Alf's gut as he heard the tone of Nick's words lash sharply back at him. Giving a long nod, he sighed, reaching into his pocket for the antacids and pulling out an empty wrapper. "I'll let Crispen know."

"Good. 'Cause, if you don't do it this time, Alf, I will."

Nick flicked the tattered papers into the trashcan and pulled another file over, easily signing the bottom of it without hesitation, the way Alf wished he'd signed the other. He stacked all of the papers into one pile, then, extending them out to Alf. Staring firmly back at his friend, tension stretched the skin along his jaw taut as both men held tightly to one end of the stack of documents.

"No more, Alf."

"Right, Nick." He nodded, taking the files from him when Nick's grip on them finally released. "No more."

Chapter Seventeen

Nick drove into Saint Adeline with Tony after finishing up some late afternoon meetings. He planned to catch Cate at MacCarthaigh's, figuring that he and Tony could tie up the last of their business for the day while they had dinner. That way, he'd at least see her before he went home. If he wasted enough time, he might even be able to wait until her shift was over and drive back to the loft together. The call he made to check in with her began to set his teeth on edge, though.

"Oh, Nicky, I'm sorry. It's going to be forever before I get there. The highway's like a parking lot. We haven't moved more than five inches in the last ten minutes."

"You all right?" He frowned, looking down at the hands on his watch face. "You want me to have Frankie come get you? I knew he should've come along with you tonight."

"Nicky, relax. It's just bad traffic. Even if Frankie was with me in this mess, he couldn't do anything about it, not unless he's learned how to fly since this morning." She rolled her eyes. "The roads are already getting slick, so I'll have to crawl once this clears up. You're lucky you're already out of this side of it. Shayne's going to be completely cheesed off by the time I finally get to MacCarthaigh's. Can you give him a heads up when you get there?"

"We're here, now. Had to park a ways off." Nick let the phone slide away from his mouth and he sighed as he and Tony approached the building. Through the window, he looked across to the bar where Shayne busily filled orders. "I'll tell him. Just, don't leave us alone here too long."

"I'll do my best." She rumpled her mouth at one corner, looking at the congestion of the road ahead. There must've been an accident somewhere further down. "The holiday season is really picking up. He'll be a little tight for help until I get there, but he'll have Jessica and that new kid we hired to cover."

"All right, see you soon." Excusing himself as he squeezed through a thick crowd of people, he went in. Slipping his cell into his inner coat pocket, he edged around the corner, just behind the bar. He gave a quick nod to his brother-in-law when a sharp look was cut his way. "Hey."

Shayne's jawline rippled lightly under his neatly trimmed beard, but he didn't stop what he was doing. "If you're looking for Cate, she isn't here. I'm too busy to entertain you until she does show up. As you can see, it's standing room only in here tonight, so if you're wanting to sit, you'll have to wait in the office."

"Nah. I'm fine."

Nick glanced at Tony, then scanned the restaurant. He'd never seen it so busy. Every booth, table, and stool was occupied. A dense line was queued out the door, as well. He stepped nearer to be heard over the din.

"I just got off the phone with her. She asked me to tell you she'll be here as soon as she can. She's stuck in traffic. An accident on the highway, or something. If I hadn't had an early meeting over here, first thing, I'd probably be stuck in it, too."

"She never used to be late." Shayne grumbled, flicking an accusatory glance in Nick's direction. "Of course, she only lived five minutes away."

"Yeah. I know." Nick nodded, perfectly well understanding what the heated side-eye had implied. "I guess the commute from the loft is a little farther in this weather than her old apartment was. I'm not too thrilled at the prospect of her making the drive, once it starts getting icy on a regular basis."

"Mm-hmm." Shayne allowed himself another quick side-glance. "Won't be long. First wave's supposed to hit tonight."

"Cate said it's already starting. I'm working on remedying the commute situation." Nick stepped back when Shayne reached in front of him for something. "I just gotta figure a way to convince her that it's for the best."

"Well, you seemed to be good at convincing Cate to do what you wanted, before." He sniped back. "Shouldn't be too hard again."

He slid a couple of bowls of potato and leek soup, along with thick slabs of soda bread onto a tray. He then quickly added two frothy, dark stouts before giving a shrill whistle to the one and only true server he appeared to have that evening. Nick watched as his brother-in-law continued to handle things as though he had four hands, instead of just the two, his shirtsleeves rolled to the elbows and a heavy dew over his red-blonde brow.

"You seem to be a little shorthanded tonight." He scanned the room again. "Cate said you might be."

"More than she knows. She's been forever getting here, and Jessica called in at the last minute. Her kid started puking just as she was walking out the door, so it's just down to me, Mom, and that new kid we hired, heaven help him. Lucky for me, he agreed to stay on after his afternoon shift ended. Bit like being set down in a shark tank to start on a day like this." He filled another tray, while simultaneously taking a drink order, and flagged his mother down. "Like I said, you can wait for Cate in the office. Don't have time to chat."

"Come on, Nick." Tony tucked the folders in his hand under his coat to keep them from being splattered by anything. "We can go over these until she gets here."

"Ah…" He spoke lowly to Tony. "Go put those on the desk in the office and come back here, will ya?"

Nick's eyes followed the quick steps of his mother-in-law, watching the chaos taking place about them. By the sound of it, Cate would be at least another half an hour or more getting there. He shrugged out of his coat and hung it on a hook behind the bar. Snatching an apron from a bin under the counter, he tied it around his waist and tossed another to Tony when he returned.

"What do you think you're doing?" Shayne gawked at him, giving a deep-chested chuckle. He doubted his brother-in-law had done a day's worth of menial tasks in the whole of his life.

"Pitching in. At least until Cate gets here." Nick unbuttoned the cuffs at his wrists and began to roll his own sleeves up. "If there's one thing I know, it's family. Like it, or not, that's what I am now. Just tell us what to do."

Shayne paused. Biting his tongue between his teeth, he let his eyes move over both men. He really wasn't in a position to turn down the offer of help, regardless of the source. After another second, he tossed them both a pad of paper.

"Right. Tony, if you'll handle those three tables over there, Nick can cover these main ones in the middle. There's a bucket under the counter, there, with spray and rags to wipe down between customers."

Noting the determined nod from his brother-in-law, Shayne leaned an elbow against the edge of the bar as he filled another pint, watching the two men set out to work. He slid the drink in front of the waiting patron and wrinkled his brow as he considered all the ways the night could still play out.

#

The crowd was thinned to a more normal capacity by the time Cate finally arrived at MacCarthaigh's. She didn't see her brother or her husband anywhere in sight. A couple of servers from the night shift were milling around from table to table, and the assistant manager she and Shayne had taken on to pick up slack was manning the bar.

"Hey, Steve." She leaned over the bar. "Where's Shayne?"

"He and Nick are in the office." He gave her a nod when she pulled her brows inward. "It's okay, Cate. I've checked twice. No bloodshed yet."

Bewildered, she made her way down the short service hall and pushed the office door open. At the sight before her, she flicked her brows in. There sat Shayne on one side of the table, Nick at the other, both with a bar glass of whiskey in hand and a pile of discarded cards between them. Tony was slumped asleep in a chair with a foot propped up on a small side table in the corner, and Sylvia was adding up figures on the calculator.

"I'm sorry I'm so late." Cate closed the door quietly behind her, making a few more passes around the room with her eyes. "A cement truck tipped over halfway between the loft and Saint Adeline. I literally sat blocked in the center lane for two hours, and then it was turtle speed once it finally did start moving again, because of the ice."

Her mother called out, waving a hand from behind the computer. "We survived, sweetheart, thanks to our two knights in shining armor. Glad everything's okay. I told those two you would be fine. My daughter knows how to take care of herself."

"Thanks, Mom. What, ah…" Cate shook her head when Nick turned, beaming softly over his shoulder at her. She walked a few steps forward, bending to press a quick kiss to his lips. "What's going on here, Sir Galahad?"

"Nothing." He cleared his throat a little. "Just mooching a drink off of your brother."

"It's a drink well-earned." Shayne held his glass up to his brother-in-law, releasing the index finger from around it to aim in Nick's direction. "I can't believe I'm saying this, but he and Tony really saved our bacon tonight."

"Is that so?" Flabbergasted by the admission, she dropped her purse to the tabletop and shrugged out of her coat. She caught the satisfied flicker in her husband's eye as she lowered onto his lap. "Just how, exactly, did they do that?"

"Nick and Tony helped stave off the thirsty hoards, ran back and forth to the kitchen, bussed tables. You name it. It was only Mom and the new kid and me, without you and Jessica. We were full up to our eyeballs, I can tell you. I think every person in Saint Adeline had a hankering for MacCarthaigh's tonight."

"Where was Jessica?" The skin between her brows creased softly and she shook her head.

"I'll tell you about it, later. It's finally died down. Now that the last shift is here, I'm going home. You two should do the same. Steve said he'd close up." Shayne waved her off, then stood to go back out and check on things at the front of the house.

"Ugh." She rolled her eyes. "The last place I want to be is back on that highway, after all that."

"Yeah, about that commute," Shayne pointed a dictatorial finger in her direction, "Nick's idea of staying at the castle makes a lot more sense than you driving back and forth. It's a whole lot closer, and a better road. You ought to listen to him."

Her lips were poised to move, though shock prevented her from speaking, at first. Had her brother really just agreed with Nick? As Shayne disappeared behind the door, her gaze narrowed on Nick's triumphant expression. "Why do I feel like I just fell down a rabbit hole?"

He shrugged, gently moving her so that he could stand. He walked a few steps to where Tony was quietly snoring and tapped his foot with his shoe. "Tony. Hey, come on. Time to go."

She shook her head. "Nicky, how in the world did you ever-"

"Since it's late and you don't want to be back on the road, why don't we just go out to mausoleum for the night?" He flicked a look back at Tony, who was gathering his things. "You wanna stay out at the house, tonight, Tony?"

"Nah, I'll go on home, unless you want somebody there. Those forty winks did me enough to get home." He yawned, stretching. "We really do need to go over these papers in the morning, though."

"Nah, we don't need anybody there, not just for tonight." Nick reached into her purse, snatching the keys from the unzipped center section. "I'll see you in the morning."

"Thanks, again, Tony!" Sylvia called out as he approached the door.

"You bet, Mrs. MacCarthaigh." He nodded, returning the smile she gave him, a hand placed lightly over his heart. "It was my pleasure. We do for family, right Nick?"

"Right." Nick lifted an open palm to her mother in parting, and ushered Cate toward the door. "You're ready to go, right?"

"Uh, yeah." She nodded, a curve deepening on her lips. "If mom doesn't need me, that is."

"You go on, sweetheart." She twiddled her fingers and went back to work. "I'll see you tomorrow."

Once they were safely out of earshot, Cate angled her head to look up at him, continuing to walk toward the door with his arm tucked around her from the side. "All right, seriously. I want to know what really went on here tonight. Why are you and Shayne suddenly so chummy, and why do you have that smug look plastered onto your face?"

"So suspicious. I am smiling like this because, A, I finally put a crack in your brother's iron-clad shell, and B, you proved my point that staying out at the family place instead of the loft, for a while, is a good idea."

"Aw, Nicky, no." She shook her head, letting it fall against him. "I don't want to stay there. It's like being in a big empty hotel."

"So? Hotels can be all right." He laughed, pressing a kiss to the top of her head as they navigated a slick portion of sidewalk together. "Room service and staying in bed late wasn't so bad when we were in New York."

"We are not in New York, and aside from that first morning, you have never stayed late in bed again. You'll be down in your father's office more than you'll be in our bedroom, and we both know it."

"Not necessarily." He passed her a mischievous grin.

"I also know that the only room service we'll be getting there is if I sneak downstairs and make something, myself, and then bring it back up, pretending to be surprised." She rolled her eyes, pointing out what she'd found to be the truth. Nick was generally up, and in his loft office, working by the time her alarm went off. "Anyway, I wanted to spend our first Christmas in our place."

"The loft was more my place than ours. We'll start looking for an actual house between Chicago and Saint Adeline after the holidays, but in the meantime, we stay out at the mausoleum. Please. For my nerves and for your brother's sanity?"

She groaned, grimacing. "Nicky, I don't-"

"*I'll* make you breakfast in bed. Late breakfast. Maybe more of a brunch, huh?" He stopped by the car, curling her in his arms as he tilted a pleading expression down at her.

"When?"

"Tomorrow."

She shook her head. "You're meeting Tony tomorrow morning."

"Come on. Everybody else thinks it's a good idea. I won't live in Pop's study, but I can still work from the office, downstairs, and you'll be a whole lot closer to MacCarthaigh's. If not, I'll worry about you every time you walk out the door."

"Nicky, I know you want your way on this but…" She shook her head, looking up into the warmth of his dark eyes, knowing there was little she'd ever deny him that was clearly so important to him. "You won't let up until I agree, will you?"

His chest shook softly, the convincing curve of his lips edging down to meet hers briefly. "You know me so well."

"Fine. We'll try it, but only for a while." She sighed, conceding, and accepted another longer kiss. "And, to think I once told you nothing between us would come so easily to you."

Chapter Eighteen

Alf paced briskly outside Nick's loft office. He had the place to himself, since Nick and Cate had moved out to the family house. Nick only dropped into the loft office, occasionally, for a file or two. Frankie, of course, had taken up an apartment in the guest house, out back of the Caprianno estate, so he wasn't there. Even so, Alf wasn't comfortable making the call while inside the building. He'd been kept on hold for what seemed an eternity.

He had procrastinated shutting down the project, holding out hope for nearly a week that Nick would change his mind. Crispen was obviously peeved with Alf's reluctance to answer calls and messages. He'd seen, and skillfully avoided, a couple of Jansen goons earlier in the week. He'd managed to explain away the 'call me' message that had been scratched into the paint on his car by telling Nick that it must've been some punks pulling pranks. The event had inspired Nick to add a few more security cameras around the outer building, all the same.

Dropping down onto a metal bench near the sidewalk, Alf began to dig into his pocket for the medicine he'd recently taken to chewing like candy. Popping a couple in his mouth, he chewed their mint chalkiness with a vigor far surpassing the need. He couldn't think of any way out of the mess, other than to try and work something out between himself and Crispen. Maybe he could work Nick out of the whole thing, totally. At that thought, the line finally began to ring through.

"Alf." The tone of Crispen's voice was thin, sharp, like the blade of a knife. "I've been trying to get a hold of you, pally."

"Yeah. I got the message. Thanks for the artwork on my car. That took some explaining. Pretty stupid move.

Set Nick on high alert." He grumbled irritably. "You know, he had extra surveillance installed around all of his offices because of that stunt? Even if I had wanted to get in touch sooner-"

"Yeah, yeah." Crispen cut him off, rolling his eyes out of boredom. He wasn't in the humor to field excuses or listen to any prattling from the old-timer. "Did you get the signature, or not? Alf?"

Alf cleared his throat, feeling that sickened pang creeping in on him again. "The thing is, Crispen-"

"Yes, or no?" He demanded. "I'm tired of playing these games with Caprianno. Did he sign, or not?"

"Not." Alf rubbed a hand lightly over the quickening pulse under his ribs. Tugging at the squeezing pressure of his tie, he waited through the silence. "Did you hear what I said?"

"I heard." Crispen gritted his teeth, chewing down his fury. Drawing a breath to keep his tone even, cool, he rocked back in his chair, nodding to the two creeps that served as fixtures in his office. "I heard you let me down, Alf. You know what that means, don't you? You do recall the conversation we had, the terms that we laid out?"

"Yeah, I remember." Alf shook his head. "Listen, Crispen. You don't need Nick. If you wanna turn your business around, I can help you, myself. I'll front you the cash for your project."

Crispen burst out with an amused laugh. "I know you've done pretty well by the Caprianno family, over the years, but you can't begin to come across with the kind of deal I'm after. You can't even provide the services we agreed upon. You don't mean squat to me. You're a used-up dinosaur, Alf, nothing but an aged bump in my road, one I suppose I'm just going to have to pave over."

"What do you mean? What is it you really want? You claimed you needed Nick's two million bucks for your new enterprise. *I* can do that." He gnawed viciously on his lower lip. "Why does it have to be Nick? What can he do for you that I can't?"

"You can't give me the Caprianno name. Nicky boy's name opens all kinds of doors into what I want, and with the provisions I've got structured into the agreement, he ends up with egg on his face when it all falls down around his ears."

"*When* it falls down?" Alf scrunched his brows in tightly, the wheels in his mind turning faster with foreboding. "You mean *if*, don't you?"

"What I mean doesn't have anything to do with you, anymore. Hey, what can I say?" Crispen chuckled meanly, throwing his arms out at either side as he gave a disinterested shrug, not that anyone but his smirking henchmen could see. "I gave you more chances than I've ever given anybody. What happens between Nick Caprianno and me, at this point, it ain't got anything to do with you."

"Nick isn't gonna sign with you." Alf lowered his voice, a long-dormant, guttural quality emerging as he gritted his words through his teeth. "If I'm going down anyway, I'll make sure Nick don't sign anything with you. I'll tell him everything."

"If I was you, Alf, I'd be more worried about my own neck." Crispen laughed again, energized by the mental warfare he knew he was inflicting on him. "See, it wouldn't really have mattered whether you helped me, or not. One way or another, I'm making it my business to ruin the Caprianno family. You were nothing but a smoother transition, an easier in. I guess that was never gonna wash. Obviously, he doesn't trust you any more than it turns out he should have. You were right about one thing. He's smarter than I gave him credit for, not that that will help him much."

"Listen to me, you little punk-"

"Nah." Crispen shook his head. "Nah, I'm done listening to you, Alf. Now, I do things my way. If Nick doesn't sign, now, I just go for his soft underbelly. It's just a matter of time before you, Frankie, Tony, Louis, and any of the other Caprianno goombahs know, first hand, just what it felt like for my father when he hit rock bottom."

"You say what you want about any of us. Nick didn't have no part of what happened to your old man." He insisted. "Besides, Nick Caprianno doesn't have the kind of weaknesses you're looking for."

"He was the reason Salvador Caprianno pulled out of business with my father." Crispen peeled his lips back into an unpleasant grin as he looked down at the photograph, tracing a finger over the face on the surveillance image. "As for Nick not having any weaknesses to prey on, oh, I think he does. I think he really, really does. In the meantime, I guess it's up to you whether you break the news to Nick, or whether I do."

"What weaknesses?" Alf swallowed the tightening lump in his throat, his heart pounding in his ears. "What kind of timeline are we talking? What are you giving me to work with?"

"I don't know." Crispen snickered crudely, swiveling his chair from side to side, continuing to stroke his finger back and forth over the photo in his hand. "I just don't know. I guess we'll just have to see how long I can manage to be patient."

"Patient?"

"I tell you what, Alf. I'll give you one last chance to get him to sign. I'm not gonna wait around, this time, though." He shook his head. "No, this time, Nick finds out when I get tired of waiting. Oh, don't get me wrong, you'll both go down, one way or another, but you could save him a lot of… discomfort, if you can get him to sign first. Less work for me. Either way, we'll be in touch. Until then, I'd watch my back, if I was you."

"Crispen!" He shouted into his cell, his face beet red and throbbing with the course of adrenaline, perspiration pouring down his entire body like a shower of salty rain. "Crispen!"

Overwhelmed by the conversation, by what he'd unwittingly brought on Nick, onto his other friends, he had to pull himself to standing. The heavy breaths that left his chest puffed out in heavy clouds of mist in the cold air. He knew, very well, that in Santino Caprianno's day, Nicky's grandfather, he'd be somewhere at the bottom of the Chicago River for what he'd been into with Jansen.

At just the thought of it, and of what he'd done, Alf pulled a pack of cigarettes from the inner pocket of his coat, attempting to light one as it trembled between his lips. Unable to get his lighter to create more than a weak spark, he ripped the cigarette from his mouth and gave a loud shout, throwing it and his lighter across the parking lot.

Feeling an intense vice-like tightening in his chest, he clutched a hand over it, finding it difficult to catch his breath. He dropped back onto the bench, frame melting until he'd slumped to his knees on the sidewalk. He rolled his eyes up at the snow-clouded sky and gritted his teeth. He couldn't let things end this way, not before he got everything straightened out with Nick.

"Sir?" A woman who had been walking her dog across the street rushed over to him. Dropping down next to him, she loosened his tie and unbuttoned the top couple of buttons on his shirt, then pulled out her cell phone. "I'm a nurse. You'll be okay. Just take some slow breaths and keep your eyes on mine. I'm calling for help, right now."

#

Alf opened his eyes to see Nick slouched in a hospital room chair next to him, a fist curled firmly against the thin line of his tightly pressed lips. The young man offered him a stern look, dropping his hand from his mouth as he folded his arms over his chest.

Oh. What had Nick heard? What did he know? Had Crispen and his cronies already gotten to him? The heart monitor began to blip with a sudden uptick of speed. Alf's breathing picked up as he studied the deep furrow at Nick's brow. Not a word. It was never a good sign when Nick was too angry to speak.

"Nicky." He started to sit up, fiddling with the iv drip in his arm. "What is all this garbage?"

"Saline and some other junk. Leave it alone." Nick scooted closer to him, his face forbidding as thunder. "You're gonna be all right. They said you had an anxiety attack, maybe a little bout of angina. Said your blood pressure was shooting out of the atmosphere faster than a rocket."

"Eh, what do they know? Doctors. Who knows my body better than me, huh? This whole thing's just a racket to try and bilk me out of a tidy wad of cash." He swung his legs over the side of the mattress and shrugged. "I just forgot to eat lunch today."

"You're out, Alf." The muscle along Nick's jawline rippled a few times. He shook his head when Alf's gaze slowly cut over to him again. "No more. You've been with the family since before I was born. You've done good by us. It's time you let us return the favor, before this gets any worse."

"Gets any worse than what?" He scoffed, searching the tables for his pants. The blips on the monitor began to slow as he realized Nick didn't appear to know about his deception, as yet. "I told you, I just forgot to eat."

"It's time, Alf." Nick held a bag with his clothes out to him, knowing he would insist on leaving, no matter what the hospital staff recommended. "I should've called you on it a few months ago when I first saw the signs."

"What signs? Ah, you're crazy, kid. I got a heart like Tarzan." He stiffened his jaw and pounded a fist against his chest, but then grasped the bedrail behind him, losing his balance a bit. "All right, so I ain't nineteen no more. I'll say when I'm ready to be put out to pasture. Now ain't it. I still… I got things I gotta get straight for you, first."

"No." Nick shook his head. "You're gonna stay with Cate and me for a while, while you get back on your feet. From there, you're gonna take it easy. You and Nadine go on a cruise. Get married. Just… take it easy."

"Eh!" He waved him off, souring the expression on his face. "Nadine don't wanna bother with getting married, now, and Cate don't like me anyway. You don't need me hanging around, stinking up the romantic atmosphere. You're a newlywed, heaven help you."

Alf silently thanked his lucky stars for the distraction Cate provided. Without her, Nick might have found out about the mess with Jansen before he had an opportunity to somehow rectify the situation. He wasn't sure how things would turn out, but at least now he had a chance to try.

"You got too much on your mind to worry about an old goat, like me. Anyway, I don't do what I'm told. Where do you think you get that from, huh?"

"I got a long list of people I get that trait from, and you know it. As far as Cate goes, you leave her to me." He shifted his eyes over at the door when the doctor came in and scowled at the half-dressed patient. "And you are coming back to the house with me when you leave here. You and Frankie can drive each other crazy out in the guest house."

Alf shook his head, allowing a new plan to roll around in his brain a little bit. Maybe it wasn't a terrible idea. Whether Nick knew it, or not, he may have just done himself a huge favor by giving himself such a houseguest.

At least, if Alf went home with him, he could keep an eye out for any funny business Crispen might try and create.

"Get off me, you croaker!" Alf barked, jerking his arm away from the reach of the concerned physician.

"Mr. Giuseppe, I really need you to get back into bed. We want to keep you for observations for at least a few more hours." The doctor flicked a glance over to Nick. "Can you tell your friend it's for the best?"

"I could." Nick laughed and shook his head. "It wouldn't do much good, though, doc."

Chapter Nineteen

Cate smoothed a hand over the pillowcase, her eyes blinking slowly as she awakened. Giggling softly at the sight of Nick sitting next to her, she wadded her pillow under her head. She smiled a little deeper when he reached to push her hair away from her eyes and allowed his fingertips to trace the side of her face. As her gaze dropped to the bed tray that sat between them, however, the lightness of her expression fell.

"What is this?" She arched an apprehensive brow at the single rose in the vase. "What's wrong?"

"Nothing's wrong. I made you breakfast. Room service." He gave her a shrug in response, aiming the easy curve of his lips at her. "I promised you, right?"

"Yes, you did." She pulled herself to sitting, still eyeing the tray with caution. "You also promised it to me a couple of weeks ago. This is something else. What's going on?"

"Cate…" His chest slumped and he dropped back onto his pillows with a laugh, scrubbing his hands over his face. "What is it you think I've done that I could've made up for it with something as small as this? Trust me, if I screw up somehow, you'll know. With bells and whistles, you'll know."

"Sounds like you've been thinking about it." She teased.

"Could you try to be just a little less suspicious?" He pulled her hand over, kissing it softly. "You know, there's a time to pick things apart and there's a time to let things be as they are. Just eat the stupid toast."

"No. Not until I know what it means." She shook her head, folding her arms. "Nick?"

"Geez, Cate." He turned his head to look out from under the arm he'd dropped over his eyes. Noting the relentless expression she had pinned on him, he laughed again, and rolled onto his side. "All right. There is a little something."

"Ah ha!" She pointed a finger at him. "What is it? What's wrong, this time? The last time you said that, Alf-"

"Nothing's wrong." He huffed a heavy breath against the pillowcase and dragged himself back up to sitting. "I just wanted to say thank you."

"Thank you?" She shifted her study of him at an angle. "Thank you, for what?"

He slid a hand over to hers, curling his fingers around it. Giving her a sincere nod of gratitude, he went on to explain himself. "I know you didn't want us to stay here, and I know you *really* didn't want Alf along for the ride, but you agreed to both, for me. It means a lot. I just wanted you to know that I appreciated it."

"You're wrong about one thing. It's going to take a lot more than a couple pieces of dry toast and some cold eggs for me to be happy about Alf being here."

"Well, Christmas is next week." He laughed, reaching a hand to smooth over one of her shoulders. "Maybe Santa can bring you something extra nice."

"I'd settle for Santa just working shorter hours, for a change." She flicked her eyes away from him. "I know you want to spoil me, Nicky, but I don't need things. I just want you."

"I have been pretty buried, lately, haven't I?" He leaned forward, grinning deeply before placing a warm kiss to her lips. He could tell that she meant every ounce of the sentiment she expressed, a sentiment that mirrored his own feelings for her. "You'll have me for Christmas, Cate. You have my word."

Alf had been living in one of the guest house apartments for nearly a week. Nick knew it grated on Cate's nerves for his friend to be there. Something about Alf, in general, rubbed her the wrong way. It was only for Nick's peace of mind and happiness that she'd allowed it. She did put in an effort for Nick, but she couldn't help the sharp, distrustful gaze she occasionally sent Alf when they crossed paths.

She shrugged, looking down at the tray again. "I know how much Alf means to you, Nicky. You don't have to keep trying to butter me up."

"Hey." He gently took her chin, turning her face back to him. "You mean a lot to me. You mean more to me than every other person or thing in my life."

She shook her head, releasing a long sigh as she looked at him. "So, I guess it's true that Italian men can charm their way into, or out of anything?"

"I mean, I don't know how successful *I* really am at that." He tugged one corner of his mouth up firmly as he considered her statement. "I mean, I have my moments, but according to you, I'm not all that romantic."

"Okay, Nick. Seriously, you just handed me a ring. No, wait. First, you slid the box at me. Then, you handed it to me." She rolled her eyes when he lifted the bed tray aside so that he could scoot closer to her. "You weren't even going to put it on for me!"

"All right, all right. I'm never gonna hear the end of that one." His chest shook lightly with laughter and he tucked his arms closely around her. "I know. I'm the one that brought it up. You still married me, didn't you?"

"Mm-hmm." She nodded, lifting her fingers to comb through his hair. "I certainly did. You didn't leave me much choice."

"So, I guess it couldn't have been *such* a bad proposal." He cocked a dark brow at her, his grin spreading to both sides of his mouth.

"Oh, Nicky, it really was. I didn't care, though, not really." She laughed again, tugging him closer by the collar of his shirt. Her lips grinned against his as she murmured her reply. "You know, I think you also promised me something else, here at Hotel Caprianno, besides just room service, which I feel fairly safe in assuming is a one-time deal."

"Ah, yeah. I think we also discussed late mornings." He nodded quietly, grinning broadly between small pecks of kisses, then reached a hand off to the side to flip the alarm clock onto its face. "Hey, a promise is a promise, and we have all day today."

#

It was a rare thing for both Nick and Cate to have the whole day off together. He had actually ended up cheating, sneaking a couple of work calls under the radar from the office while she took her shower. After the later start to their day, they had decided that they'd just as well use the rest of the morning to decorate the Christmas tree together. They'd only been halfway through when Frankie popped his head in to let Nick know about another call.

Wincing at the frosty glance she'd sent him, he apologized, backing out of the room with a soft laugh. "I'm sorry, baby. I won't take long. It saves me from going into the city, though, doesn't it?"

"Mmm." She nodded, unconvinced. "I suppose we'll also stop in at your office for just a quick thing or two when we go in for lunch and the last of the Christmas shopping."

"No." He shook his head, holding his palms up as he reached the door. "I will stay away from all other offices. No more calls after this one. No more interruptions to our day."

"I'll believe it when I see it."

She turned from him, slightly miffed over the interruption. He'd only just gotten back from a trip, a couple of days in California, the week before. As if being in a strange, too-large house hadn't been enough to contend with, she'd been left alone there with Alf and Frankie for those couple of days.

Nick had been working almost non-stop since he'd come home from the west coast. She hadn't been thrilled to hear him talking about scheduling another potential overnight trip for some time after the New Year. While he'd suggested she go along, she insisted her responsibilities at MacCarthaigh's wouldn't allow.

He winced at her angry silence. "Cate-"

"Go on." She waved a hand over her shoulder. "The sooner you finish, the sooner you can get back to help untangle all of the ornament hooks."

She checked her watch again. In twenty-minutes they'd be on their way for an afternoon alone together. Mostly alone. She'd agreed to allow a newer member of Nick's staff to go along, since Nick had contended that it would be easier for someone to drive them than it would be to constantly circle the holiday parking in the city.

The kid, Mikey, was nice, at least. He was the son of a friend, a tall, wiry kid of about twenty. He was anxious to make good in the new job, and Cate didn't mind him tagging along. Mikey felt much less like a babysitter than even Frankie, no matter how much she adored him. She'd been pleasantly lost in thought with plans for their day when Alf wandered into the room.

"Where's Nick?" His voice was clipped short.

He recognized that it was by her grace that he was permitted to convalesce there. He could also tell that she didn't care for him any more than she ever had, that it had only been her love for Nick that had led her to agree to the arrangement. Still, if looks could kill, he'd have been a dead man many times over.

"I gotta talk to him about something."

"He's on a call in the office." She worked at keeping a civil tone, but sensed that there was more to Nick's stress level where Alf was concerned than just the anxiety attack he'd suffered. "He said he'd be back in a few minutes."

"Okay." He nodded, then gestured to the mess she was working through. "Hey, you want a hand with that? I used to be pretty good with messes."

"I'll bet you were." She bit down on her tongue, sighing, and turned back to him, meeting his eyes firmly with hers. "No, thank you. Nicky can help me when he comes back."

"I can just wait in the hall, if that would be better." He nodded.

Though she hadn't said anything in reply, he observed the slight flare of her nostrils, the slightly quicker pace of her breath. Fire inside that one. Internalized, or not, it was all currently aimed at him.

"Yes." She bobbed her head abruptly, swearing under her breath when she dropped a bulb onto the floor and heard it shatter. "Maybe you should wait for him in the hall."

"Let me at least help you with that." He moved toward her, squatting next to her as she picked up the shards of green and red blown glass.

"I can do it, myself." She held a hand out to stop him from reaching any further into her task, her glare pinning icily on him. "Thank you."

He laughed, shaking his head. "Boy, you really don't like me, do ya, honey? I mean, I can tell you're making an effort, for Nick, but you really don't."

"I don't like what you do to Nicky." She clapped back. "And I believe we've discussed it before, but my name is Cate or Cathlene, not honey."

He shrugged. "I hear Frankie call you sweetheart, often enough. Of course, you like Frankie."

"That's right, I do." She looked down, wincing when an edge to the glass nicked her finger. Shaking her head with an incredulous laugh, she flicked her eyes back up at him. "Anyway, Frankie says it differently. I dare say he doesn't mean it in the same way when he says it either, as if I was some flaky cocktail waitress."

"What is it I do to Nick, exactly?" He pulled back, examining her with a sharp glance. What, if anything, did she know? "He say something?"

"He doesn't have to say anything. It's in the way he looks and acts when you try to bully him into your side of things. You talk to him as if he's a child who doesn't understand something he's already brilliant at." Her tongue was sharper than she realized, her angry words stinging back at him. "I don't know what's going on with you, and Nicky may not want to see it, but I can tell something's not right. Not with you, not between you and him. I can't say how or why, but he admires you. He thinks the world of you, and you just…"

"I what?" He stared back at her, shocked by the honest, pinpoint assessments she was capable of making. "Go on."

"Listen. You and I don't have to be friends. We don't even have to like one another. Just… promise me you won't let him get hurt. That's all I ask. Can you at least promise me that much?" She shrugged, her vision lightly fogging with the threat of tears as she went on. "I just love him so much. If anything ever happened to Nicky…"

"I understand." He nodded again, appreciating her more for the way she clearly felt about Nick than he'd ever fully given her credit for. "He's pretty well crazy about you, too. In fact, I'd say you're probably the one thing in the whole world that he…"

The words froze on his lips as he spoke them and he wrinkled his brow line. That was it. *She* was it, the key, the answer. *Cate* was the one thing Crispen could, and would, use against Nick. Of course. It had been days since Alf had had that appalling conversation with Jansen. Crispen hadn't said what he was planning to do, or when. Now, though, Alf knew exactly how he would strike if Nick turned him down again.

Maybe, if Alf could somehow get Cate on his side, she could reason with Nick. Maybe they could figure out something together, some solution to put an end to Crispen's whole vindictive battle. Alf had also come to recognize that she had more brains than he'd ever given her credit for.

"Alf?" She reached a hand forward, concerned by the way his words had just trailed off and how lost in thought he'd become. "Are you all right? Should I call somebody?"

"No." He shook his head. In that instant, he saw a deeper glimpse of what Nick saw in her. Even though she held such an intense dislike for him, she yielded a concerned regard for his well-being. "No. I'm all right, Cate. But there's something important-"

"All right, baby. I know, I said it would just take a couple of minutes," Nick called from the hallway, "but I'll help you finish the tree when we get back. You ready to go?"

Walking into the room, Nick had interrupted the true start of their conversation, without realizing it. He rubbed his hands together, already having his coat on. Taking note of the side glances shared back and forth between the two, he visibly tensed.

"Everything okay?"

She nodded, moving away from Alf, dusting her hands over the trash before taking Nick's arm. "I just… broke a bulb. Gave myself a little ding, but I'll live.

You're right. We're going to be late for our lunch reservation, if we don't get going."

Alf stepped forward. "Just a second, Nick."

It felt like firecrackers were exploding in his gut. Now that he understood what Crispen had meant, they shouldn't go anywhere until he and Nick talked. He had to say something, warn him. How or where he'd start, he had no idea.

"Can we-"

"Hey, Alf." Tony broke in as he walked into the room. "Frankie wants ya. He needs your help with something out in the guest house."

Almost grateful for the reprieve, but knowing he still desperately needed to talk with Nick, and with Cate, Alf looked intently at his boss. Just an extra moment or two might give him both the strength and an idea of what to say. "I'll just be a minute, Nick. Don't go anywhere."

Cate huffed a breath, looking down at her watch again when he'd gone. "Nicky, you've been working off and on all morning. We're going to miss lunch, too."

He nodded, checking his own watch. "All right. Let's go. I'll talk to Alf when we get home."

They were just leaving the driveway when Alf returned, his face burning with panic. He caught Tony by the arm, eyes wide. "Where's Nick?"

"They left. He said he'd talk to you when he got back." Tony shrugged him off, smoothing the wrinkles from his shirt. "What's the matter with you? If it can't wait, just call him."

Alf nodded, pulling his cell from his pocket to dial Nick, hoping to catch him before they hit the dead zone on the road that led to the highway. Something sank within him, hearing the familiar ring of Nick's phone from across the foyer. His eyes landed on the blue flashing screen from where he'd apparently placed it on the hall credenza while he put his coat on, obviously forgetting to pick it back up before they left.

Chapter Twenty

Nick and Cate had taken their time at lunch, wandered around large stores and small shops. At night, Chicago would look like a magical fairyland, with lights twinkling from the bare swinging branches. Store windows and street signs would glow against the piled-up glitter of white snow on the ground. Even in the afternoon, there was something almost magical about the Christmas season in a large city.

The sights and smells and bustle of traffic along the streets and in the stores just seemed to speak the name of the Christmas season. There were jewel-colored banners and decorative displays, trees and Santa Clauses observed with every glance. Packages of every size, shape, and color hung from shoppers' fingertips all around them.

After a lengthy search, Cate had finally found the perfect gift for Marie. She looked down at her sore feet, shifted back and forth on them a few times. One other thing that the holidays were good for were lines. Long ones. As much fun as they were having together, she dearly wanted to sit down before they went anywhere else.

"Why don't you go on out to the car with Mikey? He's waiting right there, by the door." Nick suggested, noticing her discomfort. "We're only two back in line, now. It won't be long. When I come out, we'll have him take us to that little coffee shop we found the last time we came into the city together."

"I'll wait, it's okay." She held closely to his arm, smiling up at him. "I'd rather stick it out and be here with you."

"Cate, you know it's almost Christmas, right? It might not be all good will telling you to go outside with

Mikey. The clerk might just be holding something for me at the counter I don't want you to see." He laughed, dipping his head to press his lips to hers, speaking against them with a grin. "Go on. Get out of here, will ya?"

"Oh, Christmas intrigue." She giggled as she teased him. "Something for me? Let me see, Nicky. I promise I'll do a really convincing job of pretending that I forgot what it was on Christmas morning."

"Huh-uh." He grinned harder, running a finger down the curve of her neck. "And ruin your surprise? You better watch out. You'll end up on Santa's naughty list."

"Maybe I don't mind the naughty list." She laughed again, tugging him toward her by the collar. She glanced off to the side when someone cleared their throat loudly. They'd apparently missed the fact that the line had moved up a little. "All right. I'll wait outside, but I intend to go snooping later, fair warning."

"Hey, Mikey!" Nick called out, then pecked her lips once more before she moved away from him.

A moment later, a gangly man with mousy hair was standing at the register next to Nick's. He flicked a glance down at the hand Nick had rested on the counter and grinned when he looked at him. "Been married long?"

"What?" Nick glanced down at the band on his finger, realizing that he'd been softly tapping it on the glass case. Looking back up over the man, one corner of his mouth tugged up. "No, not too long. Couple of months."

The man nodded, gesturing to the photo in Nick's open wallet. "Wow, she's a knock-out. Really hit the jackpot, there. Lucky man."

"Yeah." Nick hardened his tone in response to the curl of the man's lips. "Lucky."

Something about the way the man had smiled, something about the way he'd eyed Cate's photo, turned on some sort of warning radar inside of Nick. He flipped his wallet closed and replaced it to his inner coat pocket.

Taking his packages, he turned, looking out at the sidewalk where she had been waiting for him with Mikey. He saw her, but Mikey was nowhere around. Feeling a wave of anxiety at seeing her alone, Nick began a quick stride toward the door.

"Yeah, if I was married to a woman like that, I'd be sure to keep a close eye on her, too." The man called. "Never know how long a good thing is gonna last. Some things have a way of disappearing, right under your nose."

Nick stopped cold in his tracks, whipping around to look back at the man, but he'd already wandered away and mixed with the crowd. Feeling a fine mist of chilled sweat beading over his body, Nick burst out of the doors, his heart pounding as he scanned the sidewalk. Spotting her a few yards from where she'd been before, he moved quickly, grabbing her by the arm and tucking her against his chest.

"Nicky!" Her eyes were wide, startled by his sudden appearance, and by the way he gripped her so tightly. "What are you doing?"

Keeping her closely pinned against him, he continued to dart his eyes at their surroundings. "Where's Mikey?"

"He's right over there. The meter ran out while we were inside. Poor kid was sure you'd be livid. He said he was going to try and talk his way out of the ticket. I told him not to worry, but he was so…"

Cate's laughter cut short when she looked up at her husband again. Bewildered by the intent way his eyes appeared to shift everywhere but to hers, his quick breaths against her, she lifted a hand to the side of his face. His muscles were hard, his body rigid.

"Nicky, something's wrong. What is it?" She turned her brows down at him. "You look really worried."

"No, baby, no. Something just came up. Business. I'm sorry. I'm gonna have Mikey take you home, if I don't knock him upside the head for leaving you alone, like that."

"Oh, Nicky, don't. We were supposed to spend the whole day together, and you ended up fielding calls almost all morning. We both have to work tomorrow." She tried to smile, tried to catch his eye. "At least let me go with you to do whatever it is. I don't mind waiting."

"No. I'll meet you at the house later. I'm not sure how long this is gonna take. Listen, I forgot my phone there, so, tell Frankie…"

As Mikey came back to the curb, muttering obscenities about the ticket he'd been unsuccessful in evading, Nick scorched a hot glare at him. He finally released Cate, snatching the slip of paper from Mikey's fingers, and ripping it in half. Throwing it to the ground, Nick got within inches of his face.

"What are you doing leaving her standing there alone for a lousy parking ticket, huh? What are you thinking?"

"Nicky, it's fine." Cate shook her head, stepping between him and Mikey, thinking he looked as though he'd like to tear the poor kid apart. "Nicky, sweetheart, come on. Let's just go home. Whatever it is, can't it wait? You're so tight, you're about to bust."

"No, it can't wait." He reached around her, slamming the point of a finger hard against the front of Mikey's coat. "You get her home, and you don't make any stops on the way. You understand me? And when you get there, you find Frankie, and you tell him that Nicky said to keep Cate company because he had to see a man about some business. You understand me? Huh?"

"Sure, Mr. Caprianno, sure." Mikey nodded, his Adam's apple rising and falling quickly. "Tell Frankie that you want him to stick around and that you had a meeting. I got it."

"No. Listen to me! You tell him I want him to keep Cate company because I have to see a man about some business. You tell him word for word. You got that?" He looked back down at the baffled expression on Cate's face. Dipping his head to press a firm kiss to her lips, he squeezed her tightly in his arms. "Go on home, sweetheart. Straight home… so you'll be there when I get back, okay?"

"Nicky, you didn't bring your car." She sighed, both disappointed and confused by his behavior. "Do you want to take my phone with you?"

"No." He shook his head adamantly. "I want you to keep your phone with you. Don't worry about me. I'll be back to the house in a little bit. I promise."

Hearing the insistence in his voice, seeing the determined look in his eye, her heartbeat skipped up a little. "Nicky, please tell me what-"

"I won't be long, but I gotta get going. Okay?" He glanced back at the department store doors, then cupped her face in his hands, doing the best he could to tug a calmer smile onto his lips. "We'll finish the tree and break out some mistletoe when I get back, all right?"

"Okay." She nodded, brushing his lips with hers again before she slid into the back seat of the car. "Hey. I love you."

"I love you, too, baby. See you in just a bit." After her door had closed, he snatched Mikey by the lapel of his coat, just as he was about to open the driver's door. His voice was low, his eyes like slivers of dark glass. "You don't make *any* stops. Not for gum, nothing. You need to take a leak, you hold it until you get back to the house. You understand me?"

"Yes, sir, Mr. Caprianno." Mikey nodded obediently when Nick ripped his hand free again and stepped back, the muscle twitching along his boss' jaw. "No stops. Not for nothing."

Nick let his eyes move along the street again, his expression unshakably forbidding. "Get going."

Watching the car drive off, he turned, walking down the sidewalk to a break between the two brick buildings. He stepped into the easement, letting his shoulder rest against some of the bricks while he waited. He didn't like lying to Cate, but it was a sort of business. There was no more important business in the world to him than the business of keeping her safe.

It felt like an eternity as Nick waited in the cold, blowing wind. Rewarded for his patience, he finally observed the man from the register counter passing through the department store doors. As he made his way down the sidewalk in Nick's direction, Nick ducked back behind the brick.

Nearly passing the easement, the man gasped, finding himself swiftly snatched into the shadows of the alleyway. He attempted to wriggle free, but Nick slammed him against the wall behind a fire escape stairwell. Held firmly in place with his chest pressed against the cold brick, Nick's arm pinned against his shoulders, and his own arm twisted tightly behind him, he chuckled nervously. Feeling a chill of blood trickling from the corner of his mouth where it had grazed the brick, the man attempted to twist a look at him over his shoulder.

"All right, who are you?" The harsh tone of Nick's words offered a dark forewarning of his earnestness into the man's ear. "And, don't mess with me."

"Hey, man, I don't know what you're talking about!" Attempting to laugh off the pain, the spindly figure winced when Nick squeezed the arm behind his back a little harder. "I'm just doing a little Christmas window shopping, mister."

"Yeah? Well, I got a pretty good idea what you're shopping for, chuckles." The statement was snarled in such low depths that Nick's voice was a near hazard on its own. "Now, who are you, and what do you want with my wife?"

"Me? Nothing."

"All right, who, then?" Nick pressed him harder into the wall, baring his teeth. "Does it feel like I'm playing with you, you miserable sack of-"

"All right! Ah! Geez, man." He laughed again, flinching when his arm was twisted higher once more, his breath harder to draw against the constriction of his chest. "All right! Just ease up a little, will ya? My name's Alex. Mr. Jansen sent me to check in with you."

"Crispen Jansen?" The dilated appearance of Nick's pupils made his eyes darken, and he compressed his teeth harder. "What's the big idea?"

"Mr. Jansen's wants a signed contract. He has to get things in motion within the next few days, or he'll lose all kinds of opportunities."

"Jansen'll miss out, huh? Yeah? What a shame for him." Nick sneered, pressing his full weight against Alex again. "What's he want with Cate?"

"He wanted me to find out how hard it would be to fill his Christmas list. Turns out, it wouldn't have been hard at all to acquire what he wanted, if he'd asked for it." Alex swallowed hard against the shooting pain in his arm as Nick wrenched it harder again. "Ah! Come on, man! He also said to pass on his congratulations and tell you what a beautiful wife you have."

"I'll tell you what else she is. She's safe, and she's gonna stay that way. You got it? Huh? Make sure he understands that, too. You also remember, I know what you look like now, and I won't forget, *Alex*." Nick hyperextended the man's arm so tightly behind him that any further movement would have surely snapped the bone. "I've got a message for you to take back, in return. You tell him I had my own reasons for killing the deal, and no cheap punk he sends is going to resurrect it. You got that?"

"Ah! You're gonna break it!" Alex raised up on his toes, attempting to give his arm a little slack. "Alf said it was sure thing. He said you weren't biting, yet, but that he could still talk you around."

"What?" Stunned, Nick's grip slipped a little, but he quickly tightened it up again. "You're full of it! You really think I'd take *your* word for something like that?"

"Talk to Giuseppe, then! They been working together for months! I swear. I swear! Come on, ease up, will ya?"

Alex sucked a sharp breath through his teeth when Nick suddenly thrust him away, causing him to stumble a couple of steps. Pins and needles shot up and down the nerves in his arm, and he turned to face him. The smile tugged back onto his lips, though it wasn't as smug as it had been the first time.

"You talk to Alf, then you call Mr. Jansen. He'll be waiting. If I was you, I wouldn't wait too long to finish your Christmas shopping. I know Mr. Jansen won't."

"Get out of here! And, you tell him what *I* told you!" Nick barked, watching him walk away and then turn the corner onto the sidewalk.

Feeling sickened and breathless, Nick's thoughts swirled in his mind and he staggered back into the alleyway. Allowing his back to thud against the wall, he knocked his head against the bricks behind him, and he squeezed his eyes shut. What had Alf done? Swallowing against the dry, cold air, he rocked his head from side to side and gritted his teeth. He had to get home. He had to get to Cate.

Chapter Twenty-One

When Mikey and Cate got back to the Caprianno home, she'd gone upstairs to change into something not altogether unalluring but more comfortable, for when Nick returned. Mikey, as instructed, had gone straight in to find Frankie. He stood before him at the kitchen table, his hat twisted tightly between the fingers of his hands as he relayed the message his boss had given him.

Frankie exchanged an unsettled glance with Tony, recognizing the code phrase from the old days, one that Nick knew but had never used. "Hold on a second, kid. Nicky said to specifically tell me to keep Cate company because he had to see a man about some business? You're sure that's what he said?"

"Yes, sir." Mikey nodded, anxiously shifting back and forth on his feet. "He told me to make sure it was word for word. He told me to take her home, not to make any stops, and to tell you to keep Cate company because he had to see a man about some business."

"All right kid, all right. You done good." Frankie stood from the table, clapping him firmly on the shoulder a couple of times, then nodded firmly to Tony. "You go pick up Louis and find Nick. Take the kid with you. He can show you where he left him. I'll give Sal a call."

"Right." Tony nodded, grasping his overcoat from the hook, and then slipped it over his shoulders. "I'll give you a call when we pick him up."

"Good." Frankie nodded, lowering his voice, he glanced back and forth between the two other men. "Don't nobody say nothing to Cate. Far as she needs to know, you two are going to run an errand for Nick, and then you're gonna pick him up and bring him home. You don't say nothing else."

"Yes, sir." Mikey nodded, feeling as though he'd somehow, inexplicably gotten himself into a very hot pot of boiling water.

The skin a long Frankie's thick chop of a jawline tightened and he pulled the slim-profiled Colt 1911 he kept nearby from behind the flour tin on a shelf. Cate had put her foot down about the men wearing firearms in the house. He knew the sight of them bothered her, but he wanted to make sure it was conveniently placed, should he need to get at it. Checking the magazine, he took a few controlled breaths and slipped the gun into the shoulder holster he always wore concealed under his suit jackets.

He moved to the stove, fixing a couple of mugs of cocoa for when she came back downstairs. He was going to have to keep things as normal as possible and keep her from asking too many questions until he knew what Nick wanted her to know. Cate was sharp as a tack. It would take some fancy footwork to throw her off. Luckily, there wasn't much he knew tell her anyway, not until he talked to Nick.

All he knew was that there was serious trouble of some kind, and Nick wanted her kept safe and calm. Until Frankie found out what kind of trouble, he knew he better not let a whiff of it reach her. He wasn't even going out to the guest house to talk to Alf. He wasn't leaving her alone, for even a second.

He dialed the kitchen phone, waiting for the party on the other end to pick up. "Hey, Sal. It's Frankie. Look, I thought you should know, we got a situation of sorts. Nick sent Mikey home with Cate. He had a message for me to keep her company because he had to see a man about some business."

"I see." Sal swallowed hard on the other end of the line. A sharp prickle washed over his face and down the back of his neck as he slowly lowered the newspaper in his hand onto his lap. "He say anything else?"

"No. That's all he said. Mikey and Tony are on their way to pick up Louis, then to go get him."

Sal nodded, setting his jaw on edge. "You tell him to call me, the minute he gets home."

"Yeah. Sure. Soon as he gets back." Frankie peeked around the corner of the kitchen doorway. "Sounds like Cate's coming downstairs, now. I better go. I don't think I'd better say nothing to her 'til Nicky gets here."

"No. No, you'd better wait for him." Sal straightened his back in the chair, drawing his bushy gray brows closer together. "You don't leave her alone, Frankie."

"Nah, of course I won't leave her alone." He kept his voice low, hearing the soft whisper of her house socks growing closer to the kitchen.

Cate shuffled into the room and she smiled at him, snagging a couple of mini marshmallows from the container he had open on the counter. She lifted a brow to him. The smile he offered her in return was different. It was friendly, but... different. She couldn't quite recall seeing that expression on his face before. She held her hand out when he offered the receiver to her.

"Hello?" She gave a quick laugh, then, smiling warmly. "Oh, hi, Sal. Hey, is Nicky with you? He said he had something come up, some business meeting, or something. We were supposed to finish the tree together, only he's been gone ages. He hasn't even called."

"No. Nicky isn't here. I'm sure he'll be home soon, bella." Sal hesitated for a second.

He caught the careful study Nicoletta was making of him from across the room. He managed a passably convincing grin, winking as if he was letting her in on some secret.

"You know, this isn't the right time of year to be asking questions about Nicky making unscheduled stops."

"Ah. You think he needed an excuse to get rid of me so he could do some more shopping on his own, huh? I was starting to think something…" The slightly deeper curve at her lips began to soften again when she glanced over at Frankie, taking notice of the gun. "The way he was acting when he-"

"I'm sure he'll be home soon." Sal turned from his wife's view, squinting his eyes closed, wrinkling his forehead with concern. He only hoped his voice didn't show the strain. "Tell him to call me when he gets in. Goodnight, bella."

"Yeah. Sure, I'll tell him. Goodnight, Sal." She gave slow nod, then turned back to Frankie, hanging up the phone. "That was odd. Did Sal sound, I don't know, *off* to you?"

"Off?" Frankie forced a chuckle. "What do you mean, gorgeous?"

"I don't know. It wasn't anything he said, exactly. I just... Something in his voice sounded... almost as if he was in a hurry to get off the phone when I mentioned Nicky acting strange."

"Eh, who knows with the Caprianno men?" He handed her a mug, winking at her with a friendly curve at his mouth. "Am I right?"

"I don't know." She shook her head, her eyes judging him carefully, and she took a step nearer to him. "Frankie, if there was something wrong-"

"Hey, don't worry so much." He gently tapped her chin and offered another smile. He could tell, by the way she continued to appraise him, that she wasn't a hundred percent buying it. "Come on, sweetheart. I'll keep ya company 'til Nicky gets back. Shouldn't be too long, now."

"No. I hope not." She nodded, finally breaking her study of him as she attempted to dismiss the nagging inside of her. Certainly, she could wheedle whatever it was out of Nick when he got home. "Ah, Frankie, what's the idea of the gun?"

"Coyotes out in the side yard. Pretty brazen this year." He followed a step behind her, toward the living room, changing the subject before her quick mind teased anything away from him. "So, what are we watching?"

She laughed softly, cutting a look over her shoulder at him. "I know I'm driving Nicky crazy with it, but I'm watching my favorite Christmas movie again."

"Again?" He chuckled, following her over to the large, overstuffed sofa. "What's that, every day this week?"

She shrugged, kicking off her shoes as she moved onto a corner cushion. "I think, deep down, he likes it."

"Nicky likes whatever makes you happy." He chuckled, lowering onto a cushion at the other end, then pointed at the actor on the screen. "He used to do a great Stuart when he was a little kid. Had this part down pat."

"Ha!" She burst out a laugh of satisfaction. "I knew he liked this movie, too!"

As she sipped her cocoa and glanced out the window, that nagging sensation began to tug at her again. No matter how well Frankie attempted to conceal it, concern shadowed his reflection in the glass. It was getting dark outside, the clouds looking a bit as if they might just drop some more snow at any time.

Why would Nick have Mikey leave him in the city, rather than have him drop him at his office before they left. And why, if he was just Christmas shopping, had he gotten so angry with Mikey? Why were Frankie and Sal both so intent in convincing her that he was just shopping? And the gun, she hadn't seen or heard coyotes for at least a week. Something didn't smell right. Something *wasn't* right.

#

Frankie had spent a couple of hours with Cate, doing his best to keep her distracted from noticing that Nick still wasn't home. A task much easier said than done, especially as she kept going into the foyer or over to the living room windows to look out for the car's return.

In the end, they'd watched a couple of holiday classics and he'd helped her finish untangling the knot of ornament hooks so that she and Nick could finish the tree later. It wasn't until she'd about given up on the hope of spending the last of her evening with Nick that she'd gone upstairs to get ready for bed. When she came back down, she flipped through channels and scrolled through her phone.

Frankie finally received a quick message from Tony, about halfway through the wait. After picking up Nick, they would be stopping by the loft office to check a few things before they brought him to the house. Nothing after that. Alf had come in shortly after the message from Tony and stayed at the kitchen table with Frankie, playing cards to pass the time, all the while his face was ashen with a secret foreboding idea of what had happened.

Frankie looked up from his cards, dropping them onto the table with a sigh of relief when he heard the front door, and then Nick's voice echoing from the hallway. Nick didn't just sound agitated, he sounded angry, irate. Now that he was finally back, maybe they could find out what was actually going on.

Swallowing hard, Alf adjusted his shoulders a little. A scalding flash of tingles ran down the back of his neck when he studied the expression on Nick's face as he entered the kitchen. He could see a darkness there, a seething, nervous energy behind his eyes as he fixed them directly on him. They appeared darker, harder than he'd ever known them to be in the whole of Nick's life.

Frankie observed it too. The rigid posture, the tension in Nick's shoulders and his jaw of granite, told him that whatever had happened, the trouble wasn't over yet. The glare he held on Alf also told Frankie that Alf somehow had his finger in the pie.

"You okay, kid?" Frankie finally asked.

"Where's Cate?" Nick demanded without answering the question, or without shifting his eyes from his target.

Frankie pulled himself from his chair at the table and made his way over to where Nick stood. "She was watching some movies in the other room while she was waiting for you. She fell asleep a while ago. You want I should check on her again?"

"Thanks." Nick nodded.

"Oh," Frankie snapped his fingers as he recalled the phone message, "your pop wants you to call him."

"Later." Nicky clapped a firm hand over his friend's shoulder a couple of times as he passed, though his gaze still remained relentlessly on Alf. "Shut the door, will ya? We're gonna need a moment."

"Yeah, sure. You got it, Nicky." Frankie continued to study him. "That guy you had to do some business with, would I happen to know who he was?"

Nick gritted his teeth hard enough to make the muscle at his jaw twitch. He had to take a second to calm himself before he could supply an answer. "One of Crispen Jansen's boys. Friend of a… *friend*, it seems."

"You don't say." Frankie nodded, folding his arms across his chest. "So, how did the, ah, meeting go?"

"I'll have to talk to Alf before I know how to answer that question." Nick continued to compress his teeth, his jaw almost aching from the pressure of it, not that he cared. "Can you stick around in the house for a while, Frankie?"

"Yeah, sure." He threw a thumb in the direction of the living room. "Be right in there."

"Hey, Frankie, wait!" He caught his arm, turning his back to Alf, and lowered his voice. "I don't want anybody but you keeping an eye on her. You're her shadow from now on, yeah? Anybody even looks at her wrong, I wanna know."

"Yeah, Nicky. Sure." He nodded, shooting a suspicious glance over at Alf's guilty face. "You got it."

Nick gripped his arm firmly as he lowered to voice to an almost hoarse whisper. "You are the only person I trust with this, Frankie. You are the only one I trust with her."

"She don't leave my sight. Not 'til you say different." He lifted one of his thick hands, firmly patting the side of the younger man's face. "No worries, Nicky."

Once Frankie had gone, Nick pulled the kitchen door closed and turned back toward the table where Alf sat rigidly. The older man's throat rippled with a quick succession of attempts to swallow away the knot forming there. Nick walked a few steps to the table, observing the fine mist that had begun to gather on his advisor's forehead. Alf attempted a light smile, though he knew it was pitifully weak. It felt as if Nick's eyes were piercing through him.

"You look like a man with a lot on his mind, Nick." A few more long, silent seconds of Nick's steadfast glare forced a nervous tremor to twitch at the corner of Alf's mouth. "Sounded like something… pretty particular."

"You could say that, yeah." Nick nodded, controlling his voice well as he spoke to him. He let out a steadying breath, patting the heel of his hand against the top of a chair back. "I want to know how deep you're in with Crispen Jansen, and how much truth there is to what his little crony, Alex, had to say. And, don't try to snow me, Alf, because I've been all through the phone logs and emails. You been a pretty busy guy."

"Nick… I wanted to talk to you before you left. I… guess I should've done it a long time ago." Alf gave a quick shrug, his courage to explain the whole story waning in the moment. "I was hoping it wouldn't come to this. I was hoping I could work things out a little better, so we wouldn't have to have this discussion, ever."

"So, I gather." He folded his arms, his towering silhouette nearly dwarfing the withering figure of the older man. "Just how long you been on the take for Crispen Jansen?"

"Come on, Nick. I'm not on the take. It wasn't like that."

"We'll see." He gave a hard nod. "Who approached who?"

Alf tightened his jaw a little. "All right. Let's talk about the deal."

"This isn't about any stinking deal with Jansen! It's about Cate's life!" He lunged forward, slamming both palms against the tabletop, rattling the glasses that sat sweating onto the sandstone coasters. "I know you've been making some kind of separate deal from the one you kept trying to peddle to me. I want to know why you told Jansen that you could talk me around."

"You wouldn't talk about it, Nick! You wouldn't even listen when I-"

"Well, I wanna talk about it now!" Nick thrust the chair in front of him to the side, sending it clattering across the tile, and he leaned over the edge of the table, toward him. "You wanted my attention on this deal, you got it now! I am all ears, Alf!"

Alf shrunk back, salty droplets drizzling down the sides of his hot face. He licked his lips a few times, finally, shaking his head. "Nick, I swear to you, nobody ever said a word about Cate, in the beginning. It was never supposed to be like this."

"Well, it is, Alf! That's exactly the way it is!" He shouted, shooting an accusatory finger at him. "It is, and *you* brought this to my door, into my home! So, you better tell me every single utterance that has ever passed between you and Crispen Jansen, or I give you my word, losing whatever deal you made with him will be the very least of your worries! I swear to you, if anything happens to Cate because of this, I will do time for you. I won't care if I ever see the light of day again."

"All right, Nick, all right." He nodded, hands lightly trembling as he pulled a handkerchief from his trouser pocket to mop his forehead. "Crispen approached me with this deal months ago. You know that. I knew you wouldn't want to deal with him if you knew his reputation. Sal's right. You're a good boy, Nicky."

"Don't patronize me, Alf. The time for any connection of la famiglia is well-past." He dragged the chair back from where it had tumbled and lowered into it, opposite him, an ominous furrow between his brows. "Go on."

"Crispen knew that I had your ear, knew you trusted me. He also knew I wouldn't agree to take you the deal, not on its own. So, he found other ways to… persuade me." He blew out a long breath, an attempt to keep his breaths from a steady pant. "First off, he tried offering me a cut. Ten percent of his return, if I could get you to sign."

"I see. So, just like that," Nick pressed his lips thinly together and he lifted a hand, snapping his fingers as he nearly vibrated with anger, "after all these years, after all those years with my father, my grandfather, with me, you just turned on the family for a few lousy bucks?"

"No, Nick." He wagged his head from side to side. "No. He forced my hand!"

"Forced your hand. You?" Nicky scoffed a laugh, then gnawed his lower lip as he shook his head in disgust. "How much money have you made working for the Caprianno Corporation over the years, Alf? Huh?"

"A lot, Nick."

"A lot, yeah." He nodded, shrugging. "So, what? It wasn't enough for you to make that money? It wasn't enough to hold my family's trust, to be *part of* the family? You could just so easily throw it away, to involve us with someone like that?"

"No, Nick, no." Alf's eyes pressed closed for a second or two and he shook his head. "I'm trying to tell you, he didn't leave me no choice!"

"Well, was it worth it, this offer that was too irresistible to pass up?" His fist crashed against the tabletop again as he bared his teeth, earning him the swift flash of Alf's eyes. "Was it worth putting my family in jeopardy for change from Crispen Jansen's lousy pockets?"

"It wasn't like that!" Alf barked back, his own brows diving deeply downward.

"No? Because it sounds, to me, like you got greedy, Alf!" Nick thundered in return, jerking himself back up from his chair. Gritting his teeth harder, his face tinged a shade of magenta. "After all this time, after all the trust I put in you, you decided to sell me, my family, to Jansen!"

"He knows things, Nick, things I thought were dead and buried forever!" Alf roared, tugging at the tight strangle of his shirt collar. "Scotty's dealings with Sal are how Crispen knew so much about me, things about Tony, Louis, your father."

"You're probably talking thirty, forty years ago! Anything you did would have been covered by a statute of limitations. They would've run up years ago!"

"Some of it, sure. Some of things… no amount of time would make a difference."

Nick swallowed hard, his head falling back as he considered Alf's words. His gaze slowly moved back to where Alf waited silently. "Those things from the past, that no amount of time… Can any of them be tied to Pop?"

"No." Alf shook his head earnestly, not that he had much credibility, at the moment. "Far as I know, Sal wasn't into any of that side of things, nothing quite so… permanent as I was."

Nick raked his hands through his thick black hair, comprehending the unspoken confession. Though no one had ever come right out and bluntly admitted it, rumors of some of his grandfather's business dealings appeared to be far-reaching, even into the present. He exhaled a slow breath and flicked a look back to Alf again.

"Frankie?"

"Nah. Frankie's clean. Always has been. Sal brought him in for protection when you were born, nothing more. Tony and Louis are less squeaky, but nothing too raw, nothing… unredeemable. Me… Some of what Jansen knows could put me away for the rest of my life, or at the very least, he could expose what he knows to people that could still be dangerous to me."

"We talking murder, drugs, what?"

"The less you know about any of that the better, Nick. Sal and I agreed on that, years ago." Alf adjusted himself uncomfortably in his seat when Nick cocked a dangerous glare at him. "Jansen said that if I could get you on board, that he would not only keep what he knew to himself, he'd make it worth my while."

"I see." Nick's head bobbed deeply as he scrubbed his hands over his face, muffling a foul utterance as it left his lips. "So, I guess it's not unpardonable because it wasn't just a straight-up sell-out? Right? It was just a trade, us for you, and you made a little money, while you were at it."

"I didn't want his money… *your* money, Nicky." He shook his head, his face hard, stern. "It was dirty, made me feel dirty just to think about it. I just wanted us to all be safe. I wanted to keep him from exposing things that could give the Capriannos a black eye."

"So, because you wanted protection from what you did, however long ago it was, you offered up your friends… your *family*, and that was for *our* sake?" An incredulous laugh shook in his chest, his expression pinching firmly. "You know, I've always felt like you were like a wise old uncle who was looking out for me, Alf."

"I felt the same, Nicky." He cleared his throat when Nick's eyes hardened on him again, the younger man's nostrils flaring wide, his mouth drawn tightly down. "I wish things could've been different."

"Yet, you didn't even come to me, didn't trust me with this. Why? Why didn't you even try? How many times did I ask what it was about this deal with Jansen? Huh?" Nick extended an open palm out to him when he started to interrupt, shaking his head as he went on. "You were willing to sell me out, to throw my innocent wife to him, as collateral! Nah. Nah."

"I told you, I didn't find out about that until later, Nick. I swear. I swear!"

"You swear. *You* do." Nick's lips formed a thin line, his jaw off-set at an unrelenting angle. He shook his head, his eyes deadly cold on Alf's. "So, what's your word to me, now, after this?"

"Nick…" Alf watched him warily, waiting for him to continue. "What are you gonna do?"

Nick rubbed his hand back and forth over his mouth, taking his time. "First, I'm gonna talk to Jansen, for myself, and see if I can work something out to suit us both."

Alf opened his mouth, hesitating before speaking again. "If you can't?"

"I'm gonna talk to my father and see what kind of ties, if any, we really already have with this guy. But when it comes down to it…" Nick chest rose and fell sharply as he considered. "I'll do what I have to do to protect my family, even if that means you spend the rest of your life behind some very high walls. Even if it means I do, too."

"Hey, Nicky!" Tony tapped on the kitchen door. "Hey, Nick! You still wanna talk to the kid, Mikey, before he goes home?"

Hurt and betrayed, Nick glared at Alf as he fumed. He stood there, staring back at him, their eyes locked in silent understanding over the sincerity of what Nick had declared. Loyalty was one thing you didn't break in a family like theirs. Finally, Nick turned, walking to the door to talk to Tony. Unwilling to trust Alf with any more information, he went out into the hallway and closed the door behind him.

"That kid doesn't want to see *me*, right now, Tony. You send him home, because the way I'm feeling tonight, he wouldn't be protecting anything but Marie's dog from here out. I'll talk to him some other time. Find something else for him to do with the business, but he is never to be trusted with Cate again. Yeah?"

"Yeah, Nick. Whatever you say." Tony nodded, a little shaken by the dangerous glint he'd never witnessed in Nick's eye before. "We'll find something else for him."

Nick slowly let out a controlled breath and started back into the kitchen. "All right, Alf. Here's what we're gonna do for…"

The cold air smacked him in the face as soon as the door was opened, blowing through the access that led into the back yard. He stared at the vacated chair at the table and squeezed his eyes tightly shut. Stupid. If he'd been thinking clearly, he would've known better than to leave Alf alone. He turned again, going back into the hallway.

"Frankie!"

"What's up, Nicky?" Frankies feet skidded to a stop in front of the kitchen door. His expression rumpled, realizing what must have happened. "You want I should go after him?"

"No." Nick shook his head. "Alf's the source of our problem, but he isn't the problem. He's been stupid, careless, but he doesn't want to hurt anybody. He just wants to get away. Anyway, who knows where he is now? I'll try and call him in the morning, when he's had a chance to calm down."

"All right, Nick." He cocked his head to one side. "You want Tony and me to stay inside the house, tonight?"

"Yeah. I think houseguests would be a good idea, for now. Call that security company we used for that thing in Chicago last month. I want more guys around. Nobody we've never used before." He nodded, dragging his fingers roughly through his hair. "Not so many guys to worry Cate, though. I want the alarms on every door and window checked out, too. Our company. Our people. Nobody new comes into this house. You understand?"

"I gotcha. I guess you aren't gonna tell her about all this?" He lifted his palms between them when Nick's eyes flashed onto his. "It's up to you, Nicky. I think she's tough enough cookie to handle it. I just want to know how much to say."

"I don't know yet just how sticky things have gotten with Jansen. If Alf has gotten us into anything illegal, I don't want her to have any part of it. Aside from that, I don't want to scare her if I can take care of it on my own before it spins too far out of control."

"Okay, Nicky." He nodded. "Whatever you say."

"Thanks, Frankie." Nick nodded, finally easing in a few shallow breaths. "Where is she now? Still in there?"

"Yeah, sure. She went up and changed for bed a while ago, but she came back down to wait for you. She ain't come out since."

Nick clapped a hand over Frankie's shoulder a couple of times, then walked out of the room. "Thanks. Do me a favor. Call Pop and let him know we'll talk tomorrow."

He trudged down the hall, pressing lightly against one of the mahogany doors. An old black and white Christmas movie was playing on the screen and he shifted his eyes around the room in search of her. A calmed sensation settled into his chest when he saw her peacefully asleep on the couch.

He moved slowly toward her, his gaze running over her. The remote was only loosely resting in her palm. She looked serene and restful, reposing across the cushions in the emerald green satin nightgown he'd bought her in New York, a fluffy blanket covering the lower half of her. He outstretched a hand, allowing the back of his index finger to glide down the side of her face.

"Hey. Let's go on up to bed." A soft grin came to his lips when she only breathed in a deeper breath and adjusted herself against a chenille throw pillow. "All right, Sleeping Beauty. Your way, it is."

He slipped the remote from her hand, placing it quietly on the coffee table. Gently, he pulled the blanket back and bent forward, cradling his arms under her. Adjusting her in his grip, he began to walk toward the hall. It was on the second step of the staircase that she nuzzled her head against him, groggily brushing her lips against his warm neck.

"What took you so long, Nicky?" Her voice was barely a whisper, her eyes remaining closed. "I was starting to worry."

"Shh. I know. I'm sorry. I'll make it up to you." He pressed a kiss to the top of her head. "Go back to sleep, baby."

"Mmm. Only if you promise to join me." She yawned, nuzzling him again. "How was your meeting?"

"It was… informative. I don't want to talk about it." He pushed their bedroom door open with the toe of his shoe, then crossed over to the mattress. "I just want to go to bed and hold you close."

She giggled softly, yawning against her pillow when he gently placed her there. "You always want to hold me close."

"I always will, too." He pulled the covers up, bending to press a kiss to the side of her face.

She watched him kick out of his shoes, then tug his shirt off. Her brows dipped inward, carefully measuring the difference from his normally straight and confident posture, realizing that he'd not only locked the bedroom door, but that he'd also made a point to doublecheck the window and balcony doors.

She propped herself onto one elbow, twisting a questioning brow in the direction of the bathroom. "Nicky, is everything all right?"

"All right?" His hands pressed firmly again the white marble vanity and he held his breath for a second. After glaring back at the worried reflection in the mirror, he squinted his eyes closed as he called to her. "Sure, why?"

"You just seemed so upset earlier. I thought you were going to eat poor Mikey alive. Then, I waited and you never came in. Now, you just seem… I don't know, not yourself."

"Not myself?" Coming back into the room in his pajama bottoms, he worked at conjuring up a believable smile for her. "What's that mean?"

Walking back over to the bed, he lowered onto his side of the mattress when she pulled herself up to sitting fully. Undoing the clasp on his watch, he opened the drawer of his nightstand to place it inside, using that as an excuse so that he could check that his gun was where it ought to be.

Lowering back onto her pillow, she tilted her head at him when he glanced back over his shoulder. "Nicky?"

"It's nothing to worry you with. Hiccup with a business deal. Nothing I can't handle."

When he slid under the covers and leaned over her, she combed her fingers through his hair, resting her hand between his neck and one of his broad shoulders. There was more. It was more than business, more than he wanted to let on. No matter how he tried, she could see the truth behind his eyes, anxiety, and maybe even a shadow sadness. It wasn't like him to be secretive with her. The fact that he was hiding something from her was unsettling.

"Nicky, if something hurts you, it hurts me, too." She pressed her lips softly together, letting her fingers slide down the arm that supported him. "If I can do anything to help you-"

"It's nothing." He lowered himself to stop her words with a kiss. "You really wanna help me, Cate?"

"Of course, I do." Her eyes met his and she cupped the side of his face in her the palm of her hand. "I love you."

"Then, just let me hold you tonight." He twisted his back, reaching to snap off the light. He slid down next to her, pulling her against him. "Just let me feel you safe in my arms where you belong."

"Safe?" She felt herself smile softly. "I'm always safe with you, Nicky. Why would you-"

His lips crushed against hers as his arms clasped firmly around her. "No more questions tonight."

She nodded, though her eyes moved back and forth on his in the dim glow from the bathroom's nightlight. She wished that there was enough light for her to make a deeper study of them for some sort of explanation of his behavior. As it was, all she could do was to tuck herself closely into his arms as he'd asked. She couldn't help but wonder about the noticeably quicker thud of his heartbeat against her chest, and of the tension in his embrace.

Chapter Twenty-Two

Cate was still asleep when Nick silently crawled out of bed. He didn't want to wake her. He hadn't slept more than a few broken hours all night. Afraid to disturb her with his twisting and turning, he finally sneaked out of their room and went downstairs. He'd been trying, for the last hour, to get a hold of Crispen Jansen, and had finally succeeded. It wasn't going as well as he'd hoped.

"You seem to be under the misapprehension that I owe you something in all of this. You seem to think you're entitled to a partnership, and you seem to be under the misconception that you have something pretty substantial on me. Whatever it is, it isn't going to stick. My record's clean."

"Oh, you owe me all right." Jansen nodded. "The whole Caprianno family owes the Jansens. Your slate isn't quite so clean as you'd like to delude yourself into believing."

"Oh, yeah?" Nick nodded, pacing back and forth in front of the fireplace. "Enlighten me. What exactly have I done?"

"My old man was doing all right, until yours decided to pull up stakes. He took his percentages and all of his assets with him when he went. Others followed his lead. And, why? Because he wanted his business to be a hundred percent legitimate for his precious son… for you. Never mind all of his partners, his friends that he had to throw under the bus to do it! My father died a sad, frustrated man, barely a dime to our family name."

"Sounds like your father was in the wrong business." Nick firmed his jaw as he thought it all over.

"My father wouldn't have ruined a man who'd been good to him. He would've left him with a healthy enough bottom line for his family to survive."

"I guess that just depends on what the Capriannos decided was healthy enough for the rest of us. Certainly not to survive the way that you have, oh no." Jansen nearly trembled with rage at the dismissiveness of Nick's reply. "Maybe you don't think it's your family's problem. Maybe you Capriannos don't think the rest of us deserve anything from you, but I promise you, I'm making it your problem to solve. You either come into this venture, or…"

"Or what?" Nick's feet paused on the rug as he waited for Jansen's answer. "Go on. Can't you say it for yourself, or do you have to have one of your pathetic thugs do it for you?"

"You just come across, and hope you never find out." A mean grin stretched over Crispen's mouth. "There are all sorts of ways to ruin a man, Nicky boy. You remember that. They don't all have to with business."

Nick caught a slip of a glance at her as Cate passed by the door to the hallway, thinking again about the man in the alley had said, thinking what Alf had said. "You want the money for your venture, I'm willing to meet that. Two million dollars, outright, no strings attached. You won't owe me anything. That ought to bring a little more heft to your bottom line, give you more appeal. But that's it. The money is where our connection ends."

"Two million is a good start, Nick. Of course, I'm gonna need another million to make sure things run smoothly after the start-up costs take their toll. It is a brand-new venture."

"All right." Nick could hear her humming not too far away and he lowered his voice. "Three, but that's an end to it."

"No, no. You still don't get that you aren't calling the shots on this deal. The time for negotiations is long over." He shook his head. "This isn't a negotiation, Nicky boy. I'm gonna need something else besides money."

"What do you want?" Nick watched for her, keeping his voice at a low volume.

"We're just two little words from finishing this arrangement." Crispen grinned, feeling as though he held his prize firmly over a barrel. "Nicholas Caprianno, printed nice and neat, right on the dotted line."

"No." Nick shook his head. "There won't be anything linking us on paper. That's not the way this is going to work."

"Your signature, your public support and friendship, or… You know, your wife goes out a lot. Pretty headstrong, too, I hear. It can be a dangerous world out there. You never know what could happen."

Nick leaned forward, gritting his teeth at the receiving end of the phone. "Listen, you-"

"But with more friends, more protection for her, she might just stay a whole lot safer. I'd hate to think of what losing such a woman could do to a man like you. I'd hate for anyone to know the kind of pain my father felt when he lost everything dear to him. I wonder just how much a man's wife is worth to him, in the end, a man like you."

Knowing she was just outside, Nick managed to maintain the low tone of his voice, though it had taken on a deep, rasping quality. "If you, or any of your creeps, so much as breathe in my wife's direction-"

"Be in touch in the next day two, Nick. Hope you've given my offer its just consideration, by then. Alf knows how to get a hold of me at any time."

Hearing the line disconnection, Nick looked down at the phone, tapping the end of it against his tense jaw as he quickly sorted through it all. His eyes shifted toward the foyer, hearing Cate's footsteps coming nearer again. He dragged a hand roughly over his mouth, knowing he had to say something to her, what he wasn't sure, but something to stop her from leaving until he figured out what to do. She bounded into the room, a pleasant expression on her face and a quiet song on her lips. He hated to ruin things.

"Ah, what are you looking for?" He placed the phone gently on the sofa table behind him, continuing to follow her around the room with his eyes.

"I wanted my red velvet flats for today. I'm not sure where I left them the other night. I thought I might have kicked them under the couch in here when we were watching that movie together, or rather, not watching it." She giggled. "I think I lost an earring in the cushions, too."

Laughing softly again, she recalled the way the movie had been discarded from their attention. Thinking of it again made her heart skip up a beat, or two. She paused in front of him, leaning over the edge of the couch to press a kiss to the awkward smile on his lips.

"What are you doing just sitting in here? The TV isn't even on."

"I had a call to take."

"I hope it wasn't anything to do with that business that had you so upset yesterday. You were in knots."

He cleared his throat, watching her as she moved on. "You planning on going somewhere?"

"Shayne texted me. Someone called in sick this morning, so I'm going to have to get down there early and cover. The rub of being a partner in a restaurant, I guess. Have to cover any gaps. What are you still doing here, by the way? I can't believe you haven't left yet. Did you decide to work from home?"

"Ah, yeah." He rubbed the back of his neck.

"Well, now I really do wish I could stay." Grinning, she continued to peek under and around things. Noting the discomfort that lingered in his expression when she glanced up again, she straightened her spine, dropping her hands onto her hips. "Nicky, what is the matter?"

"I didn't really sleep great last night. But, hey, you should stay with me." He caught her hand, pulling her onto his knee, and pressed his lips to hers. "We could be lazy, drag out that mistletoe we talked about, and stay in bed all day."

"That sounds wonderful." She laughed, shaking her head as she slipped from his arms and continued on her way. "But that is what yesterday was supposed to be for."

"No, no, I know." When she turned, he adjusted his shoulders back against the tension that was gathering there, doing his best to keep his demeanor light in its firmness. "I really think you should stay home with me today, though."

"If you're trying to make up for working yesterday, I appreciate the gesture, but you don't have to." She rolled her eyes, giving him a laugh, and waved him off. "It won't do you any good either. I'm afraid you missed your shot until this weekend, buster. I can't just blow-off my responsibilities to stay here and play with you, much as I might want to."

"Come on, Cate." He groaned. "It's not like you even have to work."

She lifted a hand to sweep a lock of hair that had fallen next to her face. Staring back at him, she aimed an indignant expression. "It's not playtime, Nicky. I have a commitment there, a commitment you said you supported."

"I do, if that's what you want, it's just…" He shrugged. "Not today."

"And yet today is the day I need to be there."

"Shayne can cover." He folded his arms when she looked back at him again, her brows drawn inward in response to his surprisingly firm tone. "It won't kill him to have to do it, instead of you. I'll call him, if you want, but… you just need to do this, this time."

"No, I don't just need to." She took a few steps closer to him, bewildered by his demanding statement and by the abrupt shift in him. "What I need to do, is to go in to work. Shayne closed last night, so it's not fair for him to cover this morning. Besides, just splitting this extra shift with him is already going to make both of our days longer."

"Cate, you're not listening." He hauled himself up from the couch cushion, walking toward her, giving her a face sterner and more forbidding than he knew he'd ever given her. "Shayne's going to have to figure something else out."

"Shayne already figured something out, and I already agreed to it. It's pretty much all on our shoulders since Mom and Dad retired. That means sharing the load. You know that." She screwed her face into a full scowl, folding her arms to mirror his stubborn stance. "I'm not one of your guys. I'm not an employee, of any sort. I am your wife. You can't just *order* me to-"

"As your husband, and the head of the family, I have certain responsibilities, too." He countered, his voice growing firmer. "I didn't want to play that card, but this time, I will, if I have to."

"I thought you said you and I were equal partners in this marriage." She shook her head, cocking a questioning look at him. "So, I guess this means we're partners only when it suits-"

"Cate!" He thrust a demanding finger in her direction, walking past her with the lines between his brows forming an even darker expression than before. "I don't care if it makes you mad… I do, but this time, you're just going to have to be mad. We are equal partners, but this time, this *one* time, you need to do what I ask."

"You mean what you command. If you're going to say it, say it all. I don't know what happened in that meeting yesterday, but it doesn't give you the right to lay down the law and expect me to just cow down." Finally finding her shoes, she stepped into them. "I don't know what brought all this on, but we can talk about it when I get back."

"We'll talk about it now, because you're staying here!" His voice began to grow louder.

"No, I'm not!" Releasing a sharp breath, she moved nearer to him again, her eyes shifting over at the cell phone on the table. "Nicky, what was that call? If it's going to have this much bearing on our relationship, I think I deserve to know what's going on. Is the business in trouble? Is that it?"

"I'm trying to keep there from being trouble! I just need you here. Why is that so hard to understand?" He scrubbed his palms over his face and turned to look at her when he felt her hand curl over one of his shoulders. "I'm not discussing that call, Cate. Trust me, it's better that you don't know."

"So much for telling me that your business, any of it, was an open book to me, that you had nothing to hide from me! Nicky, I swear, if you are thinking of dipping your toes into anything illegal…"

Her fingers slipped free of him and she took a step away, her eyes flashing back and forth on his, at the uncharacteristic severity she'd never seen in them before. Feeling her own stubbornness ramping up in response to it, she tightened her jaw and moved further back from him.

"Fine. Keep it to yourself. Keep it *all* to yourself!" Her voice rose to match her own temper. "But if you won't talk to me, then I don't see any reason for me to be here."

"I have my reasons for wanting you here, whether we discuss my business, or not. Usually, yes, my business is open for discussion with you, but not this time." He began to pace back and forth. "Everyone is entitled to keep certain things private."

"You mean secret!" She shouted back. "Don't sugarcoat it!"

He held his tongue tightly between his front teeth and huffed a breath. "I am not getting into it, right now."

"Well, then, I guess we're at an impasse!" She shook her head and started toward the door. "You can demand until you're blue in the face, when you ask like this. You can just keep that bad-tempered mood of-"

"Fine!" He shouted slamming a fist down on the wet bar and making the glasses rattle. Fearful that he couldn't stop her, anger colored his complexion a darker hue. "You're right. I am *not* asking you, Cate!"

His words had been so loud and so forcefully delivered that it made him regret the startled expression on her face when she'd whirled back around. Still, it couldn't be helped. Using the seconds that had rendered her silent with shock, he worked at reducing the fierce heaving of his chest, measuring in and easing out a few slower breaths.

He cautiously moved toward her, his footsteps stopping when she shuffled back from him. She attempted to blink away the glossy sting in her eyes. He swore under his breath through the tight compression of his teeth. Scaring her had been the last thing he'd wanted to do.

"I want you here, Cate." He let out another breath, harnessing the volume of his voice as he spoke to her again. "You need to understand that I have my reasons. That, for now, is all you need to know."

Feeling more hurt by him than she thought she could ever have been, she swallowed away the tightness in her throat and lifted her purse from a side table. Shooting him a defiant stare, she tightened her jaw and angled her chin upward. Whether or not he witnessed the tear that slipped down the contour of her face, she didn't care. She knew he'd seen the willful decision behind her eyes. That was enough.

"Cate, don't do it! Don't-" Ugh! He slammed his hand against the wall with a shout when she turned and stalked out of the room. Planting his fists against the waistband of his jeans, he looked down at the floor and swore ripely. Hearing the front door slam, his head snapped back up with a huff. "Cate!"

Frankie filled the frame of the open door just as Nick started toward the hallway and he held up a calming hand. "You want I should follow her?"

Nick stopped, remaining where he was, recognizing that he was far too angry to follow her himself. His teeth clamped down tightly, and he flicked a look out the window. Turning back toward Frankie, he gave him a deep nod.

"You got it, boss." Frankie turned abruptly and set off on his way.

"And you stay with her until she gets back home, no matter what she says! And take Tony with you!" Nick shouted after him.

Pacing by the window, watching the two cars pull away, he snatched his phone from where he'd left it. Forcing his fingers to dial quickly, he called the only person he knew he could trust for advice and information, the only one who truly knew everything he needed to know.

"Hey, Pop. Yeah, I know you wanted me to call last night, but listen… We need to talk."

Chapter Twenty-Three

Sal drove up to the front of the house at a little after eleven. He pulled a plastic storage container from the passenger's seat and locked the car behind him. He'd barely reached his key to the deadbolt of the front door when it was abruptly pulled open before him. Nick must've been watching for him.

Sal's eyes ran up and down the length of his son, the sight of him tugging the inner corners of his brows down. Nick had a truly haggard appearance about him. His eyes showed signs of sleeplessness, dark shadows beneath them. His hair had been roughly dragged through so many times that he appeared almost unkempt. And for the early hour, Sal made note of the bar glass Nick held in his hand.

"Pop." He stepped aside. "Come in."

"I nearly rang the bell, Nick." Sal laughed to himself, attempting to bring a smile to his son's face. It didn't work. "With newlyweds, sometimes it's better to knock first, huh?"

"Cate's at MacCarthaigh's. It's just me and Louis here. Let's go in the living room." Nick led the way, appearing to have ignored the jovial comment that had been offered.

"Mama sent some cookies." Sal placed the container on the foyer table and followed after him. "I'll leave them there."

Nick turned to look over his shoulder at him when they'd reached the wet bar. "You want something?"

"Sure. Whatever you're having." He reached a hand to take the glass he was offered. His gaze remained on his son's controlled anxiety as the two men chose opposite chairs. "All right, so, I'm here. What happened, Nicky? Something with Crispen Jansen that you didn't want to talk about on the phone."

"I thought, when I took over, you told me everything I needed to know about the business. The good, and the bad." Nick stared intently back at his father, his elbows on his knees as his feet bounced with a nervous energy beneath him. "You gotta tell me the truth, now, Pop. No ugliness barred. Is there anything to what Crispen says? Did we ruin Scott Jansen?"

Salvador sat quietly staring back at him for a moment, clinking ice against the side of the glass as he swirled the amber contents with a flick of his wrist. He carefully considered the question. Finally, beginning to understand the situation, he placed his drink on the end table next to him. He remained, for another short measure of time, selecting his words with deliberate care. His glance flicked back up at Nick, and he sighed.

Distrust. Fear. Uncertainty. That was what appeared to be eating so viciously at his son. He recalled the agitated tone of Nick's voice when he'd phoned, the way he'd used the old code the night before. He wouldn't have used it unless there was something really wrong. As on-edge as he appeared to be, Sal knew he was going to have to work the details out for him.

"You aren't a boy anymore, Nicky. When you took over the business, I told you everything you needed to know about it, at that time." He paused, considering the choices he'd made back then, wondering now if some part of it might have been a mistake. "I told you everything that you could know that wouldn't put you any danger of backlash."

"Backlash? Jansen is making threats against Cate, Pop! I'd say that's a pretty significant backlash, wouldn't you?" Nick shot his brows down, further darkening his scowling expression. "He says we ruined his father. I need to know if that's true."

"You should know better than to even ask that, Nick." Sal shook his head. "What went on between our family and theirs was just business."

"Well, since I appear to have very different business practices than you did, back in the day, you're gonna have to be a little clearer." He nodded firmly. "I remember the day you ended things with Scott Jansen and several others. You told me there would be a time when I would come to understand why you felt the need to guard what was most precious to you. Well, today is that day for me, Pop! Keeping me out of what used to be isn't protecting me anymore, if my wife isn't safe. Don't you see that?"

"I have seen more and have known more than I hope you will ever see or know in your lifetime. Don't think I don't understand what it is to feel this fear of what you love being snatched away from you! I've worked your whole life, your whole life, Nicky, to keep you from what was passed to me!" He shot back, aiming the point of a twisting finger at his son. "Now, what does Jansen want with Cate?"

"What do you think?" Nick threw his arms out to the sides, his voice louder than before. "He's using her to get to me. She's his bargaining chip because of something to do with us, the way things were before!"

"I see."

"And he's absolutely right about that, Pop. Because, if anything happened to her, he would well and truly destroy me! Without Cate… I got nothing. She might as well be the air I breathe." Nick cleared his throat against the brokenness that threatened to overtake his voice. "I knew it from the first moment I saw her."

Sal sat quietly for a moment again, staring back at his son as he contemplated what he would say in reply. "All right, Nicky. I spent years protecting you and your mother and your sister from those business practices, those associates, that were so different from what you know. But now, I can see that it's time to tell you the rest."

Nick settled back into his chair, tightly folding one arm over the other in front of himself. "I'm listening."

"There are things in the past, in my life… my business, that I am not proud to recall. I changed that business so that you and Marie would never have the kinds of memories that I live with." Sal sighed, shaking his head. Good intention didn't always yield good results, even after so many years. "Your grandfather didn't like the idea of his daughter marrying me. He knew the family reputation. Believe me, there was a lot more truth to the reputation in those days than I hope there will ever be again."

Nick furrowed his brows as he tried to recall events of the past from his childhood. Over the years, flashes of hazy memories would crop up, and he would dismiss them as imagination, or as simply a small child's view of something he'd misunderstood. Perhaps they were more accurate than he'd realized.

"In the beginning, he was right about me. I was content just being a cog in the family business. It was just work to me. I didn't know different. It provided well for what I wanted, and I was cocky when I was young. Your mama, heaven love her, was willing to take me, no matter what the terms." Sal lightly smiled, then. "It wasn't until you came along that I started to consider wanting better for my family, but I dragged my feet. When you were only nine, there was retaliation for a business deal gone wrong. When that world began to reach its claws out for you, for Marie, I knew the time had finally come to make a break with it."

"And with Scott Jansen." Nick shifted his eyes off to the side as he worked through what his father had just told him, attempting to discover the connection. "Was he the deal that went sour? He was the one that caused you to want to change things?"

"No, Nicky, no. Scotty was just a small-time operation. He was more a middle man, a front we gave a percentage to. The son's the one that wanted to branch out. I guess he did." Sal lifted his drink again, then rolled the bar glass between his hands, studying his son. "Scotty wasn't a bad guy, but he was part of that world that I wanted to leave behind."

"Then, you're saying we weren't responsible for his business going under? You're sure?" He off-set his jaw and stared back. "Crispen holds us responsible, holds *me* responsible. He claims that if it weren't for you changing things for me, his father would never have ended up the way he did."

"Eh, Crispen was just a snot-nose kid when all that went down, just a grade school punk shaking down younger kids for their lunch money. He knew nothing about what happened. There were no hard feelings when we parted ways with Scotty, or with any of the others. Scotty wasn't much of a businessman, it's true, but we can't take the responsibility for his poor business skill."

"Crispen obviously sees it differently." Nick shrugged.

"Instead of getting out, like I did, others of my associates stayed in. Scotty's son, he didn't have the respect that I instilled in you. He was raised differently, entitled. For all the decent side of Scotty, he was too indulgent with his boy. He was no better than a cheap hood, growing up, and he's no more than that now."

"Unfortunately, I can personally vouch for the latter part of that statement to be true. His arms are a lot more far reaching than I gave him credit for, though." Nick shook his head, lifting the glass in his hand to gulp the last of its contents and then placed it aside. "At least I know I wasn't wrong when I said it wasn't us."

"You weren't wrong. Scotty made too many bad investments, too many sure-things that turned into nothing. His son turned him on to many of them with his greedy, get-rich quick schemes. The last I heard, Scotty did die nearly broke, nearly nothing to show for a lifetime of work. Did we break him, though?" He pressed his lips together, shaking his head thoughtfully. "Nah. We don't own that real estate."

"So, Crispen's just looking for someone to blame, and he's decided that we fit the bill."

A long breath passed through Nick's lips and he dragged his fingers through his hair when his father quietly nodded. His hands dropped weakly to either side of the cushion he sat on. His eyes fixed on his father as he shook his head in desperation.

"What do I do, Pop? He won't negotiate. I even tried to pay him off, more than he originally wanted. He wants the name. He wants the business. He wants someone to pay for what happened to his old man. He wants *me* to pay for it, Alf, you," he paused, rubbing a hand over his mouth and let it drop, "and Cate."

Sal adjusted his arthritic bones in his chair. "What does Alf say? Why isn't he in here? If he's the one that brought you the contact, he should be-"

"Alf's no help, trust me. Ah, Pop, you don't know how wrong we were to keep Alf in for so long. He dug the knife so deep into my back I'm surprised you can't see the blade sticking out this side of my chest." He brushed a hand over his ribs with a sickened laugh. He let his head fall back against the cushion behind him and pressed his eyes closed. "He was in on it with Jansen from the start, and he got in over his head."

"Alf was in on it?" Sal shook his head, his eyes dark under the downward turn of his thick brows. "No. You sure, Nick?"

"Yeah, I'm sure." The fingers of his right hand massaged the throbbing ache at his forehead and then sunk to cover his eyes. "Got it out of him, for myself, last night. I went out to the hall for a minute and when I went back into the kitchen, he was gone. Nobody can find him. Nobody can get a hold of him. Smoke in the wind."

Sal gnawed his lower lip, the wheels of his still-sharp mind turning quickly, going over facts and conversations from the old days, weaknesses he knew about Alf that he still hadn't shared with Nick. "You let me take care of him."

"Pop…" Hearing the tone of his father's voice, Nick lifted his head from the chair back and he arched a brow, his gaze meeting the older man's. "Legal. This all has to be above board. I promised Cate when we got married. Not a toenail over the line of the law."

"Ah, she's a good girl. She's making you a good wife, Nicky." Sal's chest shook lightly. "Cate can breathe easy. I didn't mean I would take care of Alf *that* way. Although, he's lucky it isn't my grandfather's day, or even *your* grandfather's. He and Jansen both are."

"I don't know what to do about Cate. I can't protect her. I can't even keep her home!" He shook his head, lines creasing deeply between his brows, his chest tightening up on him again. "I don't know how much of what to tell her, but I'll have to tell her something. She's so stubborn, she makes me crazy, sometimes!"

Again, Sal's chest vibrated with a deep laugh. "Come on, Nicky. That's one of the things that you love best about her, the fight, the passion. I know."

Nick nodded, though his grave expression never lightened. "Usually, yeah, but this… How do I protect her when she won't let me? I promised her I would keep her safe, but she won't… Ugh! How am I supposed to do that, tell her why, when I'm trying not to scare her?"

"It was easier for me. Mama could fight like a bear, but she never went against me when it came to business. She never asked." Sal's head bobbed from shoulder to shoulder as he weighed the question. "You should tell her, Nicky. She's strong."

"I promised her, though, Pop. I promised her she didn't have anything to worry about when she married me." Nick slowly rocked forward, his chin pressing against the fingers he'd tightly woven together. "Aside from her *letting* me keep her safe, how… How do I even do it? How do I make this right, for everybody?"

"You love your wife, Nicky, I know. I see it. And she loves you. But, love, hate, they all have choices. They all have consequences." He flicked his brows, then. "Life isn't as clean as we like it to be. Maybe it's my fault for not letting you see the messier side of my business. Maybe I shielded you from too much. We all do the wrong thing, sometimes, trying to protect what we love. You won't like to hear this, but it may come to the point that you have to break a promise. It'll be up to you to choose which one."

Nick tightened the muscle along his jaw and he swallowed hard, his thoughts filled with the options before him. Flaring his nostrils slightly, he stared back at his father, his head bobbing. He understood. It wasn't something that anyone else could work out for him, and his father was right. There would be hard choices before it was done. There would be consequences fitting whatever decisions he made. Somehow, he would have to weigh the balance.

Chapter Twenty-Four

It was late when Cate got back to the house, and beginning to sleet. Though she wouldn't have admitted it willingly, she'd been glad when Frankie had offered to drive the slick road for her. They didn't speak much on the way. She was exhausted and her heart was still bruised because of her argument with Nick, for the way he'd bossed and shouted at her. The closer they got to the house, the more her temper kicked back up, and the sorer her feelings became again.

"He ain't gonna be happy it's so late." Frankie commented as they walked up to the front door. "He wasn't expecting you to be gone all day."

She took his arm, though it appeared Nick had already thrown some salt on the pavers leading up to the door. Tony was parking the cars in the garage, so it was just the two of them, alone.

"Nicky's going to have to learn that he can't always have his way just because he has a louder voice. Anyway, I wasn't ready to come home, before now." She sighed, looking away when Frankie cocked a brow at her. "Enough with the face. Us being late isn't going to shock him. I know you checked in several times."

He shrugged. "It's what I do."

"I know." She smiled, laughing softly. She looked back up, shaking her head. "He shouldn't have made the two of you sit around babysitting me all day. I'm sorry if it was boring. It wasn't fair for you and Tony to get caught in the middle of our argument. I don't know what got into him this morning."

"Ah, we were fine. Don't worry about it."

"I've never seen him like that before, Frankie." She tried to stiffen the shudder of her lower lip, but she heard the slight tremble in her voice and knew he probably had, too. "I don't think I'm quite what he was expecting, after all."

"Just a minute, sweetheart."

Frankie glanced around to check for anyone that might overhear what he was about to say, closing the heavy entry door behind them. He kept his voice low. He wasn't betraying a confidence. Nick said he was going to tell her something. He just wasn't sure what. He couldn't let her think that Nick was unhappy with her, though. That would've only hurt them both.

"You know Nicky loves ya, right?" He tapped the underside of her chin softly so that she'd look up at him. "Huh?"

"I, ah… I hope this isn't the speech where you're going to make a bunch of excuses for him." She folded her arms, lowering her eyes between them again as she continued to replay the events of the morning in her mind. "Whatever the reason, he can't shout commands and only mean what he says when it's convenient."

"It ain't that way. Maybe you ain't looking at the big picture." He reached one of his thick-fingered hands to curl around one of her slender ones, sorry for the moisture he could see her fighting away from her eyes. "Sometimes, people don't act the way they normally do when they're scared, do they?"

"Scared?" She gave a soft laugh, shaking her head to the suggestion. "Nicky's not scared of anything. I've never seen anyone less scared of anything, in my life. It sometimes scares *me* how fearless he is. He's got you, and Tony, and that prized popgun he totes around."

"You're right. Nicky's one of the strongest guys I've ever known, and I've known him since he was just a little guy. There's one thing, for a fact, I know he *is* scared of, though. So scared, just the thought drives him about out of his mind." He made sure to hold her gaze steadily as he spoke. "If he ever lost you, he'd crack up into about a million pieces. There wouldn't be enough glue in the world to put him back together, if anything ever happened to you."

"I'm not leaving him, Frankie." She drew her brows in, confused by the intimation. "I'm mad at him, furious, hurt even, but I'm not leaving him. But Nicky hasn't been himself for a couple of days. What am I missing?"

"I think…" He shrugged. "I think you better go talk to him."

She nodded, walking past him, toward the family room. She glanced at him again, curious. There was a flickering blue light under the French doors. She knew that was where Nick must've been. As angry and stubborn as he'd been, it was entirely possible for him to still be waiting in the exact place she'd left him that morning. She only hoped he was more open to discussing whatever Frankie seemed to think was bothering him enough to do battle with her.

"Nick?"

She tapped the back of a knuckle against the door, then pressed it open. It wasn't latched tightly and it swung freely in response to the pressure of her hand. Taking a step into the room, she closed the door behind her. She knew he had to have heard her, but he didn't speak.

The only light was from the flash of the television and the warm crackling fire. In the dim illumination, she observed the continuous ripple of the muscle along his jaw as he sat in one corner of the couch, staring, but not watching the screen in front of him. His spine, which had been relaxed to a slump, curved into a stiff arc as he leaned to snatch his bar glass from the coffee table.

"Nicky," she let her thigh rest against the arm of the couch as she looked at him, "we need to talk about this morning. I think it would do us both good to clear the air."

"Now's not a good time, Cate." He made a slight glance at her as he stood and walked past her for the bottle of whiskey he'd left on the mantle. "Maybe you should've come home sooner."

"I needed the time to think." She swallowed hard, hearing the cold decisiveness in his voice. Letting her eyes scan over him as he filled his glass again, she nodded. "Are you saying you've had too much to drink to discuss it?"

"I'm not drunk, if that's what you're implying." His voice was low, controlled carefully to keep from barking his reply back at her, and he shook his head. "I've only had a couple, all today. I just wanted something to calm my nerves before bed."

"Good." She steeled her own nerves, lowering onto the arm of a chair that was nearest to where he stood. "Then, so far as I can see, it's as good a time as any to hash it out."

He lifted the glass to his lips, his left hand resting firmly on the edge of the mantle. He focused his eyes on the flame in the box, and shook his head again before taking a sip. "I told you, it's not a good time."

"Well," she slapped her palms against the tops of her legs with sharp exhalation, rubbing her hands up and down the denim, "I guess as long as you've decreed it to be so, that's all there is to it, then. I mean, that's the way this new arrangement-"

Boiling over with the anger and worry he'd been struggling to keep from blasting at her, he hurled his glass into the firebox, shattering it against the bricks. Pivoting sharply, he made quick strides over to her, pulling her up to standing. His pupils dilated, darkening aside from the flicker of reflected light, and they bored lividly into hers.

"You want to know why I was so demanding, Cate, why I thought I knew better than you did, this morning? It was because I did! Do you think I really relished keeping a secret, *any* secret, from the most important person in my life? Did you think I enjoyed fighting and yelling, demanding that this *one* time, you did as I said?"

"Stop it!" She cried, tears spilling freely down her cheeks as he shouted. "Nicky, you're scaring me!"

Getting a hold of himself again, he loosened his grip on her, letting his hands fall to his sides. Seeing the fright that reflected back at him, he dropped weakly to his knees in front of her. She could feel the wild pounding of his heartbeat where his chest rested against her legs. Looking down into his eyes, seeing them desperate with a level of fear she never expected to view in them, she brought both of her hands to lightly frame his face.

"Oh, Nicky, what's happened to you?"

"Nick!" Frankie called from the other side of the door. "Everything okay in there?"

Nick breathed heavily, needing a second or two to compose himself before he could call back. "We're fine, Frankie."

"Nicky, you have to tell me. You're not putting me off, this time." Her voice was no longer filled with the distress that had gripped her only seconds before. Now, seeing the distraught anxiety that had engulfed him, almost broken him, she wanted only to make things better. "Seeing what this is doing to you hurts me more than any shouting match ever could."

He gave a weak laugh. Letting his face slip from the soft touch of her fingertips, he dropped his back pockets onto the soles of his feet beneath him. Giving a light sniff against the emotion that was trying to free itself from him, he cleared his throat, looking off to the side. Where did he even begin?

"It might not seem like it, but I'm sorry I scared you. I wouldn't have hurt you. I swear, I'd break my own arm before I ever raised a hand to you."

"That's not what I was afraid of. I know you'd never hurt me, Nicky."

"Good." He let his head bob softly, drawing another deep breath as he looked back at the compassionate expression she held on him. "Something went wrong. Something went really wrong, and… I don't know how to fix it, Cate."

"Is it the business? Money? I told you, none of that matters to me. Whatever it is, we'll find a way to work through it together."

She dropped down in front of him, slipping her hands into his, feeling the way he gripped them tightly. It was almost as if he was afraid something would tear her away from him if he didn't. She managed to catch his gaze again, holding it steadily.

"I don't deserve you." His eyes closed and he felt himself lean into the hand she pulled free of his to place against his cheek. "I also don't know what I'd do without you. I don't."

"You're not without me. I'm not going anywhere, no matter how loud you shout." She insisted, locking her eyes onto his again when he opened them. "Please don't shut me out of something that's shaken you like this. As long as you love me, I am strong enough for anything. I promise."

"I'm not sure I'm strong enough to tell you." Nodding softly, he took a second to settle himself before he began. He pressed his lips firmly together, furious with himself for letting anything dangerous come even close to touching her. "Do you remember a deal we discussed when we first met?"

"The one Alf kept trying to push at you, sure." Her brows drew in. "I don't understand. I thought you decided against it. Last I heard you mention it, you turned it down.”

"Yeah," he nodded, "that's the one. You told me to go with my gut, to trust my instincts. You said, no matter what Alf told me, I should just let the deal go if I felt that gnawing in my gut."

"And you did." She insisted, letting her eyes flick back and forth on his as she did her best to understand. "How could a dead deal cause problems now? We talked about that ages ago, before we were even together."

"Yeah, only I didn't kill it then, when I knew I should've. I hesitated. I let it draw out, let Alf play their game." He swallowed hard. "I knew something wasn't right with him, but I didn't press him about it. You were right about me putting too much faith in him. I never thought he could screw things up so badly."

An apprehensive prickling sensation crawled over her skin. She'd never heard Nick so much as allude to anything against Alf. "What's he done?"

"I found out that he made a side-deal with a guy named Crispen Jansen, not a great guy. That was why he was pushing to get the deal through. That, and to save his own skin, because Jansen knows things about Alf that could get him in deep."

"I knew there was something. I knew it! Where is he?" She started to get up, livid for the anguish Alf's betrayal was causing her husband, but Nick caught her hand. "After everything you've done for him, Nicky! If he thinks he can do this to you and get away with it, he's got another think coming!"

"Come here, baby." He pulled her back down, smoothing a hand over the tempered flush of her cheek. If he hadn't been so overcome with concern, he would've smiled at the fierce rage she was ready to fire off on his behalf. "I don't know where he is. I haven't seen him since last night. He took off. Nobody can get a hold of him."

"But, Nicky, I don't understand. You always said Alf had your back, that he was like family to you." She shook her head. "I don't understand how he could've… It has to be a mistake."

He drew his brows in sharply, screwing his mouth tight. As his eyes shone with emotion, he gave a sickened laugh. "There's no mistake, sweetheart. He told me, himself."

"Well, maybe it's not too late for us to figure something out, some sort of compromise with this other man."

"Nah. Jansen's even more crooked than I thought. When Alf confronted him with some of the stuff Tony and Louis dug up, Jansen told him he'd cut him in a percentage, free and clear. I'd never have to know about it. All he had to do was to get me to sign the deal."

"I don't understand. Why is this man so fixated on you?" She shook her head. "Why couldn't he have just found someone else to invest in his scheme?"

A light smile appeared on his lips and he stretched a hand to brush through her hair. "Two million dollars is a lot to just dig up. With it, he has the potential to get five times the return. Without it, he gets nothing. It wasn't even the money, though. He wants my name attached to it. It'd take too long to explain why, right now, and it wouldn't help to get into it."

"And Alf was just going to let him do that to you?" She sat quietly fuming. "Nicky there has to be a way around this."

"I have been racking my brain, Cate. If there is, I don't see it." He sighed, letting his hand drop lifelessly to his knee. "Anyway, when Alf finally told Jansen he tried but he couldn't get me to sign, first he went after him, then he decided to strike back with the only other threat he thought would make a difference."

"Alf doesn't strike me as the type to be intimidated easily." She dropped down, turning to press her back to his chest as she drew his arms around her. He'd fallen silent again. "Just walk away, Nicky. This man can't force you to sign a deal."

"I can't just walk away. He was only using Alf to get to me." He pulled the fingers of one of her hands to his lips, pressing a light kiss to them, his eyes squinting tightly closed. "He knew that once Alf botched the deal, he had to find a way to coerce me into signing it."

"What leverage could he possibly have over you? It's like you told me, there's nothing dishonest about any of your businesses, that anyone could look through your accounts and see that it's all legal." She shook her head, angling a look up over her shoulder at him. "Do you really think he'd come after you?"

"He'd come after me, and not just with my business." His body went rigid against hers. He knew she could feel it, knew she could see the ripple along his jaw, but there was nothing he could do about it. "He threatened to come after the only thing I can't stand to lose."

"And that one thing, that's why you didn't want me to leave this morning." Beginning to connect the dots, she heard the quicker breaths as they left her lips, a tingle of nerves showering over her as he held her eyes captive with his. Steadying her voice as well as she could manage, she finally pushed through the shock, responding to his statement. "It's me, isn't it, Nicky?"

"Oh, baby, I'm so sorry. This is all my fault." He tilted a regretful expression, seeing the instant flash of nerves she attempted to force down for his sake. His arms squeezed tighter around her and he pressed a firm kiss to the top of her head when she'd looked back down. "I know you were worried about something like this happening when we first got together. I just never thought…”

Hearing his voice weaken, she twisted in his arms, adjusting herself to face him, burrowing her chest against the protection of his. “You told me that you were a commodity. You told me that being attached to you meant I had the potential to be one, too. You gave me the choice, and I chose you. I'd choose you all over again, Nicky.”

“Maybe I shouldn't have let you.” He shook his head, holding her closer still. “I have to go ahead with the deal, Cate. I promised you I'd keep you safe, no matter what. If that means-”

“Nicky, if you agree to the deal, your name, your family name, your reputation, it all becomes tainted. Any children we have! What about them? They'd grow up under the same shadow that your father and your grandfather did, and even you, to an extent! You can't just throw it all away. You can't just do business with people who could, and probably would, drag you into something illegal.”

“I can't take the chance of him doing anything to hurt you, either! You have no idea how close I could've been to losing you yesterday! He sent one of his guys out, following us, just to show me how easy it would've been for him to do it.” He shook his head, pressing his lips thinly together. “I've been going over and over it, ever since. No matter what happens to me, what happens to the business… If it keeps you safe, I don't have any other choice.”

“Yesterday... You mean, the man you had to see about business.” She shook her head, her eyes welling with tears. “Well, you can't do it. What if we just, ah… What if we go to the police, and we tell them-”

“Tell them that my number two guy made a shady deal with some hoods? Tell them that he's tied in with goodness knows what else, and that he's responsible for a threat against you? Expect them to believe that with my family history I knew nothing about any of it, that I'm not mixed up in it?" He shook his head. "With Alf's prior records, he'd spend the rest of his life in prison."

"It's his doing, not yours! Why should you have to pay for it?" She wedged herself even tighter into his arms when he remained firm. "If you won't go to the police, what if you just give him the two million dollars? Paying them is better than the alternative, isn't it?"

"Guys like Crispen and his goons always come back for more." He shook his head. "Anyway, I already thought of that. That was the call I made this morning. They want my name, or…"

"Or, they want me." She couldn't help but tremble a little as she finished his sentence. "So, what *are* we going to do?"

"Aside from signing, I don't know what else there is." He shook his head, dipping his head to press another kiss to the side of her face. "I don't know."

She jostled quickly, flashing him a panicked glance. "My family! Nicky, are they-"

"No." He shook his head. "Jansen made it abundantly clear that he knows you're the key to me. Your family doesn't mean anything to him."

Calming again, she relaxed back into his arms, as relaxed as she possibly could be. "How long do you have to decide?"

"Day or two, maybe. He wasn't specific." Looking earnestly into her eyes, he let his fingertips skim lightly down her throat. "Until I take care of this, you have to promise me that you will stay home. You have to promise me that you won't go out unless you absolutely have to, and that you'll take Frankie and Tony with you if you do."

"I promise. I'll tell Shayne I'm sick, that I caught whatever's going around." She sighed, softening with his touch. "You could've told me."

He nodded. "I wanted to take care of it without scaring you unnecessarily."

"I'm not scared, Nicky." She smiled when he drew his brows inward at her, obviously disbelieving her statement. "All right, I'm less scared when I know what I have to deal with, and I'm a lot less scared when we deal with things together."

He nodded again, lowering a warm kiss to the curve of her neck. "We'll figure it out. I'm not gonna let anything bad happen to you. One way or another, that's a promise I intend to keep."

Chapter Twenty-Five

Morning light, diffused by an overcast sky, had been filtering in for a while. Nick and Cate stayed up a good deal of the night, holding one another, talking things over in low voices. Though it was getting late, Nick knew she needed what rest she could get, so he let her sleep. He hadn't been able to, at all. He'd tugged a pair of jeans on, to ward off any chill, and a plain undershirt. From there, he'd moved to sit in the large window seat across from the bed.

He tucked his bare feet under him and rested his elbows on his knees. Glancing down, he realized he'd gnawed his normally manicured fingernails to jagged nubs. A faint smile edged onto his lips when she made a little noise. Her deep copper hair made a stark contrast against the bright white pillowcase. If he could simply freeze the moment, and do nothing but just watch her sleep, safe and peaceful, he could be perfectly content.

He quirked his brows up, curving his lips admiringly when she adjusted her position. The fair, silken skin of her back became exposed by the slip of the linens that surrounded her. She turned her face toward him, her long lashes slowly drawing open. The soft smile that flirted at the corners of her mouth when she noticed him made his heart swell. The pleasant sensation of the silent, loving exchange between them was swiftly replaced with a cold drop in the pit of his stomach, though, recalling the conclusion he'd come to.

"Nicky." Her voice was groggy and soft. "What are you doing over there?"

Her fingers slipped down to the fallen covers and she drew them up as she rolled onto her side to more fully face him. She stretched an arm out, puffing her lower lip at him. When he only continued to stare at her, she let her hand fall over the side of the mattress with a quiet giggle.

"Come back to me." Her smile returned deeper than before. "It's one good thing about laying low. We can stay here all day, if we want to."

What a lovely thought. His grin stretched wider as he slid off the seat and walked to her. He slipped under the covers when she made room for him. The contented sigh that whispered from her lips, with her head on his shoulder, her chest against his, echoed like sweet delight in his ears.

Being together, feeling the soft press of her kiss against him, the divine sensation of her melting in his arms… If only it could last, this moment with them tucked together, cozy, safe, everything as it should be. If only they could continue to pretend that their life was as free of care as it had been only days before.

"You're brooding." She murmured, her face angling to peer into his eyes. She ran a finger over the crease that had settled between his brows and she laughed. Her smile remained full as she stretched up to nip his lower lip with her teeth. "That somber look isn't the one I was hoping for when I asked you back to bed."

"Sorry." He pressed a kiss to the side of her forehead and smiled weakly.

She shrugged softly, her fingers beginning to pick at the wrinkles on his undershirt. "Do I want to know?"

"No." He shook his head. He was afraid of what her reaction would be when he told her the decision he'd come to during his sleepless night.

"You don't want to say, either." She propped up, her playful expression sobering, though she continued to stroke back and forth across his shirt with her index finger. "It's something you need to tell me, though, isn't it?"

"Yeah." He nodded, hesitant to have the conversation with her that he knew was coming. "I know what we're going to do. At least, I know where we're going to begin."

"I don't know why you wouldn't want to tell me that. I'm all ears, if you've come up with…" She trailed off, shifting a glance across the room to where his vision had become fixed.

At some point during the night, or wee morning hours, he had pulled her suitcases from the closet, filling them with her clothes and other necessary items. They were packed carefully, stacked next to the dressing table, glaring back at her, a painful omen of what was to come.

"Where are yours?" She gritted her teeth against the reply she sensed she was about to receive, her breaths beginning to quicken slightly.

"Cate, I-"

"No, Nicky." She shook her head, pressing a flattened palm between them, and scooted back a bit. "Where are yours?"

A slow exhalation left his chest and he tilted a heartsick glance at her. "I'm not coming with you."

"No. No. I'm not going anywhere without you!" An almost hysterical laugh escaped her as she shook her head and sat up. "Nicky, no!"

"Cate, sweetheart, it's just for a little while. I'm sending Frankie with you. He'll make sure you're all right." He drew himself up, crawling across the bed toward her as she retreated from him. "I have been thinking about it a lot longer than you have, trying to find another way, any other way, but this is the only thing we can-"

"No, Nick!" She shouted it at him, that time, vehemently shaking her head again as she reached for her peacock blue silk robe. She slipped from the bed, wrapping the slick covering around herself, and tied the sash at her waist.

"Cate!" He scrambled to his feet, snatching her by the hand before she could take off. "Come here."

"No! Nicky, stop! Let go!" She tugged and pulled, attempting to free herself when he'd hugged his arms around her. Withering in his hold, she began to sob. She stamped her foot, turning to look at him. "I won't go!"

"You have to!" He tugged his brows down, his face reflecting the anguish he saw in her expression. "Don't you see? It's the only way I can keep you safe while I sort this whole mess out."

"No! You are not sending me away! I won't..." Her fists beat against his shoulders when he wouldn't release her, her voice becoming strangled with tears, and she collapsed against his chest, sobbing. "Please, don't make me do this. You promised! You promised you'd keep me safe! I'm safe here."

"You're not, Cate!"

"I am!" Her fingers clawed at his shirt, wadding the cotton tightly. "I trust you. I'm safe with you! I am!"

Feeling his ribs crushing in on him in despair, his chin came to rest on the top of her head as she continued to dampen his shirt with her tears. Her entire frame trembled in the unrelenting embrace of his arms.

After a few moments, her body slackened against him and he loosened his hold on her. He lifted his hands to her face and tilted it gently so that she would look at him. The sight of her tear-stained cheeks, the red rim to her eyes was like a knife in his side, and he dropped his forehead against hers.

"I am so sorry, Cate. I'm so sorry." His eyes pressed tightly closed when he felt her fingers wrap around his wrists, hearing her fight against a mixture of labored breaths and sharp sniffles. "I won't make you stay away for one second more than is absolutely necessary. I promise. I promise."

She wilted powerlessly in his arms, her hands jerking to cling to his strong shoulders for support, and she shook her head. "Nicky, I can't leave you."

"You have to. I'd never forgive myself if anything happened to you."

Tears continued to blur her vision as she replied. "Do you think it would be any easier, for me, if I left you here and anything happened to *you*?"

"I won't take any chances with you. That's it. That's all there is to it. Nonnegotiable, this time." He swallowed hard, watching the tears flood down her face in recurrent streams. "I'm sorry."

As she shook in his arms, inconsolable, he dropped onto the dressing table bench, pulling her onto his lap, letting a long kiss linger against the side of her neck. His lips paused there, fearful of not knowing when the next time would be that he might do so again. The only thing he could do was to utter constant repetitions of apologies and reassurances of his love for her.

#

From the balcony of their bedroom, Cate watched Frankie load the car. She'd gone out there to be alone, to stare blankly off into the fog that had densely infiltrated through the surrounding trees. It was a perfect day for such a mournful chain of events. It felt cold and unfriendly, devoid of anything beyond the mist. She blinked into the distance, looking but not seeing, salty tears continuing to slip silently down her face.

Finishing the preparations outside, Frankie gave a long stretch. As he flicked his eyes up at the house, he startled, seeing Cate perched on a handrail of the second floor patio. For a man of his large build, his footsteps sped swiftly through the foyer and up the stairs, past the puzzled expressions on Tony and Nick's faces.

Unnerved by Frankie's urgency, Nick started up after him at a fast clip. Cautiously, Frankie moved into the bedroom where Nick and Cate slept, walking softly to the open balcony door. He shot his hand out behind him to stop Nick from rushing to her, afraid he'd startle her into a fall. Instead, they watched her for a moment, neither of them speaking.

She was silent. Long, loose locks of hair hung down the back of her puffed ivory sweater. With the seat of her jeans resting on the wide stone handrail, her feet dangled over the other side, crossed at the ankles. The palms of her hands were flat on either side of her. She didn't appear to be anxious or desperate, only quiet. Contemplative. So quiet and so still that she looked as though she might've been plucked from a painting.

"It's time, isn't it?" Without turning, she gave a nod and lightly sniffed. She lifted her fingers to swipe the moisture from her cheeks, rosy from the cold. Her voice was soft, almost a whisper when she spoke. "Don't worry, Frankie. I'm just thinking."

"How did you know I was here?" He cautiously stepped out onto the balcony, motioning for Nick to stay put at the door.

"I smelled your cologne. It's a nice smell, Frankie. I don't know if I ever told you that before, but it's nice. Comforting." Normally, she would smile as she commented. Not today. Today, she had nothing left to give anyone. As she spoke again, her voice began to betray her. "He thinks this is for the best. Nicky. He doesn't think I'm strong enough to stay."

"Nah, that ain't it, sweetheart. Tough guy as he is, Nicky just knows he ain't strong enough to let nothing bad to happen to ya." He glanced over the rail at the ground below, then flicked his eyes upward at the sky. A little-known fact about Frankie was his discomfort with heights. "He loves you."

"You know, when he first came around, in the beginning, he was a real pest about it, driving Shayne crazy flirting with me. But he made me look forward to it, every day. He made me depend on him, even then, without my realizing it was happening." She pressed her eyes closed, tears rolling down each cheek. "Nicky stole my heart, a piece at a time, and I never even saw it coming. Now, now that it feels like he's part of me… It feels like, without him, my whole world's being ripped away."

Frankie glanced back at the doors, at the sideways look Nick held on her from where he stood, his temple pressed against the white-knuckled fist that anchored him in place. Nick's eyes were glassy, his face shadowed with pure torment. Taking the last few steps closer to her, Frankie reached out, easing a hand over one of her shoulders. She was calm. There was no tremble under his touch. She simply wanted to know why her life, the beautiful, wonderful life she'd known just a couple of days before, was being snatched from her grasp.

"Come on, sweetheart. You know Nick'll find a way to make things right. He don't want you to go no more than you wanna leave." He placed his other hand on her other shoulder, squeezing lightly when her head dropped back against his burly chest. "All them extra zeros after his name, and he feels like you're all he's got in the world."

"Why can't these people just leave us alone?" Her words came out angry, bitter. "Nicky hasn't done anything to them."

"Just the way some people are, sweetheart. Ain't no use trying to figure it out." He shrugged. "Now, how about if we go downstairs and I'll fix you some cocoa before we go, huh?"

"He blames himself, you know. For this thing with Jansen… with me. He's taking the brunt of the responsibility on himself." She let out a long shudder of a sigh. "I don't blame him, though. However this turns out,

I want him to forgive himself. I don't want him to do anything that's going to cause him more trouble."

"Hey, Nicky!" Tony's voice echoed from the lower floor. "Nick! Your pop's here!"

Aside from the summons, Nick had already heard all that he could stand. Even with the danger she was in, her concern was still for *his* well-being. He turned from the door, heading back out of the room. Though men like Nick generally refused to allow tears into their eyes, his stung with a need for them.

In his chest, his heart pounded the steady roll of an angry war drum. Jansen had hurt her. He had hurt her. He would formulate a plan, but he wouldn't set anything into motion until he was sure she was safe. One thing was for sure. Jansen wasn't going to get away with any of it.

"Come on, sweetheart." Frankie held onto her as she turned, stepping back over the rail to him. "Let's go get that cocoa."

"No thanks." She shook her head, tucking her arms against herself. "We should probably be on our way. I just need to say goodbye to Nicky."

"All right." He gently nudged her chin with the bend of his index finger and smiled. "Whenever you're ready."

Chapter Twenty-Six

Cate looped her scarf around her neck a few times and slipped into the soft brown suede coat Nick had given her as an early Christmas gift. Her eyes flicked at the photo of them on the nightstand. She'd leave that for him. Walking along his side of the bed, she let her fingers skim over the warm blanket, her hand gripping his pillow as she reached it. She drew it to her face, pressing her eyes closed as she pulled in his scent. She needed to keep him with her. Tucking the pillow closely to her chest, she continued out of the bedroom.

Her feet felt like lead as her black ballet flats whispered over each step of the staircase. Pressing down against the heaviness in her chest, she gritted her teeth, willing back any further show of tears. She wasn't going to leave him that way. She wasn't going to let Jansen's venom taint their last moments together.

Sucking in a steadying breath, she lifted her hand to knock on the office door. He'd been tucked away in there with his father, discussing the whole matter. The knuckles of her right hand paused, mere inches from the wood, overhearing the low-spoken words between her father-in-law and her husband. Slowly lowering her hand to her side again, she listened intently to the conversation.

"I don't understand, Pop." Nick shook his head. He stood with his spine slumped against the edge of one of the dark bookcases, his arms tensed and folded over his chest. "How did you know where to find Alf? You know how many people I've had looking for him ever since he cut out of here, the other night?"

"Ah, not everyone knows all the secrets of the old days, Nicky." Sal mirrored his son's tightly folded arms, though he sat looking back at him from the corner of the desk. "Tony and Louis and I knew Alf in the old days. You didn't, not in that way. It wasn't hard to find him, only time consuming."

Nick nodded, setting his jaw like granite, his eyes flickering with the heat of anger behind them. "So? What happened?"

"Alf and I had… a *discussion*, regarding his options." Sal angled his head slightly to one side and he shrugged. "Don't ask me how we came to an agreement, Nick. Just know that Cate won't have to stay away too long before this is all over."

"What?" Nick's arms slowly released from their tight clasp and his posture straightened as he shook his head. "I won't bring her back before I'm sure it's safe, Pop. I won't let her be put in any more danger than I've already gotten her into."

"Of course, you won't, Nicky." Sal shook his head again. "A little while, maybe, to be sure that it's safe, but then, she can come back to you."

"How can this mess possibly be tied up so quickly?" Nick shook his head again, trying to decipher any such scenario that would allow for it to be cleaned up so easily.

Cate slowly lowered the pillow she'd been clutching to the hall chair outside the office door. She leaned closer to the room, knowing that Nick wouldn't want to burden her with details of any sort of plan. He wouldn't want to take the chance of involving her in any further risk. She recognized that he also wouldn't have wanted to get her hopes up, in case things didn't go as Sal obviously seemed to think they would.

A deep breath slowly left Sal's chest, his gaze holding firmly to his son's. "Without telling you more of our private conversation than might be good for you, I can tell you this much. I reminded Alf that he and I worked together, in mutual trust, for many years, that you were good to him, and that he should remember what loyalty in a family like ours entails."

Nick cranked his neck to one side, uncomfortable with the direction things might be heading. "Pop-"

"Let me finish. Patience, Nicky." Sal held his palms up to him. "After Alf and I talked, he decided it would be in his best interest to speak with the feds. I reminded him that I know far more about his past than Crispen Jansen could ever hope to. I went with him, to be sure he followed through without disappearing again. It's why I haven't been in touch before now."

"The feds?" Nick took a step forward. "Are you in trouble, too, Pop?"

"No, Nicky, no. Thankfully, Alf came around… or I might be." Sal shook his head.

The sincere look behind his eyes told his son how ominous the conversation must have been. No matter what he told Nick, Sal wouldn't have hesitated to use whatever means necessary to protect his family, if it came to it.

"The things Alf was involved in," Sal continued, "the things that have come back to haunt him, thankfully, they were nothing to do with me. Your grandfather, but not me. My father never let me into that side of things."

"Pop, I know the business wasn't on the right side when I was still a kid, old enough to remember the day you ended things with your connections to that side of the law."

"Any… *questionable* actions I might have been involved with, before we turned legitimate, they weren't anything to follow me this far. Alf, when he was getting started with my father, he was in bad ways. Your grandfather, Alf, they believed in practicing retribution. Vengeful retribution. I think you're smart enough to work out what I mean, when I say that. It's those things that Crispen Jansen is holding over his head."

"So, what happened with the feds?" Nick settled his shoulder against the window. "Where's Alf, now?"

"He's at the loft office. He's got a couple of plain-clothes agents babysitting him until they get what they want."

Nick lifted a brow to him. "Which is?"

Sal's chest dropped and he licked his lips before pressing them together in a thin line, taking a moment to steady himself before he came to the point of it. "I wanted to keep you out of any of this, Nick, but they need your cooperation, too."

He shifted a wary look at his father in response to the tone his words carried, not that any cost would've been too great if it meant keeping Cate safe. "What do they want from me?"

"They want you to do nothing."

"What?" Nick shook his head, pulling his brows back in, bewildered by the simple statement. "I don't understand. They want me to do something by doing nothing? What does that even mean?"

"They want you to let Alf use your name, our name, to make the deal with Jansen. He'll be wired." He held his hand up to the start of Nick's protest. "Before you say anything, I got it in writing with our lawyers. This is a set-up for Jansen only, with no legal repercussions to our family or the business. They've been looking for something on Crispen Jansen for a while, but he's been too slippery to grab onto."

"Okay." He settled back into his contemplative stance from before. "What else did they say?"

"In exchange for Alf helping them to catch Jansen, they're prepared to cut him a deal."

"A deal?" Nick threw his head back, scoffing an incredulous laugh as he began to pace angrily. "So, wait.

He racked up federal crimes, back in the day. He attempted to sell us out. He knew Jansen was going to come after Cate, but to save his own skin, he did nothing to stop it! All that, and he still gets to walk free?"

"No, Nick." Sal shook his head again. "He's not going free. He won't get a needle, but he'll be in prison for the rest of whatever time he's got left. He'll just be doing it with heightened protection, and it won't be in some scummy little hole."

Nick continued to pace, seething with irate anxiety, still feeling that Alf was getting too easy a pass for all that he had done. For the danger that still threatened to snare Cate, Nick would like five minutes alone with him, just five. The way he felt, he'd almost be willing to do time for those few minutes.

His footsteps came to a stop, realizing that this might be the best and only way to end things. "And this is going to keep her safe?"

"I believe it will." Sal nodded. "Crispen's arms only reach so far."

"How long?" Nick's chest rose and fell hard. At least if he had some sort of timeline to offer her, it might make it an easier pill to swallow.

"That, I can't tell you." Sal shook his head. "It's a faster conclusion than any other alternative would be, a safer one for her, and a more legal one for you. Weeks, maybe a few months for it to be fully tied up. The feds need to know that you're on board with this, Nick."

He stood there, fuming as his mind tabulated all of the available options. Months without her. The expression on his face was hard as steel, realizing that it really was the best option they had. At length, he nodded. "I'll do it."

"Good." Sal nodded. "Our lawyers are waiting at the loft office with all the papers, outlining our role in this. As a senior officer of the corporation, I've already signed them. Our council was waiting for my go-ahead to turn them over, until after I'd talked with you. You may still have one or two things to sign, for your protection. We'll go as soon as Cate's off."

"Fine." Nick bobbed his head again.

Sal angled a questioning look at him. "What's your plan for her?"

"Frankie's going with her to the airport. He'll give our pilot directions when they get there. I promised her I'd find a stand-in for her at MacCarthaigh's so Shayne isn't buried. I have some connections I can tap into for that."

Cate tightly pursed her lips together, her mind running over the whole conversation. So, Alf was back at the loft office. Well, after thoroughly ripping their lives apart, after hurting Nick so, she wasn't about to give him the pass that he was hoping for. She had every intention of giving him a piece of her mind before she was forced into hiding, forced away from Nick.

She lifted her hand, as she had started to do moments before, and knocked loudly. "Nicky?"

Nick flicked a strong look at his father, holding a finger to his lips, then crossed to the door. Sal nodded, understanding the gesture. Nick pulled the door open, relieved to see that some color had returned to her complexion. Offering her a smile, he stepped aside to let her in.

"I'll give you two a minute." Sal walked past them, pausing to brush a supportive kiss against her cheek, then moved off toward the foyer to speak to Frankie.

Nick closed the door, then turned. Framing her face gently with both of his hands, he leaned forward, pressing his lips tenderly to hers. He slipped his fingers lower, ghosting down the curves of her neck, tracing the sides of her silhouette, then twined them together against her low back. He sucked in a tight breath, dipping his head to let it rest lightly against hers.

"I guess it's that time, huh?" The muscle at his jaw rippled in tense waves as he gritted his teeth again. "You have everything you need?"

"You mean, besides you?" She shook her head, angling back to look into his beautiful, but troubled dark eyes. "I left something at the loft."

Nick edged back from her uncomfortably, knowing that Alf was in the office there. "I don't know, Cate. I really think you and Frankie should get going. Whatever it is, if it-"

"I hid one of your Christmas presents there last week. It'll only take a minute to grab it, and we won't be going into the city." She angled her head up at him, laying a hand flat over his heartbeat. "We might not be able to be together for Christmas, but I think I should at least be able to see you open it. Give me that much, please."

After a moment, he gave a conceding nod. "All right, Cate."

How could he deny her something so trivial after all she was being forced to give up, and for who knew how long? It was no small thing for her to walk away from their life together, her family, her stake in MacCarthaigh's. He'd grant her request, and then she'd be on her way to safety. He'd just have to make sure Alf was kept from sight when they got there.

"I can ride in with you and Frankie, then come back here with Pop and Tony afterward." He pulled the door open to walk with her to the car. "I was heading in with Pop, anyway. There's... some business I need to take care of."

"Good." She nodded, clutching his hands tightly in hers, strangely energized at the thought of confronting Alf. "That's settled, then."

Chapter Twenty-Seven

Nick's black Cadillac pulled to a stop in the parking lot of his loft office. Cate clung tightly to his arm, sensing that their time together was almost up. No matter what deal Alf had come to with the government officials, it wouldn't all be wrapped up by tomorrow. There was no telling how long it would be before she could hold her husband so closely again.

"It's going to be all right." He nodded. "I can't say more, just now, but it *will* be okay."

Nick kept his eyes straight ahead, though he knew she had angled herself to look at him when he spoke. Knowing that he couldn't have quite brought himself to retain his tough exterior if he'd looked back at her, he merely shook his head.

"Cate, I know you hate when I keep things from you, but-"

"I understand. I trust you, Nicky." Her fingers curled firmly over his arm when he finally did flick a glance at her. Her other hand came to the side of his face and she managed a brave smile. "We'll be fine."

Tensing the muscle at his jaw, he swallowed against the strangled sensation in this throat. His gaze remained steadily on hers, though his brows twitched inward in response to the surprisingly willful glint that she'd reflected back at him. What was going on in there?

The woman sitting next to him was a one-eighty from the one that had pierced his heart that morning on the balcony. She was perfectly calm, assured, as if she'd somehow stolen the strength that was beginning to abandon him at the thought of their being apart. Whatever had happened, whether or not it was all an act for his benefit, she was nearly beaming with some source of untold confidence.

Squaring her shoulders as Frankie opened her door, the curve at the side of her mouth sneaked slightly higher. She couldn't have seen the bewildered expression on Nick's face as he slid across the seat after her. He exchanged a glance with Frankie, who's own expression appeared just as perplexed by her unfaltering composure.

"Keep an eye on the car, would you, Frankie?" Nick spoke distractedly, continuing to follow after her with his eyes. "We won't be in there long."

"Sure." Frankie nodded, opening the driver's door with a baffled shake of his head. "Sure thing, boss."

Nick gave his father a nod when he reached the entrance. Sal had arrived just before them. As the two men walked in together, Nick noticed Cate hesitate when she nearly passed his closed office door. He adjusted an immediate tension in his neck when she suddenly stopped walking and glanced over her shoulder at him. Scowling, she flicked her index finger at the door.

Hearing Alf's muffled voice coming from the other side, Nick took a few quick steps toward her, shaking his head. Sal followed directly behind them. As she was several feet ahead of them, Nick wasn't quite fast enough to stop her from rushing forward and slamming the heel of her hand against the handle.

Alf and two other men, men she didn't recognize, looked over at her. Alf placed a hand against either man that flanked him, silently letting them know that she wasn't a threat. He stared at her for a few tense seconds. She wasn't deterred in the least by Nick's low-spoken utterances, or by the lightly tugging grasp he held on her. Alf watched her cautiously. She didn't look as if she knew whether she was going to cry or scream at him.

Jerking her wrist free of her husband, she made several long strides over to where Alf stood. Her eyes were like perilous, green slivers of glass as she stared him down. She managed to keep her lip from trembling with either hurt or fear, as it had wanted to. The other men glanced around at one another and gave a light shrug.

Rather unexpectedly, her hand flew freely at Alf and she clapped her stinging palm against his cheek. Undeterred by the leap Nick had made at her, tucking his arms tightly around her waist from behind, she railed at Alf, her voice loud and demanding.

"How could you? How could you do this to us, to Nicky? He trusted you! He loved you! You were his family, Alf!"

"It's all right. Let her go, Nick." Alf shook his head, waving his open palms between himself and the couple he'd betrayed. The prickling remnant of her fury left the flushed outline of her fingers on his flesh. "She's right."

"I don't need you to point out the obvious for me." Her chest heaved sharply, the dark stare she held on him filled with disdain as Nick dragged her back toward the hallway where Sal waited. "I'm certainly not asking for you to make excuses for me!"

"Nick!" Alf called just as they'd passed back through the open doorway. He settled a look on her, nodding to her. "I'm sorry, Cate. It wasn't nothing against you or Nick."

Her emerald eyes darkened. "Nothing? It may be nothing to you, but-"

"Cate!" Stone-faced, Nick tugged back as she strained against the barricade his arms provided. He flicked a quick glance at his father, then hooked his chin over her shoulder. Lowering his voice, he used a more soothing tone as he spoke into her ear. "Come on. Come

on, baby. I want you out of here before this all hits the fan.
You and Frankie should be out of town already.”

She ripped free of him when Sal pulled the door
closed. Backing away from them, her eyes stared wild and
hot at the office. Gritting down against the tears that
threatened to cloud her vision, she shook her head at Nick,
then turned for the stairs to their loft.

He started to go after her, but was impeded by the
sudden presence of the taller of the plain-clothes men from
the office. “Mr. Caprianno, I’m agent Barnes. That’s my
partner, agent Fernandez. We’d like to go over one or two
things, if you could just step in.”

“Will you give me a minute?” Nick barked back at
him.

Sal placed a hand against his son’s chest, patting it
lightly. “She’s all right, Nicky. She’s strong. You meet
with them. I’ll go talk to her.”

Nick’s attention remained on the stairs, heaving
breaths being pulled in and out from the flare of his
nostrils. He nodded, thinking he’d like to give Alf the
same or worse as she had done. He couldn’t fault her for it.
He was only sorry that it seemed to have stolen any last
moments of peace she may have had with him.

“Give her a minute, Pop.” Nick forced out a sharp
exhalation, gripping the door handle in his white-knuckled
hand.

Cate walked back and forth between the kitchen and
sitting area of their apartment. With her hands clutching
his Christmas gift tightly to her chest, angry, silent tears
screamed down her bright cheeks. Whatever else
happened, at least she’d had her chance to meet Alf head-
on before she was forced to leave.

She lifted a hand, swiping her fingers over her
moistened cheeks when she heard the footsteps behind her.
Nick didn’t say anything. She figured he was probably
searching for the right words. She’d been like a wild cat

downstairs, hadn't let him console or restrain her. She'd pushed at him when he'd tried.

"You left the balcony door cracked open when you came by the other night. Lucky every cat within a two-mile radius isn't living in here." She coughed a laugh against the emotion that strangled her words, and shook her head. A shuddered breath slipped from her lips when he didn't reply. "I won't be here to remind you to close it, you know."

It was good they had a few private moments alone, really alone. Aside from Frankie being out front with the car, everyone else was downstairs in the office. She kept her back to him, not quite able to look at him, knowing it would only be to say goodbye. Her mascaraed lashes blinked against her bleary vision.

She knew Nick was often silent when he was stricken with anger, but she longed to hear his voice. She was sure he was probably upset with her for what she'd said and done. He may have even guessed that she'd eavesdropped at his door. Whatever it was, she didn't want their goodbyes to be this way.

"Oh, Nicky, please don't be angry with me. I just couldn't help myself. When I realized that he was…" Her words froze as she turned around, her eyes widening on the man before her. She shook her head, shuffling back a step as her heart pounded against her ribs. "Who are you?"

"It's okay, Mrs. Caprianno." The stranger held his hands up between them to try and calm her. "I'm Nick's new security guy for the building. He sent me up for you. I'm supposed to walk you down to the car. He thought the back way would be better."

She took a second, letting her eyes move over him, and she took another step back, shaking her head. He hadn't come in the front door. She would've heard. She flicked her eyes back over to the arcadia door again, realizing Nick hadn't left it unlatched. No. This man had already been in the apartment when she'd gotten there.

"I don't know who you are, but I know you don't work for my husband." She continued to edge slowly back from him. "Nicky would've told me. He always makes sure I meet anyone new. And he'd never allow a security guard to just walk into our apartment. He was walking me to the car, himself."

"You know, you really are a very smart woman." The man, tall and lanky, stepped forward, sprigs of heavy damp hair falling over his eyes as he laughed quietly. "Just, keep on being smart, and you'll be fine."

"*You'd* be smart to leave here, right now. You stay away from me, or I'm going to scream my head off."

"No, no. That wouldn't be a wise thing to do." He grabbed her from behind as she turned and started for the balcony, cupping a hand over her mouth before she could make good on her threat. "You don't want to do that."

Surprisingly agile and strong for his waif-like appearance, Alex managed to hold her closely against him. He kept a hand over her mouth, his other arm squeezed around her waist. His feet scuffed backwards along the polished floorboards, tugging her with him toward the open door. The fire stairs were just on the other side of the balcony and would take them down to where Bobby waited in the back alleyway.

At the top of the metal steps, she managed to wriggle enough to bite his hand and slam her heel into one of his boney shins. As he let out a grunt, she reached for the railing. Throwing an empty flowerpot at the door, she shattered the glass. She intended to make every bit of ruckus as she could.

"Nicky!" She shrieked for him. Her gaze shifted left and right, knowing there was nowhere for her to go, that everyone she trusted was either down in the office or sitting in the car out front. "Nicky!"

Alex lunged forward, crashing the back of his hand hard against the side of her face, making her tumble and nearly fall from the top of the steps. Reaching to grab her up again, he struggled down the stairs with her, Cate fighting him each and every step of the way. She flicked her feet in and out around his, trying to trip him.

"You're gonna kill us both, you stupid- Ow!" He tugged her harder when she'd kicked him again, fighting him, literally tooth and nail, the whole way.

Having heard her scream for Nick, and hearing the shatter of glass, Sal rushed up the last of the interior stairs to the loft. Noting the grunting and shuffling sounds of a continued struggle, he tried the door handle and shouted for his son. His shoulder slammed against the door as he attempted to get it open. He hadn't brought his keys with him and he knew the lock was too strong for any further attempts on his part to work.

Nick's feet nearly slipped out from under him as he skidded out of the office and bolted for the stairwell. Agent Fernandez was close at his heels, while Barnes stayed with Alf. Nick knew his father wasn't a man apt to shout, unless there was a need. He bolted up the steps like lightening, his fingers fumbling with his own key at the lock. Frankie, having heard her last screams, had rushed into the building and joined them in hallway.

Nick burst into the apartment. Panic stung his every nerve when he saw the shattered arcadia door and the scattered bits of glass glistening up from the floor. The gift she'd gone to retrieve lay next to an overturned dining chair. The gate that led from the balcony to the fire stairs hung open and the sound of tires squealed with a shrill echo against the buildings. He ran across the loft, but there was no sign of Cate or the car that had absconded with her.

Whirling around, he blew past the group of men, streaking back down to the office. His footsteps pounded the hard flooring as he crossed the room, then wadded Alf's jacket tightly in his closed fists. The older man stumbled back, eyes wide on his once-trusting companion. He could guess what had happened. Overhearing Fernandez on his cellphone in the hallway, the news was confirmed.

"Where did they take her?" Nick's voice was guttural, treacherous in comparison to any sound Alf had ever heard him utter to him before. "I said, where are they?"

"I don't know, Nick." He shook his head, his palms splayed between them. "I don't know. Jansen ain't called yet to set up the meeting place."

"Then you call him. We'll go together." Nick thrust him back, dismissing every eye that watched him. "Call him!"

Alf shook his head. "Nick, I don't think you tagging along would be such a good move. The whole idea was to protect you."

"The whole idea was to protect *her*!" His complexion burned a deep shade of crimson as he bellowed back at him. "I couldn't care less what you think, anymore, Alf! You lost that! Now, you call him, or so help me-"

"Mr. Caprianno," Barnes began, cautiously stepping toward him to diffuse Nick's volatile temper, "I know how upsetting this turn of events must be to you, but I have to caution you against any impulsive-"

"You shut up!" He barked at the man, eyes ablaze with fury and with fear. "You think I'm gonna wait for you to do something? You hear the name Caprianno and you back up ten paces. You figure, from the reputation, we deserve whatever we get! Well, I'm not waiting around to trust my wife's safety to you. She hasn't got anything to do with any of this!"

Sal stepped forward, reaching a hand for one of the tautly flexed arms that his son used to detain Alf. "Nicky, these men, they're the good-"

"No, Pop!" He shook his head. "Whatever their plan was, I just became part of it."

"We can't allow you go with Alf, Mr. Caprianno." The man he'd verbally trounced spoke calmly. "I assure you, despite your family history, we of all people know who we're dealing with when it comes to Crispen Jansen. He's been too slippery to prosecute, in the past. A pain in our sides, to say the least. He's gotten messy with this grudge match. Alf's cooperation and testimony could've put him away for blackmail, extortion, and a number of other things. But he just crossed over into a whole new arena by kidnapping your wife. With this, we could-"

Nick shook his head, shouting back at him. "I don't know whether he's on to you, or if Alf gave him a tip-off, but he obviously thinks something stinks. My wife isn't bait! I have no intention of waiting for you to tack murder charges under his mugshot, too."

The agent attempted to appease him. "It won't come to that."

"If anyone is going after Cate, it's going to be me!" Nick fired back, then looked at Alf again. "Where would they have taken her?"

Alf flicked a look at the agent and let a long breath pass through his lips as he nodded. "Nick's right. He should be there. He's the big fish Jansen's been after all this time."

Chapter Twenty-Eight

As Crispen waited impatiently for his prize to arrive, the soles of his slick-bottomed dress shoes tapped along on the cold cement inside the metal building. He'd checked his watch a dozen or more times since Bobby had called him. The smile had spread so widely over his lips when he'd heard Cate's voice in the background of the speeding car, that he could have given the Cheshire Cat a run for his money.

Finally, with or without Alfonse Giuseppe, his plan was coming to fruition. He should've just done things his way from the beginning. Hearing the angry snap of a female voice echoing in from outside, he turned, grinning that deep grin of satisfaction again. Alex and Bobby were making their way into the warehouse, barely containing the fiery redhead in their collaborative grasp.

"Take it easy, you baboons!" She continued to wriggle and make things as difficult as possible for them. She glared at Alex. "Hey, tall and scrawny, why don't you do yourself a favor when it comes to your hair products. Learn to edit!"

Bobby let her go once they were inside. Jerking free of Alex's grasp, too, she gave him a hard shove that nearly toppled him. Shifting a look directly at Crispen, her complexion was practically glowing with anger.

She folded her arms, staring willfully back at the man who had started it all. "You wanna tell that bean rail to keep his grimy hands to himself?"

"Keep *my* hands to *myself?*" Alex scoffed, then turned to Crispen. "She didn't just hit me. She bit me, clawed me, spit, kicked, you name it. She might be little, but she's mean! Ain't that right, Bobby?"

Bobby allowed the smallest hint of a curve to tug uncharacteristically at his lips. "She did all right."

"I didn't know we were picking up a lady bobcat! After that knee, I don't know that I'll ever have kids, you know what I'm saying?"

She narrowed her eyes at him. "Do the world a favor."

"Enough, both of you! Geez!" Crispen's eyes swept back and forth between his associate and his bargaining chip, then landed on Bobby. "They like this the whole way here?"

"Nah." The other man shook his head softly. "They're pretty well calmed down, now."

Cate stomped a foot at Alex when he took a step nearer to her again, snickering when he flinched. "I wouldn't, if I was you."

"All right, all right. Alex, Bobby, get lost."

Seeing the darkening skin under his crony's eye and the claw marks on his wrists and neck, Crispen burst out a louder laugh. He was beginning to grow increasingly amused by her. He gave a deep nod, waving both men away from her. Then, taking a few steps closer to her, he circled around her as he looked her up and down.

"Nicky boy sure does like a challenge, doesn't he? You got a little bit of a temper, don't you, gorgeous?"

"You haven't seen anything." Her chest rose and fell hard as she watched him circling her. "You wanna stop the merry-go-round act? You look a shark."

"I feel a little like a shark with you around." He snickered, noticing the way her eyes hardened on him. "I'd gladly take a bite out of you."

Laughing again, he finally came to a stop in front of her. He leaned in nearer, grinning toothily with a nod, approving her scent choice. Viewing the cold hatred that radiated back him, he took another half-step toward her, inches from her, lifting a finger to stroke the side of her face.

"I like a challenge, myself, every now and then." He laughed softly. "Nick's a lucky man."

"A better one, too." She fired back at him, setting her jaw defiantly tight. "Should we go on pointing out the obvious?"

"The better man?" Lifting his arm, he nearly clapped his open palm against the side of her face, but he stopped, letting it fall to his side again. "No flinch. I like that, Cate. I like that a lot."

"I have no intention of flinching. Can't say as much for your choice of minions." She folded her arms between them, shifting her eyes back and forth on his, determined to keep from showing the fear that silently quaked within her. "It's cold enough in here. What's the matter, you didn't have any connections with a heated building? I'm going to be a popcicle by the time my husband gets here."

"Sorry." He shrugged, broadening his grin again. "Next time I invite company, I'll make sure and pick a warmer location. Hopefully, Nick's smart enough to figure out where we are sooner, rather than later. Can I offer you my coat?"

"I'd rather freeze, thanks. And Nicky's brilliant. He's probably on his way here, right now." She drew her brows down, narrowing her eyes just slightly as his slithered over the length of her again. "Why don't you just leave us alone?"

"Sorry." He shrugged, lifting a cigarette to his lips and lighting it. "I can't do that. The Capriannos have already cost me too much. It's their turn to pay the piper. What goes around, and all that."

She thought back to some of the story she'd worked out of Nick. "He was just a little boy when what you claim happened supposedly happened."

"Oh, you know about that, do you?" He wobbled his head from shoulder to shoulder, scrunching his face as he sucked in a long drag of smoke. "Well, I'm sure you've heard the Caprianno side of things."

"That would be the accurate side, then." She angled her chin sharply up at him when he blew the smoke just past her. "Nicky doesn't lie to me."

"Ah, but he doesn't tell you everything, either. Does he?" His mouth curved into a malicious smile as he laughed. "Alex said Nick hurried you away when you were downtown the other day, so I'll bet he didn't even mention our little arrangement until he had to. Kind of makes you wonder what else he might not have told you, doesn't it?"

A slightest waver tested her strength, but she braced against it, knowing that she trusted her husband. Crispen was only trying to rattle her, doing what he could to get to her.

"I'd believe there were little green men on the moon, if Nicky told me. You, on the other hand…" She laughed, shaking her head at him. "Well, I wouldn't believe word you said if you'd just sworn an oath in court. So, like I said, I'll stick with Nick's side of things."

The arrogant curve at his lips slipped a bit. Sassy little minx. "Whatever song and dance he sold you while he was romancing you, honey, it don't change the facts."

She nodded, making a play to buy time from any ideas he may have for her. "Suppose you tell me your side."

"Salvador Caprianno ruined my old man for the sake of his precious son. So, you see, it isn't Nick's fault… and then again, it is. To add further insult to injury, your husband was too worried about getting those manicured hands of his dirty by associating with the likes of me."

"Whatever happened all those years ago, it wasn't Nick's doing. As far as this deal you want goes, obviously, he was right about not going into business with a crook like you. Just goes to prove how intelligent he really is." She grinned at the way he sucked harder on his cigarette. "Tell me. How is any of this going to make up for what happened to your father?"

"It's my way of squaring the past with Sal. A son for a father, or maybe even a daughter-in-law, in a pinch. See, if Nick doesn't come through, I'll settle for you in trade. He does what I want, I just ruin his business. If he doesn't play ball, I ruin his whole life."

She knew he'd detected the hard swallow she wasn't quite able to conceal, that time. "Nicky's stronger than you give him credit for."

"Not always, as it turns out. I think we both know he isn't *that* strong." The look in his eyes morphed from a cold glint to a lighter, taunting gaze, and he laughed softly. "Let's just hope, for your sake, that Nicky boy is as devoted to you as you appear to be to him."

Although it was obvious that he took pleasure in her discomfort, she could also tell that some part of him appeared to like her. At the very least, he found her interesting. It wouldn't keep him from killing her, if he wanted to, but it had the potential to buy her some time.

"Crispen… May I call you Crispen?"

"You may. One way or another, we're gonna be old friends, by the end of the night." He nodded, his cheeks hollowing inward as he took another drag, then motioned to a large drum of some sort nearby. "Have a seat, Mrs. Caprianno."

"I assure you, Crispen, after all of this, you've definitely piqued my curiosity."

Despite what she said, she knew he could tell by her tone that she'd meant it in a far less pleasant manner than what her words suggested. She walked a few paces over to the place he indicated and lowered onto the barrel lid.

"Isn't this all a little cliché?" Her glance shifted around the large building and she drew one corner of her mouth up in a smug grin. "Really?"

"Isn't all what cliché?" He lowered onto a nearby stack of crates. "Go on."

"The slimy flunkies," she stifled a full giggle, "the dirty warehouse in a bad end of town. A warehouse run by you, I assume, or at least someone associated with you. I mean, this is probably one of the first places Nicky would look for me. It all seems a little… I don't know, lazy."

"Lazy?" The quick flash of temper that flared within him swiftly shifted to an amused chuckle. He waggled a finger at her, nodding. "You know, I like you, Cate. I do. But, as for Nick thinking to look here, well, that's the whole idea."

"Explain that to me." She cocked her head to one side. "I thought you were supposed to meet with Alf."

"Oh, I will, and Nick, too, I'm sure. But, if Nicky boy doesn't want to come across, it's convenient to have my, ah… enticement so close." He adjusted the slump of his spine, tugging back his shoulders. "I don't often respond well to demands, so I don't think I'll be answering any more of your questions."

"I've never really done well with demands, myself. What else are we going to do to pass the time, though?" She touched her fingers to the swollen cheekbone Alex had given her on the loft balcony. "I can't say Nicky's going to be all that pleased when he sees this."

"Alex tends to be a little overzealous, eager to prove himself. Moron. My apologies for the less than cordial treatment." He laughed again, placing his flattened palm over his heart in mock sincerity. "What can you do?"

"Well, I don't know what you do, but I lead with my elbow and turn to drive up with my knee. You might notice your goon walking a little funny, for a few days.” She smiled when a hearty laugh burst from his lips. “A little more conversation. Humor me. Like you said, we’re going to get to know one another pretty well before this is all over.”

“I know what you’re doing, and it’s too bad we had to meet under these circumstances. You’re an interesting woman.” He flicked some ash to the side. “If you’re hoping that I’ll get attached to you and hesitate to use you against Nick, when it comes to it, though, you’re wasting your time.”

She shrugged. “It appears I have time to waste.”

“I like your style.” He folded his arms, though the deep-set show of amusement remained. “Don’t get me wrong. I won’t say that it wouldn’t be a shame, if it came to that. I might even be almost sorry to have to do it, but all’s fair, and all that.”

“Of course.” She held her palms out, working up a believable expression of nonchalance as she silently prayed that Nick would indeed turn up soon. “Business.”

“Yeah.” He laughed again, nodding. “Yeah, exactly. Business.”

“I wish I could say the admiration was mutual. Unfortunately… I am curious why you’re anxious for Nicky to find us so easily. I can safely promise you that it won’t be pretty, once he gets here. I don’t envy you my husband’s temper. I’ve tasted it, myself, and he loves me. Thanks to you for that treat, by the way.”

“Knock you around, did he?” He flicked his brows upward. “Didn’t peg him for that.”

“Oh, no! Nicky would never resort to violence.” She shook her head vehemently, then broke into a slow smile. “Well, not toward *me*.”

“Oh, yeah?” He nodded at her, letting a cloud of smoke expel from the flare of his nostrils. “Thanks for the warning.”

"I almost shudder to think how he's going to react when he gets a hold of you. Almost." She shook her head to the tighter expression that was creeping onto his face when she said that. "Ah, ah! Don't lose your temper, Crispen. We did agree to be friendly, but you had to know I was going to stay on his side. Funny thing about me. I always manage to pick the winning team."

"Winning? That remains to be seen." Crispen's expression continued to shift into one of dark annoyance, and he sharply tossed the smoldering butt off to the side, sparks flicking up from where it landed. "On second thought, I don't know how really attached to you I am, after all."

She only drew one side of her mouth into a smug upward lift. "Well, that is a pity. I think with a little more time, we could've really bonded here."

He flashed a look at her again, narrowly glaring back at her when he heard the sound of another car pulling up outside. "I guess we'll never know. That sounds like our boy, now."

Chapter Twenty-Nine

With only Alf and Nicky in Alf's sedan, the search for Cate was deadly silent. Salvador was uneasy about letting his son go with only Alf, the two agents following them in a separate car. The only compromise that could be reached, was to permit Frankie to ride along in the backseat of the second car. Barnes and Fernandez stayed a street's length away at all times, so as not to tip off Jansen.

They'd already checked two locations, without any luck. Crispen hadn't answered his phone when Alf had called. Both Alf and Nick knew that Crispen was just enjoying his sick game of hide-and-seek. He wanted them to have to look for her. He wanted Nick to worry, every single second that she was being held, not knowing what might be happening to her. It was clear that he derived joy from making the Capriannos suffer, and making Alf squirm.

As Alf and Nick pulled to a stop outside a rusted warehouse at the outskirts of Chicago, the older man finally nodded, cutting the engine of the black sedan. "This is it. That's Crispen's car, over there. If he's got her, she'll be in there. Those two yahoos at the corner of the building are his gophers."

"I'm familiar with the scrawny one." Nick's eyes cut over to the driver's seat, studying his companion with curiosity as Alf switched off the recording device that had been concealed by the agents. "What are you doing? That isn't part of the plan."

"I'm not following no plan those government lackeys have for me. By settling things *my* way, I protect you, I protect Cate, and I wash myself as clean as I can for what I done to you. I haven't lived careful, all these years, to let anyone snatch the last part of my life from me and toss me in a cage."

"Don't think you have much say in the matter, at this point."

"You always got a say, Nick." Alf tugged the carefully positioned bugs from where they had been placed, tossing them into the center console, and pulled out a nine-millimeter that he'd had concealed there. "We're getting Cate back, then I'm getting out of here."

"Wait a second." Nick's hand shot out, grabbing the sleeve of Alf's coat tightly in the strong clutch of his fingers. His eyes bored into the older man's when his head snapped back in Nick's direction. "Get me straight on this. Cate is safe, then I don't care what you do, or where you go. But if anything happens to her, anything, I promise you, you won't be going anywhere."

Alf nodded, understanding. "I'm sorry things turned out this way, Nick. Really."

"That doesn't help much." The leather of Alf's coat made a creaking sound as Nick's fingers reluctantly allowed the sleeve to slip free again. "Let's just go get Cate."

"Right." He nodded again, a deep pang of regret settling into his chest. Pulling a couple of antacids from his pocket, as had become his ritual, he drew in a long breath and reached for the door handle. "Okay, kid. Follow my lead."

They slammed both car doors closed, each set of shoes making an echoing succession of soft steps over the cold and icy blacktop. Bobby and Alex loitered just outside the large rolling door to the building. The broader man remained quiet, as usual, while the wirier of the pair shifted on his feet in the cold. A cigarette bounced from between his lips as he chuckled at another of his own jokes.

"Shut it." Bobby's low voice made a rare appearance as he lifted a hand to his chattering counterpart. He tilted his head a little to one side, drawing his shoulders back to broaden his chest when Alf and Nick approached. "Alf. Mr. Jansen's been expecting you."

"Yeah." Alex gave his weasel's laugh, elbowing his unshakable partner as he spoke. "He's been waiting, hasn't he, Bobby?"

"Shut up." Bobby cut his partner a sideways glance, then looked back at the other two men.

Disgruntled by the slight he received in front of their visitors, Alex flicked his head in the direction of the large rolling door. "They're in there."

"Wait a second." Bobby held up a hand to them, his gaze leveling on Nick. "You got anything on you, let's have it."

Nick unzipped his coat, lifting it and twisting from side to side, showing he'd left his gun at home. After smacking his pockets flat, he glared back at the other man. "Satisfied?"

"Yeah, Caprianno don't wanna do nothin' to break the law, Bobby. He's such a good boy." Alex gave an snarky chuckle and pointed at Alf. "He don't never carry, anymore. Doubt the old man would even know what to do with a piece, at this point."

As if to prove him correct, Alf opened his own coat, exposing the inside, but was careful not to turn as Nick had. The gun he wore was safely tucked into the back of his waistband. Nick knew what he was doing. It had been smart. They'd underestimated the older man. As he'd discovered for himself, Alf wasn't a man to be underestimated, regardless of his stage in life.

"All right, go on." Bobby jerked his head roughly, then let them pass.

Nick paused a couple of steps behind Alf. Studying Alex's battered and disheveled appearance, a grin etched onto his mouth. An amused chuckle left him as he made note of the bruised eye, the claw marks on his hands, wrists, and neck. His lower lip also showed a deep split. She'd done a decent job holding him off. Giving a final laugh, Nick stepped in closer to him.

"You look a little worse for wear, Alex." The curve on his lips dropped immediately and fully, then, and the expression on his face darkened as he lowered his voice. "You better hope that she's in a lot better shape than you are. I won't play as nicely as my wife did."

Alex unintentionally shuffled a couple of half-steps back from him. He swallowed hard, giving Bobby a sideways glance. Rubbing at his shoulder, he recalled their first interaction in the alleyway. He wasn't quite so certain of just how harmless Nicholas Caprianno might be to him. He tried to find a laugh, but for once, it couldn't be summoned. Taking another step toward Bobby's imposing frame, Alex's beady-eyed gaze watched Nick disappear into the building behind Alf.

Bobby slipped a keyring into Alex's hand. "Go lock up. They ain't going anywhere 'til Mr. Jansen says so."

As he entered the vast space, Alf nodded. "Crispen."

His arm stretched to the side, flattening a hand firmly against Nick's chest when he took a broad stride toward her. Nick tilted his head apologetically at her when he noticed the vice grip Jansen held on her arm.

"You didn't have to go through all this mess, you know." Alf continued calmly. "I told you I'd be here, didn't I?"

"Ah, but you also disappeared on me for a while, didn't ya?" He shrugged. "How was I supposed to know I could trust you to keep your end of the bargain, especially after all this time? Besides, my insurance policy ensured

Mr. Caprianno would be here to do business in person. Nick."

"Jansen." Nick's eyes were clouded with anger. He was careful not to look too hard at her, or for too long, knowing he'd lose his focus if he did. His jaw rippled in flowing successions as he gritted his teeth. "I'm here. I'm ready to deal. Let her go."

"I gotta say, I'm impressed with your choice, Nick. Got a hefty temper, though. Feisty. Was that part of the appeal, for you? It was, wasn't it? Foreplay, and whatnot." Crispen peeled his grin back as he tugged her nearer to him, almost nuzzling her with his closeness. "Beautiful. Smart, too. Maybe smarter than you, even. She knows just how important she is to this whole process. Don't you gorgeous?"

"Eat dirt!" She jerked against his tight grip, shooting a glare up at the taunting expression he had aimed at her husband.

"Oh." He tsked his teeth at her, then thrust his hand upward, fisting her silky hair tightly in his fingers and making her wince. "Caprianno, you really should tell your wife that that ain't a nice way to talk to people."

"Easy, Nick." Alf grabbed onto Nick's arm as he lunged for Jansen, then gestured for him to look down.

Nick's chest heaved with irate breaths. He lowered his eyes to Jansen's other hand. The matte black metal barrel of a gun Crispen pulled from under his coat was pressed into her side. With a baiting chuckle, Jansen's sneer widened on him. They both knew who held the upper hand.

"All right." Nick nodded. "You wanna do business? That's why I'm here. Let her go, and I'll sign whatever it is you want."

"Nick, Nick, Nick." Crispen shook his head. "You still don't get that you're not the one calling the shots. We deal when I say we deal."

"Nicky…" She pulled the inner corners of her brows up in response to Crispen's tight hold. Bracing against the rim of moisture that gathered in her eyes, she stiffened in his grasp.

"Ah, ah!" Crispen released her hair and thrust her toward a makeshift table between him and Nick. "She's yours when I get your signature. Of course, I know you normally make it a point of reading every single line, with painstaking diligence, but I hope we can skip that part. Doesn't really matter what you're signing, does it, not if you want her back?"

"Go ahead, Nick." Alf nodded to him, though his own menacing gaze remained on Crispen.

Nick's jaw swelled with tension, keeping his sights firmly on his wife, his heart crashing against the walls of his chest. Leaning over the papers, he scribbled his signature on the allotted lines. Making a last scrawl, he slammed the pen down on the top and lifted his focus back to her.

"There. See. That wasn't so hard, was it?" Crispen gestured for her to move. "Go ahead, Cate, and ah, thanks for the company. Been a pleasure entertaining you."

He slid the stack of papers into his hand and grinned as he began to look them over. Cate quickly rounded the table and threw herself into Nick's protective arms. She gripped him tightly, burrowing herself against his chest.

"You okay?" He pressed a hard kiss to the top of her head, though his gaze remained on Jansen.

"She's fine. I'd be more worried about myself, if I was you." Crispen snickered, then lifted his eyes from the document.

Nick dropped his brows down, glaring in the other man's direction. "What do you mean?"

"Not one line of this links back to me. I've been pretty meticulous about that. Drives the feds crazy, know what I mean?" Crispen laughed again. "See, I figured that

Alf, here, would run scrambling to make a deal, something to save his own lousy neck. He'd want to make sure you were protected. Am I right?"

Nick stood silent, staring back at him with daggers in his eyes. "Maybe he would've thought about that. What's your point?"

"I guessed that whatever protection you might've negotiated would be limited to your business with me. That meant we couldn't really look like partners. Oh, I wanted to be, at first. But then, I thought of something even better. I would've enjoyed seeing your name under mine, of course. So long as I still win, though, I don't mind playing the middle man, just this once."

"I get it. On paper, your hands stay clean." Nick nodded.

"Very good. But, you? I'm afraid you're in bed with some pretty unsavory people, Nicky boy." Crispen shook his head in mock sorrow. "Shame what'll happen to you, to your business, when it all comes to light. Might even end up doing a little time over something of this scale. Then again, might be best to tie up any loose ends now."

"Loose ends." Nick nodded, moving Cate to stand behind him, turning himself into a shield.

"You understand. Any contradicting stories could muddy the water. I can't let that happen. Makes no difference to me if you're around to see it go down. Either way, you know what's coming, and your old man gets to watch everything he has fall apart." Crispen shrugged, then looked toward the door. "Bobby!"

Just as Nick was contemplating making a grab for Alf's gun, he glanced off to the side, noticing its owner slowly reaching to the back of his waistband. His eyes flicked back over to Crispen who, satisfied that they were at his mercy, had made the mistake of giving his full attention to the side conversation with his thug.

Nick could feel Cate's heart knocking at a quickened pace against his back and he squeezed her hand. Satisfied that they had them under their control, Bobby and Crispen didn't turn around until Alf steadily raised his arm in their direction.

Crispen managed a light laugh, not wanting to give away the intense drop he felt in the pit of his stomach. In a flashed motion, Bobby had yet another gun aimed at Alf for the one he held on Crispen. Crispen's firearm put Nick on point of target.

"Three guns. Well, it seems we're at a stalemate, boys." Jansen clucked. "If I shoot Nick, Alf shoots me. If Alf shoots me, Bobby takes Alf out. So, what are we gonna do here?"

"I guess if I get shot, I get shot." Alf growled lowly. "That's the thing about my age, Crispen, the thing you never understood. Half the time, what time you got left seems golden. The other half of the time, you really don't give a-"

"Cops! Cops! They're coming up the street! We gotta get out of here!" Alex burst through the warehouse door, bellowing at the top of his lungs, accidentally clubbing into Bobby.

Apparently, the feds only allowed so much time before they went into action after Alf had cut communication. At the echoing peel of accidental fire, Alf dropped to his knees, then fell forward, his chest thudding against the cement floor. Bobby and Alex tore off for the back exit as Nick sunk to his friend's side. Rolling Alf over, Nick met his gaze.

"I guess this squares things. I always said you was a good boy. I'm sorry, kid. I'm sorry for not doing better by you sooner." Panting, the older man grimaced, coughing a wet, bloody cough, jerking a crimson-stained hand around Nick's. "We're square, now, aren't we?"

"Yeah, Alf. Sure." Nick kept his eyes fixed on Alf's. For both of their sakes, they needed to quickly make peace. "Yeah. Sure, we're square."

Crispen, realizing he was going to be cornered if he didn't do something, knowing that Cate was a messy end for him to leave behind, aimed for where she stood, just feet from her husband. Nick glanced back just in time and sprung to his feet, running to block any line of fire.

As Frankie and a whole possie of police cars and agents crashed against the locked gate, two thunderous cracks echoed against the corrugated metal walls inside the building. Cate could hear the others getting closer. With a loud shout, Crispen fell, his gun skittering across the cement from his reach, and Alf's bloody hand dropped to the ground, finger slipping off of his trigger. Redemption.

"Cate…"

Nick looked down and staggered back a half-step, attempting to make sense of the slick merlot-color that painted the hand she had touched him with. The stain spread quickly, soaking the front of his shirt. Shifting a look back at her, he drew his brows in tightly and reached for her.

"Cate…"

"Nicky!" Her scream traveled quickly in the cold air.

She threw her arms out to grab him, feeling him slump against her, and they crumpled to the floor together. Looking down at him, at the way his face didn't even twitch in response to her pleas, she lifted his hand pressing his palm against her cheek. Feeling it slip from her fingers, she watched his arm fall to the ground beside them.

"Nicky! No! Nicky! Frankie! Sal!" She gripped his sodden shirt tightly in her fingers and shook it, his body remaining unresponsive. "Somebody, help! Somebody!"

She could scarcely catch her breath for the frantic tears that burst from deep within her as she dragged him up, clutching his limp body so tightly against her own. Hearing a scuffle of shoes just outside and the rattle of chain link, she snapped herself free of panicked uselessness and carefully laid his back against the concrete.

She heard the lock on the gate finally breaking and heard the feet running toward the building and around it. Okay, okay. Calm! He needed her to be calm. Tears flooded down her face, almost blinding her vision. She pulled her coat off, covering his torso, then ripped her scarf from around her neck. She packed it firmly over the bloody source on the upper right corner of his shirt. Choking against tears and terror, she continued to press her bloody hands against his chest, her forehead dropping against him.

"Nicky, please don't do this to me!" She threw her head back, screaming again. "Somebody! We're in here! Please! Help!"

"Cate!" Frankie came barreling across the floor toward them when his eyes met the horrible sight, police running to the other two men to check their vitals. "Nicky!"

She whipped her head up at the sound of his voice. Every muscle in her body was trembling with the fear of losing what she most loved in the world. She shook her head helplessly. "Frankie, help him!"

"Nick." He dropped down next to them.

"You have to help him!" She shrieked, looking down at Nick again. "Please! Somebody, help my husband!"

One of the officers was on the ground at her side almost before she could even finish her plea. In a split second, she'd found herself pushed back from him as they did what they could. Frankie curled her tightly against his barrel chest, his gaze fixed on Nick. He murmured quiet assurances for her, praying more than believing that they would turn out to be the truth.

Chapter Thirty

The private hospital room was quiet. Only the hushed blips of various monitors made any noises at all. Occasionally, soft voices could be heard from the nurses' station in the hallway. Both Cate's family and Nick's had come and gone several times. Only two people were permitted to stay with him. Cate had refused to leave. She'd threatened that fighting MacCarthaigh spirit against anyone that even considered budging her. Frankie stood guard outside the door, also rejecting any petitions to displace him.

The police had come and gone a few times, taking moments here and there to check on his condition or to speak with Cate. The only person who appeared to be unbothered by it all was Nick. After briefly waking up in a surgical recovery suite, he hadn't so much as stirred again in nearly twenty-four hours.

Whether it was medication or the surgery he'd needed that kept him out, no one knew. Then again, he hadn't slept much for two days before he'd been shot. The bullet had nicked a vein, causing him to lose a good deal of blood. The doctors told her that it was probably a combination of things that kept him asleep.

Cate was insistent that she would be there if any changes took place. Not even Sal or Shayne had a prayer of talking her into going home for a rest. Under the circumstances, she'd been permitted to clean up in the bathroom sink of his room and had accepted the change of clothes her mother had brought to her.

His room was dim, nearly dark. She was sleeping carefully curled next to him on the bed when his eyes began to drag slowly open, at last. A muddling confusion clouded his mind as he began to draw more wakeful. He let his head loll softly to his left and he swallowed against his dry throat. Feeling Cate breathing against him, her hand over his heart so that she could feel the reassuring thud beneath her fingers, he felt immediate relief. She was safe.

The throbbing, burning sensation in his shoulder when he shifted caused him to suck a sharp breath through the grit of his teeth. Gradually, he began to remember it all. He recalled Crispen lifting his gun toward her. He recalled Alf managing to lift his own. Then… nothing. He did faintly remember hearing Cate's frantic screams, but he'd lacked the ability to open his eyes and comfort her.

Wincing lightly, he slid his right hand over, letting it slip onto the one she held on his chest. He lifted her fingers to his lips, brushing a weak kiss to them. When she inhaled more deeply and began to bat her lashes slowly, he edged one corner of his mouth up slightly. She shifted a glance up at him, fully expecting to see him unconscious still.

"Nicky!" She gasped, bolting up next to him, and fell into an immediate blubber of tears. Sliding off the bed, she ran to the door, grasping Frankie's arm. "Frankie, go get the doctor. He's awake!"

"Cate, come here."

Nick attempted to keep the soft chuckle that he felt creeping up on him at bay. Just the very thought of laughter made his chest hurt more. He lifted a hand a couple of inches from the mattress, his fingers extended toward her.

"Nicky, Nicky." Moving back to the bed, she lowered carefully onto the edge. She shook her head, dropping her face into her hands as she uttered a string of garbled thanks.

"Hey. Hey." He reached his left arm open as wide as he could manage, curling it over her when she lowered next to him and continued to sob. His head rocked toward her and he pressed his lips to the top of her head. "It's gonna be okay, now. We're gonna be okay, now. It's over."

"Ah, Nicky!" Frankie stepped into the room just ahead of the doctor, an expression of pure relief overtaking him entirely. He shook his head, wagging a scolding finger at him as she moved out of the physician's way. "You sure gave us a scare, kid. Don't you ever do nothin' like that again, you hear me? That wife of yours, she kind of likes you, you know?"

"Yeah, I know." Nick nodded, then gave a low groan to the prodding of the doctor's hand over his wound. He turned his head to look at him, scowling darkly. "You gotta do that?"

"How about this?" The doctor pinched and prodded some more. "Can you feel all of this? Wiggle your fingers for me."

"Yeah, I feel it!" Nick grouched again. "Wiggle my fingers? I'll-"

"Oh, Nicky, just do it!" Cate swiped the tears from her face, dropping her fists onto the tops of her hips as she delved her brows down at him. "While you're at it, you just get used to doing exactly whatever else he says, do you hear me?"

"What if I don't wanna?" He squinted a playfully defiant look at her, feeling a smile hinting at his lips. "I don't do too well being told what to do, either, you know."

"Oh, I know. If anyone knows…" She nodded, then jammed a finger against her chest. "I know just how stubborn you can be, but don't you think for one second that you have any say, this time. You remember we're equal partners in this marriage, only sometimes one of us has the final say. I told you, in the beginning that I'm always right."

"And I told you, whether or not you're right, that doesn't automatically make me wrong." He countered, leaning back into the pillow when the doctor finished with him.

"Are they always like this?" Concerned, the doctor creased his forehead in a frown and looked to Frankie, keeping his voice low. "It's not a good idea for him to get worked up this way."

"Forget about it, doc. She's better than any medicine you could give him." Frankie chuckled quietly. "The only time you gotta worry about those two is if they stop arguing."

"I heard that." Nick glanced in Frankie's direction, then back at her again. "So, what if I let you have your way this time?"

"We both know this isn't the last time I'll have my way." Her voice calmed and she stepped forward to take the hand he extended to her. Her face took on a more serious expression, then, and she offset her jaw, doing her best to keep the water works from starting up again. "You do what he says, Nicky. I mean that. Please."

He squeezed her fingers lightly and nodded. "You gonna put me in time-out if I don't?"

"You're impossible. You know that? Thank goodness." She leaned forward, smoothing a hand down the side of his face and brushed her lips against his. Turning to the doctor, she folded her arms. "So, what now?"

"Now," the doctor replaced his stethoscope around his neck and he gestured for Frankie to resume his place outside the door, "my nurse will call your family contact, and Nick can get some more rest. I'll speak with you both more about recovery, later."

"More rest?" Nick flinched, suddenly and painfully recalling the reason he wasn't supposed to laugh. "I feel like I've been asleep for days. Come on, doc. You let me out of this bed and I bet I could run a-"

"Nicky, shut up." She angled a stern expression at him and lowered back onto the edge of his bed. When the doctor flicked the lights on his way out, she lifted the corners of her mouth into a relieved curve. "We both know you don't have the strength to chase me around this room, let alone run any kind of race. Just, lay back and be good, for once."

"Okay, baby, okay. You win." Already beginning to tire again, he drew in and released as deep a breath as he could manage without a twinge. "So, what happened?"

"What happened? You got shot, Nick. That's what happened." She tried to laugh, tried to keep it light, but couldn't quite manage. His weakened appearance nearly brought her back to tears as she recalled the events. "Crispen got off a shot just before Alf managed to."

"Alf." He lowered his eyes to the tangle of their fingers on the mattress and he nodded slowly, knowing his friend couldn't have pulled through. "Jansen?"

She shook her head when he glanced back up at her again. "Alf was a good shot, better than Jansen or his cronies gave him credit for. He's in a locker down in the basement."

Nick sighed, letting his head slump deeper into the pillows as he shifted his eyes to the ceiling. "The police? What happened, there? They know about Alf? What about Pop? Is there anything-"

"I'm not going to tell you anything else, if you don't relax." She pressed her lips thinly together in response to the way he was working up. "Your dad didn't have anything to do with whatever Alf was into. He was right. He's safe, Nicky. Of course, they knew about Alf. Thankfully, he appeared to be honest with them. It sounded as if they knew a lot more about him than you could've probably ever guessed."

"Yeah." He nodded, swallowing hard as his mind worked through the loss of his once so trusted friend. He gritted his teeth, clearing his throat before he went any further. "What about Bobby and Alex?"

"They didn't get far. Police picked them up. With everything they were into, kidnapping me and the way things turned out with Alf, they'll both be kissing the sunshine goodbye for a very long time."

"Cate, about that deal I signed…" He hesitated, looking away from her. "You should know that I don't know what's gonna to happen. If what Crispen said was true, I may be in pretty deep. The release we signed with the feds really did only specify a contract with him."

She shook her head again, reassuring him of the rest that he'd missed out on. "They know you didn't have a choice, Nicky. You've always played by the rules, and they know that, too. Believe me. They've kept a very close eye on you over the years, making sure you did play by the rules. Apparently, they have a mound of files on your family."

He nodded with a scowl. "I bet."

"The point is, the deal was signed under duress, and it was never filed with anyone. Alex babbled their plans like a chatterbox when they pulled him in. That problem has, more or less… taken care of itself."

"I see." He tilted his head toward the bandages on his right side. "So, what about this?"

"You were… really lucky. *We* were really lucky."

Thinking of the way she'd prayed to see those dark eyes of his for the last couple of days, she had to work especially hard not to fall apart with them finally fixed so intensely on hers again. Feeling hers beginning to gloss, she stood and walked to the window, turning her back to him. Christmas lights all over the city twinkled out of the darkness, as if nothing had happened, as if the world had just continued to go on, even though she felt as if it had fallen down around her ears.

"Cate?"

She sniffed hard, drawing her fingertips to her lips. "Just a fraction off from where the bullet went through, Nicky, just a fraction, and you would've-"

"I didn't."

Hearing a couple of strangled sobs escape her, he observed the way she'd hugged her arms around herself so tightly, in need of comfort he couldn't appear to provide her. Knowing her, she wouldn't have talked it through with anyone, no one but the police. It would have just been the relay of a mechanical series of events to them. She needed to get it out.

"Talk to me, Cate."

"Talk to you? I feel like I haven't stopped talking to you since it happened. Talking and talking, on and on, and never hearing… anything." The sight of the Christmas lights began to blur in her vision and she shook her head. "You jumped in front of me an instant before Crispen pulled the trigger."

"At least that probably lets me off the hook with Shayne." He attempted a small laugh but couldn't quite mange it.

"Don't joke, Nicky." She shook her head, sniffing, wiping another tear from her cheek. "I know you mean it to help, but you have no idea what I've been going through."

"No, I don't. You're right." He sucked his lips in, pressing them tightly together with a nod. "I'm sorry."

"The shots were so close together. Before I could register what was happening, you hit the ground. The doctor said it was the sudden drop in blood pressure that made you lose consciousness, at first. But then, when you didn't wake up, I didn't know if..."

He angled his head at her, hearing the tears thickening her voice again. "Cate, I'm-"

"And, I didn't know what to do, Nicky." She shook her head, nearly falling apart again. "There was so much blood, and all I could do was shove my stupid scarf there while I alternated between prayers and begging you to look at me."

"Cate, sweetheart, come here." He ached for what she was feeling every bit as much as he ached for the wound in his shoulder. "I'm sorry I let you down."

She snapped her head to the side and slowly turned. Dipping her brows at him, she shook her head. "Nicky, what are you talking about?"

"I broke my promise to you." Though it was difficult, he forced himself to keep his eyes on hers. He wanted her to know that he was sincere in his apology, and an honest man always looked eye to eye. "I promised I'd keep you safe, and I didn't."

"Nicky," she crossed the room, lowering next him again, "you literally took a bullet for me. You came for me when I was in trouble. You were willing to send me away, even though I know it ate you up to even think about it. You did keep me safe. You did keep your promise."

"There should've never been a need for any of that." He touched the purple shadow Alex had put on her cheekbone, deepening his scowl as he refused to give himself a pass. "I should've done more, seen more. I should've listened with an open mind when you had concerns about Alf."

"Nicky, stop." She shook her head when he began getting agitated again. "I will not allow you to blame yourself for this."

"But, you were right about him, about that deal. And what's more, I think I knew it, too. I just didn't want to accept it. If I had just let myself see it, admit it, none of this could've happened."

"Nicky, you can't take credit for the demented plotting of a lunatic." She reached to cup the side of his face in one of her hands, leaning to press a light kiss to his lips. "What if you'd never come into MacCarthaigh's? What if you'd never made me fall in love with you? What if I'd approached things about Alf in a better, more receptive way? What if I hadn't insisted on stopping at the loft?"

"I see what you're doing." He smiled softly at her.

"Good." She gave him a curt nod and began adjusting the pillows and bed coverings around him. "Then no more what-ifs. From now on, we'll both make an effort to balance our tempers with reason, and leave it there."

"And stubbornness?" He laughed weakly. "What about that?"

"I still see stubbornness as an attribute, now more than ever." She angled her head from side to side as she made her case. "Stubbornness kept you coming back to MacCarthaigh's after I'd turned you down. It also brought you back to me when I could've lost you, Nicky."

He nodded, swishing a finger over one of her hands. "Okay, Cate. Stubbornness we'll keep."

"Stubbornness we'll keep." She leaned forward again, brushing a slightly firmer kiss to his lips. "Now, get some rest before they kick me out."

He closed his eyes, smiling. "I'd like to see them try."

Epilogue

Though MacCarthaigh's was closed to the public for the night, it was filled with the murmured sounds of cheerful voices. With Nick and Cate just returning from their official honeymoon, both families had come together again. The couple had been gone for nearly a month, skipping over the worst of the heat and humidity in Saint Adeline. They returned just in time for the work on their new home to be completed.

"I'd like to say a word or two." Shayne stood from his place at the table, looking around at all of the faces. "When Nick started coming around, I admit, I was less than thrilled. I'm not a man who often admits his mistakes, but… I'll admit, now, that I was wrong. He's proven himself to be an honest, upright sort, and it's clear how much he loves our Cate. There's no doubt in my mind that she's in good hands. She'll have all the protection she'll ever need with him, whether she likes it, or not. Good luck with that, Nick."

"Thanks." Nick grinned off to the side at her, laughing, then looked back to him. "I have a feeling I'll need the luck."

"Anyway, I guess what I'm saying is…" Shayne shrugged, then lifted his beer to the other end of the table. "To my brother-in-law. You're an okay guy, Nick."

"Nicky, *not* a hood?" Mrs. Caprianno lifted a brow to Shayne, a smile peeking from the stern expression she held on him.

"Nicky, definitely *not* a hood." Shayne nodded to her, returning the smile, then looked back around the table before lifting the drink to his lips. "Nick, Cate, we're glad to have you back home where you *both* belong. Slainte!"

"Salute." Mrs. Caprianno smiled deeper, drawing her wine glass in for a sip.

"That's a nice house you two chose, Nicky." Shifting a sideways smile at him, Sal spoke when the table went back to conversation. "Plenty of room for my grandchildren, eh?"

"All right, Sal." Cate peeked around her husband with a laugh, then pecked Nick's lips when he dipped his head toward her. "They're in the plans, but I'm still not quite ready to share him yet."

"I'm only teasing, bella." Sal chuckled. "You're both young. There's time. There's time."

"Mmm." Cate glanced over at Frankie. "Are you getting settled in the guest house okay?"

"It's real nice, Cate." Frankie grinned, nodding appreciatively at the way she had made it a point to see to every detail herself.

Though they all joked about Cate not wanting a sitter, he knew that she now understood his purpose and his place a little better. She drew him in even closer than before. Since Christmas, she welcomed his company, and rarely questioned Nick when Frankie or Tony were sent along with her anywhere. It wasn't to say that she gave up her independence, merely that she had a new respect and understanding of the way things must sometimes be done.

As Nick and Cate looked around the table, they felt the unwavering saturation of love that surrounded them. The two families had become one, not just the two of them. It was more than either of them could have asked for, or expected. It was only the beginning.

- About the Author -

D.L. Ptaszynski currently lives in Peoria, Arizona with her family. She has roots in the Midwest of the United States and lived there, herself, for several years before relocating back to sunny Arizona where she was born. While she loves her desert home, her time spent in the Midwest, the people, the seasons, and the environment have taken up a special place in her heart.

D.L. spends most of her time with her family, being outside, and writing the kinds of novels she likes to read. One of the things D.L. enjoys most about writing is always having a say in the way things turn out. Her books are available in both Ebook and in paperback.

***Want to learn more about D.L. Ptaszynski and her current works in progress? Follow her on Facebook and Instagram or email the author at: dlptaszynski@yahoo.com**

Reviews are greatly appreciated. Leave an honest review for any of D.L. Ptaszynski's books on Amazon, Google, Goodreads, and on any of the social media sites in which she participates.